Holding
Battersea

A STORY OF
CONTEMPORARY LONDON

David Armstrong

Published in 2009 by New Generation Publishing

Copyright © David Armstrong

First Edition

Typeset in Georgia 12/16 pt

Adobe InDesign, Charlie Armstrong & Mary Hanna

A CIP catalogue record is available.

Acknowledgements

I would like to thank all my family and friends for their help and encouragement in writing and producing this book. Lesley Martin bore the brunt through uncounted lost hours and many 'second' readings. Our son, Charlie, was there at the end to design the cover and resolve the layout. My sister Carol always believed it was possible and kept me going. When I needed helpful readers of earlier drafts the support and comments of our good friends was invaluable. I am particularly indebted to Carole Adler, to Lynne and Ross Warner, to Ruth Zammit and to Peter Jackson.

Thanks; you all did your best. The remaining short-comings are entirely mine.

Chapter One

For years Tom had clung to the comfortable fantasy that one day some romantic holiday encounter would transform his unremarkable existence as a single, thirty-something, teacher of history. Yet again this year, two weeks at a Mediterranean resort in Spain had altered nothing except his bank account. Late one Sunday afternoon near the end of August he was returning pretty much as he had left; and still wearing those habitual blue jeans and a crumpled linen jacket over a check shirt, open at the neck.

A short taxi ride completed his journey home. A spell of warm, humid, weather had clamped an immobile lid of grey cloud over the blue slate roofs of South London, absorbing the constant rumble of traffic. The clouds diffused a silvery light which cast no shadows and made the well-mannered rows of busy Victorian houses look crisp and two-dimensional. Across the road, the broad municipal grassland of Clapham Common spread pale and parched beyond an avenue of motionless trees. Tom paid the cab-driver and stood for a moment looking up at the tall, shining, windows of his flat, made opaque by the reflected sky. He kicked open the front gate and tugged his suitcase along the crumbling pathway.

Unlocking the shabby communal door, he paused to gather-up a pile of post someone had left for him on the hall table before struggling up the gloomy stairs. He breathed again the familiar aromas of fried-food and cigarettes rising from the Pattersons' scruffy rooms below. Keys and coins in his pockets jangled in response to his footfalls on the long-defeated stair-carpet. On the first half landing he applied more keys to three separate locks and opened the door, pushing his suitcase ahead to reclaim his inner sanctum.

In the kitchen, the cold tap still dripped and now a wasp battered noisily against the windowpane. Tom sniffed the stale air, and moved towards the living room at the front of the house. Time had stood still for two weeks; a crumpled duvet lay across his bed and unread newspapers spread across the floor. He hated the annual realisation that the crisp, cool, barefoot marble of holiday hotels had yielded once more to the dull brown carpets of home. The bedroom curtains remained tightly drawn, just as he had left them. In their dust-dappled yellow light he saw the amber-toned inertia of his daily life. He grunted, swore, dropped his suitcase, tossed the letters onto an armchair and retreated to the bathroom.

The ancient taps spat and gurgled before allowing a silvery flow of tepid water. He glanced at himself in the mirror; his face looked sallow and podgy after all the hours spent travelling. He worried that his chin was looking fat and sucked in his cheeks to view a thinner face. His fingers massaged his cheek-bones, trying to dispel the puffiness below his eyes. His soft brown eyes blankly returned his unhappy gaze. With wet fingers he attempted to flick some life back into the lazy waves of his fair hair. He blamed the conditioned air of airports, planes and trains for making his hair look dull and greasy. He gave his reflection a thin-lipped scowl and turned away.

Churning the hard, dry, soap in his hands he decided he needed tea and had the kettle filled before he realised there would be no milk in the fridge. He muttered '*Oh fuck!*' and switched off the kettle. Warily, he pulled down the top sash to release the wasp but it flew up aggressively and pursued him across the kitchen.
"Argh, what?" yelled Tom, wafting away his droning attacker before ducking across the hallway and clattering back downstairs, banging each door behind him as he went.

Later, he stood more contentedly at the tall front windows of his living room, sipping tea and munching on a newly acquired packet of chocolate biscuits. A wasp lay dead on the window sill, where he had eventually squashed it using the hem of the curtain. Tom picked up the phone and dialled Barry's number, hoping that Barry's wife, Lucy, might answer. She did, and he thought she sounded pleased to hear him.

"Hi Tom! You're back!" she began.

"Apparently so. What have I missed?"

"Nothing. It's August. Everyone's away; except us of course."

"You went somewhere, didn't you? Earlier in the year?"

"A weekend at Disneyland, Paris, with three kids – four, if you include Barry – doesn't count as a *holiday*; not for me anyway."

"You couldn't have persuaded them to keep Barry?"

"Ha, yes as one of *Cap'n* Hook's pirate crew you mean?"

"Or one of The Lost Boys?"

"Don't imagine I wasn't tempted..."

"Not quite the Tuscan idyll you had in mind, I'm sure..." he said, laughing.

"No, nothing like, but at least the silly-season's nearly over."

"How would we tell?"

"People need to get serious again, even including you, my dear Tom. There's another meeting for the anti-war campaign coming up...soon."

"Oh yeah, right. When's that?"

"Mmm, hang-on, my calendar's right here on the wall...Yes, next month, on the fourteenth, seven thirty..."

"Can't wait."

"It's important."

"Do you honestly believe anything we do makes the slightest difference?"

"In what regard?" demanded Lucy.

"In everything."

He heard Lucy sigh and draw a deep breath before she continued;

"Come on Tom; not you as well? This is not like you," she said.

"Sorry. Bit tired, I think; travelling all day...it gets to you, you know?"

"Well, do cheer up. Think positive! I mean, at least you've been somewhere where they have grown-ups...Hot and sunny too. Portugal wasn't it? No, Spain! How's your sun-tan?"

"Like the rest of me, fading fast."

"Oh dear, what was it this time?" Now it was Lucy's turn to drag her words so that she sounded tired. Tom made no reply and she quickly tried again. "I know, let me guess; hot summer nights of psycho-babble and soul-searching with a divorcee from Swindon? Or perhaps wordless fumbling with a fat-bummed nursery-nurse from Dudley?" Lucy pronounced 'Dod-lie' with a nasal drawl, imitating a previous girl-friend of Tom's whom she had particularly disliked.

"That was just on the flight out," said Tom. "But thanks for your concern..."
"Ah, there, there, *bless*. Getting warm was I?"
"I could almost believe you care."
"But I do," protested Lucy. "I want to hear all about it."
"You will, I promise, just as soon as I've invented something sufficiently heart-rending."
Lucy laughed again, loudly this time and said,
"We can't go on letting these things happen to you."
"What things?"
"Random, doomed and pointless relationships of course."
"Randy and doomed? Sounds promising..."
"Stop it! You're ducking the issue."
"OK then, *pointless* I like. I'll settle for that. Surely everyone has those?"
"I don't!"
"Doesn't count; you're married."
"Tell me about it."
"Respect!" said Tom.
"No, listen; despite certain evidence to the contrary, I *do* know a thing or two about relationships." Lucy was laughing as she said this and clearly beginning to enjoy their exchange. "You wouldn't think that once upon a time, I mean *BC- before children,* I was a qualified socio-psycho-something, would you?" Tom laughed back to her and she hurried on. "And I certainly know a thing or two about women - I could tell you a lot about what makes us tick."
"Tick? I've never had one who ticked."
"Do try to be serious, I know it's hard for you," said Lucy sternly, pretending to be impatient. "Someone should get you sorted out

properly one of these fine days..."

"*Sorted!* As Barry would say..." answered Tom.

"Don't imagine I haven't..." she paused, suddenly losing confidence in her line of thought. "Oh, Tom, I'm so sorry. Here's me rabbiting-on and you probably only rang because you want to get your car back."

"There's no hurry..."

"We've been so grateful... It was a great help while Barry had his repaired."

"Like I said, no rush. I won't be driving anywhere for a while... not until school starts... God! How depressing is that? I can't believe there're so few days left before the new term..."

"I've no sympathy for you there," said Lucy. Her voice dropped to a confidential whisper, "I can't wait for Emma and Cherie to go back to school."

"Where did the summer go?"

"Over the hills and far, far away...*tiddly um tum tum*! Which reminds me, *Mister* Cork; did you manage to finish that book I lent you?"

Tom was about to answer when he heard her say "*Don't!*" and then there was a pause before Barry's voice began,

"Wotcha Corky! Listen; don't worry about the car... I'll whiz it round to you later."

He heard Lucy in the background complaining loudly, *"What are you doing Brendan? I was talking to Tom, if you don't mind!"*

"Oh dear," thought Tom, "she only calls him 'Brendan' when she's particularly annoyed." Next he heard Barry complaining, *"Well, Alice is crying,"* and Lucy saying, *"So? She probably wants a drink or needs changing..."*

"It's OK, no sweat," said Tom into the phone, "another time we'll ...." but the line went dead before he could finish.

Twenty minutes and some more tea later, Tom was again watching the world from the front windows when he saw his own car speed past and turn sharply into the side road at the end of the terrace. He winced and leaned into the bay to follow its progress, imagining the tyres scuffing against the granite kerbstones as the car bounced to a halt. Barry's untidy head emerged and moments later the doorbell rang.

"Alright, keep your hair on, mate!" called Tom as he trotted down the stairs to where Barry's torso loomed large against the coarse, wired, glass. Tom swung the door open; Barry swept past him without a word and lunged for the pile of junk-mail, unclaimed letters and flyers for pizza-delivery on the hall table.

"Hellooo, old chap, had a nice holiday?" exclaimed Tom, as sarcastically as he could. *"You're looking fit and tanned, squire... Thanks for the loan of your motor, by the way,"* continued Tom, mimicking Barry's South London accent. *"You'll find most of it in a heap just 'round the corner."*

"Sorry, mate, got a lot on my plate just now," said Barry turning to go upstairs. "Was there any proper post when you got back?" he enquired, over his shoulder. Tom remembered the pile of letters he had discarded into the armchair and followed Barry up to the flat. Closing his front door, he found Barry in the front room already sorting through the mail and separating first one and then a second cream-coloured envelope from the rest.

"Feel free," growled Tom, "there are plenty of bills... sure you don't want those as well?"

Barry suddenly sighed emphatically as if he had been holding his breath for a long time and could now breathe normally again. He collapsed into the armchair like a deflating balloon.

"Look, I'm dead sorry, mate," he began, "I just had to get these, I knew you'd understand."

"Understand what?" asked Tom. "All I understand is that you've come crashing in here like some mad bugger, and started going through my post without so much as a *'by your leave, guv'nor'*..."

"I'm sorry, it's just...." Barry tried again, "well, it's not easy."

Tom stood above him, arms folded, waiting.

"Nottingham," said Barry, looking up, "you know I've been working on a project up there for over a year now."

"Yes," said Tom, shaking his head to indicate that this was hardly a complete explanation.

"Well, I've become involved with this woman; Penny she's called. Ironically, she's a friend of Lucy's; they were at college together, back in the days... It was Lucy told me to look her up..."

Barry paused and pushed his fingers through his thick, black, curly hair, then shuffled in his seat.

"Would you mind sitting down?" he asked. "This is not made any easier with you standing over me like that."

Tom paced across to the sofa and sat down heavily, examining Barry's profile against the changing light. The sun had finally pierced the flat white sky with bright evening rays which told of distant heat. Beyond the windows, an evening breeze had started to rustle the tree-tops. Barry began again, quietly;

"She's a knock-out is Penny. Totally blew me away -- right from the off."

"And she's married, of course," guessed Tom.

"We know what we're doing," said Barry, feeling around in his shirt pockets and then patting his trousers. "Got any ciggies?"

"I actually bought you some cheap ones in Spain, not duty-frees any more of course," said Tom rising to go into the bedroom and unzip his suitcase. "They're to share with Lucy, too," he called over his shoulder.

"Hah! Guess what? She's given up again!" announced Barry. "Last week, *'kin'ell*, she had nicotine withdrawal symptoms and her period. We all suffered, I can tell you. She even gave me a hard time just because I asked her to 'phone the dentist and book an appointment for me. How loopy is that? They're so totally unpredictable."

"Who? Dentists?"

"No, *wimin*! Well, I mean Lucy, of course. Not Penny; she's something else."

"Is Lucy OK now?" asked Tom.

"Oh yeah, except she's become some sort of born-again health freak. Won't let me smoke anywhere in the house. She'll ban me from the garden next, or the street I shouldn't wonder; Christ, it's not as if I smoke in bed anymore."

Tom habitually scratched his left ear when faced with awkward facts, and now he did so fiercely.

"You do know she's right, don't you? She should want you to

quit smoking."

"Look, mate, we both feel dead guilty about Lucy," said Barry, undoing the cellophane from a packet of cigarettes and vigorously clicking the lighter Tom had offered him.

"So you and Penny are a '*We*' now are you?"

"It's serious mate," insisted Barry, "Penny's got a kid too, same as me."

"Actually, you've got three," corrected Tom. "Have had since the year before last."

"Don't remind me," agreed Barry. "Ah, come on... We don't want to hurt anyone. And we're *not* hurting anyone, except ourselves of course, so long as it's kept hush-hush."

There was a silence. Tom studied the lines around Barry's mouth and eyes, thinking how the redness of the fading light made his unshaven face look almost sinister. Barry stared back across the room, wafting blue smoke as he raised his arm to continue. His dark eyes narrowed in concentration and his heavy fingers reached nervously to pinch and stroke his nostrils.

"We feel so cut-off when I'm back in London," he said, still avoiding eye-contact with Tom. "We need to feel close, all the time. So I said she could write to me at your address," added Barry, speaking rapidly. Tom stared back at him, hoping to convey the disbelief he felt.

"Can't she use a phone?"

"You're joking! You never know who might answer. Could be Lucy or even one of the kids!"

"Your mobile?" asked Tom.

"Even worse, there's too much of a paper trail. All our phone bills give lists of calls... Pure dynamite; what if Lucy or, God help us, Penny's husband.....and then there's things like missed call alerts, ring-back and last number re-dial. You can't be too careful."

"And email? Couldn't she try sending you some hot-mail worthy of the name? No?"

"Leave off, Corky," said Barry, his big fingers plucking at the fabric on the chair-arm as his agitation increased. "That kid of hers is a right nerdy little bleeder. He'd be opening-up her messages quicker than you could say *Bollocks to Bill Gates*! No way; we couldn't have that."

Tom sighed and coughed with annoyance as he sniffed the smoke from Barry's cigarette.

"So you told her to write her love letters here, to me?" he said.

"Brilliant, isn't it? Except they're not *for* you..."

"Yeah, *brill*..." said Tom, adding, "Lucy is my friend too, you know."

"But we're mates, aren't we?" insisted Barry. "All *lads* together? I meant to get your spare keys before you went away, but there just wasn't time and anyway Lucy always wanted to come with me when I said I was popping round to see you. So I couldn't .... Then Penny phoned last Friday..."

"Taking a risk wasn't she?"

"She wanted to know if I'd got the letters. I had to tell her you were away, and she said her husband was acting dead suspicious, and to be sure to get the letters as soon as..."

"Hang on," interrupted Tom, "has this *suspicious* husband, whose wife I'm not shagging, *but you are*, got my name and address?"

"Penny fears he might have," admitted Barry, in a whisper.

"Fucking ace!" exclaimed Tom.

"She's not sure, not really sure," offered Barry.

"Oh, there is some hope for me then?" grunted Tom, peering through the twilight to where Barry sat, no longer listening, straining to read Penny's words of love in the failing light.

"God, she's sexy," murmured Barry, appreciatively, "just seeing her hand-writing on the envelopes does it for me. Do you think you could switch a light on, mate?"

Tom crossed the room to the dimmer switch and brought up the wall-lights. Barry squirmed with pleasure in the armchair; Tom turned away and flicked on the desk-lamp. The scatter of school-related paperwork instantly reminded him of Lucy and their earlier, truncated, telephone conversation. Ignored by Barry, Tom rattled down the top sashes of the bay windows. The night breeze began to refresh the room bringing with it the sharp, insistent, crackle of car tyres on the warm road outside.

"I need to eat," said Tom morosely, "and that means going out."

"I could use a drink," answered Barry, without looking up. "I've already eaten, we'd just finished Sunday dinner when you rang..." He folded the letters tenderly as he spoke.

"I hope you're not planning to leave those here," said Tom.

"No, no," grinned Barry, showing his teeth, "I'll hide them at the office; I wouldn't want you sniffing through them."

Tom turned angrily towards him and Barry held up his big forearms in mock surrender.

"Joke!" he snorted happily. "But seriously, I'm grateful to you mate."

"Don't be," replied Tom. "Just ask her not to send any more."

"It'll be alright, don't fret," said Barry soothingly. "I'm sure she'll be able to write again in a few days' time. All you have to do is call me when a letter arrives..."

"No! I don't want there to be any more letters."

"Oh come on Corky," whined Barry, "I thought we were mates; this is really important."

"And what about Lucy?"

"What about Luce? Not your concern," replied Barry. "Lucy is my problem."

"Lucy is my friend."

Barry paused, his eyes moving swiftly across to the door and then back to Tom.

"You've got to help me, there's no other way and there's too much at stake," he pleaded, watching carefully to gauge Tom's reaction. Tom stared back, as blankly as he could. Barry paused for a moment then tried a different approach,

"What Lucy doesn't know won't hurt her. *What the eye don't see...*"

Another silence ensued, broken when Tom commented quietly,

"It seems so old-fashioned, writing love-letters. I didn't know anyone still did..."

"They're so wonderfully erotic," Barry added quickly; anxious to encourage Tom's sudden mellowing. "You can say more considered things on paper, more sincere and passionate. I tell you, mate, girls just love that sort of thing! They love words; look how they bang on about the books they've read."

"Me too," protested Tom, "I do that..."

Barry ignored him and continued,

"I bet Penny starts to feel well juicy when I get going..."

"You really are deeply shallow, aren't you?" snapped Tom.

"Girls don't forget me in a hurry mate!"

"No, they're probably totally gob-smacked that such a sexist pig still exists. Christ alone knows how an attractive and intelligent woman like Lucy puts up with you."

"Huh!" grunted Barry, flattered by Tom's disparaging description. "You never met her old Dad, did you? Shit, he was a piece of work; talk about uptight! After the upbringing that old stuff-shirt gave her, man, I came into Lucy's life like a breath of fresh air; a bleeding life-force I can tell you...She thought I was dead authentic, real working class; the genuine article."

"And you think that justifies your behaviour now?"

"Leave it out, mate; I'm still up for it, aren't I? I'm pretty successful and a damned good provider -- she knows that. OK, so I kick-off every now and then, but don't you worry about Lucy. She still remembers how she used to call me *'The only living boy in New Cross'*!"

"Not *New York*? Not like the song, then?"

"Nah mate," said Barry loudly, deliberately reverting to a stronger South London accent. "It was only ever *New Cross* for us. That's where I came from and back then she loved me for it. About the time we first started going out, this band called Carter USM did well with a cover-version of that Paul Simon song, only they did it as <u>The Only Living Boy in New Cross.</u> It could've been written about me! And USM; fuck me! It meant 'Unstoppable Sex Machine'. Those were the days, Christ she couldn't get enough of me then. No wonder her old man had a purple fit after he'd met me. He soon clocked what I was doing to his *luverly* little girl; the pervy old Kraut..."

"That was years ago," said Tom dismissively. "We've all changed...moved on. I bet Lucy has...some of us have even grown up."

"Balls! You're just jealous that I've got a relationship with another woman who does joined-up writing," interrupted Barry, cheerfully. "Wouldn't you just love it if any woman ever sent you more than a postcard or managed to write you something longer than a shopping list; you miserable sod!"

Tom frowned at the insult and regretted letting Barry turn the tables on him so completely.

"OK, so why did you assume that I wouldn't tell Lucy? What gives you the right to make me an accessory in this sordid affair?"

"It's not sordid, that's the whole fucking point!" shouted Barry, pulling himself up from the armchair. "You think you're so high and morally bleeding mighty. Christ! I know you've had relationships with married women and then hidden away up here when you've lost interest. You're no better than me!"

"Yeah, so what? But I'm not married, am I? And I haven't got children."

"Huh! Wait 'til you're married with kids; getting GBH of the ear'ole every bleeding night..."

Barry stood and scowled, then flung his right arm across his chest and began anxiously scratching the upper part of his left arm. Tom stared back, concentrating on finding the words for what he wanted to say,

"Look," he began, "you can have your fun with Penny and both of you can piss on Lucy, each in your own special way; not my affair... But the letters coming here mean that I'm betraying Lucy too."

"You wouldn't tell her, would you mate? That would be betraying me, right?"

"Just let me do my own betraying," moaned Tom.

"I haven't done anything wrong," said Barry desperately.

"I really want you to know that. Penny and I, being together, it's fantastic, how can that be wrong? Why should other people be allowed to spoil that? If Luce doesn't know, how can it hurt her? And if you tell her, it'll be you who deliberately hurts her, not me. I can't believe you'd want to do that."

Tom groaned with irritation,

"That's classic, that is; blame the bloody messenger!"

They stood facing away from each other. Barry seemed to be

contemplating the large, colourful, print of an abstract painting on the wall beside the desk. Tom stared ruefully out into the darkness settling over the Common, his hands pushed deep into his trouser pockets, his shoulders raised in an enduring shrug. Fleetingly, he imagined Lucy's face smiling knowingly amidst the reflections on the window pane. Barry coughed.

"Look, let me have a spare key so I can pop round and pick up the letters while you're at work. Then your hands will be even cleaner."

"Do what you want," hissed Tom. "Just keep me out of it."

"Ah, thanks mate," said Barry, nodding towards Tom's back and smiling again. "You'll see; love conquers all. Trust me, I'm married."

Tom shook his head slowly in disbelief,

"Lust *excuses* all, you mean."

"Whatever, but it's never wrong, no way," concluded Barry. "You're bound to get a good'un chucking herself at your feet one of these days..."

"Yeah, *even me...*"

"Yeah, even you! Now, come on, let me buy you a pint. That'll cheer you up. You're probably a bit pissed-off after your holiday; coming home, getting back to the daily grind. I mean, it's always a bit of a downer, isn't it?"

Chapter Two

Two weeks later Tom went to the public meeting called by the 'Stop The War' campaign. He attended more from habit than conviction. The venue was a community hall over in Manor Street and by 7.30pm the turnout was still disappointingly small. Since the heady days of the big march eighteen months previously, public support had suffered from the wasting surrender to feelings of apathy and impotence. In Iraq, meanwhile, savage violence continued daily. No one in public life had yet described a believable exit strategy. Getting into Iraq, as they had been warned, was proving a lot easier than getting out.

Tom drifted along the rows of empty seats and yawned dispiritedly as he breathed the sickly smells of floor-polish and disinfectant. He surveyed the isolated clusters of anonymous heads. A man on the platform tapped the microphone officiously and cleared his throat. Two elderly women who had been standing chatting suddenly moved apart and there sat Lucy, several untidy rows of plastic chairs in front of him.

He sat and stared wistfully at the back of Lucy's head. Her dark curls shook animatedly whenever she inclined her head towards the grey-haired man sitting next to her. Tom gave her a minimal wave, trying to be inconspicuous, when she turned round during the ill-tempered debate. He recognised Lucy's neighbour as Colin, well known locally for his efforts to sell *'Socialist Worker'* outside Sainsbury's every Saturday morning. It seemed that Barry and Lucy may once have shared Colin's militant politics but that Barry – ever the opportunist - had nailed his colours to *New Labour* in the early days of Blairism. Lucy and Tom, like most of those who clung to the traditional beliefs of 'Old' Labour, had persistently grumbled and sniped from the sidelines right up to, and beyond, Tony Blair's election victory in 1997.

Even from several rows back, Tom could read from Colin's demeanour that the elderly Trotskyite was unhappy with the incoherent manner in which the meeting was petering out. Suddenly, Colin's younger associate, Neil, was on his feet clashing vehemently with the Chair over some esoteric point of procedure.

"You can't do that!" protested Neil.

"I just did," stated the Chair, slapping his hand on the table. "Meeting closed!"

Neil's final outburst was lost in the rush of conversation and the scraping of chairs across the pock-marked wooden floor as everyone rose to leave. Tom remained seated, watching Lucy through a forest of arms and legs whilst those around him started to don their coats or swing rucksacks and cycle helmets into place. Lucy was stooping towards Colin, offering her arm for support as he tried to rise. For a moment, Tom wondered if Colin had suffered some kind of paralysing intellectual seizure, brought on by overwhelming disappointment as yet another public meeting failed to conclude with a decision to set up burning barricades or precipitate a General Strike. Lucy stepped aside, letting Colin and Neil stride angrily away, already deep in conversation. She raised herself on her toes to seek out Tom, and smiled as she caught his eye. Lucy mouthed a greeting, which Tom took to be *'Are you coming for a drink?'*

He reached her near the exit, where she had stopped to write her name and address on one of the contact sheets. Her short, white, raincoat hung open, she pushed back her black leather shoulder bag and leaned towards the table. Standing behind her, Tom noticed how her elegantly tailored grey trousers ended neatly just above the ankles of her black boots.

"You'd better give my address," he suggested without thinking, "Barry won't like the sort of mail you'll get from this lot."

She turned her face towards him wearing a quizzical smile,

"Letters? Whatever do you mean?" she asked, and Tom

blushed horribly for the first time in years. Lucy flicked her hand dismissively across Tom's sleeve and quickly tucked it through his arm. She smiled up at him and said,

"Come on shy boy, I'm going to buy you a drink..."

As they fell in step, walking arm in arm along the street, Lucy felt the autumnal chill of the evening air and used her right hand to button her coat over her pale blue sweater. Instinctively, she drew closer to Tom's warmth and he seemed pleased, closing his elbow to grip hers more tightly. They walked towards the nearby 'Manor Arms' and Lucy slowed, pulling Tom back. A substantial contingent from the meeting bunched together in the pub doorway. Tom glanced at Lucy.

"Oh no, let's not," she whispered, with a significant nod towards the queuing politicos.

"Come back to mine for a decent cup of coffee, and then I'll drive you home," offered Tom.

"That would be nice; Barry's up in Nottingham *again* this week, Mary's babysitting and I can never get her to go home before eleven ... 'Fraid I mostly drink tea these days, 'though ...."

"I could open a bottle of wine?"

"Oooh, but *I'm a married lady!*" recited Lucy as they strolled past the last brightly lit shop fronts and looked across at Holy Trinity Church, settled grey and sombre in its own dark pools of shadow at the edge of the Common.

"Graham Greene lived here in the late thirties," he said, halting Lucy outside an orderly Georgian façade.

"I never knew," she replied, peering through the screen of black iron railings. "Shouldn't there be a blue plaque on the wall?"

Tom shrugged.

"It looks much older than most Clapham houses, is it eighteenth century?" she enquired.

"Definitely. It was built just before 1720..."

"You're such an *old historian!*" she chided.

"You know that his novel 'The End of The Affair' is set hereabouts, don't you?"

"I remember they were shooting scenes for the film on the Common a few years ago; oh and Barry going on about 'The Windmill' featuring in a Graham Greene story. Trust him to know the pub of the film of the book."

"I came across Graham Greene in my researches for the 'Doodlebug Summer' project I'm preparing for the kids in Year 9," said Tom. Lucy looked puzzled.

"It's to get them to examine local history; interview people who were their age in 1944 and find out what life was like around here sixty years ago. If you remember, a V1 is instrumental in ending the affair in Greene's story; 'robot bombs' he called them. He dates it very precisely to 17th. June 1944, and sure enough a V1 really did come down over the other side of the Common at six thirty that evening."

"That *very* evening," echoed Lucy, mocking him gently.

"I checked."

"Got any more *fascinating facts*? And tell me, *Clever-clogs*, was the famous *Mister* Greene living in this *very* house when that happened?"

"No, he was long gone, but he may have come back in the early fifties when he was writing the book." Tom knew he was being teased but, coming from Lucy, he didn't mind it at all. He was glad to have her attention.

"So did a Doodlebug kill one of the lovers?" asked Lucy. "You know I can never remember the details of books afterwards..."

"Nearly...I mean it explodes outside the house while the lover is making his way down the stairs. A few minutes later the woman, Sarah, sees his arm sticking out from under the rubble. She thinks he's dead and starts praying; she imagines making a deal with God;

'*Let him be alive,*' she prays, '*and I will believe.*' But that isn't enough, she thinks, so she adds, '*I'll give him up for ever, only let him be alive...*'"

"And is he?" asked Lucy.

"Is he what?"

"Is he alive?"

"Yes, of course he is; he's the one telling the story! Anyway, he comes round, goes back upstairs and finds her kneeling down, praying. She seems surprised that he's alive, more surprised than pleased, he thinks. She gets dressed and hurries home and that's it – *the end of the affair.* Only she doesn't tell him why, so he gets all bitter and twisted and years later – when she's about to die – he steals her diary and finds out about her promise to God. After that," laughed Tom, "he's pretty bloody angry with God, I can tell you."

"I just don't remember any of that," sighed Lucy.

"Greene has the lover, Maurice Bendrix, living over that side of the Common," Tom gestured with his left arm towards the yellow lights flickering distantly across the dark acres; "and Sarah, the mistress, lived over this side with her boring old husband, Henry."

"*Maurice* sounds deliciously French," mused Lucy, "and therefore rather sexy...Imagine if he'd been called 'Morris'; that's 'M-o-r-r-i-s', you wouldn't think he was any good in bed, would you?" she asked with an intimate smile. Tom enjoyed the feeling of flirtation but couldn't think what he might say to encourage her to continue. They linked arms again and walked on in silence. The noise of the traffic increased; Tom began to speak but realised that Lucy was not hearing him. He leaned closer, her soft dark curls brushed his nose;

"I could tell you a tale about the celebrated Mr Greene and his departure from that house back there," he began.

"OOH, do tell!" she insisted, squeezing his arm.

"You know he was famously randy?"

"Get away!"

"Well, one night during the Blitz, in 1940 or 1941, when his wife Vivien and the children had been evacuated to Oxford and he was supposed to be living here and working in London, a bomb hit that house and gutted it. Greene should have been killed, but in fact he was spending the night with his mistress. Vivien said afterwards that Graham's life had been saved by his infidelity."

"Oh yes! That's great; let's hear it for adultery, folks!" shouted Lucy, jumping ahead of Tom and punching the air with her fist so that her shoulder bag swung into Tom's stomach. He caught the straps and used them playfully to haul her back towards him. An astonished group of people stood aside to let them pass. Lucy saw him wince.

"Did I embarrass you darling?" she cooed. "I don't know what

22

I did to make you blush so red in the hall, but if I ever find out I'll certainly do it again."

"Please do," said Tom, trying to put a brave face on his confusion.

They waited for the lights to change at Cedars Road;

"This road features in <u>The End of The Affair</u> too," said Tom, "The strange rationalist character called 'Smythe' – the guy with a deformed face – Greene has him living down there."

"You'll have to lend me the book; I'm going to have to read it again, after what you've told me tonight."

Tom held open the garden-gate and she brushed past him, saying

"I do love talking to you, Tom."

Tom wanted to smile but couldn't. He suddenly felt his stomach go hollow as he remembered the latest letter, lying in wait upstairs in plain view on the kitchen table. Panic swept through him as he fumbled for his keys, certain that Lucy would instantly recognise Penny's affected handwriting on the envelope of a letter addressed to her husband, but sent *'Care of Mr T. Cork'*.

Puzzled by Tom's hesitation, Lucy stood aside so that he could unlock the outer door and they stepped into the dark hallway. Tom's arm stretched along the wall, reaching for the time-controlled light switch. In the darkness, Lucy silently intercepted his hand and pulled him towards her. She folded her arm around his neck and kissed him passionately, pressing herself against his groin. Tom stared wide-eyed into her upturned face, her eyes were closed and he gently enfolded her in his arms, responding gratefully to her kisses.

"God, I've wanted to do that for so long," she breathed. Tom cupped her face in his hands and kissed her longingly on the lips.

"Me too," he said slowly, with an involuntary shudder. "Can I take you upstairs?"

"Well I'd rather you didn't *take* me in this disgusting hallway, darling," she laughed, pressing the light switch so that a pale yellow light illuminated the stairs. Outside his front door the light clicked off, and they began another long, slow kiss. Tom felt

Lucy's tongue slide delicately into his mouth and he sank back against the wall, pulling her to him and reaching below her coat to stroke the grey cloth stretched tightly across her bottom.

"Perhaps we should go inside?" she whispered.

Tom politely took her coat.

"I'm going to risk using your bathroom," she said, slipping away from him. Tom sped into the kitchen, snatched up Penny's letter and threw it into a drawer. Then he ran the cold tap and noisily filled the kettle.

"Shall I make tea?" he called, "or would you prefer wine?"

"Don't shout, I'm right here," replied Lucy appearing in the doorway, her dark hair tumbling richly to her shoulders. She crossed the room and stood close to him, lacing her fingers gently with his;

"Just show a tea-bag to some hot water, no milk, no sugar; then come and sit with me in the front room."

When Tom entered his living room carrying the two cups Lucy had switched on his desk lamp but turned its beam to the wall. A pool of light spilled from the bedroom behind him and silver bars reflected from passing headlights swept across the ceiling.

"Leave the curtains open," called Lucy from the sofa. "I love the openness those tall windows give this room. You're so lucky to be up here on the first floor looking out over the Common..."

Tom moved towards her; Lucy laughed when she saw that he had used cups and saucers.

"What, no mugs?" she asked. "Are you trying to seduce me or something?"

"Yes, I think I am," he said, adding, "or something..."

"Come here," said Lucy, carefully placing her cup and on the tiled hearth.

They lay on the sofa in the silent darkness, her face cradled on his shoulder, their heads touching gently. They breathed in unison and sighed between kisses.

"What are we doing?" she asked.

"Being honest, at last?"

"You know this could all get very complicated, don't you?"

"My feelings for you are very simple."

"Don't tell me you're just a simple *bloke*; please not that."

"Oh no," answered Tom, "I've put up with so much from Barry to get just a little of you. I'm very big on complexity and contradictions; otherwise it wouldn't have taken me, what is it now? Four years? Five? To let you know how I feel."

"And how do you feel?"

"Can't you tell?"

"No! So far I've had to take the lead in everything..."

Tom frowned, distractedly, and began to say,

"Look, things have changed; developed – you know – it's alright, I mean we can allow this to happen ..." he halted abruptly.

"What?"

Tom closed his eyes, realising he had nearly revealed what he knew about Barry's relationship with Penny.

"This is all very difficult for me, my position is very awkward, you must see that," he stammered.

"Not as awkward as mine," she snapped.

"But there's Barry to consider..."

"Oh is there? Is there really?" she demanded, struggling to remove his arm from her shoulder and sit upright. "Let's consider Mr Brendan *'call me Barry'* Sands, spinster of this parish!"

"Bachelor," corrected Tom, foolishly.

"Bachelor! Yes I do mean *bachelor,* Mister *Clever Dick* teacher! He certainly behaves like one."

"I'm sorry," said Tom.

"Don't be; just let me cry on your big woolly shoulder. He's having another affair, it's not the first, it won't be the last, and the stupid prick still doesn't realise that I can always tell."

"Who is it?" ventured Tom.

"How would I know? Do I care? No, not any more. He's probably found some big-breasted tart up in Nottingham. That's why he has to keep dashing up there for important bloody meetings. Important, my arse!" she sobbed.

"I love your arse," said Tom without hesitation.

Lucy stared, the tears stood still in her eyes; she looked bewildered and speechless.

"What about us? After this evening, I want there to be hope for us," Tom prompted her, quietly.

"I've thought about you for a long time," she confessed, speaking slowly and carefully, after another long pause. "And I still can't decide if a relationship with you would be totally impossible or merely unthinkable."

Lucy sniffed, then smiled weakly when she realised what she had just said. She tried to look forlorn. Tom watched her and smiled back.

"But not doomed," he said quietly. "Doomed is for Graham Greene. Thank God an affair between you and me would only be impossible. We can deal with that..."

"You think?"

"I've fantasised about you for ages..."

"Typical! I sometimes wondered if it wasn't really Barry you found so very fascinating."

"Leave it out!" said Tom, imitating Barry's tone.

"Well you took your time..." she sighed. "I'd still be waiting if I hadn't..."

"Oh Lucy, darling, I'm sorry. I didn't dare make the first move.... Seriously, what if you'd not...? I mean it would've been *End of*..."

"But I did, didn't I?" she said, touching his lips with her finger. "You won't remember, but about two years ago, at someone's party, you unloaded all your pent-up romantic drivel onto me."

"Couldn't you tell it was really about you?"

"No! Certainly not! Actually, you were extremely drunk and kept quoting Leonard Cohen....."

"Oh God; was I that embarrassing?"

"*Oh yes*, and then some," she laughed, dabbing her eyes. "I was very tired – just getting over all my gynaecological troubles after Alice was born – and I didn't have the energy to crawl away. Plus I felt sorry for you; a good man going to waste; so caring but so lonely..."

Tom buried his face in his hands,

"Oh no," he moaned, "not '*caring*' as well..."

"Actually it was good for me," she continued, briskly. "I decided to find you a partner...pretending I didn't want you myself...I wondered if you'd talked so openly simply because you'd stopped seeing me as a proper woman... I'd become just this comforting, providing, absorbent ....*THING*! A sort of emotional sponge; all soggy with leaking breast-milk and the snot of human kindness. Ugh!"

"Oh Lucy, I'm so sorry..." he whispered. "Why did you say it was good for you?"

"Because it made me determined to get better; I needed to become attractive, even *sexy*, again. I decided that if I could get you to fancy me, then I would be whole again. I'd be an independent *person*; not just someone's mother, someone else's dull little housewife or, as in your case, someone's cathartic mop and bucket!"

"But you are sexy! You are now, and you were then," cried Tom. "You are formidable in the way you manage your life, your children - Barry even - and still have time to read and be politically active. You're so attractive, so alert...so involved...." He paused.

"You've stopped," she protested. "Is there more?"

"And so gorgeous..." he growled, leaning over to kiss her, but she sprang away and he had to clutch desperately at the arm-rest to prevent himself plunging onto the floor.

"Mary, *bloody* Mary! I've got to go!"

"Have you suddenly remembered you're a C-C-Catholic?" he stuttered. "Is this a delayed reaction to all that talk of Graham Greene?"

"No, you fool! Not *that* Mary, and not the bloody drink either. It's Mary the bloody babysitter! What's the time? I've got to be back before 11.30, tops."

"It's OK, it's only 10.45," he answered, "I can drive you home in no time."

"No; let me call a cab."

"But why?"

"Barry may be an unfaithful, lying bastard, but he's also incredibly possessive. He knew about the meeting tonight, *and* he asked me if you'd be there. He'll be ringing me at home soon, and if I'm not back he'll ring here and start asking sly questions."

"Has he guessed that I fancy you?" asked Tom, reaching for her hand.

"Ask him, why don't you?" challenged Lucy. "Remember he wouldn't let me talk to you on the phone that day you came back from Spain? And since then he's always dashing round to see you just when it's tea-time for the kids, so I can't come too. Tonight he'll want to make sure that we're not together. He wouldn't hesitate to give poor old Mary the third degree...and she can be pretty damned nosey too... So, please call a cab, darling, now!"

Chapter Three

Tom stood at the roadside watching the tail-lights of Lucy's cab swing into the traffic at the end of the Common. He watched until the taxi disappeared, beginning a reverie about how the Common now lay between himself and Lucy, just as in fiction it had lain between Bendrix and Sarah.

Back upstairs he re-aligned the desk lamp, sat down and attempted to resume preparing lessons. Thoughts of Lucy at once invaded his mind. He saw her turning towards him across the rows of chairs at the anti-war meeting. He suddenly remembered her irritable, Marxist, companion and imagined Colin's vituperative dismissal of Greene's work as *'petit-bourgeois tales of self-indulgent romantic complications…a distraction from the class-struggle…'*

Tom looked up at the black windows, impatient to reclaim his picture of Lucy. The darkened glass coldly returned his own, indistinct, reflection. Lucy aside, the campaign meeting had left him feeling deeply depressed. Since his time at university, he had gnawed endlessly, year after year, on the brittle bones of all the left-wing political parties. And all he had ever wanted to do was to *understand,* he told himself. Secretly he suspected that all he had ever really wanted was to *belong*…A few hours earlier he'd been tempted to give the Anti-War meeting a miss; now he knew he'd only gone because he knew *she* would be there.

These days Tom frequently found himself becalmed while political debates raged around him. Talking things through with Lucy would help, he felt sure…He remembered a comment of Sarah's which he had underlined the other day. He reached for the book, found it hidden under a swirl of papers and began flicking through the pages. Eventually he found the passage, much further into the story than he had remembered. Sarah, in a letter to Maurice which he reads only after her death, wrote:

I've caught belief like a disease. I've fallen into belief like I fell in love."

Another arc of car headlights swept across the room. He saw again Lucy's face, pale, animated and alluring, defying the drab surroundings in the hall. Looking down, he read the words

'I've never loved before as I love you...'

He read them again, this time aloud, feeling impelled to push back his chair, walk across to the sofa and bury his face in the cushion which still bore the imprint of her head.

The telephone rang and he rushed to pick up the receiver, hoping it would be Lucy. Instead her husband's voice enquired,
"How was the meeting?"
"Pretty pointless, I suppose," muttered Tom, "the usual paralysing rancour..."
"Paralytic, more like."
"Nothing was decided...except to call another meeting..."
"Huh; political activists? My arse!"
"We can't just stand aside; give up and do nothing..." began Tom. Barry interrupted him;
"Bunch of wankers!"
"They just don't like being lied to..."
"Who cares? I'm bloody sure I don't. Tony Blair's great gift to the Labour Party was his Pick 'n' Mix approach to politics...Get real."
"Totally unprincipled politics, don't you mean? No mention of Socialism."
"Fuck that; don't start on about bloody 'Socialism'."
"Scares you these days, does it?"
"Not at all; listen, I had a proper working class upbringing - not all cosy and comfy like yours. Your parents were teachers too,

weren't they?"

"So?"

"So, I had to become aspirantic; you didn't!"

"That's not a word."

"What isn't?"

"It's aspirational."

"Well bollocks to that. Listen, my old Dad worked on the buildings all his stupid life. He was in the Labour Party because he was a trade unionist; had to be; only way he could survive. He never banged on about Socialism. He was a bonus militant. He fucking knew what *the struggle* was all about. Shorter hours and better wages, that's what matters to the punters. Blair sees that."

"I doubt it. I can't imagine Blair and your old Dad having much to say to each other..."

"Now that's where you're wrong...so very wrong."

"I think not. Can't you see New Labour..."

"Leastways, never mind all that, getting back to those letters mate," said Barry, cutting across him. "We just need you to help us out for a few more weeks. Not long; there's no one I can trust like you..."

Tom swallowed and glanced across the room almost expecting to see himself embracing Lucy.

"There's been another letter, it came this morning," he rasped.

"Yeah, I know. She told me. You alright, mate?"

"Just got a frog in my throat," explained Tom. "I've probably caught a cough from some diseased child at school."

"There's a lot of it about," scoffed Barry. "So make sure you get your share!"

Clearly, Barry had been drinking and Tom pictured him lying in a hotel bedroom watching cable-TV pornography with the sound off.

"And I don't want you to worry that you're letting Lucy down," continued Barry. "If you think you're letting her down, look what I'm doing to her faith in me."

Tom was tempted to say '*She knows, you silly fucker*!' but held back when he thought of the consequences for Lucy and, after this evening, for himself.

"And don't worry anymore about Penny's jealous husband

coming after you," brayed Barry, "I think I can reassure you on that front, mate; I've thrown him right off the scent."

"What do you mean?" exclaimed Tom. "There is no scent; at least, none that leads to me."

"There are times," Barry boasted serenely, "when I am dazzled by my own brilliance!"

"Oh yeah; so what've you done now? – assuming that I care."

"Simple really. I've sat back and thought the whole problem through, coolly and rationally. Graham you see, that's her husband, suspects Penny might be having an affair but he doesn't know with who..."

"With *whom*," interjected Tom.

"Do fuck off," snapped Barry. "So, to avoid detection, I had the brilliant idea of giving Graham all the help he needs."

"You've lost me, but no matter," sighed Tom.

"So I sends him this anonymous letter, signed from *A Well-Wisher*, suggesting that he keeps a closer eye on his wife. And then, entirely coincidentally you understand, I arrange to meet him for lunch the next day: to discuss a bit of business.... And '*Graham,*' says I, straight after the hors d'oeuvres, '*You seem distracted, something on your mind old son?*' And that got him, he took the bait. '*Well yes, there is as a matter of fact, Brendan,*' says he. '*How jolly perceptive of you to notice.*' Then, of course, all I had to do was to coax it out of him and offer my services; '*Graham,*' says I once again, '*you've been so helpful to Paul and me, introducing us to all the right people up here, if I can help you out in any way...*'

"And that opened the flood gates, poured out his heart to me, he did: all his fears about being an older man with an energetic younger wife. I nearly blew it by agreeing just how *energetic* dear Penny can be. Fucking sexual athlete, if you ask me – which, fortunately, he didn't!"

"Oh God," yawned Tom.

"So anyway, he agreed that I'd be an ideal person to keep an eye on Penny *without arousing her suspicion* and saving him from the embarrassment of using any of his so-called *chums* from Nottingham. It's a very sweet deal; Graham's re-assured, I'm pure as the driven snow if word gets back to him that I've been spotted with his wife, and – what's totally fucking hilarious – I can poke his wife in peace while he's thinking I'm keeping her on the straight and narrow! Best bloody poacher in the business, turned bloody gamekeeper!" Barry bellowed the last few words.

"Oh, that's very cunning," sneered Tom, imagining Barry rolling on the bed and almost crying with pleasure.

"I'm a …..ha hah ha! I'm a *private dick*!" sobbed Barry through tears of uncontrollable laughter. "Beautiful, or what? Totally fucking brilliant!"

Tom waited, the phone held away from his ear, for the laughter to subside. He did not want to hear Barry even mention Lucy's name. Distractedly, he pursued the first apparently impassive idea that came into his head;

"It's a strange thing," he resumed when Barry's noise level had fallen, "but this is all uncannily similar to events in a book I've been reading, where the lover takes charge of the private detectives on behalf of the unfortunate husband.."

"What book is that?" asked Barry, with some interest.

"The End of The Affair"

"Oh, I know it. Graham Greene isn't it? Another bloody *Graham*, is that what you mean?"

"No… I hadn't thought of that. It's just that the cuckolded husband in the book – a man called Henry, actually – dithers over what to do about his suspicions and then finds out that the lover – actually he's an *ex-lover* at that point – has taken the initiative and had the wife followed by a private eye – a man called *Parkis*. And this all emerges during a most unpleasant lunch which the lover has arranged deliberately to be as spiteful as possible towards Henry…You said you'd been having lunch with her husband, Graham."

"I'm sure I've read it," said Barry; making no attempt to disguise a yawn, "or did I just see the film? I didn't get any of that stuff 'though. I don't see the parallel…."

"The parallel is that neither your actual Graham nor the fictional husband in the book grasp that the lover is managing the investigation to suit his own personal interests ….."

"No, don't be daft; I'm not *investigating* her; I just want Graham to *think* that I am."

"Yeah, so in both cases, the lover is controlling what the husband knows. In the book there's a real investigation because the lover doesn't know why she suddenly dumped him, he thinks she must have moved on to another affair and...."

"Nah mate, it's not like that...."

"It's never going to be exact is it? But.....oh, never mind."

"Look, gotta go," concluded Barry, obviously losing interest, "I've another call waiting, might even be The Bad Penny, *herself*. Anyway I'll be round for the letter tomorrow night, probably about tea-time. Don't worry if you can't be home, I've got your spare keys.... Just leave the letter somewhere I can spot it."

Tom said nothing. His mind was churning on the awful reminder that Barry had keys to his flat. Getting them back would, he realised, take some doing.

"See yer then...*comrade*," grunted Barry and the line went dead.

* * *

Tom put down the phone and swore softly into the darkness. He went back to the sofa and stroked the fabric where Lucy had sat. He picked up the phone and dialled; Lucy answered almost immediately.

"You were right," he said, "Barry called me just now."

"What did he say?"

Tom hesitated.

"Are you still there?"

"Sorry, Luce, the phone slipped," he lied.

"I asked you what he'd said."

"Oh, nothing."

"Come on, he must have said something. I know Brendan better than anyone, he's too calculating to have phoned you without some cover story. He wouldn't want you to be suspicious that he's suspicious, the devious bastard. Did he ask if you'd seen me at the meeting?"

"Oh yeah," answered Tom, feeling relieved, "I told him that you were talking to Neil and Colin."

"Brill; that'll give him something to worry about."

"Why? He can't be so paranoid that he imagines you could run off with one of those crusty old losers," snapped Tom.

"No darling, of course not. But Barry thinks they're dangerously left-wing, he's sure they're subversives; watched by Special Branch and MI5..."

"They're not dangerous," laughed Tom, "except when people have to cross the High Street to avoid buying '*The People's Daily*' or whatever it is they try to flog outside Sainsbury's. They're a road safety issue now, that's all. Who cares?"

"Barry does, stupid. He thinks if I'm associated with them it'll be used against him by people he's upset in the local Labour Party. You do know that our Brendan has ambitions to become an MP one day, don't you?"

"Huh; for which party...?"

"Very funny."

"Has he rung you?"

"Of course he has, I wouldn't be talking to you if he hadn't, would I? It wouldn't do for him to find both our lines engaged.... Even Brendan Sands could work that one out."

"Are you alone?"

"Course I am sweetie, apart from the girls, and they're asleep. They'd bloody better be! Apparently they gave *bloody* Mary a really hard time, had her running up and down stairs fetching glasses of water."

"I'm coming over," stated Tom.

"Darling, is that wise?"

"We can't leave things like this."

"Like what?"

"Exactly," said Tom.

"Tap gently on the front window," she whispered, "don't ring the doorbell for Chrissake."

Tom sped into the bathroom, cleaned his teeth and sprinkled after-shave across the front of his shirt before hurrying down to his car, leaving his desk lamp pouring light over his still unfinished lesson plans and The End of The Affair.

He found a parking space just up the hill from Barry and Lucy's house. A neighbour had purloined a long stretch of kerbside by placing two ancient galvanised metal dustbins in the road with a scaffolding plank spanning between them. Tom closed his car door with an almost inaudible click and moments later he was tapping on the window. Lucy had the curtains tightly drawn so he could not tell if the lights were on in the front room. Nothing seemed to be happening and he wondered if she had heard him. He was poised to tap again when the light in the hall brightened as if a room door had opened. He heard a bolt slide away inside the door.

"Who is it?" hissed Lucy.

"Harrison Ford," claimed Tom.

"Piss off, you're much too old now, even for me," whispered Lucy, gradually opening the door and smiling nervously around its edge. Tom moved inside and she closed the door gently behind him before turning to accept his embrace. He felt the pleasure of her kisses again as if they had been apart for months. His hands moved across her shoulders and felt their way down her back. She was wearing only a dressing gown and he felt her breasts press against his chest.

"You're not Han Solo; you lied to me," she said quietly when their lips parted and she took his hand, leading him on tiptoe into the front room.

The only light came from a table-lamp with a thin silk scarf thrown over it. "Actually you do remind me of an actor," she smiled, standing close, "he's French."

"Jean-Paul Belmondo? Yves Montand? Johnny 'aliday?" suggested Tom.

"No, younger; that guy who was in *Green Card*; oh you know; the bloke with the big nose. Cyrano de what-not... It's your nose what does it!"

"Well thanks a lot," sniffed Tom. "You know what they say, big nose, big...."

"Feet?"

"Come here and find out," he whispered, pulling her closer and feeling her legs opening around him. He started to say something else but she silenced him with her lips and they sank together into an armchair before sliding onto the floor. Tom opened her gown and pressed his face into her breasts before reaching for a cushion which he slipped under her thighs. He began to stroke the thick copse of hair between her legs as she undid his belt and pulled down his jeans.

Afterwards, he lay beside her on the floor clasping her to him and listening to her breathing. She kissed him softly and they both smiled as their eyes met.

" Mmm, *Cyrano de Bergerac*," she murmured.

" Je m'appelle Gerard Depardieu," he whispered.

"Did you bring the Graham Greene book for me?" she asked.

"Sorry," said Tom. "I meant to, but in all the excitement I guess I just forgot."

She kissed him again.

"You'll have to come round to my place for it. It'll be on the bedside table."

Lucy pressed against him once more.

"Are you cold?" she asked. "The heating went off hours ago."

From upstairs came the sound of a child coughing and Lucy quickly twisted away from him, gathering her gown around her as she rose. She stepped lightly into the hall and stood at the foot of the stairs, head cocked to one side, looking up and listening intently. Tom sat up, swept his hands through his hair, then slowly got to his feet pulling up his jeans and buttoning his shirt. A floorboard creaked loudly and he froze like a statue. Through the door he could see Lucy gesture urgently to him to keep still.

"That'd be all we'd need," she whispered conspiratorially, "Cherie or Alice bumbling down the stairs."

"We could say we were playing sardines," offered Tom.

"Or Doctors and Nurses, more like," she giggled. "My girls aren't daft you know, they'd know we were being naughty!" Lucy began to growl and pulled him towards her again. Now it was Tom's turn to say "Shush!" and he put his finger on her lips;

"I can smell me on your finger!" she exclaimed and held him tightly.

"I'll never wash it again!"

"Go melt back into the night, babe," hissed Lucy.

"Bob Dylan '*It ain't me, babe*' 1964," he stated, automatically.

"I don't care, but you've got to go; go now, and without a

sound."

"Hey, that's another song, maybe two..."

"Sssssh!"

"Can I phone you tomorrow?"

"I'll be hurt if you wait until tomorrow. I want to hear from you later today."

* * *

Tom looked down at his watch; it was ten past three in the morning. Gingerly, he eased open the car door and sank into the driver's seat; fearful of making the slightest sound. He released the handbrake and the car immediately began to roll down the hill. The first metal dustbin loomed in front of him and Tom tried to turn the wheel but he had not yet put the key into the ignition. The steering remained locked.

"Fuck!" shouted Tom, stamping on the foot brake just as the front of his car boomed against the dustbin. Over it went and its lid clattered away down the hill, filling the night with a harsh metallic clamour. The wooden plank crashed down, twisting sufficiently as it fell to topple the second 'bin with another resounding crash.

Sweating and swearing, Tom rammed the key into the ignition, turning it fiercely and crunching into gear as the engine roared into life.

"How was it for you, darling?" he shouted defiantly.

The car lurched forward and accelerated away as lights flickered on in bedroom windows. Lucy herself, having watched Tom's departure from behind her bedroom curtains, sank down into the darkness convulsed with stifled laughter. She heard sash windows go rattling upwards, impelled by the anger of awakened sleepers. From across the street, Mary's voice rasped loudly into the night, threatening to call the police. Lucy released the curtain and collapsed backwards onto the big bed, tears of laughter washing mascara down her cheeks.

"Oh Tom," she whispered into the pillow, "how predictable was that? All these years and we've just been an accident waiting to happen..."

From the next room came the sound of a child coughing and starting to wail. Lucy stopped laughing and groaned as she sat up.

Chapter Four

On Saturday morning Tom waited, as arranged, on the corner where Lucy's road crossed over Northcote Road. Yesterday, on the phone, she had said she would be there around 10 am, but couldn't be sure.

"And I'll have one or more of the girls with me. You won't mind will you, darling?"

And Tom did not mind. He did not mind at all. They were Lucy's girls and he had known the younger two, Cherie now aged 6 and Alice, just 2, since they were born. The eldest daughter, Emma, the eight year old, he had known since she was under a year. Thus did Tom calculate that he had known Lucy - and Barry as well, of course – for all of seven years. Normally rational, but in reality deeply superstitious, Tom regarded '7' as a magic number.

Now he stood in the grey drizzle feigning an interest in the properties displayed in the estate agent's window. He was reading through the twenty or so glowing endorsements for stunningly expensive houses and flats when Lucy suddenly appeared around the corner, hooded against the weather, and pushing a buggy which resembled a plastic teardrop on wheels. They stood together for a moment under the dripping awning of the florist's shop. Lucy smiled at him from under the dark hood of her raincoat; he wanted to kiss the rain from her nose but restricted himself to squeezing her elbow. Little Alice was chortling merrily under the buggy's transparent canopy and, as they walked towards the street market, Lucy would lean forward at intervals to call out something to Alice. As they crossed the road, Tom heard her ask,

"Shall we go and see the carrots and oranges man today, Ali?"

Gradually the trio worked their way along the crowded pavement, progressing from stall to stall. Lucy's shopping bag became fuller and fuller, weighing down the handle of the buggy. Tom bought some fruit and a couple of green vegetables. Lucy congratulated him, mocking his *New Man* status.

"Barry," she said, "assumes that all vegetables grow in plastic bags and then get frozen, except at Christmas. Then he makes a big production about coming down here to buy a Christmas tree and half a ton of sprouts. The rest of the year, we'd all die of scurvy if we relied on his choice of groceries."

"And the turkey?" enquired Tom.

"Oh yes; he's very extravagant with that. *Big gesture*! You remember the one we had last Christmas? You were there, far too big wasn't it? But he had to have it. And it had to come from the top of the range butcher, you know, back there along the road. I could hardly lift the damned thing, let alone cook it."

"That's enough about Barry," complained Tom as they returned along the other pavement. He had imagined that they would shop leisurely for a few minutes before dropping into a wine bar for morning coffee. But this was a damp Saturday morning; the market was going full pelt and all the shops and cafes were crowded. Manoeuvring the buggy among the swirling legs kept Lucy distracted.

"When am I going to see you again?" asked Tom.

Lucy was about to call out again to Alice but spotted that the child had fallen asleep. She smiled at Tom.

"I want to see you too," she said, "but it is difficult. Barry's at home now, he was still in bed when I came out. I can tell him that Alice and I bumped into you down here at the market. We've got Paul and Anna coming over this evening..." Lucy was starting to frown and look far away down the street as she rehearsed the catalogue of her commitments. "Shall I suggest inviting you over this evening?" she asked, brightly.

"Er, no. Don't do that, but thanks anyway. I'm meant to be having dinner with Sam and Rosie tonight," answered Tom, smiling broadly.

"Sam and Rose?" asked Lucy.

"The couple who live upstairs, in the flat above mine. We get on pretty well. I hardly ever see them, they're away a lot. But ages ago they suggested a meal tonight, so I can't really let them down at the last minute."

By now they were back outside the florist's once again.

"Give me a moment," said Tom and darted inside, leaving Lucy standing alongside the buggy on the pavement. He emerged a few minutes later with a big bunch of blue and yellow flowers.

"From an admirer!" he proclaimed.

"Why thank you, kind sir," she said, leaning to peck him on the cheek. "My husband will be pleased."

"Oh hell," moaned Tom. "Can't I just have bought them to cheer you up on a dull day?"

"Don't worry, darling," she soothed. "He probably won't even notice we've got any flowers, and if he does, I'll just say that you offered them as a gift for the house, or that I bought them to impress Paul and Anna. Yes, he'd go for that."

"And?" enquired Tom.

"And what?

"And when can I see you?"

"Tomorrow. Tomorrow afternoon," said Lucy, decisively. "Barry usually goes to sleep on Sunday after lunch. I shan't be doing a roast because I'm cooking tonight. So I'll give the girls their lunch soon after twelve, then suggest going for a walk across the Common. Barry will immediately head for the sofa to feign death. The girls and I will all toddle up to the swings, you know the ones, near Becky's house? And then we'll come over to you for tea."

"Tea?" asked Tom, starting to panic. "Do you mean cakes and sandwiches, jelly and ice-cream type tea?"

"No, just get some biscuits and some juice."

"Won't Barry mind?"

"'Course not, if he asks – which he won't – I'll tell him one of the girls needed the loo, and your house was closest."

"Great," smiled Tom, "I'll see you at my convenience!"

They walked up the hill towards her house. He carried all the shopping, both hers and his, weighing down his right arm. In his left hand he carried the flowers, tilting them down towards the ground. Lucy thought this looked very strange, and commented,

"You don't have to keep the rain off them. They are real flowers, aren't they?"

"It's just that I feel self-conscious carrying them like a bouquet I'm about to present to the Queen," replied Tom. "And anyway, it's stopped raining."

"So it has," she replied, flicking back her hood and fluffing her curls into shape with her left hand.

"God, you've got beautiful hair," murmured Tom.

"Stop it! Someone will see," she whispered back.

They reached her house and Lucy negotiated the buggy over the front step and into the hallway. Alice was just beginning to stir; she coughed and snuffled bad-temperedly. Tom carried Lucy's shopping inside and put it on the floor, then presented the flowers again as she turned to him.

"Thank you so much, Tom, you're so kind," she said loudly, giving him a noisy kiss on each cheek in turn, while secretly reaching her hand into his crotch and squeezing affectionately.

"Your servant, ma'am," called Tom, while crossing his eyes and miming an open-mouthed wince of pain.

"Away with you, varlet!" laughed Lucy, closing the front door behind him. Tom turned to the street, hearing Alice waking properly behind him with a tearful wail. A woman whom he assumed to be Mary was staring at him from the front window of the house directly opposite. Tom gave her a cheerful wave and stepped quickly away up the hill, feeling Mary's scowl raking his back as he went.

* * *

The next morning Tom rose early and concentrated on preparing lessons for school. He had obtained a large scale map, covering the catchment area for his school. He had also copied various facts and dates about the World War Two V1 missiles from a book published by the local historical society. The figures showed that

86 people had been killed by a total of forty-one V1's crashing down on that part of London. Another 335 people were seriously injured and 567 were slightly injured. This meant that there were nearly 1,000 casualties in the three months between the first V1 attack at 2am on 16th June and the last one on 13th August 1944. This was not the Blitz; that had begun nearly four years earlier in the autumn of 1940. The V1 raids had started one week after the D-day landings in Normandy, when civilians in London could have been forgiven for thinking that, for them, the worst of the danger had passed.

On the map, Tom had marked the impact points of each flying bomb, drawing circles around them to indicate the area damaged by the blast from the explosions. Now he was adding to the map little stickers showing where each of his pupils lived. The previous week, he had begun taking Year 9 to visit some of these sites, especially if they were near their present homes.

18th. June, five killed in Downton Avenue, just along from where Louis lives now, wrote Tom.

22nd June, at the back of Valley Road, where the new estate is. How many of them live there, he wondered?

28th. June, Barcombe Avenue, four killed. Isn't that where Leon said he lives, thought Tom, rifling through the list of addresses.

He heard his door bell ringing and jumped up. Emma and Cherie were waiting on the doorstep. Lucy was standing behind them with Alice clinging shyly to her skirt. The older girls were more confident, stepping quickly past Tom and half-way up the stairs before Lucy called them back.

"Wellies!" she shouted, and the pair turned round and darted back down to the hall where they quickly discarded their muddy boots. Lucy had already collapsed the buggy and tucked it under the hall table. Now she was bending over Alice, gently tugging off each of her tiny boots in turn.

"Ah, that's amazing," said Tom, "I didn't know they made boots so small." He took the opportunity to run his hand gently across Lucy's upturned behind.

"Careful, Sidney!" she smiled.

Tom followed Lucy and Alice upstairs. Their progress was slow. Alice climbed each rise and tread in turn, all the time clutching her mother's hand. When they reached Tom's flat, Emma was emerging from the bathroom with the sound of the flushed cistern refilling behind her. Cherie came from the direction of the kitchen bearing a large carton of juice which she had found in the 'fridge.

"I can't reach your glasses, Tom, "she complained. "They are in a cupboard too high up."

"Make yourselves at home, girls, why don't you?" called Lucy, addinginalowertone, "I'msosorryTom, theyseemtobetakingover."

"That's great," he answered. "S'OK Cherie, look there's some beakers over there for you. Pick what colour you want." Alice started forward but Lucy held her back, reaching into her shoulder bag at the same time.

"Here we are, Ali," she called. "Look, I've brought your very own special cup from home. Aren't I a clever Mummy?"

"Yes, and so beautiful," whispered Tom, bending to kiss her neck as the three girls disappeared into the kitchen.

"Is your house ready for this invasion?" asked Lucy. "Have you had everything less than two metres above floor level nailed down?"

"I was just working on a large map, which I've left spread across the floor in the front room. I think I'll just go and rescue it," said Tom, hurrying away. Lucy followed him, noticing that he really had tidied up; his bedroom looked quite spacious and, she thought, quite inviting with all the clothes put away, the surfaces dusted and the curtains pulled back neatly. She approved of the small vase of flowers on the bedside table, and noticed the Graham Greene book alongside it, as promised. She felt Tom watching her from the living room and she blew him a kiss.

"Who's Sidney?" interrupted Cherie. "You said 'careful Sidney' when we came in."

"He's my imaginary friend," said Tom cheerily. "He lives in a cobweb above the light bulb on the stairs."

"Can I see him?" asked Cherie.

"Only when it's time to go home," said Tom. "He hides when I have visitors but, if they've been very good, he sometimes pops out to say goodbye."

Cherie looked sceptical but described a circle on the carpet with her foot while she pondered the extent of her disbelief.

"I'm a maginry fren," announced Alice, speeding to find her mother.

"You've got a lot of Lego, for a grown-up," observed Emma from the floor.

"Well help yourself," said Tom. "That big box contains all the toys I possess. Some are really ancient, I had them when I was a boy. Look, there are Star Wars figures and all sorts..."

"Let me see," said Lucy, kneeling down beside Emma and quickly joined by Cherie and Alice.

"I'll go and put the kettle on, shall I?" asked Tom. "And we'll have a nice cup of hot water."

When he returned, bearing a tray with two cups of tea, some biscuits and more juice for the children, Tom found Emma busy constructing something using Lego. Cherie and Alice had made a tent from the duvet on his bed and were busy populating it with objects from around the flat. Tom stooped to pick up his calculator which seemed to have fallen onto the bedroom floor.

"That's Rex, he's our puppy," warned Cherie. "Be very careful, he has a fearful bite!"

"Good dog, Rex," said Tom, stroking the calculator as he returned it to the floor.

"I think he likes you," said Cherie, "or else he might have chewed your leg off."

"Can't keep the girls out of your bedroom, eh Mr Cork?" enquired Lucy with a wicked smile.

"Frankly my dear, I am a bit of a babe magnet," confessed Tom.

"Well in Ali's case that is certainly true," said Lucy, sitting now at Tom's desk with his map partly unrolled before her.

"It was called *The Doodlebug Summer*," began Tom. Lucy nodded,

"When we lived in Streatham, Emma's nursery school was on the site of a row of houses blown-up by a doodlebug. Yes, here it is, *Bomb Number Eleven, 8am, 29ᵗʰ June, 1944, Harborough Road. No fatalities*, thank God! It was too early in the morning for the children to be on their way to school."

"Can I see? Can I see?" called Emma, rising from her Lego construction on the floor. Tom stood behind Lucy, gently massaging her shoulders and feeling her supple response as Emma pushed back the roll of paper on the desk.

"That's one of the things I've asked the students to look for," continued Tom, "gaps in the old terraces of Victorian houses, where you suddenly find an infill of a small block of flats or a cluster of more modern houses which date from the fifties or sixties."

"How are your students responding to this project?" asked Lucy.

"It's amazing," he shrugged, "kids never fail to astonish me. I was expecting this to be a good way to get them involved in understanding historical events as they have affected the real lives of ordinary people, *blah, blah, blah...* before we go on to look at the causes of the war and all that. I was also hoping it might start them thinking and talking about contemporary issues; the 'terror' bombing of civilians, whether by cruise missiles, rockets, planes, suicide bombers. All that stuff. But no, not a bit of it."

"So what have they done?" asked Lucy

"So far, they've been really concerned to find new houses and flats built on the sites where V1s exploded and killed people. They've decided that the new houses will be haunted by the ghosts of those untimely killed in 1944. Especially by any children who were killed. That really interests them. All their responses, their whole frame of reference, is nothing like mine. Their views seem largely the product of computer games and teenage horror movies, mostly with an '18 Certificate', which they seem to watch endlessly on DVDs in their own bedrooms. *'Teen-slashers'* they call them."

Lucy turned discreetly and pulled a face at Tom, indicating that perhaps he had said enough in front of Emma, who was no longer looking at the map but listening intently. He quickly decided to persuade Emma to go back to her Lego by using the familiar teaching strategy of 'saturation boredom'.

"You probably know that the 'V' part of V-weapons stands for *Vergeltungswaffe,* I can't pronounce it properly, look there it is on this handout."

Lucy read the word aloud with faultless pronunciation." *Vergelten:* to pay back. *Vergeltung:* reprisal. *Waffe:* weapon," she continued. "The Nazis wanted revenge."

"You are obviously fluent, "said Tom.

"You forget; both my parents were Austrian refugees. Their families only came here in 1936, when they were still only children themselves. When a V2 rocket landed near where my father was living in St John's Wood, only months before the end of the war, he took it very personally. I remember my mother saying that the V2s were the worst. You didn't hear them coming. Just *Whoosh! Kerrump!* And it's *'Goodnight Vienna'*, or in her case, 'Goodnight Finchley Central'."

"Yes," continued Tom, "lots of the eyewitness accounts mention the noise made by the pulse-jets on the V1s. People came to realise that you were safe so long as you could hear them, clattering across the sky. Graham Greene called them *robots......* It was only when the engine cut out that they began to glide down to earth. That was when you were in trouble. When they went quiet, then you had to dive for cover."

"And pray," added Lucy.

"I think even I'd pray in that situation. Hemingway quotes a soldier's prayer somewhere, probably in *For Whom the Bell Tolls.* It goes something like *'Dear God, if there is a God, save my soul; if I have a soul.'* "

"That's an agnostic's prayer," corrected Lucy. "I didn't think it was specific to soldiers....."

"It's not easy relating 1944 to the present day, although some of my pupils have older brothers in the army. I wouldn't expect them to be interested in how a V1 might have affected fictitious characters like Bendrix and Sarah. But bombing civilians; that sudden, murderous interruption of the lives of ordinary people, well that isn't just history, is it?"

"Mores the pity!"

"It's something that *has* happened within living memory on their own streets and is still happening everyday in places like Iraq or Israel. It happened in New York on '*9/11*'; they all know about that."

"And it could happen again in London," murmured Lucy. "A lot of people are very jumpy about Al Queida attacking here next. Mary, for instance, won't go on the Tubes since the train bombings in Madrid. She's convinced they'll blow-up a tube train inside one of the tunnels..."

"During the Blitz," said Tom, "The underground stations were where people went to shelter from air-raids. I've got copies of some Henry Moore drawings in this lot, somewhere. They show huddled sleepers, wrapped in blankets, all along the platform at Bethnal Green, or somewhere in the East End."

"Didn't always save them, did it?" added Lucy. "Mary told me how she remembers, from her childhood, that a bomb hit Balham tube-station one night and killed lots of people who were sheltering there."

"That's in amongst these papers too," sighed Tom. "Apparently, those who weren't killed by the explosion drowned when the tunnel flooded because the water mains had burst."

"Dear Lord," said Lucy, "and to think, I used to stand on the platform at Balham every morning, on my way to work, cursing if there was a gap longer than two minutes between the trains..."

"Another strange link with the modern world," said Tom, sifting through a pile of grainy, monochrome photographs, "is that Bin Laden didn't wait for a cruise missile to fall into his hands – he re-invented the V1 in the form of hijacked airliners."

"The big difference is that the Nazis made pilotless planes into flying bombs and despatched them to crash down on civilians – the suicide bomber goes one step further in depravity. He or she literally looks his victim in the eye...." murmured Lucy.

"Can they really believe they are about to enter Paradise when they press the button?" asked Tom. "I really would like to know...."

"If that's true," growled Lucy, "it's a total perversion of any religious belief I could ever hope to understand..."

"But religions have always been associated with sacrifices. Pagans sacrificed animals – even people sometimes – to appease their Gods and the same psychosis for blood-letting found its way into Judaism and Christianity. The core belief of Christianity is a blood-sacrifice. I don't know enough about Islam but it seems they share in that tradition...."

"I'm sure they do," agreed Lucy, sadly. "Don't they call it 'Martyrdom'? I just don't know what convinces them they have no choice....And they do in fact choose to take other people with them. They can't call that 'sacrifice' or 'martyrdom'; it's plain, stark, selfish murder – that's all it is."

"Did you know that during the Vietnam conflict, Buddhist monks would set fire to themselves in public as a protest against the fighting?"

"Yes, but they only did it to *themselves* - that's bad enough, I know - but at least you could understand them to be saying '*I want the world to know that this situation is so intolerable; that a horrible death is preferable.....*' Suicide bombers aren't saying that, are they? They set out to kill others as well. They want to spread terror, nothing else."

"God help us all," sighed Tom. "We've got religious fundamentalists here, there and everywhere sharing the same barbaric belief that if you blow up enough people, the survivors will see the error of their ways and come round to your way of thinking. It never happens. Bombs just make people even angrier, even more willing to commit reciprocal atrocities of their own...."

"Dreadful thought," replied Lucy. "And to think I popped in to see you this afternoon expecting to be cheered-up."

Tom looked desolate, breathed out noisily, ran his hand through his hair and then gestured helplessly at the notes and photographs covering his desk.

"I'm sorry darling, I really didn't mean to go on...."

Lucy turned and clasped his arm,

"No it is serious. I agree people should be talking about these things. Isn't that why you teach history? By understanding the mistakes of the past might we be able to avoid them in the future?"

"I like to think so," said Tom, "but actually....*History repeats itself, the first time as tragedy, the second time as farce.*" He tugged fiercely at the lobe of his left ear.

"That's very good," she said.

"It's not original," he admitted. "It's Marx, but he attributed it to Hegel…"

"Where's it from, the famous Communist Manifesto?"

"Err, no, I believe it actually comes at the beginning of '*The Eighteenth Brumaire…*' Oh God, how worrying is it that I should still know that? It's hardly likely ever to be a question in the pub quiz, is it? There was a time, of course, when I couldn't write an essay without finding an appropriate couplet from Marx, Lenin or Trotsky for starters…My favourite was always:

'All that is solid melts in to air, all that is holy is profaned, and man is at last compelled to face with sober senses his real conditions of life and his relations with his Kind…' "

"You still know it off by heart."

"How sad is that? When I was a student, there were very few essays I couldn't work that one into, somewhere. 'Course in those days the bit about *sober senses* rarely applied…"

"Those were the days," she sighed, mockingly. "The *Good Old Days,* don't you know?"

"To be honest," said Tom, "now I mostly just go through the motions when I'm teaching; I think we all do. Every once in a while there's a little spark, a comment, a remark made by one of the kids, something that lifts and inspires you…… but frankly, we do it for the money. You must have heard Barry go on at me – he never tires of saying '*Those that can do, those that can't – teach.*' Well that's as maybe; but I'd like to see him present this stuff to Year Nine, so that they develop as historians and start to relate the past to the present, blah de blah de blah – and don't chuck the chairs around."

Lucy smiled gently at him, wishing to be sympathetic and encouraging.

"I'm glad there are teachers who still work from the heart," she said. "If I think of the people – outside my family – who have made a difference in my life, most of them were teachers. And when I think about it, the best teachers were all a bit odd…"

"Oh thanks a bunch," cried Tom. "So you think I'm odd…."

"Only in the nicest possible way," she said more comfortingly. "I wouldn't want you to be Norman Normal."

"Actually, he's called Trevor," laughed Tom.

"Who is?"

"My Head of Department, the guy who hounds me over targets and record-keeping and all that normal *stuff*."

"And your teaching?"

"Oh, he couldn't give a monkey's what I actually do in the classroom so long as the right percentage pass their assessments and – like I said – there isn't too much mayhem or furniture flying out the windows."

"Even if they do come up with elaborate fantasies that London is haunted by the ghosts of 1944," laughed Lucy. "I know it is, of course, only not quite in the melodramatic way they imagine. Hey! That reminds me, I want to borrow the Graham Greene book. I've thought about it a lot since the other day, and I just can't remember the story well enough. Do you find that?"

"All the time," answered Tom. "It's in the bedroom..."

"I know, I saw, and I promise I'll return it to the very spot."

"Hope you're a quick reader," said Tom.

"Come along girls, we've got to go now," called out Lucy, standing up and clapping her hands together loudly. She then added, with a wink in Tom's direction, "Daddy will be running up a huge bill on the phone to Nottingham again if we don't get home soon."

"Let me get my coat and I'll walk along with you," suggested Tom. "It's getting dark."

"Oh would you? You are a darling, just to the top of our road... Come on girls, Ali, Emma, time to tidy up!"

Chapter Five

During the next two weeks, Tom and Lucy met whenever they could which, sadly for them, was not very often. They spoke everyday on the phone of course, using a system Tom devised one night when fretting about Barry's paranoid strictures concerning the paper-trail left by phone calls made between lovers. Whenever Lucy felt the coast was clear for her to speak to Tom, she would ring his number, let it ring twice, then hang up. Tom, assuming he was home [which these days he generally was except during the school day] immediately dialled *1471 – 3* and there would be Lucy with her generous *"Hello, darling!"*

Lucy had to consider her children and the apparently watchful Mary. Barry's working hours were unpredictable and he gave Lucy scant information in advance about where he would be working or when. Some days he worked at home in an office he had installed in the loft conversion, other days he might phone her at lunchtime from the office in Battersea to say that '*All Hell*' had broken loose in Nottingham and that he would be going north on the next train.

"When might you be back?" Lucy would enquire.

"Sometime tomorrow," he might suggest before adding impatiently "Or the next day, I just can't tell. Don't worry, you'll manage. Pop over the road to Mary if you need help!"

So Tom and Lucy enjoyed their telephone chats, which often went on for an hour or more, especially on evenings when Barry was late; apparently *'Held up on the way back from Nottingham'*. Once, when Lucy bothered to chide him for being late, yet again, Barry threw at her, *'You've no idea just what a complicated tangle this Nottingham fuck-up has turned out to be!'*

He seemed baffled by Lucy's assurance, 'Oh I do understand, darling, I really do.'

'No really,' he had insisted, 'I don't think Paul has a clue what he's got us into doing this networking consultancy. There are just too many balls in the air!'

'I can imagine!' cooed Lucy with just a trace of irony behind her smile.

She had Tom in stitches when she related this exchange to him on the phone the following afternoon.

"Something I've been meaning to ask you," said Tom, "Why does Barry not use his real name, Brendan? I've noticed that you only use it when you're cross with him."

"I do it to annoy him," stated Lucy. "When he was at school, probably about eleven or twelve, they had a supply teacher one day who took the register and called his name out as *'Brenda Sands'*. The whole class erupted in laughter, poking their fingers at him. You can imagine! Paul still remembers it. He says Barry went red with anger, so angry that he gave off heat. From then on he just bashed-up any kid who didn't call him Barry."

"Bit of an over-reaction, wasn't it?" suggested Tom.

"Not really," she answered. "You're never to let on that you know this, and certainly you must never tell him that I told you, but *'Brenda'* was the name of the woman that his father ran off with."

"Oh Christ! That would explain it, of course."

"Anything else you want to know, any more skeletons rattling to escape from their cupboards?"

"Well, there is another thing;"

"Come on, out with it." snapped Lucy.

"I'm not sure I ought to ask,"

"Don't worry, I won't answer if I don't want to tell you," she assured him.

"OK," he said, "Here goes: how is that you know when Barry's having an affair?"

"Aha, "said Lucy, "I just do."

"No, you can't just say it's a woman's thing-a-me-bob,"

"Womanly intuition?" she suggested.

"How does that work?"

"I know, you know, I know, *dahling*," mocked Lucy.

"Seriously," persisted Tom.

"He goes to the dentist," announced Lucy. "That's an important clue."

"The dentist?"

"Yes. You heard. The dentist."

"But what's that got to do with anything?"

"Simple. He associates bad teeth with bad breath. If he's not 'playing away' he'll miss his six-monthly check-ups because he hates needles and drills, the taste of the mouth-wash, everything. But as soon as he starts checking his breath ready for what we sociologists call, *'sucking-face'*, he's off to that surgery like a greyhound out of trap five."

"Amazing," said Tom. "I'm speechless."

"Don't be," she answered. "There are loads more clues."

"Alright, how can you be so sure that he doesn't know that you're having an affair?"

"Just look at him," she suggested. "You've seen how he acts all the time with that silly, possessive jealousy of his? Which is really boring and tedious when you have to live with it... But actually, truth is, he doesn't notice *me* from one week to the next; he doesn't notice details. He's so wrapped-up in himself, he's distracted, unfocused, vain. He's the kid who wants all the toys but doesn't play with any of them. Just wants to keep them away from the others."

"Sounds really charming," suggested Tom.

"Shut up! Listen, he truly does not believe that I could be unfaithful. Not to him. Not because of me, because of him. He's always shocked when anyone doesn't like him. He loves himself and assumes that everyone else does too. As far as he's concerned, they'd be mad not to."

Lucy was talking more rapidly now, and panting for breath between sentences.

"We'd know all about it if he was onto us," she whispered. "He wouldn't keep quiet about that. There would be major fireworks, World War Three. I don't even want to think about it."

"But when he starts an affair..." prompted Tom, trying to restore the balance on his own scales of justice.

"Like I said, you can't miss the signs. There's going to the dentist, oh and he buys lots of new clothes, all of a sudden. Then he starts spraying himself every morning with one of those male perfumes that cost about fifty quid a bucket and have names like 'Chunk', 'Snarl' or 'Prong'. Something that sounds really butch so that guys like Brendan don't have to admit they're using scent."

"How do you know that's not for your benefit?"

Lucy shrieked a mighty guffaw into the telephone mouthpiece.

"Oh please!" she pleaded. "He spends hours fiddling with his hair style before he goes out, not when he comes in. He twists and turns in front of the mirror, trying to check his profile. When he gets home, he chucks his clothes on the floor and slumps on the sofa like a sack of spuds."

"Oh God; anything else?" laughed Tom.

"Yes," she answered quietly.

"What?"

"He leaves me alone," she said.

"Huh?"

"He leaves me alone, sexually."

"You mean, err....?"

"In bed; do I have to draw you pictures?"

"Oh. I'm sorry," blushed Tom.

"Don't be. Look, I have to go."

"Bye now," murmured Tom, "When can . . . . "

But she had put the phone down.

* * *

Tom heard nothing from Lucy for the next two days. He agonised about phoning her but always decided not to. He kept reminding himself that it was the weekend and Barry would be home. Tom knew he could not manage a 'matey' chat if Barry happened to answer and Lucy would not thank him for the consequences if he aroused suspicion by clamming up on Barry and asking to speak to Lucy. Tom spent the weekend swearing at every difficulty, resorting frequently to kicking pieces of his furniture. He broke a cup and two plates by slamming them down as punishment for some imagined provocation. He spent hours on the internet researching information on the V1 and V2 rockets, then followed dubious links to sites for militaria-buffs and even more seriously unpleasant neo-Nazi web sites. Eventually he endeavoured to cheer himself up by clicking onto some of his favourite pornography sites, only to become even more depressed when he found an image of a naked woman who reminded him of Lucy. He stared at the unreal size of the model's breasts and considered how outraged Lucy would be if she knew he was capable of demeaning her in this way.

From the darkness outside a gust of wind rattled the front windows of his living room, pellets of driven rain crackled against the glass and the invading draught billowed the curtains. Startled, Tom apologised out loud to the contorted woman on his computer screen and clicked through the shut-down routine. On his way to the kitchen he picked up a sheaf of notes he had made on <u>The End of the Affair</u> before lending the book to Lucy. In his depression, even the title of the novel seemed horribly apposite. While the kettle rose to the boil he read a quotation from Sarah's journal, '*I want Maurice.*' she had written, '*I want ordinary corrupt human love.*'

'I hate Graham Greene,' thought Tom as he blistered a tea-bag with a hissing rod of scalding water. It seemed to Tom that Greene had wanted to engage Catholicism as his guide, but strangely did not want to be shown how he could live his life without sin. It was the process of suffering that seemed to interest Greene. He wrote far more about the unhappiness that came after the affair than he did about the pleasures of being in love. In Greene's novel Tom saw a very personal struggle with religious belief transformed into a catalogue of hate. Could any of that, he wondered, be rendered tolerable, even comfortable, by the cleansing processes of confession and absolution?

'Forgive me Father, for I have sinned!' intoned Tom on Greene's behalf.

'Oh that's alright, my son,' he responded in a clerical voice, *'Now just fuck-orf and sin no more. Well, at least until the next time some tasty crumpet crosses your path....'*

Fortunately for Greene's life as a writer, absolution would only be temporary. The human condition could be relied upon to provoke endless further suffering; and without suffering Greene found nothing worth writing about.

Tom extracted the teabag using the back of a teaspoon and carefully dripped in enough milk to create the exact nut-brown brew he preferred. He read another line copied from Sarah's journal:

'Dear God, You know I want to want Your pain, but I don't want it now. Take it away for a while and give it me another time.'

'Blair, he's a bit of a Catholic too, isn't he?' hissed Tom as he switched off the kitchen lights and shuffled towards his bed. 'How much might that explain?' he wondered. 'When Greene was writing, what's that, fifty years ago?' thought Tom, 'religion had become a private matter, a matter of conscience. As a vital prescription for life, it was effectively ignored in the public realm. God sat at the apex of an imaginary hierarchy, somewhere above the Queen, but the business of government was conducted in her name not His.'

Tom had learned at school and later at university, that the big issues of twentieth century politics were economic and social and that the proposed answers came from ideological camps, not theological ones. Graham Greene had made Maurice and Sarah struggle with religious conviction alone and separately. Theirs was written as a private struggle. The character Smythe argued against religion in public - out there on Clapham Common, in fact, laughed Tom - but Greene didn't want to introduce a soap-box debate into his story. Smythe only mattered because he could be supposed to be Maurice's successor as Sarah's lover. When it became clear that he wasn't, Greene swept Smythe aside because his struggle with questions of belief lacked the grand anguish Greene had invested in Maurice and in Sarah.

* * *

The next morning was the Monday of the half-term week. Tom got up late and went out, intending to go shopping. He had only gone as far as the foot of the stairs when he saw, deposited blatantly on the hall floor, amidst the post for himself and people in the other flats, a familiar creamy envelope, made fat by another letter from Penny to Barry.

"Bugger!" he exclaimed and trudged back up to his flat where he deposited the envelope in a kitchen drawer. "Bugger!" he repeated, removed the envelope and took it through to the living room where he slid it into the top drawer of his desk.

"Bugger!" he said again and reached for the phone, dialling Barry's office number with quick jabs at the memory buttons. Barry's business partner, Paul, answered with a cheery *'Good Morning'* and, after a brief *'How are you?'* put him through to Barry.

"Corky," gushed Barry. "How're you doing, mate?"

Tom ignored the question assuming, correctly, that it was a formality and that Barry did not really want to know how Tom felt on this, or any other, Monday morning. Tom resisted the fleeting temptation to reply with, *'I'm pretty fucking depressed, thanks for asking, mainly because my affair with your wife is not going at all well.'*

What he actually said was,

"Fine. There's a letter here for you, came this morning."

"No problemo," breezed Barry. "Stick it in the desk drawer as per, I'll pop by on my way home this evening, probably around seven. Don't worry if you can't be in, I've got the keys on me."

"Bugger!" Tom mouthed silently; horrified to be reminded again that Barry could wander into his flat at any time. Barry's voice interrupted his anxiety;

"OK. See you later, mate. Busy, busy! We don't all get six holidays a year like you bloody teachers. Some of us have to work for a living."

"More fool you," muttered Tom angrily, trying to imagine Barry facing Year 9 after morning break on a wet Monday.

By two in the afternoon, Tom had returned to his flat bearing a new lamp he had purchased to stand alongside his desk. Nervously, he unpacked the components from their intricate packaging and spread them on the carpet. To his slight surprise nothing seemed to be missing and so he began puzzling over the instructions which came in fourteen languages, one of which resembled English.

'*Be connecting the two rods by turning them against each other.*' he read. The phone rang and he picked it up, distractedly, with a half-hearted, "Yeah?" There was a short pause before Lucy's voice said softly,

"Hello, Tom."

"Ah, Lucy," whispered Tom, "I'm so glad it's you. I've been desolate since Friday."

"I'm sorry, darling," she replied, "but me too." Tom waited for her to say more, his own thoughts were in turmoil trying to re-order something coherent from all the lines he had imagined himself saying to her during the previous weekend.

"Tom?" she asked.

"Yes, I'm here."

"Listen," she said, "you're at home today aren't you?"

"All this week," he said.

"Listen," she repeated, "can I come round now? Right now? We've got an hour!"

Tom was so thrilled to hear her say '*we*' that it was a couple of seconds before he said,

"Yes, oh Yes! Please do."

"Mary's going to have Alice until half-three. The other two are playing with friends and I don't have to pick them up until after four," she recited, "and I've told Mary that I have to visit a sick friend."

"That's true in my case," he replied. "Does this mean you're available on prescription now?"

Lucy giggled, "See you in a mo, 'bye!"

"See you, darling," he responded, already heading for the bedroom to change into a clean shirt and on to the bathroom to clean his teeth. Tom looked at his reflection in the mirror as the paste foamed around his lips, suddenly wondering when was the last time he had been to the dentist.

When Lucy stepped into his hallway, they stood apart facing each other, hesitating for a moment. Lucy frowned very slightly and whispered,

"Come here!"

Tom held her in a long embrace, their lips churning hungrily together.

"Missed you," she gasped.

"I wanted you so much. I want so much more," he murmured.

"No preliminaries, "said Lucy. "Let's go straight to bed."

"Let me undress you," said Tom.

"I don't need all these clothes," she said, unfastening her skirt at the side and letting it fall. Tom's fingers trembled as he began to undo the buttons on her cardigan. "I didn't stop to dress up," she said to his ear.

Tom slid the cardigan down her arms and sank to his knees, gently rolling down her tights and pressing his face into the curve below her navel. Lucy pulled her T-shirt over head and unhooked her bra as Tom rose to lift out each of her breasts, kissing them longingly in turn. They fell upon the bed and made love with a searching passion, each responding eagerly to the other's caresses. Tom pressed his lips to every part of her and tasted her with his tongue. Lucy bucked and shouted when she came, jagging the skin on his back with her finger nails.

Tom lay beside her, gasping and completely spent. When their breathing had subsided to something more normal Lucy rolled to face him and, bending her left arm, propped her head on her cupped hand. Tom lay on his side, facing her, reaching to entwine the curls of her dark hair before stroking her face and running his fingers gently down the curves of her body to rest on her hip.

"We can have a proper relationship, you know," she said firmly.

"I want to be with you; come in with you, go out with you, sit in silence sometimes, wake up next to you," he answered. "I want all of those things with you."

"Have lunch with me tomorrow," she smiled, "The girls will be there, we can talk - or be silent - while they're playing."

"I'd love to," said Tom, "but don't make lunch for me, let's prepare it together. That's a relationship."

Lucy kissed him passionately and rolled on top of him, feeling his recovering penis growing tall between her thighs.

"Be quick now," she giggled. "*Bloody* Mary will start to wonder where I've got to."

"Call her and say you're coming," growled Tom, lifting her above him as he entered her again and started thrusting gently upward against her. Lucy responded to the rhythm of his rising and falling, she closed her eyes and placed her hands on his shoulders, her knees clasped his abdomen and she gasped as his hands folded around her hard brown nipples.

Later, watching Lucy hurrying to dress, Tom suggested that she could truthfully tell Mary that her sick friend had made a miraculous recovery.

"Ooh, that reminds me," she said, "I want to talk to you tomorrow about that strange sequence in the Greene book where miraculous cures seem to happen after Sarah dies."

"You mean like Smythe losing his facial disfigurement and the letter from Parkis saying how his son was cured just by touching one of Sarah's books?"

"Weird isn't it?" she asked.

"No it's just Greene playing with Bendrix's bitterness and hatred. Greene was almost trying to turn the tables on himself by showing that Bendrix persisted in resisting belief even when not believing had become irrational. In the end, he's got Maurice saying to God '*I hate You as though You existed.*' And then he resents God for giving him back his *hopeless crippled life.*"

"What?"

"You know, after the flying bomb nearly killed him, but Sarah thought it had, and made her deal with God that she'd stop having Bendrix as her lover if God brought him back to life."

"Oh yes, and Bendrix mocks her for praying, he teases her about praying for a miracle; but in the context of the story, him being alive actually is a miracle in Sarah's eyes, isn't it?" reasoned Lucy, speaking with slow deliberation.

"Talking of miracles," broke in Tom, "that'll be your taxi at the door."

Lucy kissed him and hurried down the stairs. Tom stood naked on the landing watching her go, only flinching sideways behind the newel post when she pulled open the lower door and swept out.

* * *

By early evening he had enjoyed a long slow bath, reminiscing with delight on their love-making. Returning to the living room the remaining pieces of the lamp seemed to slot together easily now that he was no longer addressing them with impatience and frustration. *'Ah! The power of love,'* he mused, *'I wonder if the makers of flat-pack DIY furniture should add a note about half-way through their instructions saying that if it's not going well when you reach this point, have a damn good shag before you try again?'*

The phone rang and he reached to answer it.

"Hi!" said Barry. "Saw your lights on. I'm just parking-up, be with you in a minute. Got any cold beers?"

"Had a hard day at the office darling? Slaving over a hot secretary, as usual?" asked Tom, stopping just in time from saying something silly about having a hard afternoon himself.

"You sound a bit more cheerful," said Barry.

"I've just managed to put together a Chinese flat-pack standard lamp," boasted Tom.

"Bully for you," replied Barry and ended the call.

Tom retrieved Penny's letter from his desk and carried it through to the kitchen then took two cans from the fridge. He heard a rattle of keys and Barry pushed open his door.

"Cheers!" said Barry, accepting the can Tom held out to him. "Sorry I can only stop for one, mate. Lucy's been a bit under the weather lately, especially now it's half-term and she's got the other two at home all day as well as having her hands full with Alice."

"Oh dear," said Tom.

"Anyway, she rang just now to see what time I'd be home. Sounds as if she's had a bit of day of it; had to call on good old Mary across the road."

"Oh dear," said Tom, again.

"Then she said you'd agreed to be on stand-by to go round tomorrow because Mary's going to Roehampton to visit her sister. Thanks mate that would help. The kids really enjoyed coming here the other day."

"Don't sound so surprised," interrupted Tom.

"No, no, it's good. I'm glad. They were all talking about it. Especially Cherie, you're a hit with her. Emma doesn't say much, though. I have to watch that one, she's a smart little cow."

"I like her," said Tom.

"Anything you can do that might cheer old Luce up a bit, I know you will. She's getting a bit niggled about me being away so much, up and down to Nottingham. In fact she had the screaming habdabs with me at the weekend, a major wobbly, big-time. Demanded I let Paul take over the Nottingham account for a while. No way! Sometimes I think she just doesn't get it. Love me, love my job, I told her straight."

"Yes, that would do it," observed Tom, dryly.

"Do what?"

"Give her the screaming whatevers, like you just said."

"It's work I told her," insisted Barry, tipping his head back to drain the last drops from his can of lager. "We certainly need the money I bring in, and she's happy enough to go out spending it."

"Oh dear," commented Tom, "did you say anything to her about Penny?"

"You are joking, aren't you? I'm in enough shit already with Luce, I don't want her getting wind that I'm seeing another woman. Especially one of her old mates. At least I've got things going smoothly with Penny now," added Barry, tucking the letter coyly into his jacket. "Mind you, I sometimes wish there was a way of getting your wife to understand why you want a mistress; then they'd see where they'd been going wrong."

"Sounds a bit risky to me," said Tom. "I'm sure I saw that in a play once. It all backfired predictably because the wife started behaving like the mistress, while the mistress – wanting to supplant the wife and secure her own future – starting behaving like the wife."

"What happened?" enquired Barry, sounding genuinely interested.

"Bloody chaos! Poor sod went home for his tea and slippers

and there's the wife in bra and suspenders wanting him to have his wicked way with her on the kitchen table. Then he trots round to the mistress for an uncomplicated shag only to find she's gone all homely, dressed herself in a chintzy apron and is lifting an apple pie out of the oven."

"I can't see either Lucy or Penny going for any of that," said Barry. "Penny's very up market you know, she really gets off on me being her bit of rough...She had a new kitchen put in last year, all stainless steel and blue lights. Looks like the bridge of the Starship 'Enterprise', absolutely spotless. I don't think she's even found where the bloody oven is yet, let alone how it works."

Barry opened the fridge door and helped himself to another can of lager.

"Don't mind if I do," he said, "and anyway, the bloody Nottingham project's started going well at last. I've sweated tears of blood on that one, I can tell you. I've earned my bit of R & R with Penny on the side."

"Good," said Tom, "I'm sure Lucy would understand if you could only find the words to tell her."

"Yeah, cheers," laughed Barry, "through a megaphone from a safe distance, wearing a cricket box and a flak jacket! Christ did I ever tell you about Paul?"

"What about Paul?"

"You don't know this, right? In case anyone ever asks," Barry continued, "but a year or so ago, when Anna had just started her new job up in town, she came back earlier than expected one afternoon and there's Paul going hammer and tongs with the au pair girl on the sofa in the front room. Bra and knickers strewn across the floor, the whole lot! Try and fast talk your way out of that one, mate."

"Oh dear," said Tom, remembering the first time he had made love to Lucy in the middle of Barry's front room.

"And do you know what was the very first thing Anna said? This still cracks me up, I can tell you," roared Barry.

"Obviously not," murmured Tom.

"She said, hah, women eh? You wouldn't believe how their minds work. She said, '*Mind my new cushions!*' Can you believe it? Not '*Fuck me, what's all this then?*' No it was just the cushion covers; them's what she thought of first. Of course she gave Paul a right roasting afterwards and she's never going to let him forget it. And the au pair had to shoot back to Holland or Denmark or somewhere a bit smartish. Sad really, she was pretty little thing, and obviously a goer. Wouldn't have minded a bit myself, but not in the front room; I ask you!"

"No," agreed Tom with a weak smile, "not in the front room. Now, about my spare keys," he ventured, "I'd really like them back, if I could...."

"Don't worry, old son," said Barry with the can against his lips, "there's going to be changes, very soon. Just between us girls," he whispered confidentially, "Penny's about to give her old man the heave-ho. Then, when he's off the scene, we won't need the letters anymore. I'll be able to phone from the office anytime and she can send me e-mails. It's all going to get a lot easier."

Barry dropped the empty lager can into the kitchen waste bin.

"I'll be off then," he said. "See you soon, and hey, you must come to our fireworks do, back at our place, after the big display on the Common."

"What? Are they having one out here this year?"

"No, mate, not here. We always go back to Streatham for the fireworks, remember? We meet up at Paul's house and then walk over to the Common. Bye now."

"When?" called Tom.

"On the fifth, of course. You should know that, being a bloody historian!"

"Bye," muttered Tom, closing the door.

Chapter Six

All was peaceful when Tom entered Lucy's domain just before noon the following day. Lucy greeted him tenderly and showed him Emma building a Lego village in one room while Cherie and Alice painted exuberantly in another. Sheets and sheets of paper were being covered with boisterous waves and swirls of colour. Tom felt he could admire the confidence of their brush strokes and the uncompromising speed with which they pursued their ideas. Lucy laughed cheerfully to hear him encouraging the girls with a very passable imitation of the critic Brian Sewell. Cherie redoubled her efforts while Alice insisted that he should take up a brush and produce a '*painting of your Mummy*' to compare with the piece which she had just finished. Tom had to admit to Alice that he couldn't paint 'a mummy' anything like as beautiful as hers, but offered to paint her favourite character from a nursery rhyme.

"Little Miss Muffet!" squeaked Alice without hesitation.

"But don't paint the spider," ordered Cherie. "Alice hates spiders."

"Alrighty," agreed Tom. "A Little Miss Muffet, with her tuffet, but without the spider."

"What's a tuffet?" asked Cherie.

"One of those," replied Tom, painting a large brown squiggle with added purple dots.

"Oh, yes, I see," nodded Cherie.

"Me see! Me see!" demanded Alice, then plunged off her stool as she tried to clamber nearer to Tom. He reached down and lifted the crying child, comforting her as best he could while she wailed and tears streamed down her face. Lucy peered anxiously in at the door and smiled encouragingly when she saw Tom was winning against the tears. Instinctively, he began to recite the nursery rhyme, with Alice joining in slightly behind him. Carried along with her increasingly gleeful response to his recital Tom launched himself into an operatic spoof of Miss Muffet imitating something he remembered from television when, as a child, he had watched Dudley Moore sing *Leetle Miss Muff – it* in the style of Peter Pears and Benjamin Britten. When he came to the dramatic entry of the spider, Alice squealed again and threw her arms around his neck. Tom jumped up, stood Alice alongside him and then they both ran away from the spider, seeking sanctuary with Lucy.

Lucy stood laughing in the middle of the kitchen while Tom buried his face in her neck and Alice burrowed into the generous folds of her long skirt.

"Save us, mummy!" they both cried, "Save us from the big, bad spider!"

"Where's that naughty spider?" demanded Lucy. "Why I'll huff and I'll puff and I'll blow his house down."

"No, no, that's all wrong," called Cherie from the dining room. "That's in the Big Bad Wolf."

"There's not a big, bad wolf in this house as well as a spider, is there?" quavered Tom, giving Alice a look of terror.

"No. We chopped him up, the bad wolf," insisted Alice, stamping back to the dining room to remonstrate with Cherie.

Lucy darted across to close the door and then swept Tom into her arms and kissed him with passion, pressing her hips forward so that her pelvis rode against his thigh. She only broke away from him when the sound of raised voices from the other room became too loud and she clapped her hands calling out,

"Lunch is ready, everyone must wash their hands! Right now, please!"

Tom sat in a big chair with his back to the garden.

"That's Daddy's," said Emma.

"Emma!" said Lucy, "Tom's our guest; he can sit where he wants."

Emma frowned.

"If I can choose," smiled Tom, "I'd like to sit where Emma is and have Emma sit where I am."

Emma glanced at Lucy,

"Sit where you like," snapped Lucy, busily sawing a large circle of pizza into many segments of different sizes. Tom stood up and pushed back the big chair. Emma wriggled into his place, carrying her smaller chair as if it were an appendage attached to her bottom. Tom carefully manoeuvred his chair into its new place, managing to wobble the cat's saucer of milk as he did so. Milk splashed onto the floor all around the saucer.

"Sorry, puss," said Tom, looking at Lucy who merely shrugged and went on distributing pizza and salad. Alice gestured with a fish finger and stated authoritatively,

"Hermione always spills her milk, she won't mind."

"How do you know?" challenged Emma.

"There," said Lucy, sitting down, "has everyone got what they want?"

"Mmmm, yes thanks," said Tom.

"Don't speak with your mouth full!" commanded Cherie, glancing artfully at Lucy.

"Cherie!" snapped Lucy, and then they all giggled.

"Isn't this fun?" said Tom.

They sat, all four of them, around the big table at the far end of the kitchen, plates were passed to and fro and Emma walked over to the fridge to fetch another box of fruit juice, while Alice embarked on a confusing story about the supposed adventures of Hermione, the cat.

"Don't you think I look very '*Clapham*' today Tom?" asked Lucy, lifting up the hems of her long blue skirt as if she were performing a curtsy while still seated. Tom wanted to say, 'I'd love you in anything, or nothing,' but managed a more restrained,

"The play-dough around your bottom is an interesting touch."

"What?" demanded Lucy, jumping up. "This was clean on this morning." She craned her neck first left then right, trying to see behind her.

"Emma," she insisted, "have I sat in some play-dough or not?"

"Bit," replied Emma, looking up briefly from her crescent of pizza.

"Damn!" said Lucy, unfastening her skirt and shifting it around her waist.

"God!" she snapped when she saw the white marbling imprinted on the blue fabric. She scooped up the hem, then angrily dropped the skirt to the floor and stepped out of it.

"Mum! Your knickers! Tom's here!" screeched Emma.

"Oh he's a big boy, I'm sure he's seen knickers before," replied Lucy, scrubbing at the marks with the dish cloth. "This stuff isn't supposed to leave marks, you know. Maybe it's not Play-dough; I know, it's powder paint. How did that get there? Excuse me Tom," she called over her shoulder, "I've got to put this in to soak."

Tom and the girls sat at the table in a slightly awkward silence as they heard Lucy's feet go pounding up the stairs in a great hurry.

"Tom," said Emma, "can we watch the Harry Potter video after lunch?"

"I'm sure you can," he replied, "but I'd better check with your Mum first."

"She'll allow it if you ask," commented Cherie, "'cos you're a teacher and you can tell her it's about school."

Lucy returned, wearing a much shorter skirt, and Tom smiled his approval.

"Watch it!" said Lucy with a wink in his direction. "That's enough of me looking like a proper *'Between the Commons Matron'*. Barry *will* be disappointed, yet again. He says he's doing his bit to conform. You know he wants to get some big, four-wheel drive people carrier? A monster of a car. I'll never drive it, I couldn't park it, but they all use them for the school-run round here."

"Not much call for four-wheel drive, off-roading in Clapham," agreed Tom. "Bet they all want you to believe they've got country cottages down in Dorset or in the Cotswolds."

"Most of them have," moaned Lucy. "You should see the number of Countryside Alliance stickers on the cars in this street."

"Yeah, they're all for fox-hunting, I'm sure," snorted Tom. "There's more blooming foxes live within a one mile radius of this house than there are in the whole of blinking Dorset. But you don't see the toffs in their red coats galloping around the wheelie bins of Clapham, do you?"

"Jane next door claims their jeep-thing was essential about two years ago when it snowed heavily one night and they drove all the way to the top of the hill without spinning their wheels."

"Oh good," said Tom.

"No it wasn't," laughed Lucy, "because the grit lorries hadn't done the side roads and so Webbs Road and all those streets up there were totally grid-locked, and so they had to abandon the jeep and walk back home again. Serves them right."

Lucy turned to Alice, gently removed her bib and wiped food from around her mouth. Alice was almost asleep, but still clutching a fish-finger.

"Come along, Ali, beddy-bies time for you," she said. "And Emma, you two can watch a video provided you don't argue over which one."

"Harry Potter!" called Emma and Cherie in unison, clattering down from the table and dashing into the front room.

"Excuse us, Tom," said Lucy. "Sit tight and I'll just put this one down for a nap, then we might get a bit of peace. Put the radio on if you want to hear the one o'clock news."

Tom smiled after her, reached to switch on the radio and then rose and began clearing the table. He was busy with the washing-up when Lucy returned, closing the door behind her. She walked over to Tom and hugged him from behind. Tom turned to clasp her and they kissed for a long time.

"Ugh! Wet hands, mister!" squealed Lucy, jumping back from him, "I can feel a wet patch on my back!"

"Better take your top off, then," suggested Tom.

"Watch it!" laughed Lucy. "You've already had your knicker-treat for today."

"Emma really responded to that didn't she?" said Tom. "Think she'll tell Barry?"

"Doesn't matter, either way," said Lucy with another wink.

"It was all perfectly innocent, wasn't it?"

"Perfectly," said Tom.

"Coffee?" she asked.

"Show us your knickers."

"One lump or two, vicar?"

They sat at opposite sides of the table, sipping their coffee, the radio burbling quietly in the background.

"If I hear Jack Straw mention the moral high ground just once more, I'm going to puke bone-marrow!" said Lucy suddenly, stretching across the table to silence the radio. "How many children do they think have died since we invaded Iraq?" demanded Lucy.

"*We* didn't invade Iraq, that's the whole point."

"You know what I mean. They can't drop their bombs on cities and say they're only targeting the insurgents," she insisted.

"They call it *collateral damage*," said Tom.

"I don't care what they call it; 'Surgical strikes', my arse! They use technological euphemisms to distance themselves from the consequences. *'Collateral damage'* is bits of people's arms and legs blown across the street. Mentally, they're all in denial. It's the same technocratic excuse as that old German guy used when he tried to explain why he'd made rockets for Hitler. You know who I mean, the Americans captured him and then he designed all their missiles and space rockets...They didn't care what he'd done for Hitler."

"Do you mean Werner von Braun?" suggested Tom. "The Yanks were just glad they'd nabbed him before the Russians did."

"That's him," she continued, using her accomplished German accent. "*My job iz to make ze rockets to go up. Vair zey are coming down, zis iz not my department.*"

"Are you comparing us to the Nazis?" asked Tom.

"Look at those helmets the American soldiers wear now," she said. "With their sun-glasses and desert camouflage, don't they look just like Rommel's Afrika Korps, or whatever it was?"

Tom nodded.

"At least in Vietnam, the Americans wore those softer, rounder helmets. They didn't look so bloody sinister." she concluded.

Tom leaned back in his chair and smiled agreement at her.

"Yeah, you'd think they'd use an image consultant, wouldn't you?" he said. Lucy had got the bit between her teeth and reached up to her shelf of recipe books, plucking down Tom's copy of The End of the Affair.

"Have you read it again, already?" he asked.

"Oh yes," she said, flicking through the pages. "There's several bits I wanted to discuss with you." Tom smiled and leaned forward, resting his hands on the table.

"Maurice Bendrix and Henry," she said, "what a pair of horrors they both were."

"They were very different from each other."

"But horrors, none the less," she insisted.

"It was a long time ago, and it was fiction even then," said Tom, "and things were very different in those days."

"It's not that long," she continued, "only fifty years. There're plenty of people still alive from those days. But those two men, they can't even be decent to one another. Look at that dreadful lunch Bendrix inflicts on Henry at his club. The very idea of men having 'clubs'; I mean places where they could go and be *safe* from women. They could sit there, bigoted as hell, surrounded by similar old buffers and served by obsequious lackeys who knew what they meant when they asked for '*The Usual*'."

She was into her stride now and Tom sat back, folding his arms, content just to listen.

"And women! Just look how Greene uses women. They're all either prostitutes, invisible nameless menials or impossibly beautiful *femmes fatales*. Interestingly, their femininity is more likely to be fatal to themselves than it is to their blokes."

"I don't know Greene's work well enough," interrupted Tom. "I just read this book because of finding where he had lived and then it was mentioned on a web-site about Clapham and the Blitz."

"And children, for God's sake!" continued Lucy. "He just makes them seem a sickly encumbrance, like Parkis's son."

"Mrs Bertram, Sarah's mother," said Tom, "I don't think she fits into any of your categories."

"No, I agree," responded Lucy." But she's hardly an attractive figure either, is she? She has a spoiling role. She's predatory and she's after Henry for money. Then Maurice has dinner with her, and why does he do that? Only to prevent himself from starting an affair with Sylvia, the '*sweet young thing*' he's just lured away from the dreadful Mr Waterbury."

She looked directly at him and Tom nodded his agreement.

"See," she resumed," pretty women just gravitate helplessly to the most attractive man available. Sylvia had settled for Waterbury until Maurice came along. Then she trots after him like some soppy spaniel; silly bitch! And Greene wants you to know that he, himself, is the most attractive man available. Nobody ever suggests that he's put anything of himself, autobiographically that is, into the character of boring old Henry."

"Mmm, well yes," added Tom, "and you could equally say that Greene doesn't identify himself with the rationalist Smythe, or Parkis or of course the celibate priest, Father Whatsit."

"Father Crompton," replied Lucy, flicking urgently through the pages of the book. "And look at the *'happy ending'*. Two blokes - the ex-lover and the cuckolded husband - strolling off to the pub together. He's got Maurice mixing up love of God with love of women; then protesting that he's too old and too tired to learn how to love either of them. See, here, the very last words in the story, *'leave me alone for ever.'* But he's not alone, is he? He's living with poor, benighted, bloody Henry. Henry who sleeps with a silly smile on his silly face"

"I bet I do that," said Tom.

"I'll let you know," snapped Lucy.

Tom felt he should speak now and gently lifted the book from Lucy's fingers as if this would add some authority to his views.

"Greene, or rather Maurice, does say at the beginning and again at the end, that this story is a record of hate..."

"But," broke in Lucy, "at the beginning he says he hates Henry and he hates Sarah. At the end, Sarah's dead and Maurice is living in Henry's house saying things like *'I have to be strong for both of us now.'*

"He hates God," continued Tom. "But I think Greene only wrote that to give Maurice a flaw, something that would set him apart from Greene. It's having Maurice hate God that lets Greene deny that Maurice is truly Greene himself."

"Huh?" uttered Lucy. "I think you've lost me there."

Tom ignored her confusion and pressed on with his own question,

"Can you see me doing that with Barry?" he enquired.

"Doing what?" she snorted.

"Sharing a house."

"No I fucking can't!" exclaimed Lucy, clasping her hand to her mouth and whirling round to make sure none of the children had slipped into earshot.

"It's OK," Tom assured her, "the telly's still raging away in the other room."

"If I'd thought," said Lucy, "that I'd be the sort of mother who parks her kids in front of the telly in the holidays....."

"They all do it," said Tom.

"Not round here, they don't," she complained. "Not them. No, they all rush around doing elaborate programmes of piano lessons, dancing, gymnastics, fencing, yoga, foreign languages, extra Maths... Anything to improve the little darlings."

"Yeah, and they've all got pots of money, live-in Nannies and au pairs, and then when the kids are about seven or eight, they ship them off to boarding school. Then I guess it's a bit of a novelty having them come home for *the hols*. They probably all go skiing, or at least off-roading at their second home in the country."

"Oh, fuck, I'm such a dismal failure," moaned Lucy, slumping forward with her head in her hands, "I don't do any of that."

"You're here for them when it matters," said Tom, reaching to take her hands in his.

"You won't criticise me darling, will you? Not in the cruel way that Barry does?"

Tom stood and circled the table to put his arms around her shoulders before kissing her neck through the thick tresses of her hair.

"Be careful, darling, the girls..." she said kindly.

"I know," he answered, stepping away and filling a glass with water from the cold tap,

"Ooh, I'd like some water," said Lucy.

"I'll find you a clean glass," he said.

"I'll drink from yours, don't be silly," she chided, then added very quietly, "it's not as if we haven't exchanged any bodily fluids, is it?"

"Barry's started reading The End of the Affair now. Imagine that. He just picked it up on Sunday morning and sat there, reading, for about two hours; unprecedented. I had to rescue it from him..."

"Cor, blimey Guv'nor!" exclaimed Tom, mocking Barry's accent, "but it ain't got no pictures!"

Lucy frowned,

"That's not fair; he's surprisingly well-read. He just wouldn't want any of *the lads* to know that he reads books. Anyway, what was it you asked me about Barry just now?"

"Nothing, I just wondered if you could imagine Barry and me sharing a house like Bendrix and Henry do."

"Of course," giggled Lucy. "You mean the lover and the husband?"

"Yes."

"I can see the two of you in the pub, crying into your beer and complaining about how badly women have treated you."

"I'm not like that, am I?" protested Tom.

"No, but you might try to help Barry. That's your nature, and you don't realise that he'd never lift a finger to help you."

"He does, sometimes," argued Tom, wondering why he too had now come to Barry's defence.

"No," said Lucy, "Barry does you favours; he does them because he enjoys the feeling of patronage it gives him. He likes to feel that he is distributing his largesse to a few selected recipients who'll be suitably grateful. But never forget, it's your gratitude he wants. He likes having people beholden to him. For all your intelligence my darling, you're a complete sucker when you come up against a calculating, selfish bastard like our Brendan."

Tom wanted to protest that this was unfair, but remembered that he had yet to recover his house keys from Barry. Instead he said to Lucy,

"But you married him!"

Lucy stood up slowly and turned to Tom, very deliberately placing her hands on his shoulders so that he faced her squarely.

"And that," she began, "is probably why I've come to love you. If I'd known you before I married Barry, I'd still have married him; every time. I've had to learn about living together the hard way. Learning by doing, I think it's called. Now I know what you get with a man like Barry, and that's why I can see the value of having a man like you."

"I don't think that makes me feel very happy," whispered Tom.

"It wasn't meant to, but it's true none the less," she confirmed. "Barry is the type of guy who woos and wows his women. He likes the chase, but afterwards his heart's not in it for the long term."

"Don't I have any wow?"

"Frankly, no," said Lucy flatly. Tom pulled a face. "But you do have something else. Let me finish. Barry will carry on doing what he's good at, which is having affairs. But you, my darling, will be having affairs with the women Barry has married and then neglected."

"Oh," he complained, sourly, "frustrated housewives, I suppose, who've had the Brendan Sands experience and find themselves less than totally fulfilled?"

"Precisely, Tom. You've got it. I love you for being the caring sort who can actually see what life might be like for me. I've been so distressed I even looked up the word 'husband' in the dictionary not long ago, soon after Barry started disappearing up to Nottingham for days on end. It's so simple. When it's used as a noun it does mean a woman's partner in marriage, but as a verb it means to look after, *to care for with art and skill*."

"So you want me to be a verb, not a noun?" asked Tom.

"Yes," said Lucy, "I want you to be my *doing* word."

Tom held her fingers to his lips and kissed them as sensually as he could, knowing that the videotape might be nearing its end in the front room. He yearned to tell Lucy that Barry was having an affair with a married woman, and to question where that left her theory. He was painfully aware that he could not tell Lucy about Penny without disclosing his own complicity in passing the letters to Barry.

"I'd like to be your gerund," said Tom as sweetly as he could.

"What?" laughed Lucy. "Trust you to come up with some obscure word no one's ever heard of. Unless you mean a gerbil? We've got one of those upstairs in a cage. They're not very attractive; I wouldn't want you to be one of those."

"No," smiled Tom, "it's a grammatical term, from the Latin. It's a noun formed from a verb, usually ends in *ing*, like when someone's said to be '*in the running*' for example."

"I'm glad that's settled," said Lucy.

"I want to be the man who gives your end a good *ing*!"

"Tom! And to think you used to be so shy; I love it when you talk grammar to me, *clever dick*."

Chapter Seven

Lucy rang soon after nine the next morning. She let the phone ring twice then Tom called back.

"Hello sleepy head," she began, "you sound as if you're still in bed."

"I am," he replied. "Can you come round?"

"Don't be silly!" she exclaimed. "But I just wanted to say again how much I enjoyed talking to you yesterday."

"Me too."

"No, it really matters to me, having the chance to talk to someone who isn't eight years old, or less. I tried telling that to Barry, do you know what he said?"

"I can't imagine," said Tom, "but I'm starting to have conversations with your Emma which are far more interesting than the laddish banter I generally manage with Barry."

"Exactly!" exclaimed Lucy. "Imagine how I feel; refereeing disputes over Barbies, Lego and felt-tip pens all day, negotiating what clothes they're all going to wear and then Mr Wonderful comes home and his first words are, *'What's for din-dins, babe?'* Give me strength."

"You were going to tell me what he said?"

"Ugh, the last time I told him I needed adult conversation he tried to make lots of smutty jokes as if I'd said I wanted to watch one of his pathetic *adult* movies."

"Oh dear," said Tom, habitually.

"Then he suggested asking *Bloody* Mary over each day for what he calls *a cuppa...*"

"I've never spoken to Mary," observed Tom.

"Well Germaine Greer she ain't," snapped Lucy. "But, come to think of it, they do look a bit similar."

"Oh dear," said Tom. "Can I see you today?"

"Love to; can we do the swings again and then come over to you afterwards?"

"Sure, but call me when you're leaving home and I'll meet you at the swings."

"Are you sure you want to do that?"

"Yes, 'course I do."

"Great," said Lucy, "but that's not why I called. Before I forget I want to make sure you can come to our party on the sixth, that's the Saturday after next. Will you?"

"Love to. Barry also said something about going to the fireworks at Streatham on November the fifth, and having a party afterwards?"

"Oh yes, I'm glad he suggested that. Do come with us. We'll meet at Paul's house first. You know where that is, don't you?"

"I know the road, just remind me of his house number."

"69. *Soixante Neuf*," she replied. "I'm surprised you forgot that."

"I'll remember it now you've told me," he laughed.

"Seriously, I'd be glad if you came. There's always such a big crowd and I like to have one adult for each child, in the dark and all."

"Was it Cherie who used to get really scared by all the bangs and flashes?"

"She still does, and this will be the first time I've taken Ali. Emma's OK, she's a real tomboy. Hah! Tomboy, we'll put her with you, *Tom -- boy*!"

"What, in case I'm frightened?"

"No, silly, so you can give her the history. About Guy Fawkes blowing up Oliver Cromwell and all that stuff."

"Actually, it wasn't Cromwell. The Gunpowder Plot was in 1605, way before the Civil War. It was James the First and his parliament they planned to destroy."

"See, I knew you'd be able to tell her about it."

"I can't believe," remarked Tom, "that we still have an annual public celebration of religious bigotry on this scale. Do people realise that the 'Guy' they're burning represents a religious minority? I can't believe that anyone more tolerant than Ian Paisley – and that is pretty much everyone – could possibly regard that as something to celebrate..."

"But you will still come with us, won't you?"

"Sure, I'd love to. Burning Catholics? A fine old British Tradition! *Part of our Christian Heritage, init?* We could probably get a grant for next year's party from the Heritage Lottery Fund if we apply in time."

"But remember," stressed Lucy, trying to stop Tom's ranting, "the party at my house will be the next day. The kids will be too tired after we've been to Streatham, so I've decided....."

"You've decided. Good on you."

"Yes, *I've decided* to have a few friends round on Saturday evening. There'll be other littlies there too, so we'll have sparklers and safe stuff in the garden about six-thirty and then sausages and drinks afterwards for the *growns and wrinklies.*"

"I've just thought," said Tom, "The Presidential Election will be over by then. Maybe we'll really have something to celebrate, if Bush loses?"

"Don't count your chickens...see you at the swings, bye"

"Lucy hang on," called out Tom, "I need to let you arrive first,"

"Why?"

"I don't want to look like a paedophile, hanging around the children's play area."

"Are you serious?"

"I'm a teacher; we have to be alert to that kind of thing. As a single adult, especially a male, I can't go anywhere near a play area without at least one child in tow to give me respectability."

"I suppose you're right," said Lucy. "I've never thought of my children as bestowing 'respectability', but I guess when you see an adult with a child it does make them seem more established, more a part of the community."

"I'll try not to look too shifty," laughed Tom.

"Some hope," she replied. "Look, I'll call you when we're ready to leave."

Tom timed his arrival so that Lucy was already inside the fenced-off play-ground when he strode across the wet grass. The children were darting about like quick-silver, eager to try all the apparatus without pause for breath. Lucy wore a long, dark blue, woollen coat and an even longer brown crocheted scarf.

"You made it," she said, squeezing his elbow as he rested against the fence beside her.

"At least I'm not the only man here," observed Tom.

"No, but we are the only couple. See, he's having some '*quality time*' playing with his little boy; those three Clapham Matrons are chatting about house prices ..."

"Prices here, or in the Dordogne? What's the betting?"

"The other two, over by the climbing frame, are au pairs, and I'd love to know what they're discussing so earnestly in Romanian, or is it Polish?"

"Could be house prices too," suggested Tom.

"More likely ironing or the iniquity of their working hours."

"They should be discussing boys," tried Tom provocatively, expecting Lucy to release a feminist volley at him. Her response surprised him.

"I do hope so," she said. "I wish there was some way we could show that we are not a married couple. I want those three posh tarts to know that you're my lover, not my boring old spouse. He's toiling away at his office, just like theirs."

"Do you think they care?"

"You bet they do," said Lucy. "Those women consume. They devour life. They do perfect! They keep tabs on everything that's happening or to be had."

"Go easy on them Luce," said Tom, startled by her vehemence. "They've just got loads of dosh and they know how to spend it."

Lucy narrowed her eyes, taking in every detail of the women's appearances.

"No," she began, "it's more than just money. They're educated and ambitious. They had careers before they opted for this. I'd say they are *driven*. Having a family is the next big project for them. They are single-minded and determined as if their lives depended on it. And in a way they do; well their self-esteem anyway."

Tom followed her gaze and saw three well-dressed women talking and watching their toddlers at play. He turned back to Lucy and frowned. She continued,

"Barry has always been disappointed that I haven't become like them; that I didn't make some la-di-da friends as soon as we moved over here from Streatham. Now, my old friend Penny, she'd fit in with them instantly."

"Penny?" queried Tom, feeling the familiar cold, inner spasm at the mention of her name.

"The one I was at college with? The one who lives in Nottingham. Barry's seen her and her boring-billy husband a few times since he's had that contract up there."

The sight of perfumed, cream-coloured envelopes addressed in Penny's 'head-girl' script in flowing blue ink filled Tom's mind; he could not think what to say but managed to continue looking vaguely puzzled.

"You've met them, you know," continued Lucy. "Penny and the dreadful Graham stayed a night with us last Christmas and I'm sure you were there in the evening. Penny's very striking, very cool; you could easily imagine her chatting languidly with those three."

Tom stared across the play-area and muttered a deliberately non-committal,

"Oh, well, yes."

"Don't stare so obviously," whispered Lucy, physically twisting Tom by his shoulders. "But, when you can, look at their clothes; so carefully chosen, smart but casual, clearly expensive, subtle combinations of autumnal shades, worn once or maybe twice before...Huh, then look at me; cat-hairs on this," she plucked at her collar, "and a smear of Ali's breakfast on my sleeve. This is my winter coat, it must be at least four, no five, yes; *five* years old. I remember buying it when Cherie was still in a baby-sling. Apart from my white raincoat, I don't have other coats to mix and match. This," she brushed her sleeve vigorously, "this is bloody it!"

Tom put his arm around her small frame, feeling her thinness and her angular shoulder blades through the soft navy-blue material. He smelt her perfume and breathed her in.

"I want to kiss you," he said.

"Don't, Emma's looking at us."

He felt her body tense again under his fingers as she continued,

"And look at their kids, Tom; all sweet cheeks and destiny. They've turned motherhood into a spread sheet on their laptops. They're highly competitive, and boy do I know it! And if enjoying the illicit attentions of a wayward lover is this season's fashion accessory, they'll all want one. I bet Penny's got some guy on the side; I know I would have if I'd married that boring arse Graham!"

"Oh dear," said Tom, fearful that Lucy would never forgive his complicity in Barry's liaison with Penny.

"Penny–pots-a-money we used to call her. Bored housewives, nothing to do all day, 'course they're all at it, who can blame them?" chuckled Lucy.

"So things could be looking up for me then kiddo?" laughed Tom, anxious to steer the conversation away from any further mention of Penny.

"Watch it," warned Lucy, kicking his ankle with her black leather boot,

"You're mine, I saw you first, and anyway they would soon tire of you...."

"Why?" demanded Tom, petulantly.

"Because you're always banging on about leftie politics, or history or religion or books. They would only be interested if you had a late-model Porsche and a large portfolio!"

"What?" squealed Tom, "I've never had any complaints..."

"No silly," she soothed, "I mean your investments, your stocks and shares, your *standing in the City*, not your todger! And I thought you were a new man, not an old-school phallocrat."

"I am," he protested ducking and twisting as Lucy poked her fingers into his ribs. "But change the subject," he pleaded, "Emma will think we're having a row."

"No, she's just trying to earwig our conversation," said Lucy, offering a wave and a totally insincere smile in the direction of her scowling eldest daughter. "She'll know this isn't a row. She knows a row is what Barry and I have. That gets her really upset and she throws herself between us. It's heartbreaking."

"I'm sorry," repeated Tom.

"Don't be; just go back to what you were saying on the phone about George Bush."

"Why don't I take you shopping? I could buy you new clothes."

"Bush!" she insisted, "I know you hate shopping. You don't even buy clothes for yourself. Anyway, I've had my rant for today. I feel better now and I want to talk about George Dubya."

"The election is only next Tuesday," stated Tom, "I so want to see Bush humiliated. I so want to see *Regime Change.*"

"It'll probably be a feeding frenzy for lawyers again, if every state counts like Florida did last time they may not have finished all the court cases before Christmas," suggested Lucy, wrapping her scarf another turn round her neck as she felt the temperature falling.

"No, I think Kerry's got a good chance," continued Tom, "to win it outright. He's not very inspiring, but Bush is such a muppet, surely..."

"No, you're wrong there, I fear," said Lucy. "The religious right are going to turn out with a vengeance and there are millions of them."

"Where?"

"Out in the square states, where no one else ever goes. Places that don't register with Hollywood or get shown on TV, except in documentaries about tornadoes or films like Fargo or Paris, Texas. Small towns where no one has a passport because they don't ever intend to leave *the good ole US of A.* The America we know about just flies over them, commuting between New York and the West Coast. But they're down there alright, and this time Bush is going to get them voting."

As they talked, Lucy took hold of Tom's arm and walked him over to the line of swings where Emma and Cherie were trying to lift Ali's small but bulky figure into one of the 'baby' swings. Emma looked imploringly towards Lucy,

"Come on!" she mouthed.

"Good job I've learned how to lip read," muttered Lucy reaching to lift Alice high enough so that she could wriggle down into the chair of the little swing. Tom laughed and stepped away to start rocking Emma and Cherie in their swings. With one hand for each, pushing firmly into their backs as each returned, he soon had them squealing with delight at how high they were flying. He felt very contented standing there under the skeletal roof of the tall black trees, hunching his shoulders inside his jacket to resist the blustery wind and not yet minding the cold seeping into the bones of his feet.

"I was thinking, religion really has come back into politics hasn't it?" sighed Tom, stepping back from the danger zone and turning to Lucy, "Who would have predicted that happening, say ten years ago? We have compulsory religious studies in schools, and now these ridiculous 'faith-based' schools are springing up. Don't the silly burghers read history? Why would they? Some of them don't even get Darwin."

"Calm down dear, not in front of the children. And anyway, 'history' is not exactly immune from manipulation, is it?" laughed Lucy. Tom frowned, his eyes following the swings back and forth as she continued. "I can still remember my father saying that in Russia, under Stalin, only the future was certain, the past was totally unpredictable."

"I know what you mean," he replied. "There are photographs where Trotsky was originally in the front row, then after a few years he's in the back row, then he's not there at all – and Stalin, who was never there in the first place, suddenly pops up in front of everyone. Quite amazing!"

Lucy stood quietly watching her children play and the slow procession of traffic in the distance. The chilly breeze picked up again and rustled the carpet of crisp brown leaves, blowing them against the low railings of the fence. Curls of her dark hair fluttered against her forehead and she swept them back with repeated, almost nervous, gestures.

"Have you noticed," asked Tom, "how we mention religion so much more since…, well, since when? Since 9/11? Why is that? We're not what I'd call *'religious people'*. We grew up in a secular society which we thought was acceptable to people of all faiths and of none. So when did we lose our secular politics, our good old left versus right ideological division between Labour and Capital?"

"I want that back," said Lucy. "I don't want religious divides in politics between Prods and Catholics, or between Christians,

Jews, Moslems, Sikhs, Hindus or any others. It's nonsense, it's retrograde, it's incomprehensible."

"That's pretty surprising," said Tom, nodding in agreement, "less than fifteen years since the Berlin Wall came down, and already we're nostalgic for the dear dead days of the Cold War, Thatcherism and the Miners' Strike. Days when everyone knew where they stood."

"Did we?"

"No, of course not," he admitted. "I never sorted out whether I was a Commie or a Trot or a Socialist, or a Social-Democrat or even an Anarchist or anything else in the great menagerie of the left in the last century. But I'm sure I believed then, and I still believe now, that everyone should be free to choose whatever religion they want, or have none of it."

"You can't separate religion from life," broke in Lucy. "You can't put it away in a sealed box marked 'private'. If you have religious convictions they will affect your views on issues regardless of whether they are public or private."

"What, like Catholics opposing divorce, birth control and abortion, you mean?"

"Yes. Absolutely. That's their right. I may not agree with them; that's my right. I shouldn't make them disobey their creed, but they have no right, none at all, to stop other people getting divorced, having access to contraception or to legal abortions."

"Of course" added Tom, "fair enough, if you profess a religious belief it should be confirmed in the way you try to live your life."

"Exactly!" said Lucy, rather loudly. "And that's why I find Graham Greene so annoying; it's right there in the disparity between the Catholic faith he espoused and his own shameless infidelities."

"What? Are you objecting to him having affairs?"

"No, of course not," answered Lucy, curling towards him. "No, I'm just annoyed that he could make his faith into such a big deal without it seeming to affect the way he conducted his life. It's as if religion was something he talked about and wrote about rather than did."

"Maybe he enjoyed feeling guilty? But at least he made it clear that this was a private dilemma. He wasn't laying it on anyone else."

"More likely it was sheer arrogance, you know that sort of *'Only little people pay taxes.'* creed. In his case it would have been *'Only little Catholics need to resist the sins of the flesh'.*"

"Don't do as I do, do as I say," sniggered Tom

"What I'm trying to say," continued Lucy, without glancing at him, "is that there is a place for religious conviction in politics; it's important for politicians to have ideals about which they are passionate. You know that as well as I do, otherwise they're just shallow little opportunists who don't know what they think until their spin doctor has run a focus group on the issue."

"Sounds like your husband," said Tom.

"Tell him that, not me!"

"That's exactly my problem with New Labour. Apart from opposing the war in Iraq, the main reason why I can't see myself voting for Blair in the next election is that New Labour has failed to understand it has to have a purpose. *Modernisation, targets, private finance initiatives* all those things, they're just bollocks if there is no clear purpose behind them. The purpose of the Old Labour Party was never to make capitalism – the system - work more efficiently. If Blair had ever grasped that concept, then he wouldn't look so baffled when his own people try to tell him why they're against university tuition fees, or more privatisation; things like that."

Lucy glanced away from him. Her eyes were following the children, now circulating happily amidst the climbing frames, ladders and slides.

"Martin Luther King," she said after a pause. "Now there's a man who knew his Bible and took his religion seriously. He saw the Civil Rights Movement as his Christian witness. He couldn't have turned aside from that struggle and still have been a Christian, even when he knew that the Klan would kill him. You wouldn't be talking like this if we'd had someone like him in the White House."

They paused and allowed themselves to fall silent while both frowned intently, mustering their thoughts. Tom was desperate to say something that Lucy might find both conclusive and endearing.

"It's not funny," Lucy began again, "we've got all these religious folk intent on going to heaven. And me too, I sometimes think. But then I'm like the bishop or whoever it was who noticed that people all want to go to heaven; but not just yet, thank you very much."

"That's changed," said Tom grimly. Lucy turned to him, the smile fading from her face like a passing shadow. "That's how they persuade young men to become suicide bombers, they promise them instant access to four and twenty virgins in paradise."

"Don't set me off on Islam! To me it's outrageous the way Moslem men treat women. The Ayatollahs and the Taliban are some dreadful anomaly left over from the Middle Ages, if you ask me."

"Of course they are. The Koran is, so is the Bible. That's when they were written. They tell you exactly how to survive in a patriarchal, pre-industrial society, with no welfare-state, and in a hot country, at least fifteen hundred years ago."

"Why the 'hot country' bit?"

"Pork," he replied. "Jews and Moslems don't eat pigs; and why? Because pigs eat rubbish and pig-meat goes bad quickly in warm weather, and gives you food-poisoning. So it's a survival thing; *Darwinian*, you might say."

"This is becoming pointless," she laughed. "We're bound to agree, you and I, that people should at least be free to choose. You can't have democracy without freedom of conscience and free speech."

"Maybe you have to be non-religious to believe in religious freedom? Once you've '*got religion*' doesn't it sort of take you over? These new fundamentalists, all of them – Evangelical Christians, Jews, Moslems – want a theocracy not a democracy. They don't want debates and votes. They've got the answers, they're all there, written in their sacred texts. What's to vote on?"

"Women's rights, for a start," affirmed Lucy. "And the freedom to criticise religions, and to make fun of religious hypocrisy. The very idea that there could be such a thing as a *Holy War* would be ridiculous if it wasn't so tragic!"

"Remember a few years ago," continued Tom, "when the *fatwah* was put on Salman Rushdie for writing <u>The Satanic</u>

<u>Verses</u> ? I heard a discussion about our blasphemy laws on the radio one morning. They had representatives of various different faiths giving their opinions. The Rabi, the Bishop, the Mullah, all huffed and puffed, agreeing with one another how they should all be protected from blasphemous comments on their beliefs. And then the interviewer turned to a Buddhist and asked him for the Buddhist view.

" '*Well*,' said the Buddhist, quietly, '*I'm not entirely sure that it's possible for a Buddhist to blaspheme, but if it were, I suspect it would probably be very therapeutic.*' Took the wind out of the other guys' sails, completely; nearly converted me to Buddhism on the spot."

"Oh yeah, and where are the Buddhist extremists when you need them?" asked Lucy. "Where are the guys in long, saffron robes going round perpetrating random acts of kindness and completely un-provoked generosity?"

They both laughed at this until Lucy raised her voice and called across the play area,

"Alice! Alice! Ali, that's far enough!"

"Round them up and we can go back to mine for tea and biscuits," suggested Tom, hopefully.

"Alright," accepted Lucy, "but enough of all this heavy duty politics and stuff. No more once we've left the swings."

"Agreed," he said, "but talking of swings,"

Lucy halted, turning to eye him suspiciously; Tom grinned.

"I was only going to mention," he remarked, "that there's an image in <u>The End of the Affair</u> when Sarah writes - in her Diary I think - a description of how our minds swing back and forth like a pendulum. She wonders what it would mean if the truth were to be located somewhere along the arc of the pendulum, but not at its resting point. She asks 'what if' the truth lay at an angle to the vertical, it would be nearer to one extreme view than it was to the other, but certainly not at the extremes and not in the dead centre either. Sarah suggests that we'd really be attracted to, and want to believe, a truth that required the pointer to stop at an impossible angle."

"I can just see that idea appealing to you, Tom Cork," she nodded. "You're a life-long member of the awkward squad. That's why Brendan might be an MP one day and you never will, even though you know far more and you're a better human being all round. He's never going to worry about some awkward truth stuck out at sixty degrees from the normal and impossible to acknowledge safely. But you would, it would really matter to you, wouldn't it?"

Tom grinned back at her and, grateful for each other's presence, they linked arms as the three children gathered around them.

"Can we go to Tom's, oh can we, oh please?" shrilled Cherie.

"Well, it's getting late, and it's a bit awkward," began Lucy. "What do you think, Tom?"

"Awkward, huh?" he relished the hurt. "You know me, I'll go for awkward every time. "

"Hurrah!" shouted Cherie, pausing to check that she had understood this strange exchange correctly, before throwing up her hands and shouting another 'Hurrah!' while skipping away to fetch Ali's buggy. As she went she chanted in time to her skips,

"Awkward, awkward, let's be awkward!"

One of the Clapham Matrons stood aside, condescendingly, to let Cherie go past but then stared after her with hands on hips, frowning and tut-tutting at the lyrics of the child's skipping-chant.

Chapter Eight

On Friday evening Tom arrived at Paul's house just as Paul and Anna, their son and daughter, with Lucy, Barry, their daughters and a tall, grey-haired, man were all muddling their way out of the front door, ready to set off for the firework display. Glancing at the knot of dark figures caught in the street lights, Tom was suddenly aware that this would be the first time he had seen Barry and Lucy together since his affair with Lucy had begun. He stopped the car and sat for a few moments looking at the animated figures through the mist of condensation rapidly clouding his windows.

"Hi Tom," called Paul as Tom strode away from his car, pulling an old grey parka jacket over his shoulders and zipping the front.

"Tom's here, Lucy, we can all leave together," continued Paul as he greeted Tom with a warm handshake. Paul was a similar height to Tom but had much broader shoulders and the beginnings of a paunch which made him appear stocky. Paul had a kindly, soft face which seemed to smile readily, judging by the lines of wrinkles spreading below and around his blue eyes. Paul's dark brown hair was increasingly flecked with grey and he wore it slightly long, such that he frequently needed to sweep back his forelock when it fell over his eyes.

Lucy stood on the footpath with Emma beside her.

"Here's Tom, Emma," said Lucy softly, "are you going to take his hand and show him the way to the fireworks?"

Emma stood still and silent, wrinkling her nose, obviously reluctant to move towards Tom. While Emma hesitated a smaller, hooded figure detached herself from the larger group and hurtled towards Tom.

"Can I go with Tom? Please, please!" shrilled Cherie as Tom caught her flying torso under the arms and swung her up into the air, staggering as he absorbed her momentum.

"That alright with you, Tom?" asked Lucy. "Emms you take my hand, Daddy's got to look after Alice."

"Put me on your shoulders Tom-tom," insisted Cherie and Tom swung her up above his head, relieved by her lightness, and let her settle on his shoulders with his hands holding her booted feet. Cherie ruffled his hair and called,

"Look at me, look at me, Gran'pa Simon!"

They processed up the incline towards Streatham Common, Tom walking alongside Paul's wife Anna, trying hard to hear what she was saying and to avoid catching the heels of her son Jason who was walking at an erratic pace just in front of them.

"Do keep going, Jason," called Anna.

"Can't, there's too many people," he snapped back.

Tom saw that Jason was right. Up ahead, at the top of the road, the knots of pedestrians coming up the hill had coalesced into a huge throng which now moved awkwardly onto the dark slope of Streatham Common. Tom saw Lucy turn, instinctively doing a head count of her children. He smiled broadly, patted Cherie's boots and felt her wriggle as she waved to her mother. Suddenly Barry was alongside him, bearing Alice grizzling quietly on his shoulders.

"This should be fun, mate, providing it doesn't rain, and I'm sure it won't," said Barry.

"Alice needs to blow her nose!" called Cherie from the darkness above Tom's head.

"Ugh, *Lucy!* I'm getting all snot in my hair, I can feel it," complained Barry,

"Alice, stop that!" he called, tossing his head back and provoking a wail from Alice.

Lucy intervened.

"Here, let me take Ali," she offered. "Emma, you take Daddy's hand now."

Tom looked across in time to see a smile of sheer delight on Emma's face as Alice was handed to her mother and Barry happily stretched for Emma's small hand. Lucy smiled at Tom and then flicked her eyes up and down to indicate that events were turning out exactly as she might have predicted. Tom was about to say something supportive when the crowd began chanting a $5 - 4 -3 - 2 - 1$ countdown in response to an incomprehensible loud speaker announcement. Cherie slapped her hands against Tom's ears in time with the chanting and could not hear Tom's protests because a series of enormous bangs and flashes rent the dark sky above them. The fireworks had begun.

Tom planted his feet well apart on the slippery grass as Cherie threw her head back to admire the huge expanding balls of white, blue, yellow, red and green sparks which pumped brightly, faded and then vanished in the blackness above their heads. The glowing beads of light were always racing outwards from the original explosion long before the sound of the bang reached them. The vast aerial display was emanating from launch-pads somewhere further up the dark hillside and several times the tumult of crashing light rose to a crescendo and died away. Each time Tom thought that must be the Finale, only to be staggered by another, even more awesome, cacophony cracking the night sky and reverberating from the windows and walls of the distant houses on the far side of the Common.

He glanced at Lucy and saw her comforting Alice. The child was obviously overwhelmed by the whole experience and was burrowing desperately into Lucy's coat collar. Lucy said something to Barry who waved her away and excitedly pointed out a falling star-shell to Emma. Tom's head was jerked upwards as Cherie again gripped his ears and tufts of his hair. When he looked back, Lucy had vanished into the crowd. Tom remembered Lucy worrying that Cherie would again be frightened by the noise and the flashes. A flurry of excited kicks against his chest from her little red boots convinced Tom that Cherie was now relishing the excitement.

The display ended and the crowd broke into straggling applause. Tom looked around expecting to find himself surrounded by strangers but there were Anna and Jason standing next to him;

Paul and Cassy came weaving towards them through the throng.

"Did you like that, Cherie?" called Anna, facing Tom but speaking to a point somewhere above his head.

"Best yet!" announced Paul. "They must be practising for the opening ceremony of the twenty-twelve Olympics!"

"Huh! If London gets them!" muttered Tom.

"It'll be Paris, you'll see!" commented Anna. "We won't get them here, not after Iraq."

"What on earth are you burbling about? The war's got nothing to do with it," said Paul derisively.

"It has," insisted Anna. "You've no idea how unpopular your government has made us in the world."

"Oh, it's MY government now, is it?" challenged Paul. "You voted for them too, I seem to recall."

"Never again!" responded Anna, drawing Jason to her side and turning for home.

"Oh, and who else is there?" Paul called after her before looking imploringly at Tom. "You don't want the Tories back, do you?"

"Lucky the rain held off," offered Tom, feeling less than entirely successful in his sudden role as a matrimonial umpire.

"Come back to our place to have a bit of nosh and a warm up," invited Paul, trying to retrieve his previous good humour.

"He means a bite to eat, or some 'supper'," called out Anna, her lips pursing in an embarrassed smile. "My God, Paul, you sound more like Barry every day!" she added in a fierce whisper which Tom was not supposed to hear.

* * *

The front entrance hall of Paul and Anna's house was a sea of coats, scarves and discarded Wellington-boots when Tom entered, having remembered just in time to lift Cherie down from his shoulders before risking her head against the door frame. Cherie darted away into the house, hopping from one foot to the other as she removed her boots without a pause. Tom felt suddenly light and experienced a mildly floating sensation as his back eased from carrying Cherie for the past forty minutes.

"Let's get you a drink, mate," said Paul, patting Tom on the back and propelling him gently into the living room.

Tom spotted Lucy through the archway, busy with Anna, dispensing cups of juice and biscuits to the children. Barry swept towards him holding out a large glass of red wine.

"Thanks," said Tom, moving so that he had a clear view of Lucy and Anna. Lucy looked tired and slightly strained. He noticed that her first response to every demand from her children was to breathe out the briefest of sighs before she managed to smile. Anna, by contrast, looked polished and coolly immaculate. Her blond hair was gathered neatly in an elegant bun, adorned with a ribbon which sparkled with blue jewels. Her eyes had a quick, darting, intensity which always made Tom look away whenever their eyes met. Freed from the folds of the padded jacket she had worn for the firework display, Anna looked poised and slim, her pink sweater clinging tightly to the waist of her smart blue jeans.

"There'll be eats in a mo," said Barry, "when the girls have finished dealing with the kids. Have you met Paul's Dad?"

"No, but I've heard a lot about him. Pleased to meet you," said Tom, shaking hands with a tall, bespectacled man with thinning grey hair, who rose from an armchair to greet him. Although dressed entirely in black, Simon had a surprisingly youthful appearance. The circular lenses of his eye-glasses made him look slightly owlish but his dark eyes conveyed intelligence and his wide mouth easily formed a broad smile.

"Simon Traynor," said the man.

"Tom, Tom Cork. Don't get up."

"Like a second father this man has been to me," said Barry, laying his hand affectionately on Simon's shoulder. "In fact, Simon, you've been more of a father to me all these years than my real dad ever was. Have you noticed, Tom," he continued, "how my girls all call him Grandpa Simon?"

Simon smiled benignly from behind the silver-wire frames of his glasses.

"Yes, Jackie and I are very fond of your family Brendan. Very fond. Jackie will be sorry to have missed this, but she can't risk going out on these cold nights."

"That's a pity," said Tom, politely.

"And," persisted Barry, "this man, at seventy three, you don't mind me giving away your secret do you Si? - You don't look a day over fifty even now. Anyway; this man, Tom, knows more about computers than a whole bus-load of teenage whiz-kids. I tell you, Paul and I would be lost without him. Absolutely, up shit-creek without a paddle, that's where we'd be."

"Oh no, no. Providing you are sensible, and cautious with money, you'll manage alright, the pair of you. *You'll have to one day*, I keep telling them, Tom," he added, laying the slender fingers of his right hand on Tom's sleeve,

"They've just got to learn the great lessons business has taught me over the years and which I'm always trying to pass on to them."

"I know exactly what you're going to say, Dad," interrupted Paul.

"And that is?" enquired Simon, raising his eyebrows and looking up over the rims of his glasses.

"*It never ceases to amaze you*," recited Paul and Barry, almost in unison, "*that we always have time to do every job twice, but are always much too busy to do it properly in the first place!*"

"Sounds like my father, too," grinned Tom, "He never tired of telling us, *'Thar's two ways a' doing any job, an' wun of 'ems proper like!'* "

"I didn't know your dad came from up north," commented Lucy, joining the conversation.

"He didn't," blushed Tom. "He just had these sayings he would come out with, and somehow they always sound more convincing if you try to say them like Fred Dibnah."

"Sounded more like Monty Python to me," snorted Barry. "Come on, let's eat!"

The whole party, adults and children, thronged around a generous buffet spread out on a large table in the dining room. Tom and Lucy manoeuvred adroitly to be next to each other as they shuffled along. Lucy picked up two small, brilliantly red cherry tomatoes and placed them on Tom's plate either side of a gherkin he had just selected. She began to giggle at the effect this created and at Tom's sudden blushing. Smiling, Tom pierced the gherkin with his force and endeavoured to plant it on Lucy's plate in retaliation.

"*Fork off*, Corky!" she spluttered, nearly losing the food from her plate as she dodged away from him.

"Children, please!" called out Anna, who had been observing their flirtation with some interest.

Oblivious to Anna's gaze, Lucy took her plate to an armchair in the other room, where discreetly, or so she thought, she patted the armrest, indicating that Tom should sit there. Barry, meanwhile, stood with his back to the darkened windows, his feet planted slightly apart, holding a full plate and chewing vigorously. He paused to lick his thumb and forefinger before addressing the room;

"Bush got re-elected I see. You were wrong there Tom. That Michael Moore film didn't have the impact you said it would after all."

"Don't know what you mean about '*re-elected*'," replied Tom, quickly swallowing a crumbly piece of quiche. "This is the first time he's actually been elected on the popular vote."

"Oh, so maybe his first term doesn't count then. Do you think that means we can have eight more years, not just four?"

"God, I hope not," interjected Lucy, eager to defend Tom from Barry's intention to mock him so publicly. "My money's on Hilary Clinton for 2008, they'll be ready for her after four more years of Dubya in the White House."

"You've got to admit," resumed Barry, still addressing Tom very directly, "the man's a political genius."

"What?" spluttered Tom and Lucy almost with one voice.

"Well, look at what he's done. First, he makes all you clever leftie academic know-alls think he's a complete plank. Then he brushes aside all your liberal angst about regime-change in Iraq, speaks directly to the ordinary people of America and manages to beat Kerry 51% to 48%! He also now controls the House and the Senate, and what has he promised his electorate?" Barry paused, noisily biting into a piece of celery from his plate.

"I dunno," shrugged Tom in the silence that followed.

"To bomb the *cheese-eatin' sorrenda monkeys?*" suggested Lucy, trying to affect a John Wayne-style drawl.

"Who?" asked Anna.

"The French," explained Paul.

"No, no, no," resumed Barry. "There you go you see, under-estimating him again. The only things George Bush has promised to do are to oppose gay marriage and not to allow human cloning. That's it! Not peace, not victory, not jobs, not welfare, health-care or schools. None of your usual goodies."

"So, what?" prompted Anna.

"So that's his trick. He picks-up on two way-out notions that are never going to happen, builds them up into an imminent threat to life as we know it, then makes sure the simple-minded consumers understand that he's the no-nonsense kind of guy who'll stop all the *Washington* nonsense. And bingo! Bush wins the election with a blank cheque to do whatever the hell he wants."

Barry slowly swept the room with a big grin as he finished his explanation before turning to put his plate down on a side-table and pick up a glass of wine.

"Do we think there's a lesson there for Tony Blair?" suggested Paul.

"Absolutely there is," agreed Barry. "Don't promise the electorate what you will do, re-assure them with a short list of things you won't do."

"Like what?" asked Lucy.

"Alistair Campbell can be relied upon to think of something."

"He's one of the things Blair should promise not to bring back," said Tom.

"No worries, he's back already mate," announced Barry confidently. "The old team; Alistair Campbell and Peter Mandelson, they're in there, behind the throne, planning the election strategy. Stick with New Labour, mate, it's the wave of the future!"

"Be careful," warned Tom, "politicians who get too cocky can suddenly find themselves waving goodbye. Remember Neil Kinnock? Hailed as '*The next Prime Minister*' on the eve of the '92 election and then flushed down the toilet thirty-six hours later."

"Oh dear," said Lucy, trying to make her voice sound fragile with mock-grief, "and now we've got this ridiculous tabloid *shock-horror* about David Blunkett and the paternity of some married woman's child."

"She's not just any 'married woman'," chipped-in Barry, "she's the publisher of the <u>Spectator</u>. Kimberley something her name is..."

"Quim?" suggested Paul with a malicious grin.

"No Paul! It's Quinn! And don't be so crude!" snapped Anna.

"And then there's Blair and Brown," continued Lucy, brushing her skirt towards her knees, "Behaving like a married couple in the throes of a particularly unpleasant divorce. As the top three men in a government Blair, Blunkett and Brown are not waving but drowning, if you ask me."

"Don't panic!" called out Barry. "That's all just media hype and froth. This time next year we'll be safely into an historic Third Term, and Tony will be planning a smooth hand over to his chosen successor..."

"Oh, so it's not Gordon Brown then?" enquired Tom, trying to make the question sound innocent but aiming to rankle Barry's 'Blairite' reflexes.

"Hah! Gordon Brown? *Gordon Bennet* more like!" scoffed Barry. "No, I have it on good authority from those in the know that Tony's successor won't be his gloomy neighbour." Barry tapped the side of nose with his left index finger as he spoke, "You watch Ruth what's her name? Kelly, that's it; she's just been moved to the Cabinet Office...." he suggested and coincidentally a staccato burst of noisy explosions from a firework outside in the street rattled the windows.

"The plan is for the succession to jump a generation and ensure the continuation of the Blairite Third Way up to 2020 and beyond," he roared above the din.

"God, they really make them sound like gunfire, don't they?" cried Lucy, clearly startled by the continuing heavy slapping sounds echoing ominously from outside. Anna brushed Lucy's shoulder reassuringly with her finger-tips and moved behind Barry to draw the curtains across the tall windows. Paul began offering to re-fill glasses from a newly-opened bottle of red wine.

"Did you hear about the assassination of that Dutch film-maker, Theo van Gogh?" asked Paul as he tilted the bottle towards Tom's glass.

"Yes, how awful," said Tom. "Wasn't that the same day as Bush's election?"

"I don't see the connection," frowned Anna.

"There isn't one," answered Paul, "at least nothing direct, but I'm certain that the killing wouldn't have happened without 9/11 and its aftermath in Afghanistan and then in Iraq."

"Why is that?" asked Simon, sitting back in his chair as Anna collected his plate.

"Theo van Gogh was a journalist and a deliberate controversialist. He was quite well known in Holland. He was shot about eight times, then stabbed, then his throat was cut."

"Ugh! But why?" demanded Lucy.

"For insulting Islam, the killer left a letter pinned to his body with a knife," answered Paul.

"That's obscene, and grotesque. In Holland did you say? It's awful and unbelievable," she cried.

"He was very hostile to the teachings of Islam and he made his criticisms sound as provocative as possible. Then he made a film about the mistreatment of Moslem women..."

"But that needs saying," insisted Lucy. "Moslem women are oppressed. I feel like shaking them when I see them walking along in their black headscarves. That's so obviously a symbol of ownership and control imposed on them by men."

"They're generally driving Mercs whenever I see them," suggested Barry. "Doesn't seem to be too much hardship involved in that, is there?"

"In places like Saudi Arabia," commented Simon, "women just aren't allowed to drive cars or even to walk down the street unaccompanied."

Lucy rose to her feet and joined Anna in collecting empty plates and glasses. Tom retained his plate, jokingly holding it away from her,

"Have you noticed," he enquired impishly, "how we men are all sitting down while you and Anna have done all the fetching and carrying?"

"Hey, watch it," said Paul. "I've been dashing around with this bottle keeping your glasses filled."

"Yeah, that's man's work," boasted Barry, playfully raising his arm to ward off the blow he expected from Lucy.

"This is no laughing matter," she stated angrily. "I won't allow you to trivialise women's issues. We're talking about access to education, to jobs and - ultimately - the right to control our own bodies. It doesn't get any more serious than that."

"In Saudi," explained Simon, "women are able to have jobs and go to university; it's just unthinkable for them to mix with men from outside their family. University professors conduct tutorials with their female students via the telephone."

"At least they can go to university," said Anna. "Under the Taliban, Afghan girls couldn't even go to school."

"Our children all seem to have gone very quiet," observed Lucy, cupping a hand to her ear as if listening intently. "Can I just pop upstairs and see what they're up to?"

"I'll come with you," offered Anna. "I'm sure Cassy will be looking after them. Jason, you can be sure, will have disappeared into his lair."

"Going back to Theo van Gogh," said Tom, turning to address his remarks more directly to Simon. "His death really has shocked the Dutch. They have cultivated toleration as their way of life for so long now and this has rocked their foundations."

"Yes, I can imagine," answered Simon. "There are liberals like us beginning to question whether tolerance has only resulted in disintegration. They are shaking their heads as if mystified by the lack of integration by the large Moslem community into mainstream Dutch society."

"That's where 9/11 is relevant," added Tom. "Since then, Moslems in the West seem to feel themselves to be suspects. They probably feel isolated, even paranoid."

"You can't 'suspect' a whole religion," said Barry, "We've just got to keep tabs on the extremists. That's actually what David Blunkett's been doing, with precious little support from the Lib-Dems and from some folk even within the Labour Party."

"Habeas Corpus, the presumption of innocence and the right to a fair trial: these are what we are defending!" exclaimed Tom. "They shouldn't be the first things we chuck away just because some idiot tries to blow-up a plane with explosives hidden in his shoes."

"That's different," began Paul. "We are similar to the Dutch, we have a pretty relaxed and tolerant society where immigrants have, by and large, been welcomed...."

"Not with open arms," put in Simon. "But certainly in very large numbers. The majority of children born in Holland this year will be born to Moslem parents."

"So what *do* you do?" asked Tom. "When your tolerant society tolerates an intolerant religion, some of whose followers cannot tolerate free speech?"

There was a pause. Tom took a sip from his wine glass and scanned the room.

"Well go on then," suggested Barry, "unveil your answer, I assume that was a rhetorical question."

"No," said Tom, "I was describing the dilemma. I don't know the answer, but it worries me that if we don't find a solution pretty soon there will be a violent backlash from racists and from our own religious bigots."

"That's what's already happening in Holland and in France and in Germany and Austria," lamented Simon.

"But Tom," sneered Barry, "do you never imagine that you could be at all bigoted, or even racist, yourself?"

"Look, I try not to be, OK?" sighed Tom. "Some of my best friends etc. but I'm getting uneasy with multi-culturalism when it stops anyone from being critical of practices which are, frankly, either plain daft or simply barbaric."

"Whoa, steady boy!" called Barry. "You work in the People's Republic of Lambeth, remember?"

"Don't I know it," moaned Tom, but added with a smile, "when it comes to religion I try to be equally hostile to all religions."

"D'you know, Tom," said Barry, starting to sound angry, "you're obsessed with religion as an issue in politics because you used to follow a political ideology which operated like a religion. Then you lost your *religion* and to hide your disappointment you go around attacking anyone who still has a religion. You're an ex-commie who's become a born-again fucking crusader for atheism!"

"Christ!" blasphemed Tom, shaking his head in the silence that followed. "Who rattled your cage?"

"Tom believes in religious freedom," commented Lucy as she and Anna came back into the room and resumed their places. Both looked slightly disconcerted that the conversation had become so fraught while they were out of the room.

"Kids alright?" asked Barry in an aside directed at Lucy.

"Mmmm, they're happy as Larry," she answered, swallowing the remainder of her drink. "Cassy's being an angel with Cherie - who's completely in awe of her anyway. Alice is fast asleep on Cassy's bed and Emma is in Jason's room playing some totally unsuitable computer game with him."

"Didn't you stop her?" demanded Barry.

"Certainly not, she's really happy and, as far as I could tell, she's winning."

"I'd better go and see for myself," said Barry, grunting loudly as he struggled up from his armchair and strode across the room.

"Sorry," said Paul.

"I just hope it isn't *Vice City* or something like that," said the departing Barry over his shoulder.

"No, I can assure you he hasn't got that one," Paul called out. "It's probably *Amanda Croft* or whatever she's called."

"Lara," said Simon, "It's *Lara Croft*."

"Amanda was that au pair girl *we* had, if you remember, Paul," said Anna, with great acidity.

Tom quickly hid his smile behind his near-empty glass.

"So, what did we miss?" enquired Lucy, boldly. "Anything or nothing?"

"I think we'd all agreed," suggested Tom, "That people should be free to practice any religion or none."

"Can't argue with that," said Anna.

"Tom and Barry both put down '*Jedi Knight*' as their religion on the last Census," said Lucy.

"That seems a bit silly," said Simon. "I remember someone saying that if any faith had at least ten thousand followers claiming membership, then the authorities would have to give them a box to tick on the next census form."

"That was the general idea," agreed Tom. "I'd say that being a Jedi was pretty harmless compared with the bloody history of Judaism, Christianity and Islam...."

"Which all claim to worship the same God but find atheists more congenial than other believers who tread a parallel but different path," interrupted Lucy.

"Yes, but '*Star Wars*' was entirely fiction," insisted Anna.

"You don't think The Bible and The Koran are made-up?" enquired Tom. "Do you think they're all true?"

"Of course they are," said Anna. "For believers they are the actual Word of God."

"Err, no, surely not," replied Tom. "That's why they're called '*Believers*', isn't it? Because they have faith that what they believe to be true, actually is true."

"Tom, you can't say any religious belief is untrue. All religions contain many truths," countered Anna.

"Well, what about, say, 'Flat Earthers'?" argued Tom. "If I tell you I *believe* the Earth is flat, then I'm asking you to believe something that we all know is untrue."

Simon, who had been listening quietly to these various exchanges, decided to intervene.

"I'd say," he began, "that we all know planet Earth isn't flat but we do behave most of the time as if it is. We think of Australia as being over there, not down there. We are used to looking at the world shown flat on Mercator's projection." Simon paused as if expecting one of the others to speak. No one did so he shrugged and carried on. "Hopefully, there are still tribes out somewhere in the rainforest who believe there are gods in the trees, in the wind and in the rivers. I might not share their pan-theism but I bet they have a better grasp of their ecology than most visiting scientists. I think it might be very difficult to establish which of their beliefs is completely untrue, and which of our 'scientific' beliefs is absolutely true."

"I thought scientists no longer dealt in 'truths', don't they now talk in terms of probabilities rather than 'Laws'?" suggested Tom, after another pause.

"This is all getting very heavy, for a party," complained Paul. "Should I put some music on?"

"These are important issues," replied Simon. "We certainly should be talking about them."

"Theo van Gogh," asked Anna, suddenly, "was he related to Vincent..."

"Oh yes," replied Tom. "According to his website he was a direct descendant of Vincent's brother, also called Theo..."

"And now he's dead, because some fundamentalist didn't like what he said," observed Lucy, sadly.

"What's almost worse," continued Tom, "is that there are already some commentators who are saying he was too provocative, too out-spoken, that he had it coming, that he went too far..."

"I hate that," said Anna. "That's so utterly spineless! It's like saying that a rich man is asking to be robbed or a pretty woman is asking to be raped."

"*May the Force be with You!*" proclaimed Barry, charging back into the room. "Say, who d'ya have to sleep with t'get a beer around here?"

"For God's sake, Brendan!" cried Lucy. "We're having a really serious discussion here."

"*Sorry,*" said Barry, with heavy emphasis. "Aren't we meant to be celebrating Guy Fawkes' Night? No? Wasn't he burnt alive as an example to us all?"

"The survival of Parliament, that's worth celebrating," declared Simon. "For all its faults, and for all the centuries it took to evolve, democracy remains the worst form of government we know of...... except for all the others."

"Pardon?" said Lucy.

"I mean," explained Simon, "that despite all the spin doctors, and hype and ego-mania of individual politicians, parliamentary democracy is better than any other system we've been able to cook-up."

"What this country needs," growled Paul, addressing the stem of his wine-glass, "is a damned good spin-bowler, not another bloody spin-doctor."

Anna stared at him with her eyebrows raised and shook her

head.

"Politicians, especially Labour ones," complained Lucy, "always seem to start off being radicals and firebrands, and then they get elected and can't wait to make compromises."

"Given a choice between government by force or government by fraud, I'd choose fraud every time. The body-count is so much lower," answered Simon.

"But it is still fraud then, isn't it?" said Tom.

"Well, it probably has to be." Simon pressed his finger tips together as he positioned his elbows on the arms of his chair. "It's that balancing act between good-government and self-government. Total self-government is anarchy which is a great idea but doesn't work for very long in practice. Strive too hard for good government and you soon get experts popping up who promise to make the trains run on time; and we all know where that can lead......."

"So where is the fraud you both seem willing to accept?" enquired Anna.

"It's there in the way that we are only really a democracy once every four or five years when there's a General Election; in between times we have an elected dictatorship," said Tom.

"Even elections aren't that democratic," added Lucy, turning towards Tom. "You keep saying how, with first-past-the-post, more people can vote against the winning candidate than voted for him..."

"Or her!" shouted Barry, trying to be provocative.

"Yes, indeed, *or her*," accepted Lucy, "although we do still deny the vote to peers, convicts and certified lunatics," she snapped back. "And you, Tom, also complain that you can't vote *against* someone without having to vote *for* someone else."

"That's why I think there is going to be a very low turn-out at the next General Election, and lots of spoiled ballots from people who say '*none of the above*' when they look at the list of candidates and what they stand for."

Anna breathed out noisily;

"People who don't use their vote make me sick. Look at the lines of black people who queued from early morning to vote in that first election in South Africa; people who said they could die happy now that they had achieved their life's ambition – just to cast a vote. And anyway, if you don't vote, strikes me you've no right to moan about anything the government does for the next five years."

"You'll never stop lefties like Tom from complaining," chortled Barry. "It's a way of life with them. You watch, he'll get all precious about how he can't vote New Labour because of Iraq and then he'll have a right royal whinge when he finds that the Tories are back in by default."

"Actually, what interests me as an historian," cut in Tom, trying to drown out any further words from Barry,

"Oh, stone me! Pray silence for the great *historian!*" mocked Barry.

"What interests me," persisted Tom, "is that from the seventeenth century *Levellers* until after the First World War, 'democracy' in this country was a subversive idea, resisted at every turn by the ruling class. It was all about *we the people* trying to take control. But now, now that we've got votes for all, we find that democratic politics is really all about how *they* control us."

"Oh here we go," said Barry. "Here comes the old ultra-leftist bit, never mind parliament, man the barricades! Bring on the *Dictatorship of the Proletariat* or some such total bollocks."

"Lobbyists, spin doctors, media barons – they're all out to determine the agenda and manipulate opinion," said Tom, speaking quickly and raising his voice to drown-out Barry's heckling. "I mean, just look how difficult it is even for someone as accomplished as Tony Benn to put across an alternative viewpoint within a ten second sound-bite – without being made to look ridiculous…"

"Maybe he just is ridiculous," shouted Barry. "Ever consider that?"

Tom shook his head and looked down, wondering how best to continue without displaying too openly the resentment he felt against Barry.

"It worries me," began Lucy, eager to quell the evident antagonism between her husband and her lover, "when any politician starts claiming to have a mandate from the people to do this that or the other, unless they all stood on single issue platforms."

"But then it would be a referendum, not a parliamentary election," resumed Tom, initially grateful for her intervention. He then suddenly frowned and visibly bit his lip to restrain himself from continuing; afraid now of drawing attention to his frequent and lengthy conversations with Lucy. He need not have hesitated.

"Well, Lucy," said Paul, breaking the silence that had followed, "you and Tom certainly seem to spend enough time discussing politics with each other, I don't know how you do it." Anna shot him a fierce glance, intended to say 'stop right there', and Paul returned a puzzled look which he exaggerated by scratching his head. Barry sailed obliviously into his own explanation,

"Politics is Tom's way of chatting-up birds," he laughed. "Sad, isn't it? Actually, he's just a bit slow and doesn't realise what a turn-off it is. Lucy feels sorry for him and lets him try out his patter on her in the hopes that one day she can get him to see the light. She's on a mission to get him married off; poor bugger!"

Anna's eyebrows shot upwards and she pretended to be suddenly busy collecting their used plates. Tom looked at Lucy, who turned away and smiled, weakly, when she caught Simon also looking at her.

"I think," Simon announced soothingly, "that we have reached the point in the evening where we should all agree to differ on politics, on religion and even on how to light love's unpredictable fuse. I, for one, have a strong feeling that we could carry this on for the rest of the night and dawn would find us none the wiser."

"More wine, anyone?" enquired Paul.

"Can't, mate. Driving, aren't I?" replied Barry, gruffly.

Later, they said their goodbyes and Tom departed while Lucy was upstairs preparing her children for the journey home. Tom drove distractedly and received a chorus of impatient blasts on the horn when he failed to respond immediately to a green filter light on the one-way system.

"Fuck off! Fuck off!" he yelled at the neon-bright street, and resumed his brooding thoughts as he wondered just how much

Lucy and Barry talked about him between themselves, and whether they were as dismissive of his foibles as he and Lucy were when they mentioned Barry.

"Fucking Brendan! Fucketty, fucketty, fuck, fuck, fuck!" he shouted, pounding on the steering wheel.

Chapter Nine

Tom was plodding up the stairs to his flat carrying two bags of groceries from the supermarket when he heard his phone ring twice then cease abruptly. He put down his shopping in the hallway and hurried through to the living room to dial Lucy's number. She answered at once.

"Where have you been?" she asked. "I've been trying for ages."

"Just down to the shops, it's Saturday morning you know," he replied.

"Don't get tetchy. I could have imagined you doing far more interesting things."

"Come around?" tried Tom.

"I'd love to darling, but I can't. I just wanted to thank you for keeping Cherie so happy at the Common last night and....."

"S' OK," interrupted Tom, "my ears have nearly recovered."

"What, from all the bangs and crashes?"

"No, not that. From Cherie, she practically tugged them off every time she leaned back."

"Oh God, has she made you look like Prince Charles?"

"In your dreams, lady!"

"Seriously, 'though," resumed Lucy, "did you notice any tension between Paul and Barry last night?"

'Tension between Paul and Barry?' wondered Tom, wanting to tell her how jealous he had felt seeing her with Barry and knowing all the time that she would be going home to bed with him. And then there was his concern about how much Anna, and even Paul or Simon, might have guessed about their affair. That was what he would call 'tension'. That was what he wanted to discuss with Lucy but found he could not even begin. He knew it was cowardly of him but he decided to wait until Lucy mentioned the subject, or at least until there was a moment he judged more opportune.

"Are you there, Tom?" asked Lucy.

"Tension?" he resumed suddenly. "No, can't say I did. I don't know Paul all that well; his Dad's nice isn't he? No, he just seemed his usual affable self with me. Why do you ask?"

"He phoned here at about half nine this morning, I answered and told him Barry was in the shower and he just grunted '*Tell him to call me back immediately. At the office,*' and slammed the phone down. No goodbyes or see you tonight or anything."

"Oh dear," said Tom.

"Will you stop saying that?" said Lucy, very firmly. "It's really annoying. I always think you're being so patronising when you say your pathetic '*Oh, dear*' as if you want to sound sympathetic but really couldn't give a stuff!"

There was a pause while Tom absorbed the anger he heard in her criticism.

"I'm sorry, Lucy," he said. "I'd never mean that with you."

"Well that's what it sounds like, so just stop saying it, OK?"

"Right," said Tom. "Where's Barry now, did he go to the office?"

"Yes, he scuttled off very quickly as soon as I'd told him that Paul sounded so cross."

"Did he know why? I mean did he say anything?"

"Humph! He certainly didn't tell me, even if he knew. No he just said something like '*Silly arse, what's he getting his knickers in a twist over this time?*' and slammed out of the house."

There was another pause while Tom fought against his reflex to say '*Oh dear*' once more.

"Do you think it's anything to do with Anna?" he ventured.

"Anna?" snorted Lucy. "What?"

"Well, Paul and Anna weren't being all that nice to each other last night, I thought."

"Didn't seem so very unusual to me. That, my darling, is how most married couples are with each other. You should hear Brendan and me sometimes; hardly a kind word between us for weeks."

"I just wondered if maybe Barry had done something to upset

Anna, and then she'd told tales to Paul..." speculated Tom.

"No, Anna's like me. She knows better than to get between Paul and Barry. They're like an old married couple themselves. They've been thick as thieves for so long now - it must be about thirty years. It's since primary school anyway. Anna has never liked Barry, but that's never worried either him or Paul."

"Do you like Paul?" asked Tom.

"Yes. Yes I think I do. Years ago I was a bit jealous that he and Barry seemed so close, but then I just accepted it and now I'm actually quite pleased he's got Paul to prop him up sometimes."

"And Simon....."

"Oh yes. They're both totally in awe of Simon, even now. It's like they revert to being schoolboys when he's around. He seems to be some sort of Father-Confessor, Doctor and Headmaster, all rolled into one, for both of them."

"So maybe Simon said something to Paul last night. What time did you all leave?"

"Mmm, could be, I suppose," pondered Lucy. "We left not long after you did; the kids all got a bit grizzly because it was so late. Time will tell. I just hope we can keep the 'fireworks' in the garden tonight. I don't think I could cope with Brendan in a bad mood while I'm getting ready for a party."

"Let me come round and help," he suggested.

"Better not," she sighed. "If Brendan comes back like a bear with a sore head I don't know at the moment whether I'd try to placate him or just chuck everything up in the air and come running over to you."

"Christ!" blasphemed Tom.

"Well at least you didn't say '*Oh dear*' this time, my love," she finished.

* * *

Paul and Barry rented a suite of offices in a converted Victorian warehouse building over near Battersea Park. Finding the gates to the courtyard locked, as was usual for a Saturday morning, Barry parked his car in the back street and hurried round to the main entrance where his key would let him gain admittance.

The heavy security door slammed shut on its self-closer behind him and at once he was alone in the cool twilight of the interior and suddenly aware of the hushed, unfamiliar, weekend quietness. He swung open the glazed doors to the stairwell and mounted the stone steps, his footsteps ringing an echo from the hard surfaces all around. The cleaners had preceded him that morning and the steps had a freshly-mopped dampness which gave the air a noticeable tang of disinfectant.

On the first floor, Barry unlocked the outer door to their offices and slipped into the even darker interior. He flicked on the wall lights, glanced at the empty space behind the Receptionist's desk and walked through to the main office. Paul was seated at the book-keeper's desk, the computer screen in front of him gave off an eerie blue light which accentuated the furrowed lines on Paul's forehead. He had heard Barry enter, in fact he had heard his footsteps all the way up the stairs, but he restrained himself from looking up or showing any sign of greeting.

"What's eating you, mate?" began Barry, never one to endure a pregnant silence for very long.

"Money," replied Paul, quietly. "Lots and lots of lovely money."

"What about it?"

"It's disappeared," stated Paul, flatly, sweeping his forelock back from his eyes.

"Gone where?"

"You tell me."

"Have you asked Simon?"

"Don't try that," snapped Paul. "Dad told me I had to sort this out with you. He's not going to bail us out anymore. In fact, what he actually said was, *'I'm not going to nursemaid you two anymore'. That's it, make or break time for you two.'*"

"So what do you want from me?"

"An explanation would be a good start."

"Of what, exactly?"

"Let's cut the crap," said Paul speaking more forcefully and turning in his chair to face Barry directly. "Since last July, you have drawn four cheques for which you have written nothing on the stubs. Antonia asked me about these, I told her to ask you and apparently you said you couldn't remember. You made her think they were to different suppliers and that the bank statements would eventually show the amounts, which she would then have to link up with an invoiced amount."

"Well?"

"So now we know. The bank gave Simon details of the last cheque – the fourth – yesterday morning. They weren't payments to suppliers, they all went to you. Thousands of pounds over and above your normal drawings."

"So Simon knows, he knew about this last night but never said a thing?"

"Correct. And he isn't going to say a thing; not now, not ever. He's very clear that this is between you and me. We either sort this out by ourselves or we don't have a future."

"OK," said Barry, resting his bottom on the edge of a desk and folding his arms across his chest. "So I've drawn a few extra quid for myself, I can explain everything; we need to spend money to make money you know."

"Sixteen thousand quid *extra,* as you put it, to be precise, and no paperwork to show where it's all gone," stated Paul, coldly.

"Oh, that does sound a lot; are you sure?"

"Very, it's all here, look," Paul pushed the heavy box-file of bank statements across the desk, scattering other papers and pens as it went. "Four cheques; all paid to you – see I've highlighted them in pink – total sixteen K. A nice fat number wouldn't you say?"

Barry slumped forward, staring glumly at the dense columns of facts on the top page of the file.

"Why on earth didn't you at least write the amounts of each cheque on the stubs?" continued Paul. "Didn't you think we'd want to know? Did you think we wouldn't find out? Four cheques for around four grand each time? Or were you just in denial, yet again? Were you thinking *'If I don't write anything down, it's not really happening'*? You idiot!"

"Calm down, calm down," soothed Barry, sensing he might get the upper hand if Paul continued to lose his temper. "I was putting in a lot of extra hours in Nottingham, working all night at least once a week, it took a lot of doing but you and Simon were really happy that I was bringing in the business. You weren't that interested in what it was taking out of me!"

"Are you saying this is all payment for a bit of overtime?" rasped Paul, waving his hand contemptuously between the file and the computer screen.

"A bit?" roared Barry. "Fucking days, weeks and months, mate! And we were charging some punters four or five hundred quid a day for my time!"

Paul turned away and pulled a large envelope from among the other papers on his desk.

"I'm glad you mentioned Nottingham," he said coldly. "By unhappy coincidence, look what arrived in the post this morning."

Barry stretched out his hand and took the envelope, tugging out its bulky contents. These consisted of a covering letter from a firm of estate agents and a lengthy contract document covering the lease of a luxury flat in a fashionable part of Nottingham.

"This should have been marked for my attention," complained Barry.

"But the lease is quite clearly in the name of this company," countered Paul. "You, me and Simon are all *jointly and severally*, or some such legalistic bollocks, to be the proud tenants of a very well-appointed, fully-furnished, three-bedroom, two bathroom luxury apartment! And very nice too, at nearly seven hundred pounds a fucking week!" he added scathingly.

"It's not that much," protested Barry.

"It bloody is, when you add-in the service charges and the compulsory insurance premiums and car-parking permits and so on."

"Fuck me!" exclaimed Barry.

"No thanks," said Paul. "You've got yourself a mistress up there haven't you and now she wants you – correction *us* – to set her up in a rather splendid little love nest so that you can have a nice cosy shag once or twice a week. And you'll be back here afterwards saying you need to finish early because you've *been on the job all night*. Too bloody true!"

"Look, we need to be in Nottingham for the long haul. The Consortium are that close," Barry held up his right hand with the thumb and forefinger trembling only a centimetre apart, "to signing a deal for us to re-programme all their ticketing so that over-the-counter, telephone and on-line bookings are all integrated in one system with no glitches."

"Don't they have hotels up there? The whole office could stay every week in five-star luxury for the sort of money this place is going to cost us. It's just not on. Cancel the contract, or pay for it yourself," ordered Paul. "I'm sure Lucy' will be very understanding...as ever!"

Barry stared at him dumbly, his mind racing to come up with a convincing argument to save the apartment Penny had chosen; the place she had insisted should be available before she would consider leaving Graham.

"You've got to learn to think big," was the best he could manage.

"Do me a favour," snorted Paul. "Here's what we do, you dump the flat, you stay in a decent hotel - as and when necessary - and get a grip on costs so that all the profits don't get, err...don't get, err, pissed up the wall."

"That's disgusting," objected Barry assuming, correctly, that Paul had come close to making a particularly indecent analogy relating to his activities with Penny.

"OK, so you do want me to tell Lucy what you've arranged for your accommodation in Nottingham?" enquired Paul, trying to sound as oily and annoying as he possibly could.

"Fuck off."

"And about the sixteen grand," returned Paul, sensing that this was the right moment to lay down his terms in full. "You and I are supposed to take equal amounts from the business. Our finances couldn't stand it if I took an equal sum out this year, so basically you owe me eight grand. That's fair, then we'll each have had the same income."

"I haven't got that amount, and you know it!" snapped Barry.

"I'll accept instalments, easy terms, but I want that money," insisted Paul.

"Did Simon tell you to take this line?" snarled Barry.

"Nope," smiled Paul triumphantly. "I told you before; he insists that we sort this one out by ourselves. He's not even complained that you've let him down, even though you obviously have. Those are my terms, take it or leave it, but remember," he finished, narrowing his eyes and staring directly at Barry, "Simon and I have two votes to your one."

"Yeah, and you're his son, I know, I know. Yeah, yeah, you had a smashing Dad and mine was a complete fuck-off!'"

"No!" shouted Paul. "Not because I'm his son, and not because of your Dad. It's because I'm right and you're in the wrong. That's why he'll back me."

"Blood is thicker than water, mate," replied Barry standing up and turning to leave.

"Don't talk to me about *thick*," sneered Paul. "You're the one who's being bloody thick."

"I need to think this over," pleaded Barry, suddenly changing tack when he saw Paul's resolve. "I'll see you Monday and tell you the best I can offer."

"Think away, think away," replied Paul. "Just be sure you think your way into agreeing my terms, that's all."

Barry left the office, petulantly leaving all the doors open behind him as he went, knowing full-well that Paul would feel impelled to follow after him, shutting each one so as to restore the security of the building.

* * *

Tom spent a restless afternoon, wondering whether Lucy might suddenly appear at his door, with or without her kids in tow. He sat at his desk, thumbing through the pages of textbooks in a desultory attempt at doing some lesson preparation. He had two piles of exercise books he should have started marking, ready for Monday, but he flipped open the first one, grunted when he saw the spidery handwriting inside and dropped it on the floor. He rose, walked into his bedroom and began sorting through his shirts trying to decide which to wear that evening. The phone rang.

He let it ring, hoping it was Lucy and that the bell would stop after two cycles. The ringing continued. Tom picked up the handset and said "Hello." The line went dead as if someone had waited for him to answer and then hung up. Angry, he dialled 1471 and a recorded voice informed him that the caller had withheld their number. Moments later the door bell rang and, again hoping it would be Lucy, Tom felt a surge of nervous anticipation which forced him to put his hand inside his trousers to adjust the discomfort of his suddenly aroused penis.

Opening the door of his flat, Tom was confronted by the sight of Barry's lithe figure charging up the stairs, taking them two at a time.

"Glad you're in mate," gasped Barry, "need to use your phone!"

"Did you ring just now?"

"Yeah, needed to check if you were here. Didn't have the keys on me, Mrs P, downstairs, let me in, she was on her way out," panted Barry. "Had to park a long way down that side street, it's a bit of a run from there."

"Thanks," said Tom sourly. "You didn't want to speak to me then?"

"No, sorry, mate" answered Barry, stepping past him. "No battery left on my mobile, used it a lot today already."

"Well, there's my phone," said Tom, pointing with his thumb in the direction of the living room, "Tea or a beer?"

"Look, mate, it's a bit awkward, I've got to phone Penny. Bit of a crisis. She should be arriving at her mate Cynthia's about now. You don't mind if I close the door do you? I'll join you in the kitchen when I've finished."

Tom shrugged emphatically, turned around and walked away as Barry clicked the living room door shut behind him.

"Oh Jesus," muttered Tom. He desperately wanted to phone Lucy but knew that he couldn't. If he told her that Barry was in his flat she would want to know why. Instead, he sat in the kitchen taking slow, careful sips from a can of lager, trying half-heartedly to engage with the Prize Crossword in the 'Guardian'. It was another forty minutes before he heard the living room door creak and Barry's heavy footfalls coming through from the front of the flat. He looked up as Barry entered.

"Better?" enquired Tom.

"Sort of," responded Barry distractedly, helping himself to a beer from the fridge. "I'll have to shoot up to Nottingham first thing Monday."

"Oh dear," said Tom and then, correcting himself for Lucy's sake, added, "Oh bugger!"

"Huh?" asked Barry.

"Got to stop saying *Oh dear*," mumbled Tom.

"Right!" Barry made a loud slurp as he swallowed a mouthful of lager.

"Hear you've been working today," said Tom and then suddenly froze when he realised Barry would now know he had spoken to Lucy. Barry was staring at him, fiercely it seemed and Tom, distinctly flustered, swept imaginary crumbs from the newspaper crossword before explaining,

"Yeah, I phoned your house to see what time it would start tonight. Lucy said you'd gone to the office."

"Right," said Barry." Well, I reckon we'll let some fireworks off for the kids around six or six thirty then we'll have a bit of a piss-up afterwards. How did Lucy sound when you spoke to her?"

"Bit frazzled, getting things ready for the party I suppose," suggested Tom. "I offered to pop round to help but she said no."

"Fuck," said Barry, "I wish you had. I'm in for a right old tongue-lashing then."

"Oh dear," said Tom.

"Oh fuck!" said Barry. "Where's the justice, eh? Penny's just given me a right old going over and now Lucy's about to do the same."

"What's upset Penny?" asked Tom, unable to conceal his curiosity.

"What hasn't?" grunted Barry. "Basically, she wants to leave her old fella – that's Graham – but only if I'll set her up in an expensive apartment until the divorce settlement enables her to extract enough dosh from *yer man* for her to buy her own house."

Tom regarded him from beneath raised eyebrows, but said

nothing.

"That's all very well," continued Barry, "but I'm not made of fucking money, am I? And this flat she wants is going to cost a shed-load. So now I've got Paul yelling in one ear and Penny screaming into the other..." he scratched his upper arm fiercely and snorted angrily, "and if Lucy wants to start having a go she'll have to join the fucking queue. I can only take it from two of them at a time."

"That's not fair!" exclaimed Tom.

"Fair?" yelled Barry. "What's fucking *fair* got to do with it?"

"Well, I mean, err, well Lucy, I mean, she's not to blame here, is she?" he stuttered, desperately trying to disguise his reflexive support for Lucy.

"No, well that's as maybe," sniffed Barry, suddenly quieter, "but we wouldn't be in this mess if, well, if she was a bit more understanding..."

Tom stared at him blankly, completely at a loss as to what to say next.

"Penny, Christ!" exclaimed Barry. "It was all going so well. She seemed to understand. We'd have a good laugh, go to a club, have a meal and few drinks, a good shag of course – huh, always a good shag... And then, thanks very much, see you next week. Why not? Why couldn't we do that, I mean go on doing that? Why do they always want to change things?"

"Make progress you mean? Develop the relationship?" suggested Tom, with genuine concern.

"But it isn't development is it? If it ain't fucking broke, don't fucking fix it. Why can't they see that? They say they love you, and like what you do, and then – next thing you know – it's not good enough, it's all got to change. Got to be more *meaningful*! Give me fucking strength, I ask you!"

"That's what Penny wants is it, a *meaningful* relationship?"

"That's it. That's what I have had her saying for hour after hour on the phone today. She just can't see that what first got me, what I first loved about her, was her style, her independence, her willingness to just *go for it*. And now what am I getting? *'Oh Brendan, I'm so desperate, you've got to save me, I can't go on like this, I need you, poor me, oh woe, I need you...'* Fucking hell, get a grip woman, that's what I wanted to say."

"And did you?"

"Almost, but, well no, not exactly. I said I'd go up there on Monday. I think I said I needed to hold her in my arms, some such bollocks. Oh God!" Barry held his head in his hands. "I need to tell her to be patient, but that'll be a new experience for her. *Patience* is not a quality you'd associate with Penny. I don't think she's ever had to be *patient* ever before in her whole fucking life."

"So you've just let her go on hoping?" suggested Tom ruefully, pulling the ring on another can of lager and sliding it towards Barry. "You've delayed the inevitable until Monday, that's all."

"I'll think of something, don't you worry mate. I'll think of something, I always do."

Chapter Ten

A rocket soared into the night, high above the rooftops, as Tom walked down the hill towards Lucy's house. Percussions and flashes emanated at random from the darkness behind many of the neighbouring houses. Tom knocked firmly on the front door just as a series of bangs and banshee howls came from a firework exploding somewhere out of sight. He waited; then knocked again. Through the ancient leaded glass he could see a figure emerge from the dining room and turn towards the kitchen. He seized the moment and knocked again, more loudly.

A large, elderly, woman with untidy grey hair and wearing a floral apron opened the door and blocked the hallway.

"Hi, I'm Tom," he stuttered, stepping back from the threshold.

"I know," said the woman gruffly. "You can't be too careful."

She stood aside to let him enter the house and closed the door behind him,

"I'm Mary," she confirmed. "I got caught out on Halloween."

"Oh dear," said Tom, and paused, expecting some further explanation to come from Mary.

"Go on through," she said. "They're all in the back, except Mrs Sands and little Alice. They're upstairs watching from the bedroom."

Tom was about to say "*I'll just pop up to say hello to Lucy,*" when Mary said firmly,

"Barry's letting them off, I'm sure he could use some help. Paul hasn't turned up you see."

Out in the tiny back yard, Cherie jumped for joy when she saw Tom emerge from the back door. Tom took her hand and looked up, waving at the black windows above, hoping Lucy was watching from one of them.

"Mary says you're letting them off!" ventured Tom with a grin. "Smells like it too!"

"Glad you're here," scowled Barry. "Shine that torch on the box again, Emms."

Emma had a press of young children and some adults corralled behind a rope at one side of the little garden.

"Mount Vesuvius!" announced Barry, stepping up to a bucket filled with sand mounted on a box next to the right-hand wall.

"Dad!" whined Emma, "you said I could tell them the next one."

"Sorry, love, lend Tom your torch and then you step forward and announce it again."

"What was it called?" she hissed loudly.

"Mount Vesuvius," whispered Barry. "Do us a favour, Tom. There's a hammer and some nails on the plank down there, just next to the bike. Take those three Catherine Wheels from the box and pin them on the fence posts, will you? I want them to be the grand finale."

The fat yellow light from 'Mount Vesuvius' continued long enough for Tom to find the nails and stumble over to the fence posts. Behind him Emma shrilly announced, "Silver Blizzard!"

There was a delay; Emma could be heard complaining,

"Dad, it's gone out!"

"No; stand back Emma. Just be patient!" Grandpa Simon's voice came from somewhere in the shadows. Tom could see the fuse glowing dully alongside the firework then with a sudden pop the cone burst open and fierce silver sparks crackled upwards. Seizing the opportunity provided by the flickering light, Tom quickly nailed each wheel to the posts, checking that they all rotated smoothly.

Emma gleefully lit the first which swayed on its axis for a few seconds then burst into life, roaring and hissing as it spun aggressively discharging its cargo of sparks and flames. The next one started similarly but two seconds into its performance the nail fell out of the woodwork and the firework expended its anger pointlessly amongst the flower pots.

"Tom!" complained Emma, "You didn't fit that one properly. Dad, you've gotta nail it properly!"

Barry gave Tom a playful slap,

"Bad boy!" he mocked before giving the next nail a couple of heavy blows. This time the nail proved too tight for the wheel to rotate at all and the final event comprised the static disc burning itself out in a golden halo of futile effort. Emma watched silently, biting her bottom lip rather than criticise her father.

Simon called for three cheers for Emma's fireworks and several excited little throats shrilled their approval. Simon took charge of lighting sparklers for the children while Tom and Barry dropped the burnt-out fireworks into a bowl of cold water. Stepping back gratefully into the warmth of the kitchen, Tom was pleased to be greeted by Lucy who passed Alice to Mary before planting a chaste kiss on each side of his face.

"Let me get you a drink, my darling," offered Lucy with a sly wink.

"What are you having?" he enquired, politely.

"Lotsh and lotsh," mocked Lucy. "I've been quietly knocking back the vino all afternoon, ever since I heard about your secret tryst with my husband in fact."

Tom frowned at her, about to question what she meant. Mary scooped up Alice and flounced out of the room.

"S'alright," continued Lucy, "he told me he'd called at your house for some 'Dutch courage' before coming home to face my wrath."

"He just turned up, what could I do?" asked Tom.

"Nothing. There's nothing to do. Nothing anyone can do; the silly bugger has got us into a right financial disaster this time," complained Lucy, pouring herself a large glass of red wine and swallowing most of it in two or three gulps. Tom continued trying to look puzzled.

"There's a cash-flow problem at the business. We've got to put up more dosh to save it and our share runs into thousands. About two grand each month, for the next six! We've just reviewing our assets, to see if there's anything we could flog," spat Lucy. "And that didn't take very long." She gazed around, waving her empty glass as if looking for a re-fill. "Seems it's all my fault," she continued. "Seems I don't bring in a single penny...just muck about with the kids all day long...Don't know what I can do. What would you suggest, Mr Corky? You're very knowledgeable about the wicked world. D'ya think I should head over to Bedford Hill and join the tarts on the streets? Brendan didn't object when I suggested it..."

Tom stared at her in disbelief.

"P'raps you don't think I could earn enough turning tricks to make it worthwhile?" she sobbed.

The garden doors opened and Simon ushered in various visiting parents and children. Lucy gazed at them, looking stunned. To Tom's surprise Mary suddenly reappeared from the hallway, thrust Alice into Tom's arms and embraced Lucy, sweeping her out of the kitchen. Alice wriggled energetically, stretching towards the incomers,

"Pa Simon, Pa Simon!" she called.

"Hello my duckling," he responded, accepting her from Tom. "Did you like the fireworks this time, little one?"

Suddenly the kitchen seemed full of people. Cherie singled out Tom and dragged him through into the front room to sit next to her on the sofa. She thrust a story book into his lap.

"Read!" she commanded.

Tom sat on the sofa reading a story first to Cherie, then to Emma and several other children who gathered around him sipping juice and liberally spilling crumbs from biscuits and slices of pizza. Alice burrowed through the visiting children and curled up on the cushion beside him, thumb planted firmly in her mouth. Eventually Tom arrived at the end of the story and concluded that they had all lived happily ever after, even though those words did not actually appear in the book. Simon stood over him, still dressed all in black, smiling benignly.

"Have a well-earned break," Simon suggested. "What story shall we have next children?"

Tom escaped back to the kitchen while the assembled youngsters transferred their attention en bloc to Grandpa Simon. As he entered the room Lucy suddenly stood in front of him, sipping a large tumbler of water which clinked with ice cubes.

"Dear kind Tom, let me kiss you, I'm so sorry about earlier," she said quietly. Tom stood still and enjoyed the pressure of her lips at the side of his mouth. Barry appeared from nowhere and slapped Tom on the back just as Tom's arm was spreading to encircle Lucy's waist.

"Get in there, my son!" crowed Barry. Lucy sprang away from Tom who turned towards Barry in open-mouthed astonishment. The room seemed suddenly quiet and Barry stood still, obviously flustered.

"Well, you might as well," he roared. "She's always got a headache by the time I get home!" An embarrassed silence engulfed the room. "This bloke I met in Nottingham last week," persisted Barry, "said his wife always had a headache whenever he suggested a bit of *how's your father*. So one night, she's gone to bed first, right? And he comes up stairs carrying a glass of water and a box of aspirins. *'Here you are, dear,'* he says. *'What's that for?'* she asks. *'Your headache, sweetheart,'* says he. *'But I haven't got a headache!'* she protests. *'Jolly good!'* says he, jumping on the bed. *'Gotcha!'*"

"There's soup, sausages and baked potatoes," announced Mary, clattering a saucepan lid and releasing a blast of hot air from the oven door. The guests gathered round and Lucy joined Mary in handing out bowls, plates and slices of warm baguette. Barry made an attempt to introduce Tom to some of her friends,

"This is Jane and Oliver, from next door," he began, "Rufus and Sally we know from Emma's school ...."

Tom tried to register the list of names and link them to faces but soon lost track. He noticed how Barry was particularly solicitous towards Jane and a friend of hers, possibly called Sophie but Tom had lost concentration when she was introduced. Tom recognised Sophie, if indeed that was her name, as one of the three mothers whom Lucy had described as 'Clapham Matrons' when they had met at the swings during half-term.

Mary handed them each a bowl of steaming soup on a plate with a chunk of baguette balance precariously on the rim. Tom sampled a spoonful of the hot liquid. Someone dropped their spoon with a ringing clatter on the tiled floor and everyone stepped back, fearing the soup was about to follow.

"Where do you teach, Tom?" asked Jane.

"At a comprehensive over in Streatham," he replied. "*Hettie Thrales*', do you know it?"

"That's jolly worthy of you," she trumpeted in reply. "Pretty uphill toil I should imagine?" Before Tom could offer his view, Jane had swept on; "Ollie, you must have a chat with Tom. He can give us the low down on schools we need to look into as a fall back for William; in case he doesn't get in at Dulwich or Westminster…"

"Well we're very selective these days," replied Tom trying to sound donnish and superior. "We're heavily over-subscribed every year."

"Imagine!" breathed Sophie. "Are you a rugger school?"

"Fortunately not," said Tom. "We've had several kids get trials with 'Palace and Fulham in recent years; and a spin bowler taken up by Surrey……"

"Asian, I bet!" snorted Oliver. "All mine are mad about cricket, can't stand soccer. They say that's just for the blacks."

"What do you mean, '*your Asians*'?" challenged Lucy, pausing as she gathered up the soup bowls. "Do you keep them as pets for breeding or something?"

"Gosh no," replied Oliver, seeming quite oblivious to the aggression in Lucy's voice, "I'm an accountant, not a farmer…Most of our trainees are Asians these days, and damned fine number crunchers they are too!"

"You know Tom, I could swear I've seen you somewhere before," frowned Sophie. "Are you and Lucy very close?"

"Oh you probably have," gushed Lucy, swaying slightly as she spoke. "He's my very own *Common Man*. He's *The Man on the Clapham Omnibus*, don't ya know? I keep him to help with outings, taking the children to the swings, that sort of thing. He'sh an ash-olute treasure! An' always 'vailable in the hols, so useful! Downright *spiffing* wouldn't you say?"

"Luce, can I have a word?" intervened Barry, taking her elbow insistently and guiding her out into the hall.

"That's it!" proclaimed Sophie, poking Tom on his chest. "You and Lucy must have been at the swings when I was there with my little brood; at half-term…"

"Bit of a swinger are you old boy?" enquired Oliver, biting the end off a well-cooked sausage.

"Ollie, fetch me another glass please," ordered Jane. "And Ollie, you've had quite enough."

"But I'm not driving," he complained. "We only live next door, darling."

"Precisely!" said Jane icily.

"Righty ho, you're the boss," muttered Oliver. "Glass of white was it?"

"Everyone alright?" enquired Barry, returning without Lucy.

"I'm afraid we must be making a move," announced Jane. "Can't have another late one."

"Me too," added Sophie. "Thank you so much for inviting us, I must gather my two. Are they in the drawing room?"

"In the front room, err yes," stumbled Barry.

"Your wine, my darling," said Oliver.

"We're going," whispered Jane, fiercely. "Going with Sophie… Don't want to leave William and his friends on their own in the house too long," she explained to Barry. "You never know what boys'll get up to these days."

"Yeah, dead right," he answered, gruffly.

"Sorry, old boy, you know how it is," said Oliver, shoulders drooping and an exaggerated 'hang-dog' expression on his puffy, pink, features.

The departure of Sophie, Jane, Oliver and various children led to a rapid exodus from the party. Lucy came downstairs looking slightly red-eyed but wearing fresh make-up, and bid a fond farewell to Sally, Rufus and their three children. Mary came and went between the kitchen and the other rooms clearing plates and collecting glasses from the mantelpiece and from other, more vulnerable, perches. In the living room, Simon continued his epic of story reading for the children. Mary eventually subsided next to Emma and smiled encouragement to Simon.

Tom found Lucy and Barry sitting in the kitchen; they fell silent when he entered. Tom looked at each of them in turn, and began to say his goodbyes.

"Sit down, Corky," ordered Barry. "Have a drink for Christ's sake, you're making me nervous. Here!" He poured a glass of red wine and slid it across the table. "Lucy thinks you might be able to settle an argument we keep having."

Tom frowned, trying to anticipate what might be coming next.

"I never get to drive our car," said Lucy, glumly. "Even when Brendan's at home and not using it, he still doesn't want me driving it."

Barry shrugged silently and looked at Tom.

"I feel so out of practice," she complained. "I've hardly driven at all since I passed the flaming test, and that was well over a year ago now."

"I just don't want you practising on my car," insisted Barry. "You'll never be able to park it."

"Our car!" she corrected him.

"Hire one," he answered.

"Using what for money?" she barked, then banged her elbows on the table and rested her head on her hands.

"Why don't you just take her out for a couple of refreshers?" Tom suggested diplomatically, looking at Barry.

"I don't want him anywhere near me when I'm driving!" cried Lucy, shaking her head. "He'll just criticise the whole time and shout at me when I do the slightest thing wrong..."

"Well get Mr 'wonderfully-calm' Cork here to take you out driving," said Barry, dismissively, adding, "in his bloody car, not mine! Then we'll see how long it is before even he starts shouting at you." Barry refilled his wine glass and gulped another mouthful.

"Yeah, I don't mind," said Tom, hopefully, and was rewarded with a melting smile from Lucy. "It is insured for any driver."

"That's settled then," said Lucy with an artificial brightness. "Tom Cork you're going to get me driving again, with confidence."

"Fine," beamed Tom. "We'll start tomorrow, Sunday afternoon; should be quiet enough. About two-ish, how would that suit you? We'll still have a good couple of hours of daylight left..."

"Have another drink mate," grunted Barry, sliding the bottle across the table again. "You'll bloody need it!"

The three of them had all drunk far too much and sat in a stupefied silence for a few moments before Barry began to trill tunelessly, "*Baby you can drive my car! Beep, beep! An' baby, I love you! Beep, beep!*"

"Lennon & McCartney; The Beatles; 1965," responded Tom, automatically.

"You bloody academics, you're all so fucking anal," sneered Barry. "You have to bloody dissect and classify everything, don't you?"

Lucy and Tom stared at him, surprised by this sudden, vehement outburst.

"You just can't enjoy something for what it is, for your gut reaction to it, can you? You're not happy till you've killed it stone dead and put it a neat little box, are you? Bloody Paul's the same and see, he couldn't even be arsed to come around here tonight!"

"Brendan, you're drunk. Tom's very kind, and I'm sure Paul had his reasons," replied Lucy.

"Oh yeah, he'll have had his *reasons* alright. Nice little, tight little accountant's reasons! The tight-arsed git...And Tom, huh! Ever wondered why he can never keep a girlfriend for more than a few weeks, or haven't you noticed, sweetie?" Lucy frowned at him, her face darkening with anger.

"I tell you, he just bores the pants off them," said Barry, answering his own question.

"I thought that was the whole point," stated Tom, trying to match Barry's aggression.

"Huh? You what?"

"That. Getting their pants off," explained Tom with a foolish grin. Lucy grimaced despairingly and turned away from both men.

"Not through boredom," slurred Barry. "Through charm and your manly charisma, and putting a bit of cash about," he claimed, visibly preening himself behind his wine glass.

Lucy grunted again and made a face at Tom, who was too inebriated to understand her desire to change the subject. He stared at Lucy, smiling broadly and trying to think of something to say that might please her. Alcohol made Tom soft and silly, Barry it made loud and belligerent.

"Knickers down the ages...." began Tom. "A six volume history, lavishly illustrated..."

"You pompous prick!" shouted Barry. "Life is one fucking long episode of *University Challenge* for you, isn't it?"

"They're not episodes," insisted Tom. "They're rounds, it's a quiz show; a *competition* you moron!"

Barry pushed back his chair which scraped loudly across the floor tiles. He stood up, swaying unsteadily and bracing himself against the edge of the table.

"That's enough!" proclaimed Lucy, leaning over the table between the two men with her arms outstretched. "You're both *alcoholically challenged* and I need help to get the real children into bed."

"You should put him to bed first," grunted Barry slumping back into his chair.

"I just might!" said Lucy, tweaking Tom's ear painfully and leading him out of the room as Barry emptied the last of the red wine into his glass and sat staring glumly at the rings of spilled wine all across the table.

* * *

Tom began his walk homeward feeling drunk and disconsolate in equal measures. His face was set in fierce concentration as he sought to counteract the stumbling uncertainty that had invaded his legs. His head was pounding and his thoughts of Lucy were punctuated by the flash and bang of fireworks still echoing around the close-packed houses.

Rockets blazed dramatically above the rooftops or danced distantly in the black sky. Deafening bangs smacked against his ears and, from a neighbouring street, a car alarm joined the general discord of the night. Treading familiar pavements, he soon emerged from the enclosing streets to face the dark, brooding, expanse of the Common. He paused at the kerb, swaying with drunken deliberation as his mind took in the stream of passing traffic. With a sudden lurch he strode purposefully into the road. There was a squeal of brakes, several car horns sounded and headlights flashed before he reached the refuge of the shadowy grassland under the black trees.

To his left was the playground, looking forlorn and ghostly quiet, all the bright colours of the equipment muted to shades of grey in the borrowed light. Another enormous firework erupted in the sky behind him and Tom suddenly thought of London under attack from the Luftwaffe and from Graham Greene's 'robot' bombs. He leaned against the rough bark of a tree and stared around at the jagged roof tops, silhouetted intermittently by the glow of fires.

Sounds of revelry and pounding music mixed with the surly rumble of traffic and the thud of explosions. In the distance, police sirens rose and fell and a vehicle with a skipping blue light on its roof raced along the far side of the Common before disappearing into the night. Tom resumed his journey, his carefully polished shoes sliding and squelching in the muddy grass. A sudden unevenness in the ground caused him to stumble, lose his balance and crash full length upon a harsh and gritty surface. His hands and knees felt grazed and painful as he rolled onto his back to face the spangled darkness above him. He realised he had tripped on the remains of one of the Second World War air-raid shelters which still scarred the Common.

Another rocket seared a fiery trail across the sky and expanded into a huge puff-ball of silver light. Tom imagined the elephantine bulk of a barrage balloon floating massively over-head, tethered to this spot on the Common by steel cables which flexed in graceful catenaries. He watched the white fingers of search-lights probing the night-sky and illuminating tiny aircraft, like silver fish, dipping in and out of the cloud base. He willed their savage destruction.

He felt the ground shake beneath him as nearby anti-aircraft guns barked their response and angry yellow flashes puffed black smoke among the fragile planes. The vision was so real that he curled his forearm across his face to shield his eyes from the whistling bombs and blinding chaos. The raid pounded on, the far horizon glowed with fires raging along the riverside and in the city beyond. Smoke billowed *in memoriam* above the roaring world. Tom closed his eyes. He imagined himself walking with a limp, as Bendrix had done after nearly being killed by the doodlebug. He stretched out both arms to stabilise the world even though he was already lying on the ground. He thought of Lucy going to bed with the drunken Barry. His stomach felt hollow, his throat suddenly burned and he realised he was being sick into the wet grass. He smelled the rancid wine in his vomit and his stomach heaved again. He retched until his stomach was empty and his eyes bulged with tears. He wiped his mouth and nose on the sleeve of his jacket and slumped, groaning, onto his back. The threatening sky rotated above him; he closed his eyes as the nausea came and went.

Sometime later, he rose uncertainly to his feet, bending forward to brush ineffectually at the mud and leaves and worse adhering to the knees of his trousers. He staggered on across the grass, threading erratically between the trees, grateful to be recovering the sanctuary of the present time and the comforting familiarity of the neon streetlights now guiding him home. He hated Barry and Bendrix and Graham Greene and Guido Fawkes, all with an equal and indiscriminate passion.

Chapter Eleven

A cold grey rain fell briefly in the early hours of Sunday morning, washing the last of the smoke and cordite smells from the sullen air. Tom slept late. Rising briefly at about nine to drink a pint of cold water he then retreated quickly beneath his duvet, sheltering his defeated senses from painful humiliation by sound and sunlight.

Soon after midday he staggered to the bathroom and stood under the shower, gradually turning down the heat until the shocking cold of the powerful spray forced sensations to reclaim his body. He spent a long time in front of the bathroom mirror combing and re-combing his hair, trying to make himself look different. He envied Barry his natural curls which made Barry's hair look attractive no matter how untidy it was. He envied Barry waking this morning next to Lucy, although he was glad enough that she could not see him right now. Tom grumbled through a litany of familiar complaints about his own hair. When it was this long it went into greasy waves which he hated. If he had it cut short it either stood on end looking all spiky or, when very short, it just made his face look fat.

Finally, he splashed water on his hair again, scrubbed it harshly on a towel, combed it firmly backwards then tried to give it a stylishly ruffled appearance using his finger-tips. The result, within seconds, he viewed as yet another disaster and, flinging the comb into the bath, he strode into the kitchen to stand, naked, drinking tea and eating toast.

Eventually, he looked at his watch and hurried to dress, selecting a check shirt and a new pair of blue jeans. He felt reassured by their tight fit and un-faded dark-blueness. He discarded his familiar baggy sweater and rifled his wardrobe for a hardly worn brown leather jacket. Pausing to admire himself in the mirror he resolved to wear this jacket more frequently – but not to school – before flicking at the front of his hair and giving his reflection an ugly V sign. He snatched his copy of <u>The End of the Affair</u> from the bedside table where it had languished recently under a half-empty glass of water. Vengefully, he flung the book across his living room and it slid to a halt on the floor, its pages shuffled up against one of the back legs of his desk.

* * *

When Tom pulled up in front of Lucy's house the only available parking space looked only an inch or two longer than his car. He thought for a moment before engaging reverse gear and aiming the car diagonally backwards into the gap. Lucy, who had been watching for his arrival from the front window, suddenly appeared at the passenger's door, pulled it open and pushed herself into the seat. Tom turned his head nervously, wanting to smile a greeting at her, ready to apologise for his drunkenness last night. He flinched when he saw the determined set of her facial expression and the hard light in her dark eyes.

"Don't start on at me, just get moving!" she commanded, impatiently.

Tom twisted again to check for traffic, and steered the car back into the road. Lucy was suddenly waving briskly out of the side window.

"There's Mary," she called, suddenly sounding pleased. "God she was such a star last night; don't know what I'd have done without her. And you weren't much help."

"Lucy, I'm so sorry..."

"Don't be. Just shut up and drive."

"Where to?"

"Anywhere! I don't care, so long as it's far away from here."

They drove in dismal silence past Wandsworth Common and down Burntwood Lane until Tom turned off into some quiet residential streets and pulled up at the side of the road, with the engine running.

"How about you driving along here?" he suggested as kindly and positively as he could. Lucy looked at him for a moment and then burst into tears. Tom switched off the engine and pulled her close with his left arm.

"Oh God! Oh God! Oh God! I'm so sorry," she sobbed. "I didn't mean to be like this with you."

"You can do anything with me, *that's* the whole point," whispered Tom.

"It's all such a mess!" she continued. "We've got loads of bills he says we can't pay; and look at last night - Barry behaving like a pig one minute and then sucking up to the neighbours like mad the next. As if they don't see through him; and who cares what they see through anyway?"

"I'm sorry, I only wish..."

Lucy blew her nose on a crumpled tissue she had tugged from the sleeve of her cardigan.

"It was worse after you'd gone, if that's possible. I think Simon and Mary put the kids to bed. I was out of it..." She blew her nose again, loudly, as if trying to expel her memory of the disastrous evening into the tissue.

"Mary's seen what he's really like, she told me so."

"When?"

"This morning. She came over; I think she was worried we might not have survived the night."

"That was good of her."

"She a very caring person. I'm so lucky to have her nearby...Not like that stuck-up cow Jane, next door..." Lucy broke down again, her upper body heaving each time she sobbed. Tom pulled her closer and pushed his face into her hair, kissing her scalp until he located her ear.

"I love you," he stated and she convulsed more vigorously.

"How can you? You can't!" she spluttered.

"Can't help it, I just do. It's a bitch, isn't it?"

Lucy tried to laugh and cry at the same time and managed to turn her face for him to kiss. Tom felt the dampness of her tears on his cheek.

"Take me to your flat," she whispered. "Please, darling Tom."

"But what about your driving…"

"Fuck that! I shouldn't be behind the wheel in this state; even if it is your car…"

Tom started to laugh. Lucy gulped, her hand slapping across her mouth;

"Oh God, I sound just like Barry, don't I? Oh help me, please Tom, you've got to help me…"

At the flat, they hurried into Tom's bedroom and made love in the soft afternoon light. Lucy lay still, feeling Tom subside and slip from her. She kissed him and whispered, "Don't go to sleep darling. We can only be as long as a driving lesson might have taken. I must be back by nightfall; Barry knows I wouldn't drive in the dark."

Tom muttered a complaint which went unheard; Lucy rose and hurried into the bathroom to wash away the incriminating scent of sex. Tom reached out for her and felt the warm but empty sheet where she had lain. He found her in the living room, standing very still and gazing out over the Common. She held a white towel in front of her but her back was naked. Tom came close and stood behind her his skin pressing gently on hers.

"Let's pretend it's summer," she said, surveying the cold blue sky of the now cloudless Sunday afternoon. "If you ignore the bare trees, the Common looks like this around nine o'clock on a summer evening," she continued. "What time is it now?"

"Just after three, I think. Let's pretend we're going out for dinner and then you're going to stay the night with me."

"Pretend away," she sighed, leaning back into him. "That's all this is, isn't it? Pretend, pretend, pretend…"

Tom spread his arms to enclose her, cupping her breasts snugly in the folds of the towel.

"I don't have to pretend," he began, "I really do love you."

"You think you do," whispered Lucy. "You probably just feel sorry for me…"

"No I don't."

"Well you should. I mean, I'm so pathetic, I hate myself."

"You're beautiful," whispered Tom into the nape of her neck. Lucy twisted in his arms until he held the towel to shield her back from the windows and he felt her nipples against his chest and her pubic hair brushing his legs. She began to ask him something but he smothered her mouth with his lips and swayed her back towards the bedroom.

"You like me because I'm an easy lay," she replied pushing her hips against him.

"That too," said Tom before he could stop himself.

Lucy broke out of his embrace, clutching the towel to her chest with her fists, her eyes bright with anger;

"And my children? Where would they be while we shagged our stupid brains out and indulged in candle-lit dinners?"

Tom said nothing; he stepped back from her.

"And Barry?" she continued, pursuing him, jabbing the air with her finger. "He'd go ape if he knew about us. Not because he loves me to distraction, but because he can't bear to give up anything he owns.

"He doesn't own you and he doesn't own me," protested Tom, backing further away.

"I'm tied to him forever and a day because of the children. You do realise that, don't you?"

"When did I ever make your kids an issue between us?"

"No you haven't, I mean you don't. And I'm so grateful for that, believe me," said Lucy, her voice suddenly softening. Her hands dropped to her sides.

"Well good. You know you can rely on me; and I can stand up to Barry..."

"I wouldn't recommend it!"

"I don't mean physically. I can't see us fighting over you."

"Barry's too clever for that. People under-estimate his intelligence all the time because of the way he speaks."

"Yes I know he uses that..."

"And he manages to manipulate you pretty well, doesn't he?" argued Lucy. "For all your cleverness..."

"No," lied Tom; thinking immediately of Penny's letters and Barry's retention of the spare keys.

Lucy moved towards the bedroom, intending to get dressed,

"We're only together this afternoon because of his grace and favour," she said over her shoulder.

"Well that's where he's pretending," retorted Tom. "We're

not the only ones. If anyone's deceiving themselves and being deceived it's him. We know more about him than he does about us."

Then he halted abruptly and sucked in his lips, fearing he had come close to speaking Penny's name. Lucy bent to pick-up her knickers from the carpet and Tom reached out to grasp her naked buttocks.

"No, darling, we can't," she protested, breaking free from him and gathering more of her clothes from the end of the bed. Tom threw himself across the duvet and began punching his pillow, huffing and puffing to exaggerate his display of frustration.

"You need to dress too," she laughed, "unless I'm supposed to have walked home after my imaginary *driving lesson*? That would look pretty damned suspicious, don't you think?"

"I'd rather watch you getting dressed first," he exclaimed, propping himself on one elbow and facing her. "Anyway, Barry would feel totally vindicated if you walked in saying I'd lost my cool and chucked you out of the car."

"That would mean no more driving lessons, *dah stoopid*! Pass me my bra, it must be under your duvet somewhere."

"No!" teased Tom. "Let me keep it as a memento of today? Something to fondle during the long, lonely nights."

"Pervert," she snapped. "Next thing you'll be asking me to dress in fishnet stockings and suspenders..."

"Ooh, would you?" gasped Tom, rolling away from her as she grabbed a pillow and swung it down on his head.

* * *

Before dawn on Monday, Barry drove north alone on the M1 motorway, heading for Nottingham. Frowning into the murky light, he gripped the wheel in silent determination. Unusually for him the car radio was silent and he heard only the deep rumble of the car's engine, the swish of the tyres on the wet road, the dragging squeal of the wiper-blades and the frequent, pulsating, toc-toc-toc of the indicator lights. His fingers drummed impatiently on the padded centre of the steering wheel as he slowed in the obscuring spray behind a swaying van which had trundled into the fast lane as it strained to overtake two enormous trucks rolling northwards, side by side.

Barry had slept badly and risen early, fumbling for his clothes in the darkness of the bedroom. Reaching into the wardrobe for his suit, he stubbed his toe on the leg of Lucy's dressing table and grunted at the sudden stab of pain.

"Put the light on if you can't see," commanded Lucy in a husky voice from deep inside the duvet.

"I didn't want to wake you," muttered Barry.

"I'm not awake," she droned, flatly. "Just do what you need, find your stuff and let me get back to sleep."

"Where's my yellow shirt?"

"There are three shirts I ironed last night hanging above the radiator in the front room."

"Sorry; and thanks," he whispered. "I need to be in Nottingham before 9."

"When will you be back?"

"Tomorrow? Dunno, I'll phone you, bye."

"Huh," yawned Lucy.

Barry scooped up his clothes and shoes and stumbled downstairs to get dressed. While the kettle was boiling water for his coffee, he trudged all the way up to his office in the loft conversion where he retrieved his briefcase and his overnight bag. As he began to drive across London, negotiating the empty streets with confident ease, his thoughts had returned to the problem that had kept him awake since 2am.

"Penny, penny, penis, Penny," he had muttered as he sped past Marble Arch and halted abruptly at traffic lights on the Edgware Road. "Penny wise, pound foolish, penny for your penis!" he exclaimed. "The pen is mightier. The penis might. The pen is mightier than the penis. Penny might, Penny bright. Penthouse Penny. In for a penny. Oh yeah, you're in for it Penny! Well and truly, good and proper!"

The motorway landscape grew grey in the first glimmer of morning light, black fields and hedges now stretched further as the eastern horizon became pink then pale orange. Squalls of black rain came and went, the wipers pumped vigorously to clear away the greasy water sprayed by the thundering wheels of each truck he passed.

"OK, so somehow," mused Barry, "I've got to break the news to the mighty Pen that there isn't going to be a luxury apartment for her to move into directly she leaves Graham. And whose fault is that? Is that? Is that?" he repeated in time with the resumed clicking of his flashing indicator lights.

"I blame Paul. Fucking Paul!" he exclaimed. "Why couldn't he just keep his long nose out of it? It's my money too, so what if I spend it on Penny? Spend a penny, piss on Penny, piss on the lot of them..." he groaned.

"OK, but she'll think I'm weak if I blame Paul. So who else? Lucy? Nah, Penny wouldn't see it that way. Which leaves Graham; Penny leaves Graham, what does Graham do? Does he take it on the chin? Up the arse? Lying down? Lying? Who's been lying? *Sorry, doll, you can't leave Graham just now because I've been lying. Lying, moi? Yes, lying moi! Lying me fucking head off!...* Head? Gimme head! Head 'em off at the pass! Pass? Pass the buck. The buck stops here. The buck stops her! Buck the system. Fuck the system. You can't buck the system. Fuck the buck. Fuck a duck. I'm screwed, fucking screwed. Royally fucking screwed."

Barry responded to a road sign announcing a service area just ahead, and eased back on the accelerator, guiding the car diagonally across the traffic lanes and onto the slip road. Soon he was sitting at a shining table in the all-night motorway café stirring packets of brown sugar into his grey coffee. The rattle of trays and plates emanated from the self-service counters behind him and the aroma of bacon fat drifting across the room made him feel slightly nauseous.

"Graham!" he said abruptly and out loud, dropping the spoon into his saucer. "Maybe I could phone Graham, arrange a meet; get him to put the brakes on Penny. What can I give him that'll do that? Tell him the truth? Ha! Now that would be a novelty. *Sorry to be the one to tell you this old boy, but my investigations have revealed that your wife really has got a lover. Someone's poking your missus and you didn't know? How would you, if I didn't tell you? What's the old saying? 'You never miss a slice off a cut loaf?' Well, never mind, the husband's always the last to find out. Mind? You don't mind do you? Mind if I do? Mind over matter, old boy, mind over matter. I don't mind and you don't matter! Oh, and by the way, old boy, that someone is ME ...Tee hee, gotcha!"*

Barry lit a cigarette breathed deeply and blew smoke across the table. One of two women at the next table coughed theatrically, glowered at him and pointed at the *'No Smoking'* signs. Barry smiled back, picked up his coffee and swaggered across to the section where smoking was still tolerated.

"Money," he said aloud as he sat down and dragged a flimsy tin ashtray towards him. "That's the idea, that's what really moves Penny. That's what pushes her buttons. If I could find a way to make her believe that there is some financial advantage for her in staying under Graham's roof a while longer. Then we wouldn't need the flat all ready for her to move into; not yet, maybe not for a while....." Barry stirred a vortex of bubbles into his coffee and then stalled the whirlpool abruptly with the flat of his spoon. He took a sip of the liquid and made a face when he realised how much it had cooled during his reverie.

"But I can't make Graham seem more attractive," his thoughts resumed, "unless I can get at the key to what made her marry him in the first place. Penny, oh pretty Penny, the penny dropped... Drop the Penny." He drained the cup and said "Ugh!"

"Penny fooled, pound for pound," he paused, frowning intently at his empty cup and then looked up, smiling. "But of course," he thought. "That's it; *Ulrika!* What if Penny could be persuaded that Graham is about to put some – or all – of his property holdings into her name, purely as a ruse to protect them from potential creditors? She'll see immediately what a terrific advantage that would give her in negotiating the divorce settlement. Bingo! Ha, yes! Graham, you sad bastard, you don't stand a chance, you're going to be a hapless victim of my lowly cunning and your wife's well-bred greed."

Barry looked at his watch; the time was nearing 7.30am. "I'll stop again after nine," he thought, "call Graham at his office, ask if I can pop in for a chat, drop a few hints about my investigation into what a good and faithful woman his dear lady wife is; just to make damned sure he will want to tell Penny tonight that he's had a meet with me today, but ensuring that he goes all coy about what we discussed. Rely on Penny to assume that we talked about her; and Bob's your fucking uncle. She'll steer herself in the right direction, *no worries*!"

For the first time in two days Barry smiled happily and leaned back in his chair yawning and stretching, straightening his spine as he clasped his hands energetically behind his head. Then he stood up quickly and, whistling nonchalantly, made his way to the toilets before resuming his journey north.

His meeting with Graham later that morning went even better than Barry's natural optimism had persuaded him was possible. He had driven first to his usual hotel and checked-in, booking a table for two at lunch. Then he called Penny from a pay-phone in the hotel lobby.

"Guess who?" he breathed when she answered.

"Bazza!" she exclaimed,

"You've just caught me, another few seconds and I would have been in the bath." She paused, collecting herself before changing to a colder tone of voice. "Anyway, I'm not talking to you, remember? Not after Saturday..."

"Forget Saturday. I'm picturing you getting into the bath. Mmmm, that's nice," cooed Barry. "Let me hold that thought..."

"Down, Fido!" she giggled, but then stopped again and continued more sternly. "We've got a lot to talk about. I haven't forgiven you for all the hurtful things you were saying. Don't you ever put me through that again."

"I'm here to make everything right, my darling. Just like I said I would. Fancy some lunch around one-ish" he enquired, jauntily.

"Where are you? I was planning to do a little Christmas shopping, to cheer myself up."

"The usual place, I've booked a table."

"Have you booked a room, you naughty boy?"

"Yes, I have. I 'ave *bonked* ze room, *Madame*," he replied.

"Can we eat in the room, darling?" she enquired. "There's loads of people I know – and who know me – in town at the moment, and Graham went all peculiar again because you made me dash over to Cyn's on Saturday."

"Come on, it's not my fault if Graham's got a thing about Cynthia!"

"Most men have *a thing* about Cynthia," snapped Penny. "Graham's the only one who's hostile, all the others are like putty in her hands."

"Not me babe but whoa, hold on a mo, you've given me an idea...a very splendid idea, splendidly wicked..."

"Don't you start getting ideas about Cynthia! Not even in jest, I don't want to have to kill you; least ways, not just yet."

"No, no, nothing like that... You're my girl!"

"Well, good. So why did you have to upset me so much, at the weekend, you bastard?"

"That's all behind us now. I promised you I'd get it sorted didn't I? And look, less than twenty four hours later I have. How's that for service, eh?"

"I still think you've got some explaining to do, Cynthia says she couldn't believe that stunt you pulled; cancelling the lease on my new flat..."

"Trust me darling, I keep telling you, I'm the boy!"

"Yes but are you a *good* boy?" she whispered.

"Lets forget about being good," laughed Barry. "Just you get your lovely self ready for Bazza.""See you at one," she replied. "But whatever it is you've cooked-up this time it had better be good; and I don't mean the luncheon menu."

Chapter Twelve

Barry took a taxi to Graham's office, scornful of the crowds of Christmas shoppers who seemed to swirl in frantic disorder around the extravagant window-displays. He pushed the door-bell and spoke his name into the entry-control system. A buzzer sounded and the outer door vibrated. Barry pushed it aside and entered the peaceful, perfumed, inner world of *Shennan & Associates, Financial Consultants*. The clamour of the Christmas rush died away as the door closed with a breathy sigh.

A slender, blonde, receptionist ushered him into Graham's spacious, book-lined office.

"Graham!"

"Barry!"

Graham rose from his desk and glided across the carpet. The two men shook hands enthusiastically, and Graham directed Barry to a group of four, richly-upholstered, leather armchairs.

"Coffee?" Graham enquired.

"No, sorry, bit pushed for time, old son," smiled Barry. "Got a working lunch at one."

Graham waved away the blonde who had stayed solicitously beside his desk. There was yet another reassuring sigh as the heavy oak door closed behind her.

"I really want to thank you for all the introductions you've given me up here," began Barry. "Paul and Simon will be coming up in the New Year and we'd like to give proper recognition to the help you've afforded us..."

"Tish, tish," said Graham. "Pleased to be of service, but there is something you might..."

"A favour? Just name it," offered Barry.

"Well, it's all this business with Penny," began Graham, taking Barry completely by surprise.

"How is your dear lady?" blurted Barry. "Haven't seen her for ages," he lied.

"Yes, Penny," continued Graham, "this is really quite difficult, I'm afraid." He looked away.

Barry nodded, narrowing his eyes, speculating frantically about what Graham might say next.

"I don't know how to put this," said Graham, leaning forward in his chair and reaching towards Barry with his right hand, "but have you found out anything? Any evidence of infidelity? It's been a while since you said you'd, err, *look into it for me,* and frankly, we've just had the most appalling weekend. Everything she did and said seemed calculated to raise my suspicions and make me jealous."

"In what way?" enquired Barry, trying to sound as innocently concerned for the survival of Graham's marriage as he possibly could.

"They say, don't they, that a husband is always the last person really to know the kind of person a woman, I mean a wife ..." Graham's right hand dangled ineffectually in the air between them. Graham stared at it briefly, rotated his hand and then closed his thumb into the palm to push awkwardly against the fat gold band of his wedding ring.

Barry felt very tense and breathed out slowly.

"I'm ready to listen," he said as calmly as he could manage. "But let me assure you, here and now, that you can be one hundred percent sure of Penny."

"Really?" asked Graham, clearly doubting the news. "Really and truly?"

"Ooh yes," said Barry, soothingly. "Scout's Honour, most assuredly so."

"But on Saturday," blurted Graham, "about mid-morning, she took a phone call and, I don't know, I just felt certain that she was talking to some man. But when I asked her, she flew off the handle and rushed upstairs and locked herself in her bedroom. And I'm sure she made more calls, on her mobile, but when I went to listen at the door, I think she must have heard me. She turned the radio on so I couldn't tell whether she was talking or whether there were just raised voices on the radio..."

"Not good, not good at all Graham. What were you thinking? She's not the kind of girl who'll react calmly if she thinks she's being cornered, or spied on. Didn't you think to call me?"

"I did, I did! But your mobile number was engaged for ages too; and I didn't want to leave a message..."

"Oh sorry," coughed Barry. "I had a lot of work to get through on Saturday. I saw the 'missed calls' but I didn't know it was you calling. My phone log just said 'Caller withheld their number'; could've been any silly tosser trying to sell me useless crap!"

"I even called your office," continued Graham, "and some chap told me very curtly that you'd gone out, and he'd no idea when you'd be back."

"Oh I am sorry; you just can't get the staff these days, can you?"

"But it got worse after lunch – well we didn't have any lunch to speak of – then Penny rushed out saying that she had to visit that dreadful woman Mrs Miles, Cynthia Miles. Do you know her?"

"Yes I do," said Barry slowly and deliberately. "I've looked into Mrs Miles' affairs and general lifestyle quite closely, on your behalf of course, and I have to tell you, to tell you..." Barry frowned and bit his lip, his fingers dug into the soft leather of the armchair, his mind raced as he tried to calculate whether this was the moment to reveal the flash of inspiration that had come to him during his conversation with Penny earlier in the day.

"Mrs Miles," he resumed but paused again. "Mrs Miles, is ... is a very attractive woman and, well quite frankly – I can be frank with you Graham can't I?" Graham nodded solemnly and drew back, looking even more concerned.

"Well, to cut a long story to the bare bones," continued Barry, "Mrs Miles and I, *Cynthia* and I, have embarked upon a romantic liaison..."

"A relationship? An affair?" spluttered Graham, completely astonished.

"Yes," admitted Barry, bowing his head, "and your dear wife who, as you know is very close to my Lucy, well Penny got wind of it and became very upset, as you might imagine, on Lucy's behalf, so to speak..."

"My dear chap, I had no idea," said Graham. "Do please forgive me. I'm not one to intrude on matters of the...err, heart, as it were..."

"Well of course, only to be expected, in the circumstances. Each to his own, you know. But things came to a bit of a head this last weekend; there were lots of phone calls. Naturally, Penny was involved – I'm desperately sorry that she was so upset – but you can just imagine her position! She's a good friend to both Lucy and Cynthia; and I like to think of her as my friend too..."

"Oh my dear chap, what can I say? How could I get things so utterly out of proportion – to have been so utterly mistaken. I feel such a fool!"

"No, no, not your fault, not your fault at all. Entirely understandable, I'd say," murmured Barry, trying not to smile as he heard his own voice starting to sound more and more like Graham's.

"What can we do to cheer you up? Are things on the mend?"

"On the mend?" snapped Barry.

"Err yes, I don't know quite how to put it. Forgive me for being so clumsy......"

"It's OK. Look, to tell the truth, Penny has agreed to meet both myself and Cynthia privately, in my hotel, over lunch, to give us the benefit of her advice and guidance. I know you'll understand if I say no more at this stage and ask you, please Graham, to say not a word about this to anyone. I mean anyone, not even to Penny. We're on a *Need to know basis*, and all that...I'm sure you get my drift....." Barry tapped the side of his nose with his forefinger, deliberately making the gesture as theatrical as he could.

"Of course, of course, mum's the word!" responded Graham.

"No, seriously, Graham. I shouldn't have told you, I promised Penny and Cynthia I wouldn't," Barry shook his head from side to side and stared down at the deep pile carpet. "Please don't say anything – not a single word – to Penny. I only told you this much because, well because you'd got so much the wrong end of the stick..."

Graham rose to his feet, smiling sympathetically, and reaching out with both hands. Barry also stood but stepped back when he caught sight of Penny's portrait in a silver framed photograph on

Graham's desk. The blue dress she wore reminded him instantly of the first time he had made love to her, tearing hungrily at that same dress in the spare bedroom at the top of Cynthia's elegant townhouse. Graham waited patiently guessing, wrongly of course, that Barry had again been overwhelmed by sadness and regret.

"Thank you so much!" gushed Graham, unable to bear the silence any longer.

"For what?" asked Barry, puzzled by Graham's sudden gratitude.

"For being so open with me, of course. I can't tell you what a relief...."

"But not a word to Penny," Barry reminded him, anxiously, before adding, "you know what they're like."

"Absolutely," agreed Graham. "Absolutely my dear old chap... Can't live with them, can't live without them; that's what I always say."

As he spoke, Graham turned to hold open the office door and so missed the triumphant leer which swept across Barry's face.

* * *

Barry returned to the hotel and relaxed in the bar with a tall glass of expensively chilled lager. Selecting a comfortable chair, he sat in a position where he could watch the hotel entrance and foyer. Taxis came and went in a busy procession and eventually he glimpsed Penny stepping from one of them. Her long coat parted sufficiently as she walked for him to see her slender legs emerging from what was clearly a very short skirt. Her vivid auburn hair was swept across her forehead in attractively contrived disarray. Her pale skin offset the dark make-up applied around her bright blue eyes and the rich crimson gloss of her full lips. It seemed to Barry that Penny always floated on a cloud of exotic perfume. He sprang eagerly to meet her, clasping her intimately with his large hands as he planted improbably chaste kisses on her soft cheeks.

Penny slipped off her coat knowing that Barry would take hold of it and lay it carefully across a nearby chair. She sank elegantly into the generous cushions of a small sofa and smoothed the dark red suede of her short skirt. She folded her long legs and crossed then delicately at the ankles, her long neck curved gracefully from the black ellipse of a simple, collarless, blouse. Barry stood back, admiring her quietly.

"Dry, white; with ice," she said in answer to the question he was about to ask.

"So what was this bright idea you suddenly had but couldn't tell me on the phone?" she enquired when he returned with their drinks and sat in an armchair, facing her.

"Never mind that now sweetheart," he answered hurriedly, "there've been important developments, this very morning..."

Penny arched an eyebrow and turned the stem of her wine glass in her fingers.

"I went to see Graham earlier today..."

"Was that wise?"

"Oh yes, most assuredly so..."

"Christ, don't *you* start talking like *him*, it's bad enough already when Crispin does it!"

Barry smiled patiently and puffed up his chest in preparation for announcing his latest *coup*. "I told him I was meeting you for lunch today..."

Penny's mouth opened in astonishment.

"Meeting you *and* Cynthia in fact," he added proudly.

"Have you gone mad?" she snapped.

"Not at all," he countered, "I've made him feel very confident that we are a perfectly innocent threesome."

"Does he even know what a *threesome* is?" gasped Penny, reaching for her glass.

"No, not like that!" exclaimed Barry. "But let me tell you the really good news."

"What?" she asked, becoming impatient with Barry's uncharacteristic circumlocution.

"I've not only persuaded him to trust you completely, I've made him feel guilty that he ever doubted you... I've told him he needs to make a significant gesture to prove how much he trusts you. I've planted the idea in his mind that he should put most of his property into your sole name."

Barry sat back, expecting to wait a few moments for this development to impress Penny before receiving her heartfelt gratitude. Instead, Penny merely looked quizzical, wondering to herself where this was leading.

"It's perfect," he hastened to assure her. "Just think of the divorce settlement he'd have to agree to if 'Bridge House', the Spanish villa, the farmhouse in Brittany and all the investment properties were in your name, not his!"

Penny set down her wine glass again and smiled cautiously, "Yes, I see," she said quietly and then frowned as the questions began to mount in her mind. "So how long will that take? What happens to us in the meantime?"

"No worries, babe," smiled Barry. "We carry on as we are, we can go on meeting just as often, we just have to hang on in there until your negotiating position is as strong as ..."

"But what if....?" she began.

"No, no, none of that," warned Barry, reaching his hands towards her. Penny's mouth twisted in anguish and she looked away from him.

"It's alright for you," she whispered, "You don't have to live there, with him. God knows how I'll get through Christmas..."

"Me too, honey, I know how you feel," he said, moving quickly to sit beside her and extend a protective arm around her angular shoulders.

"No you don't, you obviously don't," she said firmly. "You forget that part of the arrangement; I mean what we agreed about the apartment, was that we were going to stop deceiving Lucy. We were going to come clean with her and you were going to move your home-base up here. You were coming to live with me!"

Penny shuddered and the finger tips of her left hand quickly brushed the outer corner of her eye. Her head remained resolutely turned away from him.

"We will, oh we will, babe," he soothed. "I only want to do what's best for you, if we move too impetuously you could be left with only the clothes you stand up in..." he paused for emphasis, then continued. "Luce will bleed me dry, you know that. She'll use the kids to make sure I don't get a brass farthing from the house...

We'll be starting over, you and I, with little or nothing...except debts..."

"Oh bloody hell," she sighed. "I don't love him, I never have. I can't bear him near me. If it wasn't for Crispin I'd have left two or three years ago. And now that he's away at school, I thought...." She clasped her hands together in her lap, her fingers lacing tightly as she struggled to control her emotions. Barry noticed a narrow band of her clear skin appearing between her blouse and the waist band of her skirt.

"I need to know how long... I need to have some hope, something to look forward to," she said quietly, almost as if speaking only to herself.

"Come on, darling," breathed Barry, bending his head closer to hers. "It's going to be hard for both of us..."

"Much harder for me; much, much harder. At least you loved Lucy, once upon a time..."

"But I love you now, my little darling," he breathed directly into her ear. "And talking of much, much harder..." Barry's right hand stroked her knee before inching slowly up her leg, one finger-width at a time.

"Stop it!" she snapped. "I don't know if I can, not right now."

Barry sank back, flopping away from her;

"OK," he said abruptly, "Plan 'B'. We run away together right now, to the Pacific or the Caribbean, anywhere far, far away. Send them all faxes or emails saying *'Happy Christmas! Love from Brendan and Penny!'* We'd be travelling light, believe me. We'd only have what we stand in which, in your case, is delightfully little... Then, sometime in the New Year we'd re-appear, totally skint of course, to face the music. Is that what you want?"

"Huh!" she sobbed, "you've always said *'There is no Plan B!'* It's one of your most favourite expressions."

Barry smiled and stared out of the window where the grey afternoon was closing in and lights were coming on in all the surrounding buildings.

"I only want to do what's best for us," he repeated.

Penny reached down and extracted a tissue from a slender hand bag at her feet. She touched her nose delicately,

"I must look a sight!" she exclaimed. "OK, I'll stick it out, but not for long. Something's got to happen and pretty damned quick. I need to see us being together. It's got to be soon. Lucy's got to be told…"

"OK, OK, I'll tell her, but I don't know how we can stop her getting straight on to bloody Graham."

"When?"

"When what?"

"When will you talk to Lucy?"

"I talk to her all the time."

"I mean about *us*!"

"Straight after Christmas."

"Why not now?"

"Oh come on, darling. Use your loaf; just imagine me going up to Lucy with '*Happy Christmas, old girl – oh and by the way I'm off. I'm moving in with Penny. Yes that's right, your best friend, as was! She sends her love, by the way… Now then, now then, dry your eyes, Luce, for Chrissakes. Oh, and where's me Christmas Pud?*'" Barry swept his right hand through his hair; "Blimey O'Reilly, that would make it a proper memorable Christmas for the kids too, wouldn't it?" He relaxed back into the cushions on his armchair.

Penny snuffled some more, folding the tissue smaller and smaller.

"No, OK, you're right; I'm sorry. We'll have to wait, won't we? But just make me feel that there's hope…" she whispered.

"Of course there is, baby. Of course there is." Barry paused for what he thought was a decent interval before turning towards her and enquiring, "Shall we order lunch, my lovely?" Penny winced.

"I couldn't eat a thing," she murmured. "But I suppose we could go up to the room; I think I'm ready to be comforted properly now."

Chapter Thirteen

In each of the few short weeks remaining before Christmas, Tom and Lucy rarely managed to be alone together. Sometimes only briefly and sometimes when they met by contrived and carefully choreographed 'accidents' either down at the street market or further along the road at Ottakar's bookshop or in the big department store at Clapham Junction. One memorable evening, with Barry again away in Nottingham, Mary baby-sat while they went to an early evening film at Clapham Picture House and then hurried back to Tom's flat to eat dinner and make love between courses. *'Inter-course intercourse'* Tom called it in one of his more clumsy asides, but at last they were both starting to rely upon their relationship despite the constant reminders that it was illicit and all its joys were borrowed.

For Tom, Christmas in recent years had always loomed like an ugly blot on the already grey and dispiriting landscape of mid-winter. He hated the nagging adverts about 'gifts' and stubbornly refused to send cards. He told anyone who might listen that, were he a Christian, he would rage against the unrestrained commercialisation of Christmas.

"Well thank God you're not!" exclaimed Lucy during one of their late night phone calls when Barry was away yet again. "The kids love Christmas," argued Lucy in some exasperation. "Don't you remember waking-up early on Christmas mornings to find lots of lovely presents at the end of your bed?"

"Of course I do. My brother Ralph and I loved that when we were kids. But that's the whole point, you grow out of it, you move on. Christmas should be entirely for kids, it should be part of growing up – a rite of passage - that you get your last Christmas prezzies when you're sixteen or something like that. After that, well you're an adult and all you get is a splendid mid-winter blow-out. You know; the annual ritual of getting pissed and eating too much and falling asleep in front of the telly."

"Oh yes, all very traditional!" mocked Lucy. "You quaint old fashioned thing you."

"It's the pagan festival of mid-winter; the winter solstice – the point of no return when they killed and ate any livestock they could not keep alive for the rest of the winter....The early Christians just chose to call it *Christmas*. Turkeys have about as much to do with *Christ – mass* as the Easter Bunny has to do with the Crucifixion!"

"You're impossible. I don't have time to listen to all this. Unlike you, I've got a normal life..."

"Do you call what we have *normal*?"

"No! And don't start..."

"Start what, exactly?"

"Going on. Whinging."

"I don't whinge."

"Huh, don't make me laugh. 'Course you do; all the damned time!"

"How d'you think it feels for me? Does that ever cross your mind?"

"How does what feel?"

"Thinking I'm sharing in your life but always being reminded that really I'm not sharing in anything at all..."

"You knew I was married..."

"I hate seeing you with him; knowing you'll be going home with him...Sleeping with him."

"Stop it. Stop right there!"

"Why? Why can't I tell you how it feels for me?"

"I don't have...I mean I can't...Don't make me go there."

"Go where?"

"Right round the bend!"

"That's not fair..."

"Tom, just listen to yourself; I can't take anymore of this. God you can painful at times!"

"Lucy?"

"Good – *bye!*" she shouted and slammed the phone down.

Three days of silence followed and Lucy was therefore somewhat surprised when, at mid-morning on the Saturday before Christmas, Tom knocked on the front door with a Christmas tree over his shoulder - albeit one still tightly cocooned in grey plastic netting.

"We've already got a tree!" exclaimed Lucy. "There, in the front window." Alice wound past Lucy's skirt and looked suspiciously up at Tom.

" 'Nuther tree," said Alice, pointing upwards.

"I know, but this one's mine. I'm just taking it home and I wondered if anyone might like to help me decorate it this afternoon?"

"Meee!" screeched Cherie appearing from nowhere and suddenly pushing past Lucy.

Tom stared questioningly at Lucy; Cherie and Alice both followed his gaze and looked up at her too.

"Oh pleeeeze!" implored Cherie.

"Good Lord, this is a turn up for the books," exclaimed Lucy. "Do you have any idea what *decorating a tree* with these two might involve?"

"Piece of cake, compared with Year Eleven on the last day of term I shouldn't wonder."

"Well good luck, mate!" said Lucy. "I hope you're not expecting me there to referee."

"You're not invited," said Tom, tartly.

"Ner!" said Cherie, sticking out her tongue at her mother.

"I'm going to carry this tree home; then can I come and collect the girls about one o'clock? I need them to come down to Woolies with me to choose some decorations, and then we'll go up to my place and *do* the tree."

"Blimey," said Lucy, dryly.

"Then, if we feel like it, we'll phone you to come over and inspect our handiwork later on."

"I can't wait."

True to his promise, Tom returned and soon set off again with Alice riding in her buggy and Cherie trotting alongside with one hand clutching the handle. Emma refused to join them and watched their departure from the front window, slowly twisting a silver bauble in her hands.

"Tom's tree won't be as good as mine." she announced proprietarily as Tom and her sisters moved away down the hill.

"You don't think he's a bit of a bloomin' kiddy-fiddler on the quiet, do you?" whispered Barry as Lucy waved again and closed the front door. She shot a fierce frown at him and stabbed her finger in the direction of the open door to the room where Emma was.

"For God's sake Brendan; of course he's not! He's just making an effort to be more normal."

"Seems dead weird to me," he muttered. "What's he want a tree for anyway? I'm sure he told me last night in the pub that he'd be going to Strasbourg for Christmas, staying with what's 'is name, you know his brother?"

"Ralph," said Lucy. "His brother's name is Ralph and they – him and his wife and family – live in Luxembourg not Strasbourg. Tom's staying with them for Christmas and the New Year."

"My, my, you're very well up on Corky's arrangements, aren't you?"

"And I also know that Ralph is an accountant and works for the EEC Court of Auditors, so there," said Lucy, defiantly.

"Well jolly good, at least we won't have to invite the miserable bugger to have Christmas dinner with us *again* this year!" snorted Barry and stamped upstairs to his office.

"So don't bother feeling sorry for him," she called after him, adding loudly, "I wouldn't mind going away for Christmas!"

"So why don't you go with old loppy-lugs to Luxembourg or wherever?" he suggested over the banisters.

"I'd love to, but he hasn't invited me!"

"Yeah, and neither has Prince Charming. Poor little Cinders; if only she could find her fairy Godmother, six white mice and a bleeding pumpkin!" shouted Barry as Lucy disappeared into the kitchen, slamming the door loudly behind her.

Emma slipped from the front room and stood silently in the hallway, staring impassively first at the unfamiliar sight of a closed kitchen door and then gazing up the stairwell as she heard the more distant sound of the office door also closing.

It was dark by the time Lucy and Emma rang Tom's doorbell and were ushered upstairs by Tom and Alice. Inside the flat, all the lights were off except for the pale glow of Tom's bedside light with a pillow-case draped over it, which provided just enough illumination for them to fumble their way towards the front room. Ahead of them they could see the multi-coloured lights now adorning the Christmas Tree and, as they came nearer, Cherie stepped silently from the shadows and stood in front of the lights wearing one of Tom's white shirts and with silver wings strapped to her back.

"Oooh!" breathed Emma in jealous appreciation of the tableau and Alice clapped her hands in sheer delight.

"Oh Tom, that's lovely," smiled Lucy. "You're not such a dreadful old cynic after all."

Tom smiled and said "Tea, anyone?"

Cherie lunged forward and grabbed Lucy's hand, pulling her into the room. "Put the big lights on now, Mum," she commanded, "so as you can see all our decorations."

"Gosh, you have been busy," remarked Lucy as the density of items on the tree became apparent.

"You've overdone it," sneered Emma, kicking aside a step-ladder which lay folded flat on the carpet. "That's far too much stuff, you can hardly see the tree anymore," adding haughtily, "don't you know when to stop?"

"And how *did* you get that fairy right up there at the top of the tree?" asked Lucy, choosing to ignore Emma's petulance.

"I put it, I put it!" insisted Alice.

"Well, actually," explained Cherie, "Tom did climb up to the top of the ladder, carrying Alice so that she could reach..."

"I'm quite glad I didn't see that," muttered Lucy, with a friendly smile directed at Emma.

"Mmm, me too," agreed Emma, adding pompously, "sounds a bit dangerous."

"I think it looks lovely," said Lucy to Tom as they sat drinking tea while the two younger girls, now supervised bossily by Emma, reduced some of the excessive baubles and silvery fronds weighing down the lower limbs of the tree.

"Pity no one will be here to see it over the holidays," she added sardonically.

"Huh, I'll be back a day or so before Twelfth Night," he replied.

"See, you *do* know all the details of Christmas. You just pretend that you don't."

"Now, talking of *details*," announced Tom, "Santa heard that I'd be away at Christmas and so he popped by the other day with a few presents. He said he might not find me, abroad in all the snow and that... And then there were three presents left over, delivered here by some mix up at Santa's sorting office – *you just can't get the elves these days* – so I've put them in this bag," he added, reaching deftly behind the sofa to produce a large shiny, red, plastic, carrier-bag. The three little girls stared at him in wonder.

"Does anyone know to which house these presents should have been delivered?" he enquired.

Emma's and Cherie's hands both shot into the air and Alice fell forward with an eager grunt.

"I think that's settled, then Mr Cork," laughed Lucy. "Thank you so much; we could offer to take those off your hands, couldn't we girls?"

* * *

"I'd love to see you again before Christmas," said Tom when Lucy phoned him the next afternoon, adding, "I'm not booked on the Eurostar until Wednesday morning."

"Tuesday," said Lucy firmly, "I've got stuff to do tomorrow and anyway it'll take a few phone calls to arrange things for the girls to do. No use relying on Brendan to be at home during the Office Party Season. I don't think he came home sober any day last week. But if *you* could just be at home on Tuesday afternoon; can you do that?"

"You bet!"

Tom waited in nervously, fearing that last minute complications would foil their plans. Two o'clock came and went and it was nearly three before he heard a brief ring of his doorbell and Tom hastened downstairs to welcome her.

"You should let me have a key," she suggested, as he puffed up the stairs alongside her. "Or are you just horribly unfit?"

"No, I think it's just nerves," he explained. "I was worried that something would go wrong at the last minute and you wouldn't be able to come."

"That nearly happened, it's not easy to farm out the kids so close to Christmas, even for a couple of hours; what with people going away, or rushing around the shops, or – like me – just waiting for a quiet moment to enjoy another nervous breakdown." Tom started to kiss her but Lucy wanted to be held close until she had finished talking.

"Emma and Cherie have gone to Sally and Rufus, *'good ole Mary'* came to my rescue, yet again, by having Alice. Did you notice my bag?"

"Yes, I was going to ask why you've brought your own towel. Don't you trust mine to be clean?"

"No, it's my brilliant plan," proclaimed Lucy. "Mary said I looked *'Done in'* and I said *'I'd love to go to the Leisure Centre and have a nice peaceful swim for an hour or so, without any children to worry about.'* And she said, *'Swimmin'? At this time of year? Rather you than me, girl.'* – she thinks I'm raving mad anyway – so here I am. My costume's wrapped in the towel. It's great, I can go back with wet hair and all glowing and Mary will say, *'That trip to the pool 'as done wonders for you, my girl!'*

Tom pulled her close again and this time she accepted his lips and the long, searching kisses they gave her.

"You'd better be getting changed, *my girl, if you're goin' swimmin'!*" he said, imitating Mary.

"Well, perhaps just undressed, that would be a good start, don't you think?"

"Oh! Hang on a sec!" he said, falling backwards across the bed and reaching beyond it.

"What? Don't you want us to undress this time?"

"Just open this first," he ordered, pushing a large, soft, parcel towards her, gaily wrapped in Xmas paper.

"What's this, Mr Cork?" she enquired in mock anger. "Do you think I'm a child? A child in need of a Christmas present?"

"Err, yes, frankly my dear, I do."

"Oh, Tom," she exclaimed as she tore away the wrapper to reveal a winter coat, the same colour and design as her old one but new and fresh and clean, and from a much more expensive label.

"Oh Tom!" she repeated.

"Try it on, it's your size."

"Oh it's lovely. How predictable that you'd know my size. I've lived with Brendan more than ten years and he hasn't a clue what sizes I take in shoes or clothes, or anything…"

"We just have to hope that he doesn't enquire how you've come by a nice new coat."

"Huh!" she scoffed, "that's where you've been so clever in matching my old one. He'd never know in a month of Sundays, and even if he did I'd just say I'd had it cleaned, and he'd lose interest." She paused, looking thoughtful, "Mary will notice, 'though; she'll spot it at once. But that's OK, I can tell her the truth – well some of it – she likes you now, and she'll like you even more when I tell her how kind and thoughtful you were to buy me an expensive, but useful, present; all because you know we're having a hard time financially…"

"Whatever," said Tom, peeling the new coat from her shoulders and letting it fall to the bedroom floor alongside the old one. Gently he lifted her skirt and reached inside her knickers, stroking the rough skin of her buttocks before settling into the soft, moist forest where her legs met. They made love carefully and slowly, murmuring softly before subsiding and lying still, completely absorbed in each other's breathing.

Eventually, Tom rose from the bed and strode into the bathroom, turning on the taps and adjusting the temperature of the incoming water. Lucy joined him, poured some gel into the warm water and stepped in, beckoning him to join her.

"You'll have to take the tap end, you're such a gent," she giggled.

"I'd better be careful not to mention that to Mary when I'm singing your praises..."

The water level rose in the bath, the room filled with steam and Tom pushed the bathroom door with his heel before sinking into the water facing Lucy. Her toes tickled his armpits and he gently touched her nipples with his. Water slopped gently over the side of the bath, wetting the towels scattered across the floor.

The phone rang. Tom closed his eyes.

"Ignore it," he murmured. "You're here, who else would I want to talk to?"

"That's the difference between an optimist and a pessimist," whispered Lucy. Tom looked enquiringly at her, then, seeing her eyes were closed, asked, "What is?"

"A pessimist gets out of the bath to answer the phone, an optimist knows they'll ring back," said Lucy, running her fingers lightly through the beads of moisture glistening on her forehead.

"Did you get that from a Christmas cracker?"

"Or is it maybe that an optimist," murmured Lucy dreamily, closing her eyes again and frowning to recall a long-ago quotation from deep inside her memory, "is someone who expects everything to turn out for the best in the best of all possible worlds? And a pessimist is someone who believes it has ....."

A key rattled in the lock of the front door and they heard Barry's voice call out,

"Hiya Corky! Anyone home?"

Lucy gulped and slid lower into the foam. Tom leapt out of the bath in an arc of silvery spray, grabbed a wet towel from the floor and threw his weight against the bathroom door.

"Oh there you are," called Barry cheerily. "Funny time to be having a ... Whoa, knickers on the floor! Sorry, old son, is this not the best time?"

"No, it bloody isn't!" exclaimed Tom hotly. "Could you just go away?"

"Sorry, just wanted to leave this here," answered Barry.

"This what?" asked Tom.

"It doesn't matter what," whispered Lucy fiercely. "Just get rid of him!"

"What did you say?" called Barry, slurring his words slightly.

"He's drunk!" gasped Tom, in horror. Lucy closed her eyes and sank back beneath the bubbles, her dark hair floating languidly on the surface.

"I'm going out to him," Tom announced to Lucy's dark shape in the water.

Girding the towel around his waist, Tom eased open the bathroom door, pulled the chord to switch off the light and stepped into the hall, ensuring he kept one hand on the door knob and that his body blocked any view into the bathroom.

"I'm sho sorry, mate," repeated Barry. "I do seem to have caught you on the job....as it were..."

Tom stared at him: speechless at the sight of Barry standing at the side of the bed, with a child's bicycle resting against his thigh.

"Anyone I know?" enquired Barry.

Tom lunged forward to pick up Lucy's new coat before Barry again wheeled the bicycle over it. Barry's eyes fell on the second coat.

"Bloody hell!" he exclaimed. "You've got two of them in there! You lucky bastard, not those lesbian twins from the pub is it by any chance?"

"Would you please just fuck off out of here!" shouted Tom with as much authority as he could muster when standing naked, except for Lucy's pink towel, water dripping off him and forming a soggy pool at his feet.

"I just need you to do me a favour," persisted Barry. "I've got this bike as Emma's Christmas present, I just need to hide it here until the big day. There's nowhere I can put it at home where the cunning little cow won't unearth it..."

Tom heard Lucy, stir angrily in the water behind him.

"Yes, of course, just leave it there," barked Tom. "And for Chrissake give me back my keys!"

"Calm down, calm down," smiled Barry. "You'd better get back in there pronto, mate. Sounds as if they've started muff-diving again, without you!"

Tom took a deep breath and clenched his fists; Barry stepped back and began reaching into his pocket for the keys, then he suddenly paused;

"Sorry, no can do, old son. No can do," he said, shaking his head.

"Give me the fucking keys!"

"After Christmas. After Christmas," repeated Barry, tapping the side of his nose. "Santa needs to pop round on Christmas Eve to get the fucking bike doesn't he? And this Santa won't be using the bleeding chimney. No way."

Tom raised one hand to his head in a gesture of despair, only just remembering to hold on to the towel with his other. Barry threw back his head and laughed loudly as if noticing Tom's embarrassment and the pink towel for the first time.

"Nice towel!" he roared. "Dead butch! Seeing that, I'd have thought you were gay if I hadn't caught you at it with a couple of birds in the bathroom. Get in there my son! Wait 'til I tell the lads; they'll be well impressed. You know what they say; *A bird in the bath is worth, is worth....a hand up the bush...* Or something like that. How does it go?"

"Will you please just sod off?"

"I'm going, I'm going, keep your shirt on... Ha ha, seems you haven't. Corky caught with his pants down. Don't hesitate to call me if you ever need a helping hand with those two. Cor, fuck-a-duck!" And with that Barry swept out of the door and away down the stairs. Tom dropped the towel and jumped to slide home the two shoot-bolts on the door.

"He's gone," breathed Tom, opening the bathroom door again and pulling the light chord. Lucy was standing up in the bath, shivering and wrapped almost entirely in the plastic shower curtain. Tom took a dry towel from the cupboard and reached towards her, realising as he did so that she was sobbing.

"I do not fucking believe you!" she cried bitterly, her voice cracking with shock and outrage. "Why the bloody hell has my fucking husband got keys to your flat?"

"Last summer, when I was going away, I asked him ...I mean, well, he offered..."

"Just think," she spat, "if Brendan had come barging in a few minutes earlier he would've found me spread out on the bed with your face between my legs!"

"I'm sorry, I didn't...."

"And the way he talked to you. Men, ugh! You're all so disgusting. Do you tell *The Lads* about your exploits with me? Do you boast about *having me*? *Oh that Lucy Sands, she's a right goer! Can't get enough; gagging for it she is! And nice tits too, considering...*"

"Considering what?"

"Considering I'm a mother of three!" she barked and pushed past him into the bedroom.

Tom followed tentatively behind her. Lucy looked up and scowled at him, snatching up her clothes and pulling them on rapidly and angrily.

"You've had a shock......" he began

"Too fucking right I have."

"I don't talk about you," he muttered. "Not to anyone..."

She sat heavily on the bed and pulled on her leather boots.

"Let me drive you home, at least to the top of your road."

Lucy nodded, and turned to look at Emma's bicycle.

"It's nice," she said, wiping her eyes. "I told her we couldn't afford one this year. She'll love it. She'll love *him*, even more than she already does. Even 'though the heartless bastard calls her *a little cow*..." Lucy broke into sobs which shook her whole frame. Tom went to put his arms around her but she pushed him away. He picked up her swimming costume and went into the bathroom. She heard him running the basin taps to soak the costume, then wringing the water from it. Tom reappeared with the damp costume wrapped in a plain white towel.

"Leave the pink one here," he said. "Even Barry might recognize that if he sees it again today. Everyone has a white towel, somewhere."

Lucy sobbed once more, and raised her head with a fleeting smile. She stared again at the two navy blue coats lying side by side on the bed. She hesitated, then reached for the new coat and thrust her arms into the generous sleeves.

"Thank you, Tom," she sniffed, head still bowed.

"Happy Christmas, my darling," he whispered.

Lucy snuffled again and reached towards the bedside table for a tissue.

"God! My eyes must be so red; I can't go home looking like this; I bet I look like a constipated panda. Oh fucking merry hell!"

"Yes you can; just complain about there being too much chlorine in the water...That's what always happens to me."

"But I'm not you, am I? I'm a married woman, I've got kids. Oh it's all such a horrible mess. I can't be here, I can't be there. I can't be *anywhere* at the moment."

Tom sat beside her on the bed and reached around her shoulders with his left arm, expecting her to soften and bend towards him. She didn't; Lucy sat stiffly, her head bowed, staring uncomprehendingly at a small curl just above the skirting board where the corner of a piece of wallpaper was coming away. They sat for several minutes in dreary silence, both feeling utterly miserable. Eventually Lucy coughed, stood up and reached for the plastic bag containing her swimming things which Tom still clutched in his right hand.

"Are you giving me a lift home?"

"Of course."

"Tom, you're still stark naked; don't you think you'd better..."

"Oh God," he scowled, "I'm such an idiot, give me two minutes."

"Yes, Tom, I will. But just accept that I'm going to need time to get over what happened just now. And thanks for the coat..."

"Wear it with my love," he said from inside the sweater he was pulling over his head.

"Don't start me off again," she complained. "But yes, yes I will, yes I will; and I'm sorry it never even occurred to me to buy you anything."

"Good, I'm glad. I love you"

"I love you too, despite all ...despite, you know...."

Tom, now wearing sweater and jeans but still standing barefoot, kissed her tenderly, "Happy Christmas, Lucy my darling," he said very quietly. "I'd do anything for you."

Lucy stifled a sob and began to laugh but stopped when her nose began to run. She crushed another tissue against her face and said firmly,

"It looks as if you might have to," before blowing her nose very loudly.

Chapter Fourteen

The New Year was only a couple of days old when Tom returned from Luxembourg. Clapham felt cold and looked grey. His flat took hours to become warm again even though he had turned up the thermostat as soon as he had opened the door. Still huddled in his coat, Tom sat hunched in his kitchen sorting through the post and taking occasional sips from a large mug of tea. The light was fading fast and the noise of a television programme rising from the flat below was scratching at the edges of his attention. He stood up, deliberately scraping the legs of his stool across the floorboards and stamped heavily across to the light switch.

'Best to let the Pattersons know I'm back now,' he thought, letting a pile of old newspapers drop to the floor with a resounding thud. Apart from the inevitable quarterly bills and the junk mail offering credit, his post contained only a few late Christmas cards, including one from Paul & Anna showing the pyramids rather incongruously blanketed in snow. Anna had written '*So much for global warming! See you in The New Year, I hope!*' in her affectedly casual 'artist's' handwriting, ending with a large **X** which overran the edges of the card.

Further down the pile Tom found three brightly coloured envelopes all addressed to him in a child's writing and obviously delivered by hand. The blue one, which he chose to open first was a 'thank you' letter from Emma, carefully stating her appreciation of the doll's house furniture he had given her. The green envelope contained a drawing of a very gaudy Christmas tree below which Cherie had written her name in big, round letters. Finally, he slit open the yellow envelope to reveal a colourful abstract expressionist piece by Alice; confirmed by the '*Love Alice X*' which Emma had written in one corner. He checked the discarded envelopes in the bin to be sure that there was no card or message from Lucy.

'Oh well,' he thought, 'at least there's nothing from Penny either.'

Tom dragged his suitcase into the bedroom and let it bounce heavily on the bed. Moving into the front room he switched on all the lights before drawing the curtains to close out the cold black rectangles of the windows. Brushing against the Christmas tree caused a shower of sharp, green pine needles to rattle down through the decorations and onto the carpet. Tom frowned, picked up the phone, dialled Lucy's number and counted thirteen unanswered rings before he dropped the handset back onto its cradle. He slumped on the sofa, staring glumly at the cheerful lights blinking on the tree and trying to imagine where Lucy might be.

* * *

The next morning her phone again rang unanswered and Tom fretted, puzzled by her absence and the fact that the answering machine had clearly been switched off. Driving home from work on Wednesday evening he took a detour past Lucy's house and saw that there were no lights on even at six in the evening. Tom held back from calling Barry on his office number deciding that it might seem strange for him to phone for no obvious reason and just saying '*Happy New Year*' did not strike Tom as being sufficient. For the first time he actually found himself wishing a letter would arrive from Penny giving him an excuse to call Barry at work.

"Shit and cabbage!" he exclaimed, pacing irritably around his flat where the gloomy shadows did nothing to lift his mood of uncertainty and depression. 'Saturday,' he thought, 'If there's still no answer by then I'll try knocking on Mary's door; she's bound to know where they are. Now get a grip, there will be some perfectly reasonable explanation...' Tom opened a bottle of red wine, poured a glass and drank it in a few quick swallows. Automatically, he refilled his glass before carrying it and the bottle through into the front room. He sat at his desk intending to catch up on some over-due lesson preparation but every few minutes he wriggled uncomfortably in his chair, increasingly aware of the sexual nature of his longing for Lucy.

'Why is she doing this?' he wondered. 'If she was planning to be away, she could have let me know somehow; it wouldn't take much." He found himself feeling unaccustomed anger towards Lucy. 'Surely she realises I must be wondering where she's gone? This is to get back at me for the bathroom incident... She wants to punish me for that with some nasty surprise of her own.'

Tom swung round in his chair and tugged savagely at the lobe of his right ear. He finished his glass of wine and poured another, emptying the bottle. His glance fell on the coffee table and Anna's card. He looked at his watch; 'Nearly eight thirty; can I phone Paul and Anna?' he wondered. 'To thank them for the card? And possibly to enquire if they've seen Barry and family lately?'

Paul's voice answered, sounding quite gruff, and Tom could hear the commentary to a televised football match rising and falling in the background.

"It's Tom, Tom Cork," he began. "Sorry to interrupt your evening, I just wanted to say 'Happy New Year' and thanks for the card....."

"S'alright mate," sang Paul. "You'll have to excuse me I've got a filthy cold and you can thank Anna for the card; she does all that stuff. Hang on a mo, I'll pass you over...*It's Corky*," he hissed.

"Hiya!" trilled Anna cheerfully, and Tom heard the TV commentary recede as she carried the phone out of the room. "You'll have to excuse Paul," she continued. "He's really been quite ill with this dreadful flu-bug – not even been to work for two days – and he's just staggered down now from his sick-bed to watch the football with Jason."

"Oh I'm sorry," said Tom. "I just wanted to say thanks for the card and be amongst the last to wish you a happy New Year!"

"Thank you," returned Anna, "and season's greetings to you too! Did you have a good one? On the continent, weren't you?"

"Yes, went to see my brother and his lot; jolly cold over there at this time of year, I can tell you. White Christmas and all that. Did

Lucy tell you I was going away?"

"Yes, I'm sure she must have; and now of course they've swanned off to Florida, lucky old toffs, eh?"

"Florida!" exclaimed Tom.

"Yes, it was all very sudden. Between you and me I think things got a bit strained over Christmas – well Barry's not the easiest person to live with, is he? And then just before New Year he suddenly announced that he'd booked them ten days in the Florida sun. Someplace down near Miami, on the Keys, I think..."

"Oh, that must have come as a surprise, didn't it?"

"Well Lucy wasn't at all keen at first – typical of Barry not to give a thought to clothes or packing or anything – but you know what he's like!"

"Don't suppose the kids will mind missing a few days of school..."

"Oh, they haven't gone," said Anna.

"What?" snapped Tom.

"No, it's meant to be a second honeymoon type of thing. It's just the two of them."

"Lovely," growled Tom, suddenly sitting down involuntarily as his legs went hollow beneath him. He reached for the wine glass.

"Alice is staying with Pa-Simon and Jackie, Cherie's ensconced with their friend across the road..."

"Mary," breathed Tom.

"That's right, Mary; and Emu is staying with a school friend."

"Oh, good," said Tom.

"I hope it's done Lucy good. She certainly looked as if she needed a break. Didn't you think?"

"I guess so," he muttered, adding darkly, "Barry too, wasn't he always dashing up and down to Nottingham last year?"

"Paul says that's what put the strain on their marriage, him being away so much.....and between you and me – no, I'd better not say..."

"Say what?" growled Tom.

"Oh, you know what he's like; fast and loose."

"Humph!" grunted Tom. "Yep, that sounds like Barry."

"And then Barry pulled off some big deal for the firm just before Christmas; so even Paul couldn't begrudge him a bit of a break," she added, dropping her voice to a conspiratorial whisper.

"No, I suppose not," said Tom flatly.

"Anyway, Simon's picking them up at Gatwick - Sunday afternoon I think – so they'll be able to tell us all about it when they've got over the jet-lag or whatever."

"Whatever," echoed Tom.

"Look, you must come to dinner soon," offered Anna, adding archly. "You and Lucy have become really good friends, haven't you?"

"Yes," he agreed, wondering how much Anna knew or might have guessed. "Yes, that would be nice."

"Good, that's a date then. I mean, I'll call you to arrange something. No use waiting for Paul to get off the pot."

"Wish him better from me, won't you?"

"I will. Thanks Tom. Goodnight, see you *very* soon!" and she was gone.

Tom dropped the phone, drained his wine glass and threw himself onto the sofa with a loud cry of anguish.

"Fucking, bloody bastard fucking hell!" he wailed. "A *second honeymoon*, what's that all about? Fucking great piles of fucking excrement! Fucking hell Lucy, how the fuck could you?" With that he rolled heavily onto the floor, jumped up and kicked angrily at his swivel chair, sending it smashing against his desk and causing the self-assembly lamp to rock and crash to the floor, extinguishing its light.

"Bugger!" exclaimed Tom. Bending to retrieve the toppled lamp his sleeve brushed against the Christmas tree, causing a great shower of needles to clatter down, joining the crunchy, green drift on the carpet below.

"Oh, for fuck's sake!" bellowed Tom, savagely. "That fucking does it!"

He tore open the curtains and threw up the lower sash of the middle window. A rush of cold air and the whir of passing traffic blew into the room. Tom reached for the lowest part of the tree and lifted it above his head. The merry coloured lights still blazed and every movement sent a cloud of green needles raining down over him, onto the furniture and the floor.

"Out you bloody go!" he yelled, thrusting the entire tree, lights, decorations and all, out into the darkness. He let go and the tree disappeared, the long lead of the extension cable whipped across the floor and sprang straining onto the window ledge. Tom brought the sash back down with a mighty crash, trapping the red plastic cable. He strode towards the kitchen where he snatched up another bottle of wine and wrenched out its cork.

Wine splashed in dark maroon pools on the worktop all around the glass and Tom gulped down half the bottle with no enjoyment and hardly a pause for breath.

"Bugger me sideways," he growled and stomped into the bathroom to snatch Lucy's pink towel from pride of place on the radiator. He pressed it to his nostrils, breathing deeply to absorb into himself any lingering traces of her scent. Sobbing angrily, he threw the towel onto his bed, unzipped his trousers and masturbated frantically, ejaculating his semen onto the crumpled pink folds.

"Lucy, Lucy, how fucking could you?" he cried bitterly before falling forward and scouring his hot face across the bedding.

* * *

Tom lay in the darkness, his eyes closed, feeling the room sway and rotate around him. His head ached and he could hear a distant pounding which he thought might be his heart. The pounding grew louder and more insistent. He was suddenly aware of the muffled, distant sound of Mrs Patterson's voice calling to him from a long way off.

"Mr Cork! Mr Cork! What *is* going on in there? Mr Tom Cork, will you open this door at once?" Tom sat up, and scrapped his fingers through his unkempt hair. He rolled across the bed, and reached down to pull-up his jeans which were still tangled around his ankles.

Mrs Patterson's fleshy arms swayed unattractively as her fist pounded again on his door.

"Wait 'till my Jack gets home!" she called. "You can't carry-on like this. We've had enough." Now she slapped the door rhythmically using the palms of her hands. Tom stood, zipped his fly and shuffled into his slippers.

"Alright, alright," he called loudly, checking once more that his trousers were properly zipped and the belt buckled. "What is it?" he demanded, pulling open the door and swaying unsteadily.

"I'll give you *'What is it?'* Mr Cork!" exclaimed Mrs Patterson, stepping back towards the stairs as if afraid of what he might do next. "It's a disgrace, that's what this is," she proclaimed, the large hoops of her habitual gold earrings bouncing with indignation against her fleshy neck.

"I don't know what...."

"Don't you go giving me any of that *don't know* old soap," snarled Mrs Patterson, her red lips curling angrily but with a high note of fear breaking into her voice.

"Look Mrs P, please calm down and tell me exactly what hash upshet you," said Tom, trying desperately to sound re-assuring, and not as drunk as he felt.

"I can't believe you don't..." The timer switch snapped off the stair lights and Mrs Patterson uttered a throaty gasp. In the darkness, Tom's hand flew instinctively to press the familiar switch and then he reached towards her, suddenly fearing that she might jump back and tumble down the stairs.

"Keep away!" she cried, clutching the newel post for support. Tom relaxed gratefully against the wall,

"Show me," he invited. "You walk down the stairs first and I'll follow you....."

"There!" stated Mrs Patterson when they were outside in the front garden. "What do you mean by *that?* It's an outrage! A bleedin' blasphemy, as I should say such a thing." Tom stepped past her into the darkness, feeling the coarse tufts of wet grass cold and slippery beneath his feet. He turned to follow her stabbing finger and, looking up, saw his bedraggled Christmas tree, lights still blazing, suspended upside down by the electrical cable issuing from his brightly lit window. Strands of silver foil, flickering garlands and sparkling orbs dangled chaotically, twisting and clashing in the blackness. As they watched, the tree swayed ponderously, caught by the cold wind, and tapped eerily against the glass of Mrs Patterson's front window.

"Oh!" said Tom.

"I want it gone... Right now! Oh yes indeed," she insisted.

"I'm sorry, I didn't realise....of course I'll..."

"Humph," she grunted, *"Didn't realise, my arse!"*

"I said I'm sorry. I'll remove it; I've had some bad news..."

"Bad news? Disastrous News I shouldn't wonder; having your Christmas decorations still up after Twelfth Night, that's asking for trouble. You can't just chuck them out the bleedin' winda!"

"Vengeance is mine, saith the Lord," muttered Tom.

"What did you say? I heard you! Another blasphemy or such like, wasn't it?"

"No, it can't be 'blasphemy'; you shee this tree ish a purely pagan symbol. It's ign...ignome ...ignominious end can only be upsetting to the old Norse gods...."

"You're pissed, and now you're talking bollocks! It's against Christmas, that's what it is."

"No, no, it can't be. It'sh not Christian, not a Christian thing at all..."

"Get it down!" ordered Mrs Patterson, flexing her bulky forearms and blocking the pathway to the front door. "Some of us respect Santa and the Baby Jesus. We don't need this sort of bleedin' nonsense." Tom opened the palms of his hands towards her in a gesture of hopeless despair.

"OK, I'm sorry Mrs Patterson. I didn't mean any harm; I'll go and let it down right now."

As he waited for her to step aside and permit him back into the house, another icy gust swept in from the Common, this time bearing freezing rain and sleet. The rain quickly drenched the tree-lights which flickered briefly and were then all extinguished instantly with a loud *Pop!* Tom gazed upwards; the yellow rectangles of light had vanished from his windows. His entire flat was now also in darkness. The soaking of the tree-lights had tripped a circuit-breaker.

"There now," proclaimed Mrs Patterson with considerable satisfaction. "I knew it! You've gone and blown-up the bloody electric as well!"

* * *

"Hello, Tom," said Lucy on Monday evening when he answered the telephone. Tom had waited so long for this call and had agonised endlessly about what he might say to her. In the event, the sound of her voice left him speechless.

"Are you there, Tom?" she enquired softly.

"Sort of."

"Sorry, I've been away," she whispered.

"I know, Anna told me..."

"I think we should talk," she suggested quietly.

"Not like this. Can I see you?"

"I don't know...."

"Lucy, for Christ's sake..."

"Don't shout at me."

"How can I not? What's happening?"

"What?"

"Where are you? I need to see you!"

"Not now, you can't. Not right now. I was just calling you quickly. Brendan will be back in a minute."

"Fuck Brendan!"

"No Tom, don't..."

"Fuck Brendan! That's what you fucking do now, isn't it? *Fuck Brendan*, for fuck's sake!"

"Tom, just stop; he *is* my husband – you knew that."

"Stop! Oh yes *stop;* like turning off the bleeding tap! I wish I could. Oh how I fucking wish I could!"

"I've got to go, there's the door..."

"Fuck off then; see if I care."

Click. Lucy had put the phone down.

* * *

For the next three weeks Tom lived like an automaton. He went to work, he came home, he ploughed through schoolwork - marking books and preparing lessons. He shopped, he cooked and ate simple, dull, meals. He slept. At school, in the Staffroom, he sat glumly pretending to read a newspaper, hoping that no one would say more than 'Good Morning' to him. January became February, the temperature dropped and snow fell most days but seldom settled for long. Fierce snow-ball fights erupted around the school whenever there was even the most delicate mantle of white crystals adorning the worn grass and ugly tarmac.

"I see your lot are heading for trouble with the Lords over this legislation to deal with terrorists," sneered Eric Bridgeman, a Technology teacher. Tom raised one eyebrow and lowered his copy of *The Guardian* very slightly.

"They're not *my lot*, actually, Eric and I think the House of Lords might be doing the right thing for once."

"Oh you think we should just let the bastards run around unchecked and not chase after them 'till they've blown us all up?" spat Eric, leaning forward in his chair, blood pumping aggressively into his reddening forehead.

"No, of course not, but I do believe in *habeas corpus* and the Rule of Law."

"Habeas my arse! Lock 'em up and throw away the key. We're dealing with fanatics here, you know." insisted Eric.

"You might feel better but we'd be no safer if they imprisoned the wrong people."

"Whose side are you on?"

"The side of the law; the Rule of Law. It's all there in *Magna Carta* if you care to look," smiled Tom. "In amongst all the feudal stuff about forests, measures for wine and ale, removal of fish-weirs, protection of widows and heirs...Eight hundred years ago they decided that we didn't want arbitrary arrest and imprisonment in this country."

"Bloody load of old bollocks, if you ask me!" exclaimed Eric.

"I didn't."

"Didn't what?"

"Didn't ask your opinion," snapped Tom. "Actually, I don't give a toss what an ill-informed bigot like you has to say. I'm only distressed that we've got a government stuffed full of lawyers and they seem to have lost touch with the basic principles of Justice."

"That's my point, they're all a sodding waste of space," grumbled Eric.

"Language, please boys!" called a woman's voice from somewhere behind them. Tom let the outspread newspaper collapse onto his head and torso.

"Roll on death," he muttered.

Later, wrapped in a long coat and a black scarf, Tom strode through the mayhem at the end of the school-day, threw his briefcase onto the back seat of his car, and generated a cloud of billowing exhaust fumes as he savagely revved the cold engine and crunched the reluctant gear-box into reverse.

"Look at that bloody idiot!" said Eric to the Head of Science. "Bloody airy-fairy Arts graduate, you see. Not got a bloody clue. He'll tear the guts out of that bloody engine – it's people like him that run the bloody country you know!" The elderly chemist nodded his complete agreement before they both returned into the school building to avoid having to intervene in a particularly vicious incident of bullying which was developing amongst a swirling knot of pupils down by the school gates.

* * *

Chapter Fifteen

On Sunday evening Tom had arranged to go to the pub with Jack and Joan Patterson in an attempt to restore neighbourly harmony following what he now, privately, ridiculed as *'The Great Pagan-Symbol Blasphemy'*. It wasn't any such thing, of course, but Tom enjoyed the guilty pleasure of feeling superior which such a grandiose title conferred. When he rang their door-bell soon after 7.30pm Mrs Patterson, 'Joanie' as she liked to be called, declined to venture out. She did, however, seem very content, and generally placated, by the notion that Tom would be paying for several pints of ale and not a few whisky chasers for her husband.

As they walked across the Common, Jack kept up a comprehensive diatribe about the state of the country and Tony Blair's personal responsibility for it. So one-sided and irrational were most of his comments that Tom several times heard himself offering alternative explanations much more favourable to the Prime Minister. He was quickly reminded that Jack's views were firmly held and supported by a suite of deep-rooted prejudices which would not be shaken by Tom's appeals for evidence. Tom hunched his shoulders and wrapped his scarf across his mouth and nose, anticipating a fairly gloomy evening listening to Jack's explanation of how every current social and political ill – from indiscipline in schools to drug-resistant hospital *super-bugs* – was entirely the fault of foreigners. According to Jack, the principal villains were the French who, he maintained, were being allowed by Tony Blair to inject the Russian *mafia*, *'millions'* of Moslems and half the population of sub-Saharan Africa into Britain through the Channel Tunnel.

"Even as we speak," muttered Tom disparagingly, following one particular outburst which had somehow linked increases in the price of diesel fuel to lorry-loads of British lambs being burnt alive by rioting farmers in the French countryside. Tom felt some relief when they entered the smoke-haze and warmth of the pub. He hoped that the buzz of conversation all around them would quieten Jack who had immediately settled his heavy body at a table near the bar. Jack loosen his padded jacket, incongruously decorated with sporting logos, and stroked a massive hand across the grey stubble of his cropped hair. He smiled broadly, confident in the knowledge that Tom would be supplying the drinks.

Tom carried two pints of bitter and Jack's whisky chaser to their table and stood to unwind his scarf and discard his coat before sitting.

"Hi, mind if we join you?" called Paul turning awkwardly on a stool at the bar, while reaching to tug at Barry's sleeve.

"Of course not," answered Tom, startled. "Sorry, didn't see you two there."

"We're refugees from the Sunday night crap on the box," grunted Barry.

"And all that nausea about unfinished homework," added Paul.

"Shush, don't let him hear you say that; he's a bleedin' teacher!" said Barry, winking at Tom who curled his lip in response.

They brought their drinks over, Barry nodding in recognition to Jack while Tom introduced him to Paul.

"Oh yes, I've often bumped into Barry when he pops round to Tom's place," said Jack, smiling cheerfully at Paul.

"Huh, long time no see," laughed Barry. "Haven't seen much of you since Christmas have we, Tom?"

"Not seen you at all," said Tom flatly. Paul looked puzzled, glancing first at Tom and then at Barry.

"Been pretty busy myself," announced Barry. "Surprised you haven't hooked up with Lucy and the kids though. Has that moron-factory where you work made you do some work, at last?"

Tom merely stared into his pint, deciding not to rise to the bait of Barry's unpleasant teasing.

"How was Florida?" he asked, glumly. "I heard you'd been away..."

"Fantastic! Great place, I could really live there, lads; great climate, go-getting society, big steaks!"

"Lots of guns, devastating hurricanes and all run by George Bush's brother," snapped Tom.

"Der, you're just like Lucy, she carped-on most of the time too -- miserable old cow. Don't think she even left the hotel except to get to the airport."

Tom flushed angrily,

"And you?" he snapped back.

"Yeah, I was fine; like I said, loved it. I tried something new everyday. Went big-game fishing, chased alligators around the Everglades; never a dull moment. And I played lots of golf, drove everywhere, hired a fantastic Humvee. Christ that was some motor, I can tell you.... Yeah, I loved it; can't say the same for *her indoors*, 'though. She wanted to walk everywhere; I had to tell her straight; in the States people just don't do that. It makes you look like you're too poor to drive or get a cab. And then she whinged that she didn't want to eat out or even go shopping because the air conditioning made everywhere too cold! In fact, before you came in, I was just saying to Paul; wasn't I, Paul? *'There's just no pleasing some people'*."

Tom frowned but Jack chimed in with,

"Cor, you can say that again, mate!"

"Well, women anyway," added Paul, "There's no pleasing women; I mean you try forgetting their birthdays or the wedding anniversary, anything minor like that. Just see what happens. Christ, they'll go completely potty on you."

"Too true," agreed Jack, ruefully.

"No bloke would do that," continued Paul. "I mean I've known Barry longer than I've known my wife, but would he mind if I forgot his birthday?"

"Certainly would, mate," laughed Barry. "It would be your round!"

"Anyway," said Paul with a shrug, "I can't forget your birthday nowadays because bloody Anna always reminds me about it.

'Don't forget it's Barry's birthday next Tuesday fortnight,' she whines, 'and your mother's at the end of the month'. God help us."

"How do they do that?" asked Jack, with apparently genuine interest. "How do they always know when it's someone's birthday or whatever?"

"Fucked if I know," shrugged Barry, swallowing the last of his pint. "Drink up lads, it's Paul's round, what'll you have?"

"What we should do," announced Barry when he and Paul returned bearing a tray laden with drinks, "is get Anna to tell Paul to tell me when Lucy's birthday's coming up, and vice versa. That way we'll never be in the shit, ever again."

"October 27th," said Tom without hesitation.

"What is?" asked Paul.

"Lucy's birthday," answered Tom, staring defiantly at Barry, who shrugged and said,

"Sounds about right."

"How'd you know?" asked Paul.

"He's got a good memory," laughed Barry. "But he's got no wife, and so no bloody birthday to have to remember. The girls all think it's such a waste, him being single... the lucky sod."

Tom glowered at him.

"Cheer up, mate!" chided Barry. "You look as though you've lost a fiver and found a penny. Whoops, mustn't mention Penny must we?" Barry roared with laughter and nudged Paul, who also seemed to find the mention of Penny hilarious, even 'though the nudge had caused him to spill some of his beer.

"And there's another thing!" exclaimed Barry. "Sex!"

"Oh, I wondered how long it would be before we got onto sex," sneered Tom.

"They say that most normal men think about sex about once every thirty seconds," announced Jack. "You're not fucking *gay*, are you?"

"Not so far," said Tom coldly. "But I'm sure that gay men think about sex at least as frequently as heterosexuals."

Jack shook his head blankly, clearly puzzled by the suggestion that gay men might have a sex-drive similar to his own.

"Women are just from a different planet," claimed Paul.

"Unless they're lesbians!" roared Barry, then he, Paul and Jack all threw back their heads and laughed heartily. Tom smiled, not caring that his smile was disdainful.

"Take my wife…" began Paul.

"Please, take my wife!" spluttered Barry, sounding like an old-time music-hall comedian.

"There you are, you see," said Paul. "Ask any married man, we've all been there."

"Certainly have," agreed Jack.

"What are you talking about?" asked Tom.

"Sex, of course," explained Barry. "You want it, the missus doesn't, so what do you do?"

"Go and get it on with some other bird," stated Paul enthusiastically.

"And then see what happens when the missus finds out," added Barry.

"Cor, blimey, there'll be merry blinkin' hell!" said Jack.

"Too bloody right," confirmed Paul. "It's no use saying to the wife '*But I gave you first refusal, my dear.*' That cuts no ice with them, absolutely none at all….And don't I know it."

Barry put his hand on Paul's shoulder in a theatrical display of sympathy;

"No," he said almost despondently, "they give you endless grief if they think you're playing away matches; even when they've turned you down themselves." Barry then shook his head as if completely at a loss to understand the unfairness of it all.

"I just don't believe you two," said Tom, slumping back in his chair. The others stared at him. "Surely you're supposed to be in committed *relationships*, aren't you? Don't you want to discuss these things in private with your partners at home? Not like this, so crudely, with your mates down the pub? I mean, you've both got brilliant, intelligent wives. You don't know how lucky you are. You need to be a bit more sensitive to their feelings; perhaps that's where you're going wrong?"

There was a long pause. Jack frowned, staring down at the table, trying to assess whether it was an insult that his Joanie had so obviously been omitted from Tom's praise for the absent wives. Meanwhile, Tom looked first at Barry, then at Paul. Jack felt impelled to break the silence by observing,

"Bloody hell, we can tell you're not married, mate. *Relationships,* my arse!"

Paul and Barry both laughed and Paul asked Jack;

"Here, d'ya know the one about the marbles in the jar?"

"What's that?" asked Tom, cutting in before Jack could answer.

"Well, Tom," began Paul, "if you ever find a bird you want to marry...."

"And who wants to marry *you!*" added Barry, gleefully.

"Well, every time you have sex in the six months before you're married, you put a marble into a jam-jar," continued Paul.

"Make love," corrected Tom.

"Sex, make love, whatever," said Paul hurriedly.

"There is a difference," insisted Tom.

"*Course I loves ya, fucks ya don't I?*" recited Jack, mumbling into his beer.

"Then after you're married," continued Paul, raising his voice, "you take one marble out of the jar every time you get your end away..."

"And see how long it is before the jar's empty again," Barry chipped in.

"Ten years at least, if ever," muttered Jack, with feeling.

"If you're lucky!" concluded Paul.

"So stay single as long as you can, mate," advised Barry.

"Biggest mistake I ever made," grunted Jack, his heavy lips turning downwards at the corners of his mouth. "The most expensive too," he added. "And of course my little Joanie, well she wasn't one for having proper sex before marriage..."

"It's sex *after* marriage mine seemed to get all bloody huffy about..."said Paul.

"Cheer up, for God's sake," ordered Barry. "You're nearly as gloomy as poor old Tom here."

"Yeah, take our advice mate," suggested Paul. "We should know. You don't want to go buying a book if you can join a library instead."

"Marriage doesn't seem to have affected your behaviour very

much," snapped Tom, looking directly at Barry.

"It bloody well has," insisted Barry. "I only get away with more than the average punter because I can still manage some pretty nifty footwork," he boasted.

"Here, have it away on your twinkle-toes and get us another round in," suggested Paul, holding out his empty glass.

When Barry asked who wanted another pint, Tom shook his head and pointed to his glass which was still more than half-full.

"I need a slash," said Tom, easing his way out from behind the table. "Back in a mo…"

"Your round next, neighbour," said Jack, quite unpleasantly.

"No worries," replied Tom disdainfully, over his shoulder.

Coming out of the *Gents,* Tom paused momentarily in the corridor before heading out into the car park, tugging his mobile phone from his jacket as he walked. Once outside, he scrolled down to Lucy's name on the display and called her. When she answered, Tom spoke quickly;

"It's Tom, don't hang-up, I have to see you. I know you can talk."

"What? How?"

"I'm at the pub, with Barry."

"Well, bully for you!"

"I mean, I'm outside…Paul's in there too…I bumped into them. It doesn't matter, but I know you're alone."

"Might be…"

"I know, alright? I know he's not there…not where you are. At home, I mean."

"Is that so? Well aren't you the clever one? No surprise there."

"Lucy, for God's sake!"

"Calm down. OK, yes, let's talk. It's just that I wasn't expecting …it's a bit sudden,"

"I don't mean now. I mean face to face to face. I need to see you."

"I'm not sure Tom. It's tricky; what do you want to say? I guess you're very angry with me, aren't you?"

"Not now…"

"You mean you were angry, but you're not angry anymore?" she asked.

"No. I mean I'm freezing my nuts off out here. I can't talk now; I told them I was going to the bog..."

"Oh Tom, I don't know...Everything's so topsy-turvy. I don't know what I'm doing; not any more...I need time..."

"Lucy, listen. What about tomorrow morning, after your school run?"

"Won't you be at school yourself by then?"

"No. I'm going to phone in sick. Flu or something, everyone's got it."

"What about Alice?"

"Can't Mary...?"

"I'll ask; you see I do want to see you. I think; well part of me does anyway."

"Which part?"

"Don't start! What I mean is that I *have* missed you. Yes, you should know that."

"Where can we meet?"

"Not here...."

"Come to mine?"

"No."

"In a shop, as if by accident..."

"No. Someone might see..."

"Might see what?"

"You might make a scene. I don't know....."

"Lucy!"

"You might want to kill me or something, I don't know, do I?"

"Don't be so stupid. It's me, Tom, remember? Get a grip, for Chrissake!"

"Alright, alright, calm down. I know; look, I'm sorry, OK?"

"So where?"

There was a long pause before Lucy replied,

" Sainsbury's, in Wandsworth. You know where I mean?"

"Yes, very romantic. We could have 'trolley-rage' next to the cucumbers, I suppose?"

"Shut up. Drive around the car park at half past ten. On the dot, I do mean *exactly*. I'm not going to hang around. I can watch for you from inside, as if I'm waiting for a mini-cab. When I see you, I'll come out, then it'll seem as if you're giving me a lift."

"Do we need to be this paranoid?"

"It's my way or not at all."

"OK, OK. I'll be there, ten-thirty tomorrow morning. Good; that's good."

"What's good?"

"Seeing you again."

"Perhaps. I don't know..."

"I do!"

"Tom, please, don't be so..."

"So what?"

"I don't know. Look, we'll talk tomorrow. OK?"

"Yes."

"Right."

Chapter Sixteen

Lucy walked towards Tom's car carrying a shopping bag that contained only two packets of breakfast cereals and a box of tissues.

"Mini-cab, love?" joked Tom, gliding down the electric window.

Lucy smiled weakly and opened the back door. She placed her bag on the seat. It toppled sideways and the box of tissues slid out. Tom looked at the box, then at her.

"Are those for me or for you?" he enquired as she moved into the passenger's seat alongside him. "If they're for me, one box might not be enough."

"I thought you were meant to have flu," she said flatly, staring straight ahead.

Tom drove out into the traffic.

"Where to?" he enquired.

"Anywhere. Away from here."

They drove in silence. They came to a set of traffic lights and Tom turned right because that was what the car ahead of them was doing. He followed the same car, turning left and then right again. They pulled up in a traffic jam near Southfields station. The way ahead was blocked so Tom turned left when the lights changed.

"That's the All-England Lawn Tennis Club," he announced. Lucy flicked a glance towards him and at the blur of buildings passing by on the right.

"Are we in Wimbledon, then?" she asked flatly.

"Yes. We must stop; I can't talk to you if I can't look at you – even if you refuse to look at me..."

"I'm not. But don't stop near houses. I don't want to talk with any windows watching."

"Windows?"

"You know what I mean. Find some kind of open space."

"Wimbledon Common is up here somewhere; if you don't mind having *The Wombles* watching you?"

"That'll do. I had almost forgotten how light-hearted you can be..." her voice tailed away and Tom moved his left hand as if to pat her, but then held back. Lucy relaxed a little and sank into her seat.

Tom made an awkward left turn out of the traffic and wound along a narrow lane with the first open space of the Common on both sides. He slowed, hesitated and then parked behind a couple of other cars under the leafless branches of a chestnut tree. He turned off the engine to give some finality to the first part of their journey. They sat in silence, feeling the car buffeted by the wind.

"Where is this again?" she asked.

"It's the start of Wimbledon Common, a sort of bald hilltop just beyond what they still call 'The Village'."

"How fucking twee!" she sneered. "It just looks so cold and empty."

"*Appropriately bleak*, I'd say," muttered Tom. Lucy delved in her handbag and took out a packet of cigarettes.

"When did you start again?" he growled.

"In the States."

"Huh! I thought smoking was socially unacceptable in the *Land of the Free*."

"There's a lot about America that would surprise you," she said. "For instance they're not all over-weight and they don't all wear cowboy hats and carry guns."

"Barry seemed to love it, the way he went on about it in the pub last night."

"He said he'd seen you..."

"He said you were unhappy there and stayed in the hotel all the time..."

"It suited me. I slept a lot. I read a lot. He went out a lot. That suited me too."

There was a long silence. Tom gripped the steering wheel with both hands; Lucy fumbled for her lighter.

"If you're going to smoke that thing, can we get out of the car?" he asked.

Tom held the car door open for her while Lucy looked around. She clicked the lighter a few times, but each flame was flattened and extinguished by the wind before she could apply it to the tobacco.

"It won't light with you holding the door open," she complained.

Tom pushed the door closed and stood back. Inside the car, Lucy lit her cigarette and blew a cloud of blue smoke which filled the interior. Then, realising what she had done, she began flapping her hands frantically to dispel the fug and pushed open the door.

"Sorry," she said, looking down as Tom turned away and shuffled awkwardly across the coarse grass. She hurried to catch up with him, pulling her coat – the one Tom had given her – closer and tightening the belt. The tip of her cigarette spilled ash rapidly and she took only a few shallow puffs before discarding the white tube into the wet grass.

Tom turned back and stamped it emphatically into the mud. Ahead of them was a wide grassy space fringed with swaying black trees and distant houses.

"At least you won't want to kiss me now," said Lucy, drawing the forefinger of her left hand across her clenched teeth.

"Oh but I'm afraid I do, damn it!" answered Tom.

She stopped beside him; the uneven ground made her seem shorter, her face was below his shoulders. He reached for her and she stepped into the gentle cupping of his hands. He held her face. He pressed his lips to hers and felt tears starting from behind his eyes.

"God, Lucy, I've missed you," he began. She pressed closer. "Before you say anything, I want you to know that I am still in love with you," he whispered.

"That's not fair," she murmured but made no effort to move away.

"Why?" he asked tipping back his head so that her face came into focus once more.

"Because that cuts the ground from under... I mean, it's like a *conclusion*; you can't start with a *conclusion*."

"Why not?" he complained. "Everyone else does, in all sorts of ways. Look at politics or philosophy; we all start with our conclusions and then search for the facts that fit ......"

"But *in love*; it's so final and in its own way oppressive....."

"It doesn't have to be. And it's not as if it's a matter of choice – I didn't *choose* to fall in love. On balance I would have preferred just to be friends..."

"Friends who had sex?" she challenged.

"Ah! That was my downfall. When I got to know you, I mean intimately, I mean......"

"You mean you had *Carnal Knowledge*, in the Biblical sense?" she smiled teasingly.

"Yes, well truthfully, that is just what I do mean; if you insist – when I tasted you on my tongue – I realised that I was a goner. I became yours, I wanted nothing and no one but you."

"God, Tom," she breathed. "No one has said anything like that to me ever before."

"I firmly believe," he said, enfolding her with both his arms, "that no one has felt for you before in the way that I feel..."

"No, no, this is all going too far and too fast; you're not supposed to say that yet, I didn't expect....."

She broke away from him, shaking her head and ruffling her hair vigorously.

"I need to think," she grumbled.

They were walking now, arm in arm, beside a shallow pond of grey water, its silver surface combed into charging wavelets by the sweeping wind. A flurry of icy rain stung the side of Tom's face. He turned to Lucy who had stopped to watch the frantic flapping of a coven of black-winged crows, calling harshly and disputing the turbulent air above the far trees.

"I didn't mean to hurt you," she said quietly, her eyes following the ragged formation of birds.

"I had it coming," admitted Tom. "I didn't realise how much you meant to me until I thought I'd lost you..."

"You didn't lose me," she replied. "I mean, I'm not a *thing* – not an object to be lost and then found again."

"I didn't mean it like that," he countered. "I was referring to your absence. Suddenly there was this cold dark void in my life; it was where you had been. How would you describe that?"

"Winter; in Clapham," she suggested turning her smile on him.

"Sorry, I probably deserved that. Getting a bit heavy wasn't I?" he said. "We men aren't any good at talking about relationships.... are we?"

"You are."

Tom stood back from her, and gazed up at the sky, thinking how it appeared so much bigger here, now that they were away from all the usual enclosing buildings. Lucy stared down at the ground, repeatedly stubbing the toe of her small black shoe against a tussock of grass. He watched, sensing that she could feel his eyes upon her.

"Stop looking at me," she insisted.

"I know," he suggested, "come here. Now, stand with your back to me; that's it and lean back, resting your back against mine. There."

"It's like one of those 'Trust Exercises' we did in Drama when I was at college...... Oh, that's good. Now, can we say things, whatever we like, without turning around?"

"We can try."

"This place reminds me of somewhere, but I don't think I've been here before."

"Déjà vu?"

"Hey, this isn't _Catch 22_. Don't start all that '_déjà vu, presque vu, jamais vu_', stuff on me. I couldn't cope with it right now; and remember – I only have to step away and you fall over backwards."

"You too, you too," he replied. "But when you are ready to trust me, can we sit down and talk?"

"Why do I find it easier to talk to you on the phone, where I can't see you?" she asked.

"I'm going to move," he warned and felt Lucy straighten her back in anticipation. "Come and sit with me?" he suggested, walking a few paces to a wooden seat and sitting down. Lucy watched him and then followed but sat at the very end of the bench, facing away and with her back to him. Tom's left arm rested on the back of the seat and his hand touched her shoulder.

"Seriously, Tom," she resumed, lowering her voice. "I'm a married woman, I've got three children and – I haven't told you this before – I can't have any more."

She felt Tom's hand move and she called out,

"Don't move! Stay behind me; I don't want to turn around 'til I've finished!"

Tom relaxed his fingers and felt the tension in her upper body.

"After Alice, there were complications. You remember I was so ill? I had to go back into hospital. And then suddenly that was it. No more children. I didn't mind at the time, but Brendan did. He was very upset, he'd wanted a son, but it wasn't to be. Unusually for him, he didn't let on; I mean he didn't throw his disappointment at me. But then, one morning, about a year later, he hadn't come home and that was when I realised that one day one of his affairs might turn serious. He might decide someone else could give him a son... There, I've said it!"

Lucy kept her head bowed and he sensed she was rubbing her eyes. Tom moved his finger tips along the collar of her coat and touched the back of her neck.

"What would you do if he left you?"

"That's quite a question..."

"You must have thought about it..."

"I hadn't until sometime last summer. I never thought that either of us could leave the children, then one day I looked at him – the children were in the same room – and I saw that he could just switch off from them. And that's when I knew that he could; I knew that he could leave them."

"And how did that make you feel?"

"Me? Feel? Me, I felt nothing, I don't remember feeling anything at all. I suppose I should have been shocked or angry. But I wasn't. Maybe I felt a bit sad for the children, but not hopelessly sad. I think I knew that he'd still see them and provide for them...."

"Have you discussed any of this with Barry?"

"No. He won't. He's in denial. His own childhood was so fucked-up by his father leaving. He can't face that, I mean he can't face that as a pattern he might repeat."

"Has he admitted he's had affairs?"

"What? Brendan? Our Barry? Good Old Bazza? 'Course not; don't be daft. His mind doesn't work like that. After our miserable time in Florida…"

"Anna said it was a *second-honeymoon,*"

"And you believed her I suppose? I mean, like, she would know the intimate details of our lives?"

"Maybe Paul told her. Maybe that's how Barry described it to Paul?"

"I don't care…"

"Well I do. I mean I did when I heard it from Anna. I hated the very idea. It made me feel physically sick if you must know. I was very, very jealous."

"Oh, Tom, no; it wasn't like that at all. I think I was only," she paused and took a deep breath, "*nice* to him once; the whole time we were away…"

Tom stared blankly down at the grass around his shoes. He wiped his eyes with the back of his free hand.

"*Nice* to him," he said quietly. "Is that how you think of it?"

"Yes, yes I do. So there, if you must know, I only let him have me once during the whole fortnight we were away."

Tom lifted the edge of his jacket and struggled to extract a handkerchief from his trouser-pocket. He blew his nose into it and then leaned forward again, still looking intently at the grass.

"Because of you," she whispered.

"Is that true; really true?"

Lucy's upper body stiffened and her hands suddenly clenched as if she were struggling to control them. She breathed slowly; in and then out again, pacing her anger.

"Would I come out here with you, and sit like this, if I was just going to tell you a pack of bloody lies?" she hissed.

"Thank you," said Tom meekly. "Thank you very much. I…"

Lucy raised her head abruptly as he spoke and her right hand pushed her hair back from her face.

"Don't thank me!" she shouted. "You don't have to do that. You knew I was married…" Her voice dropped again. "Now listen, Tom. Just listen to me, please. I was about to tell you something else before you went all paranoid on me. What was it? Where did

I get to before you started on about being jealous?”

“You said you’d had a miserable time in Florida…”

“Yes, and then…argh, I know, that was it. On the plane coming back from Miami, I watched him eat one of those airline meals – you know on one of those plastic trays where everything is segregated into little packets and compartments…”

“And?”

“And he ate the contents of each compartment, one at a time; polished them off completely before he started on the next. And that’s how he lives his whole life. Everything he does he keeps separated into little compartments. He deliberately makes it like that.” Lucy twisted her upper body, half turning towards him. She held up one hand with the fingers splayed and began listing Barry’s activities, touching her fingers as she counted them out. “There’s his work, there’s the girls, there’s Paul, there’s Simon, there’s the lads at the pub – including you – there’s his past, there’s his future…”

“There’s you!”

“There’s his other woman…”

“Are you sure about that?”

“Sure about what? Yes, of course I’m sure he’s got another woman on the go, and I’m equally sure that he’s just the same with her or, if she’s not been boxed-up yet, she bloody soon will be.”

“I’ve just thought; would she have been as upset about him suddenly darting off to Florida with you as I was? What do you think he told her? Did she give him grief, knowing that he was taking you on holiday?”

“I should worry about that? About how she felt? Christ, Tom, I think not!”

“Just a thought…” Tom hesitated, fearful that he might let something slip, that he would accidentally say the name ‘*Penny*’ and reveal his collusion in Barry’s deceit. He tried to move the conversation from any mention of the mistress.

“I imagine your idea about separate compartments puts a lot of brain-strain on Barry. Must do, mustn’t it?”

“It would if he was normal. If he had normal emotions…”

“It does sound a bit mental…”

“Huh, *psychotic* would be more like it. Barry’s very clever. Well, cunning and clever. It's all very intricate, but he can do it – years of practice I suppose. I couldn't, I couldn't consciously do that; couldn't be a different person in different situations at different times of day....I couldn't remember which lies I'd told to which people."

"It sounds like a classic description of alienation; a recipe for a breakdown."

"Oh no way," she scoffed, "not him. It's me that's had the breakdown, not our *Bazza*."

"Maybe he had his long ago in his childhood and never got over it. Don't the shrinks talk about *blockages* or something?"

"Probably, I mean I'm sure they do, but I thought it was '*closure*' we were all meant to be seeking these days."

"Well, that too. But maybe Barry just developed this compartmental technique as a strategy for dealing with things as they were back then; when he was a kid. When he found that it worked – or it seemed to work for him anyway – I guess he just went on using it."

"Yes, why wouldn't he? You'd have to know him intimately for a long time to see that that's what he does...It's taken me however many years to sus it out... And I'm married to the bastard!"

"Do you think Paul knows? Could you talk to Paul about him?"

"Humph, no way. You said yourself, '*Men aren't any good at talking about relationships*'. I can't imagine Paul being very articulate about his relationship with Anna; so there's absolutely no chance that he'd be analytical or helpful about Barry's relationship with me. Anyway, they're close – him and Barry. They're like brothers. Paul clams up if I ever try to get him talking about Brendan....I found that out years ago."

Tom shifted his weight on the seat and breathed deeply while Lucy twisted once more so that she resumed staring away from him.

"I missed you dreadfully," he said. "All over Christmas and the New Year. I had to phone Anna when I couldn't find you. I drove past your empty house some nights..."

"Our Christmas was absolutely dreadful," said Lucy, interrupting him. "Hell on acid...Brendan was either irritable or pissed most of the time, then I exploded at bedtime on Christmas Eve – I choose my moments – and I just told him to fuck-off and live with his tart up there in Nottingham!"

"Kin'ell, Lucy; what did he say to that?"

"Denied it, of course. Blanked me completely. What he actually said was '*You've got no proof!*' and I said that those words were as good as a signed confession to me."

"Then what?"

"He turned on me of course; when his back's to the wall, Barry always counter-attacks."

"What? Does he suspect something? Does he know about us?"

"No, of course not. Huh, come on Tom, you can be bloody sure he'd have mentioned it if he'd known!"

Lucy paused, her shoulders heaved; Tom waited for her to continue.

"He accused me of not supporting him enough. He said that I didn't '*lift his spirits*'."

"Lift his spirits?" exclaimed Tom. "What? I don't fucking believe him."

"That was what he said; his exact words. I was '*gobsmacked*' as they say. He said I was scruffy and unsophisticated. He said I had no style..."

"What? That's so unfair! Compared with who? Sorry, with *whom*?"

"I think he'd like me to be more like Anna, or this drop-dead gorgeous career-girl called Antonia – *can you imagine, dahling?* - who's just started working for them; for him and Paul I mean. Or else he'd like me to be all stuck-up, snobby and *dead posh* like Jane, next door. You know the sort of thing, more accomplished, polished, cool and sophisticated. Someone who remembers to shave under her armpits! A woman who is aware of fashion and trends; an opera-buff, a Friend of The Tate..."

"But you are!"

"Am I bollocks! I'm not a *Friend* of any ruddy art gallery and I don't know *nuffink* about opera and high culture..."

"Nor does Barry, for Chrissake!"

"No but he wants a woman with style, with flair and, alright, *savoir-faire*, except he calls it '*savvy fair*'. Anna would do, except he doesn't fancy her – he thinks she's cold – and anyway she's Paul's...that puts her out of bounds by the curious logic of planet Barry."

"She's nice. I like Anna."

"Well maybe she's more your type? Barry calls her *The Ice Maiden*. He means she's frigid."

"She's probably just antagonistic to him because he has so much sway over Paul. I'd say she was pretty cool. That's not the same as being *frigid*."

"I used to think Anna and I were pretty similar...when her kids were little; before she went back to work."

"Well, you are...in a way. But you do swear more than Anna does, that's for sure. Your swearing is more graphic and sophisticated than hers; abso-*fucking*-lutely!"

"Well thank you, kind sir. It's nice to have one's talents appreciated..."

"I appreciate your talents; all of them."

"We were talking about Barry, if you remember."

"Oh yeah, so we were. He was whingeing that you didn't measure up to his fantasy about *posh-totty*."

"Pretty much... and so we came to Christmas Day – that was a total blur I can tell you – but fortunately we were over at Paul and Anna's for Christmas Dinner. After that, well I suppose Brendan just got into my compartment for a few days and took me away to Florida – to fix me."

"And did he?"

"Did he what?"

"Did he fix you?"

"Would I be here if he had?"

They sat in silence again. The wind blew coldly against them. Tom said,

"I would like it if you turned around properly now."

"No, I can't, not yet; I've got more to say before I'm finished."

"Go on...."

"I met you today because I intended to tell you that we have to stop...."

"Intended?"

"Listen. I've thought of every possible variation. I was going to tell you that I still love Brendan; that I'd decided to be a good and faithful little woman. I wanted to push you away from me. Kick you away if necessary. To make you hate me or despise me, if need be..."

"And is that what's coming next?"

"No!" she sobbed, spinning around and pushing her face into Tom's chest. He raised his arms awkwardly, ready to catch her if she started to slip from the seat.

"You must be very uncomfortable, with your body all twisted like that," he said, shifting along the bench and encouraging her to move into a less tormented position.

"I can't do it. I can't hurt you," he heard her say into his jacket. "I want you. I want you to love me. I want this to work even 'though I don't see how it can..."

Tom lifted both his arms high above his head so that his body was completely open to her. It suddenly occurred to him that to anyone watching he would look like an exhausted soldier, surrendering. *'In a way'*, he thought, *'that's just what I am'*. Lucy shuffled until she had turned round completely, then she lifted her face from his chest; her eyes were red and tears were starting down both cheeks. Tom brought his arms down and hugged her in wordless communication.

"We have to talk about living together, somehow, someday, you and me," he whispered.

"Don't be so utterly bloody daft!" she sobbed loudly. "I've thought that one through. It doesn't add up. It doesn't work... We can't; there are the children – they go where I go – don't you see? That's when I decided that I needed you to hate me...."

Tom shook his head slowly.

"Lucy, Lucy, darling Lucy," he murmured.

They sat in silence until Lucy shivered and whispered that she was just too cold to think anymore.

"Would you take me home?" she asked. "Take me to your place first, have your wicked way with me, use me, then take me home and dump me on the doorstep. I don't care who sees us!"

"Dear God," muttered Tom.

"I want to be warm again."

"Warm? You will be. Come back to the car."

"I want to make something happen," claimed Lucy as they stood up. "I want to stop all this double-dealing; I want to be honest about my feelings – my love and my anger - both! I've got to stop being torn apart by all this; it's too much. Much too much. Something's got to give before I go completely round the bend. It's got to be resolved. Nothing seems normal any more..."

"Maybe I should talk to Barry; tell him how we feel about each other..."

"No! Not that, I don't want you two deciding what to do with me. I'm not going to be *negotiated* between the two of you."

"You talk to him then. Tell him you're going to live with me."

"But I'm not, am I? I mean I might not, I haven't decided – there's the girls, they couldn't live with us at your place....."

"Why not?"

"There's only one bedroom, you idiot."

"Then I'll have to come and live with you..."

"No. That's where Barry lives."

"Then he'll have to go."

"Oh yes, and are you going to break that news to him?"

"If I have to."

"You don't have to. I don't have to. I don't *have to* anything. I don't have to have a man at all; have you thought about that? Maybe I should cut myself free from both of you?"

"You could. If that's what you decide. I'd be sorry, but I'd wait for you..."

"Sorry? What you'd be more sorry than Brendan? Is that why I should live with you? Because you're *sorrier* than he is?"

"What makes you think Barry would be sorry? Sorry at all? Maybe he'd just switch over effortlessly to his mistress...."

"Oh like changing channels on the TV, you mean? Yes I can see Brendan doing that; he'd use the remote of course..."

"Yes, if he could find it."

They had been walking along, making their way back to the car. Lucy suddenly halted and screeched with laughter. Tom stopped too, stunned by her sudden change of mood.

"It's not *that* funny, is it?" he began.

"It is, it is," wailed Lucy, now sobbing with laughter, and breaking into a Cockney bass voice which she intended should sound like Barry at his most homely: "*I wanted to dump the missus, you know like, switch her over for a little bit of something tasty I fancied on the other side, but blow me down – Gordon bleedin' Bennett – I just couldn't find the bleedin' remote, could I? Fuck me, I thought, what've the bleedin' kids done with me bleedin' TV remote control box?*"

"*So what d'ya do, Baz?*" asked Tom, doing his best to sound like Jack Patterson.

"*Well, what could I bleedin' do, mate?*" grated Lucy. "*Just 'ad to bleedin' sit there, didn't I? And put up with all her usual load of old bleedin' bollocks! 'Snot right, is it? I mean, I bleedin' ask you!*"

Tom then hugged her fiercely, squeezing her to him and feeling her breasts compress against his chest. He began planting staccato kisses on her cheeks, nose and forehead.

"Lucy Gardener, I want you to be my lover. Always. I have to have you in my life…"

"Huh," sniffed Lucy, "so we just carry on as before?"

"Yes," he answered firmly, "let's do that. It's like Simon said about democracy, isn't it? '*It doesn't work but the alternatives all seem so much worse…*"

Chapter Seventeen

Tom answered the phone to hear Anna's voice brightly inviting him to dinner,

"Saturday evening, do say you'll come. Lucy will be here; and Barry."

"Thanks. That would be nice."

"Well, we are all fully paid-up members of *the chattering classes* and this close to an election I'm sure you'll all have plenty to say..."

"Not to mention Charles and Camilla finally getting hitched, and the new Pope," he laughed, "Whoops, I don't mean the Pope's got married, no he's still an ordinary run-of-the mill seventy-eight year old, celibate, ultra-conservative blah blah."

"I take it you don't approve?"

"What's to approve? He's supposed to have a billion followers world-wide, but I gather that millions don't necessarily swallow the Church's line on condoms for example..... Err, sorry, maybe I should re-phrase that?"

"Tom! You're getting as bad as Paul and Barry."

"So sorry, but why did TV and all the papers assume everyone would be interested in the papal succession? There's been wall-to-wall coverage morning, noon and night since the death of John-Paul. *'Very Old Man eventually Dies'* : big news! I would have liked his successor to take the name *'George-Ringo'* – now that would have been NEWS."

"Oh Tom just stop it! You are incorrigible; but listen, you might have to be on your best behaviour..."

"Like always!"

"Barry and Paul have invited this goddess called *'Antonia'* who now works for them. It's quite funny really, she's their ultimate fantasy woman and they've both been winding each other up about her for months."

"Funny, Barry's not mentioned her to me at all. He's usually like an open book to his mates when he's being lecherous…"

"Oh dear," laughed Anna. "Not good news for poor Lucy then? Maybe he seriously fancies this *Antonia?*"

"Don't you worry that Paul might fancy her too?"

"Let me worry about him," she said quickly. "He knows he can look but he'd better not touch…"

"So; am I the token *'spare bloke'* to balance up the numbers and enable you and Lucy to give Antonia the once over?"

"I'm sure I've no idea what you mean, but yes, something like that," she replied coldly. "It would really put their noses out of joint if you got off with her; I'd like that."

"Can't promise anything; she might not be my type. And, realistically, I'm not likely to be hers, am I?"

"Oh, and what is your type, Tom?" she enquired archly. "Apart from Lucy, of course…"

Tom breathed in and then out again very deliberately.

"Whoops," said Anna.

"Best not to go there," he began.

"It's OK, really. Your secret's safe with *Aunty Anna.* See you Saturday; half-seven for eight?"

"Thanks. Thanks a lot."

"Don't you mean *Thanks a bunch?*"

"No, that's ironic, isn't it? I thought *Thanks a bunch* was meant to sound slightly derogatory."

"Is it? I don't know," said Anna. "I suppose I'm just trying to keep up with my kids…"

* * *

Tom pushed the button on the bell and the elaborate front door was soon opened by Paul, who carried a handful of cutlery and looked particularly distracted.

"Hi, it's yourself," muttered Paul.

"Sorry to disappoint," teased Tom. "Were you expecting it to be Antonia?"

"No, no, not really," stuttered Paul, now truly flustered. "I was just taking these into the dining room; for the table, you know... Didn't realise the time...Anyway, come-on in, Anna's through there in the kitchen, I'll be with you in a mo..."

"Tom! Hi, thanks for coming," trilled Anna, darting forward to kiss him lightly on both cheeks, then stepping back and running her hands down his arms while scanning his appearance from head to toe.

"Nice suit," she purred. "You've really made an effort; and cool shirt," she added wafting her hand across the front of the collarless white shirt he had purchased specially, earlier in the day.

"Looks as if you're going for an interview with some pansy design company," commented Paul, returning to the kitchen.

"*I* told him to raise his game," insisted Anna. "I told him that the very lovely Antonia would be here and he should get his act together."

Now it was Paul's turn to raise a sceptical eyebrow and give Tom the once over,

"Humph! Not bad, well not by his standards anyway. I thought his wardrobe only contained baggy pullovers and ragged-arsed jeans."

"Do feel free to carry on as if I'm not here," laughed Tom, proffering the expensive bottle of red wine he had been clutching.

"Oh, thanks, mate," said Paul, examining the label. "Look Anna, not cheap plonk either; *Chateau bottled* Claret, no less."

"And he's made an effort with his hair," said Anna with a smile.

Tom raised his hands in mock surrender;

"OK," he said, "I give up, but at least I tried."

"Nah, you'll do fine mate; very good," said Paul, punching him lightly on the upper arm. "But don't expect to get anywhere with Antonia. Not if she sees that old wreck of a car you drive. I shouldn't think she opens her legs for anything less than a Porsche – or just possibly the latest Audi Quatro TT Sport..."

"Paul!" snapped Anna. "Stop being crude and get the poor man a drink. Large G&T is it, Tom?" Then, as an aside intended for

Paul's hearing, she rasped, "Maybe he doesn't need his car to be a posing pouch; not like some I could mention."

"Ouch!" said Paul.

"An Audi quarter-to what?" queried Tom, declining the offer of gin. Turning away from Anna, Paul made an exaggeratedly sour face for Tom alone to see and then poured them each a glass of red wine.

"Well, it's all under control," announced Anna primly. "You have finished the table haven't you, Paul? – Oh! The water, take in those two jugs, if you please – now, Tom, lets go through into the other room."

Tom stood looking at a large abstract painting which filled the chimney-breast above the marble fireplace.

"That's nice," he said. "New isn't it? I mean I think I would have noticed it if it had been here last Guy Fawkes..."

"Do you like my painting?" asked Anna. "I bought it for Paul at Christmas, I'm not sure he gets it really, but I like it. When did you say you were last here?"

"Bonfire Night, remember? The big display, up on the Common..."

"Has it been that long? My, how time..." Anna stopped short when the door bell rang. "That'll be her," she said. Tom looked puzzled. "Well it can't be Barry; he never bothers with the bell, just slaps the face of the door and shouts '*Come out! We know you're in there!*' – or something much worse."

Paul ushered Antonia into the living room and introduced her, first to Anna and then to Tom. Tom stood and offered his hand, she grasped it firmly and looked into his eyes. Paul spoke,

"This is Tom. He's a poor, unfortunate, teacher on whom we've taken pity. We've got most of the chalk out of his fingers, and look – no leather patches on the elbows of his jacket."

"Ignore Paul," smiled Tom. "Everyone else does. You can tell it's a long time since he left school, can't you? What is this *chalk* of which you speak, old man?" Tom then added a loud aside directed at Antonia, "you'll find that like most computer-geeks he's compulsively jealous of anyone who does joined-up writing or reads books without pictures."

Antonia laughed politely and sat down in an armchair facing Anna.

"I'm so pleased to meet you at last," she began. "Oh! And is that the famous painting? Oh, I must take a closer look.... May I? My oh my; it's so rich..."

Antonia sprang across the room and Tom caught the sensual waft of her perfume as she passed.

"Such sumptuous colours," she exclaimed. Tom stepped back and parked his backside on the arm of a chair, watching as the two women moved to examine the painting closely. He thought how similar they looked, they could almost be sisters. Anna was clearly the older of the two by seven or eight years which, he thought, puts Antonia at around thirty. He could see just how pretty she was; he watched her brown eyes scanning the canvas and her eyebrows arched elegantly as she expressed her enthusiasm for the work;

"Oh I just love the way he uses paint; look at the energy in these brush strokes!" she trilled; flicking aside the full, soft curls of her auburn hair to reveal the sparkle of diamonds adorning her pendant earrings.

Tom noticed that Anna too was now studying Antonia rather than the painting. The younger woman was herself a picture of casual elegance. She wore loose-fitting, perfectly cut, dark blue Armani trousers beneath a simple red top decorated with a white wave-pattern. The top seemed held in place by a large bow on her right shoulder revealing her long arms, bare and tanned. As Antonia moved her hand to indicate a detail on the painting, a broad, diamond-studded bracelet slid busily along her slender wrist.

"And this colour here, why it's just so gorgeous you want to lick it, don't you?" she announced.

"Lick it?" queried Paul advancing across the room, holding towards her a tall glass of gin and tonic clinking with ice cubes and properly adorned with a slice of lemon.

"Calm down, dear, you wouldn't understand," laughed Anna. "Antonia has just responded heart and soul to the painting – just like I did when I first saw it."

"Has she dear? Oh I'm so pleased. I do hope Barry and thingie get a move on. I'm starving and the guests are already threatening to lick the art," replied Paul. "Do you like it Tom? Be honest; don't just say what you think the girls want to hear."

Tom jolted; he had been concentrating on catching a glimpse of Antonia's armpits, curious to know if she shaved them. Quickly he moved his gaze upwards, appreciating her breasts momentarily silhouetted against the last daylight in the window. He was about to speak when they all turned in response to a loud slap on the front door and the sound of Barry's voice booming, *"Drink! Drink!"* from outside.

Very soon Barry was in the room and holding out both hands to Antonia:

"How's the most exquisitely gorgeous data-base in the known universe?" he enquired smoothly, embracing her and kissing her properly on her pink lips. Tom and Anna exchanged glances as they both noticed how willingly Antonia curved her back to accept Barry's arms around her, and the little backward flip of her left ankle as their lips met.

"Barry; you Philistine! We were just discussing fine art when you burst in," chided Anna. "And anyway, where's Lucy?"

Barry turned around, shrugging his shoulders as he did so.

"Dunno; nipped to the little girl's room, I shouldn't wonder. Probably still trying to put her face on for Tom's benefit. My! My! You have made an effort, haven't you?" he whistled, running his eye over Tom. "Wicked suit, squire! Been along to Oxfam this afternoon have we? Pity they didn't have your size..."

"Oh, don't you start," replied Tom. "I've already had the benefit of Paul's razor-sharp wit, thank you."

"Take no notice of them," laughed Antonia prettily. "You should hear the two of them when they're supposed to be working. They're quite a double-act; they have the rest of us in stitches most of the time."

Barry beamed, holding out his arms as if receiving the applause of a large audience. The door opened behind him and Lucy slipped into the room.

"Lucy, darling," called Anna, encouragingly. "You look lovely, come and meet Antonia."

Tom watched her as she was led across the room. Her face looked tired and she was clearly wearing a lot of make-up which failed to disguise the dark crescents under her eyes. She seemed uncertain and almost timid as she held out her hand to Antonia,

"I've heard so much about you from Barry," she said quietly.

"Nothing outrageous, I hope?" smiled Antonia.

"Oh no, he's always singing your praises. *'Beautiful and intelligent!'* he says; as if that's completely unheard of amongst women."

"I've told him a million times not to exaggerate," said Paul, adding hastily, "not that I disagree of course! Not that you're not.... What was it you said Luce?"

"Oh, Paul! That's a double negative, I can't sort it out for you, can I?" laughed Lucy, suddenly regaining more of her usual humour.

"You're in a hole, mate," said Tom. "Best to stop digging."

Paul raised his eyes to the ceiling and waved an apology towards Antonia.

"I know," he said, "let's get ourselves into the dining room." And he called out to Anna in the kitchen, "Ready or not, we're coming!"

Tom watched Lucy intently. She had not yet glanced at him since she came in. His anxiety drifted away as she held back, letting the others leave the room first. She waited until he was next to her, and then gently stroked his arm:

"Nice *whistle and flute*, darling," she said, smiling broadly, mocking Barry's accent and tugging playfully at Tom's sleeve.

"Glad you like it," he answered quietly.

"I've decided I could love you in anything or nothing," she whispered.

"Cor, blimey!" was all Tom could manage in reply, feeling his face starting to flush with pleasure and realising that they were again within earshot of the others.

* * *

When they were all seated around the table, and starting their *hors d-oeuvres*, the conversation soon turned to the General Election.

"I'm in Battersea," announced Antonia, self-importantly.

"Oh, whereabouts?" enquired Tom.

"At the top of one of those big mansion blocks overlooking the park," answered Barry, and they all turned to look at him.

"That's conveniently close to the office," noted Anna, frowning slightly as she paused with a forkful of crab held midway between her plate and her lips.

"It's Labour held at the moment," said Antonia, eager to move the focus away from her personal situation, "but by rights it should be Tory."

"No way!" said Barry, suddenly eager to disagree with her. "Our five thousand majority should be safe enough, even with the way things have been going this last week."

"If the Labour vote drops because of low turnout and the Lib-Dems vote tactically, we could have a close result," suggested Antonia. "What's the situation over here?"

"Safe Labour, I'd say," answered Paul. "Fourteen thousand majority over the Lib-Dems last time and the Tories safely in third place."

"Maybe nowhere is *safe Labour* anymore," suggested Tom.

"Meaning?" challenged Barry.

"After the rocky time Blair's had this week on Iraq – and from that on the bigger issue of *Trust* – I think there might well be an extraordinarily low turnout combined with a large number of spoilt ballot papers put in by people who want to say '*None of the above!*' "

"That's not right," countered Barry. "Michael Howard's personal attacks on Tony Blair – calling him a *Liar* – "

"That's very *un*-parliamentary," put in Anna.

"But what if it's true?" asked Antonia.

"It was nearly enough to make me vote New Labour on the spot!" exclaimed Tom. "I mean, being called a liar by Michael Howard; when he's such a creep himself."

"No he's not. He's running a very effective campaign, and he tells it how it is," replied Antonia, her eyes flashing like her jewellery.

"It's not effective if it makes ultra-left old has-beens like Tom come back to voting *New* Labour," laughed Barry.

"Actually I don't think Blair *lied* to me over Iraq," said Tom. "I just think he made a series of appallingly bad decisions until, in the end, he persuaded himself that this country should follow America into a land-war in the Middle East."

"How could he do that? How could he not have been forewarned? Doesn't he have experts all around him?" demanded Anna.

"Oh yes," answered Tom, "and a closed circle of cronies who tell him what they think he wants to hear. But the real problem is that he has no principles; the Labour Party is led by a man who operates entirely pragmatically..."

"Oh leave it out, mate," blurted Barry. "As ever you're flogging a dead ideology which everyone else abandoned long ago..."

"Or never fell for in the first place," added Antonia, sharply.

"I'm just so disappointed," muttered Tom, shaking his head slowly. "Socialist politics do involve making a principled analysis; not just playing it by ear on every issue, day by day."

"I hope you're listening to this young Paul," chortled Barry. "Teacher will be asking questions at the end of the class...."

Paul giggled boyishly and flicked a piece of bread across the table at Barry. Barry put his hand up and pointed at Paul with the other. He started chanting:

"Sir! Sir! Please sir!"

"Oh, what's the point?" complained Tom. "Every time I try explaining something that might involve you holding two thoughts in your heads at the same time, you and Paul have to behave exactly like my Year Eleven leavers."

"Huh! Think what it's like to live with one of them," called Anna, fixing her gaze on Antonia.

"Ooh, but I do love it when Tom gets all petulant, don't you Anna?" teased Lucy.

"Can we get back to the real issues?" complained Antonia, sensing Anna's growing hostility and wondering, as she sipped another glass of wine, whether to placate her or get ready for some actual, or at least metaphorical, hair-pulling.

"Huh, tell that to your friend Michael," snorted Tom.

"Well I think we can win this time in places like Putney and even Battersea," insisted Antonia, her voice rising shrilly as the wine fuelled her annoyance.

"*Are you thinking what we're thinking?*" whispered Lucy maliciously, trying to mock one of the Tory Party's current posters.

"Apart from you, Antonia darling," soothed Barry, "I don't know anyone in Battersea who'd vote Conservative." He grinned broadly and waved his wine glass to encompass the table. Antonia's lips clamped shut and she pouted hotly, breathing out but saying nothing.

"I bet you Mary votes Conservative," suggested Lucy, affectionately. "She's a proper old working-class Royalist and a true-blue Tory to boot. You should hear her go on about Winston Churchill and the late Queen Mother visiting Battersea in the war. Mary was there, frantically waving her little Union Jack in their faces..."

Anna noticed the colour rising on Antonia's neck and a nervous flicker visiting the soft skin over her collar-bone.

"Anyway, what's so special about Battersea?" asked Anna, anxious to restore a friendlier aspect to the exchanges. "It's all very gentrified these days. I'm honestly surprised it was ever a New Labour seat in the first place."

"It has," announced Tom, affecting his most pedantic voice, "the highest percentage of people who travel to work by motorcycle of any constituency in the country."

"I'll drink to that," called Paul, adding, "Cheers!" as he and Barry flourished their glasses, clinking them together over the centre of the table.

"More vegetables, anyone?" enquired Anna, rising to retrieve the serving dishes from the warming trolley beside her. Tom paused, focusing all his powers of concentration on steadying the bottle he was levelling towards his wine glass.

Antonia decided to try a different tack. Shaking her hair gently and then scooping it away from her eyes, she stretched her jewelled fingers to touch Tom's hand and said;

"Tell me Tom, how did a smart young chap like yourself come to be left behind in politics?"

"Hah! *Left behind*! Ha hah; I like it!" spluttered Barry, emptying another glass of wine.

"Oh it's a long, sad story," offered Lucy, mischievously. "And I have to warn you it does involve frequent strong language and occasional nudity…"

"Lucy," giggled Anna, "that makes it an '18'!"

"More like a '38' in his case," sniped Barry.

"How many times?" complained Tom. "There you go again, talking about me as if I'm not here…"

"Oh, darling!" smiled Lucy, blowing him a kiss across the table.

"Look," resumed Tom, "in 1997 we all voted for this strange blob called *New Labour* because, frankly, anything had to be better than the Tories under Major and Lamont and all that crew…"

"And not forgetting Michael Howard. He was one of them," slurred Paul.

"*I mean, well frankly, you know,*" continued Tom, trying to sound like Tony Blair. "New Labour's political theories make about as much sense when you read them backwards as they do forwards."

"Paul, will you *please* hit him if he goes all the way back to the debate over *Clause IV*?" asked Barry and everyone laughed, including Tom.

"And I do believe that Blair has never grasped just how many of his votes came from people who were against the Tories rather than actually *for* New Labour. I mean, under our system you can't vote *against* anything, you have to vote *for* something else."

Lucy yawned, and Tom frowned at her.

"So when Blair was returned with a huge majority again in 2001?" queried Lucy, sorry that Tom had noticed her yawn.

"The electorate were giving him the benefit of the doubt," answered Tom. "But this time, in 2005, I think we're either going to see half the electorate not voting because they can't perceive any difference between the two main parties, or else we're going to see the triumph of 'valence politics'."

"The triumph of what?" asked Anna, turning to Paul.

Paul looked particularly baffled; frowning intently as he trawled through his memory.

"*Valence means the ability of atoms to form compounds,*" he stated, looking even more confused.

"Actually," said Tom, "in this context, *Valence* refers to the electorate's assessment of the overall competence of rival political parties. It means judging politicians as managers; asking how they are likely to perform in achieving desired objectives..."

"So does that mean," interrupted Barry, "that you get a low turnout at elections when the electorate are basically happy with the government and a high turnout when they want change? When they want to bring in a new set of managers?"

"I don't think the valence model is either that simple or that predictive," replied Tom. "I think it was originally developed as an alternative to the old way of explaining voting behaviour, which was based on social class."

"Hang on," put in Lucy. "No, no, listen. I don't think it's the behaviour of voters we should be questioning; it's the behaviour of political parties. Just stop and think how *they've* changed." Her eyes swept around the table as they all paused from eating and drinking, their attention engaged by the resurgent passion in Lucy's voice.

"Just compare," she resumed, "Thatcher's Tory party of the nineteen-eighties with Harold Macmillan's '*You've never had it so good!*' party of 1959: or compare Blair's New Labour with Attlee's post-war administration."

"Christ, Lucy, Tom's supposed to be the bleeding history nut! Have you been spending too much time with him, or something?" asked Barry.

"You've never had it; *so good!*" chortled Paul, turning to Barry for approval.

"Please! Let her finish," called Anna.

"No, it's OK," said Lucy. "That's all I wanted to say. I'm not upset, not in the least - we all know that these two keep their brains in their trousers. Finish what you were saying Tom."

"Err well, err I think I was just saying that the valence model sees voters as consumers ...."

"Which they are," observed Paul, eager to say something

that might relieve him from the contemptuous stare Anna was directing at him.

"I mean," continued Tom, "that New Labour was the result of a deliberate decision by a small group of people to re-position the Party so that it would maximise its appeal to the largest possible number of voters."

"Yeah, to win elections; to gain power. That's the whole point, der – stoopid!" argued Barry. "Ideological purity is no earthly use if it means that the democratic process will ensure you are permanently excluded from power. We've been through all this before; remember Michael Foot?"

"*Longest suicide note in history*," proclaimed Paul.

"It's not enough just to *understand* the world, you know," insisted Barry. "The point is to change it!"

"Do you realise that what you've just said is a direct quote from Karl Marx?" asked Tom, grinning sardonically. Lucy nodded her approval and opened her mouth as if about to speak.

"I couldn't give a monkey's!" exclaimed Barry. "The trouble with you and with all the rest of the 'chattering classes' for that matter, is that you're all so busy trying to understand everything – trying to keep yourselves *informed* – that you never actually *do* anything! You never take any action; none of you. In practical politics you do bugger all! You sit around at your precious meetings or march up and down Oxford Street but all you really want to do is to carp and criticise. Just because you know all the big words doesn't mean your vote counts for any more than mine, mate! They don't weigh them, you know? You think you understand exactly what's going on but the real movers and shakers can safely ignore you lot. Bunch of political bloody eunuchs you lefty intellectuals! The *real* working class wouldn't have any time for you, they never bloody have had. I know, mate, because I'm one of them!"

"And he reads *The Sun*," confirmed Lucy, nodding sagely.

"All I'm trying to do," countered Tom, resentment undisguised in his voice, "is to put forward a summary of one explanation concerning how we find ourselves in 2005 with two major parties having almost exactly similar programmes..."

"No they're not," objected Barry.

"Actually they are," said Antonia, soothingly. "Even on public spending and taxation it's fiscal year 2011 before their programmes actually diverge. The Tories are not arguing about cuts in actual spending; it's always cuts in the rate at which spending is set to increase. That's probably why Michael Howard decided to attack Blair personally: he wanted to say that he'd do the same things as Blair – only do them better."

"Dead right!" called Tom. "The main parties are all agreed on the desired objectives of economic prosperity, good schools and an effective health service. They're making their pitches to us as rival management teams....elections have become a process for implementing a sort of circulation of elites....that's why they use words like *cleaner* and *tougher* - because, basically, they are offering more of the same; just *managed* better."

"I agree!" called Anna, again to everyone's surprise. "That explains why the Liberal-Democrats are now more radical than Labour; the Libs know they won't form the next government so their programme can be a bit more risky – they know they won't have to make it work in practice..."

"Maybe that's where the *Trust* issue surrounding Blair has the potential to throw a spanner into the works," said Lucy. "Some voters will be happy with New Labour, generally, but very unhappy with Blair because of Iraq - OK I'm talking about myself now – so who do I vote for?"

"You vote Conservative in Battersea, of course," said Antonia, loudly.

"No, sorry, my dear, you evidently don't understand," countered Lucy. "I could never vote Conservative; I'm sure that if I tried, just as my hand held the stubby little black pencil they give you, as it hovered over the box where you mark your X, I know I'd be overwhelmed by some kind of cosmic seizure and my hand would drop off, or I'd be hit by lightning.....something dramatic like that."

"No, no, don't be so silly!" snapped Antonia, throwing herself back against her chair. "You might even get to enjoy it. For you, voting Conservative would be just like committing adultery and you won't know what a pleasure that is until you've tried it!"

With that, Antonia lifted her wine glass, drained it and so

missed the startled looks which shot to and fro between the other five people at the table. When Antonia set down her glass a couple of seconds later, Lucy was staring quizzically at Barry, while Tom was suddenly intent upon brushing a few breadcrumbs along the table cloth. Anna was smiling reassuringly at Tom, Barry was staring fiercely at Antonia and surreptitiously gesturing '*sssssh!*' with one finger held to his lips. Paul pretended to be busy pointing the neck of a wine bottle at the nearest empty glass.

"Wow," said Tom, still frowning at the cloth but unable to endure the continuing silence, "tricky business, politics!"

"And anyway," began Lucy, feeling stung into a response, "didn't you see Michael Howard on the box the other night actually saying *he* would have attacked Iraq to bring about regime-change even if it was held to be illegal? So don't ask me to get into bed with that bastard."

"Lucy, please!" called Barry.

"I'm not," hissed Antonia. "Least ways, not into *his* bed!"

"Blimey!" said Paul. "I thought we were talking about the election. Did I miss something?"

Tom held out both hands over the table.

"Ooh, err, look out," called Barry, laughing in desperation, "Tom's about to conduct a séance: *Are you there Comrade Trotsky? OOOO, Ohhhhh!*"

The sight of this made everyone laugh, including Antonia and Lucy. Anna smiled at Tom and said,

"Finish what you were saying, it was interesting. But try not to incite anyone to throw plates; this is my best dinner service."

"Well, all I wanted to add was," he resumed, "the observation that Blair is operating without reference to any recognisable body of socialist principles and consequently he's completely out of touch with ordinary Labour supporters..."

"Focus groups!" said Barry. "Try to keep up! We use focus groups to refine policies these days. They keep us much more in touch...The polls show..."

"Blair on TV the other night," intervened Anna, "did not strike me as being a man '*in touch*'."

"Frankly, I'm shocked and stunned!" announced Antonia,

looking at each of them in turn. "Barry's been telling me that you're all firmly on the side of Tony Blair and New Labour, but now I find that none of you has a good word to say for him."

"I have!" piped Barry.

"You don't count, Baz, darling. You're just a chancer – and a charmer – we all know that," laughed Antonia.

"My, my, Brendan. She *has* got your number alright," commented Lucy, sourly.

Another silence descended and this time Paul was the first to break.

"Let's go into the other room," he suggested. "The chairs are more comfortable in there, and I'll bring in the coffee…"

"Great," said Barry, "I'm just going to pop out the front for a fag."

"No coffee for me," said Lucy, following Anna into the kitchen.

"Hey boys, what about Chelsea winning the premiership, then?" trilled Antonia, still angry and now slightly tipsy. She anticipated that Anna and Lucy were about to be thoroughly bitchy about her over the dirty dishes in the kitchen and so decided she had nothing to lose by playing the *ladette* card. Paul trotted eagerly behind her into the living room, delighted to engage in speculation about the outcome of tomorrow night's semi-final matches in the Champions League.

"I think Liverpool can do it…." he began.

Lucy set down a pile of plates on the kitchen worktop and stood very still. Anna closed the door and then touched Lucy gently on her arm, trying to gauge her thoughts.

"He's gone," said Lucy. "This time he really has…he's not just having fun anymore; he's serious about this one."

Anna stroked Lucy's arm and craned around to look into her face, hidden as it was by the tresses of her hair. Lucy smiled briefly and tossed her head and shoulders as if throwing off an oppressive weight. Anna crouched to slip plates into the dishwasher.

"No worries," called Lucy with an obviously forced cheeriness. "I could feel myself detaching as I watched him watching her… He notices everything about her, follows her every move. It's almost as if he is offering his own willpower to inflate her next breath. That's not Barry, not our Brendan....not *my* Bazza. She has changed him. He is fascinated by her; he wants her so much I bet the hairs on his arms all point towards her like compass needles..."

"Oh Lucy," said Anna sympathetically, loading cutlery into the washer, "isn't it just plain, old-fashioned lust? Man facing forty, nubile beauty in her late twenties – offering to help him feel young again? Have you seen the silly grin on Paul's face when she looks at him?"

Anna snapped shut the dish-washer and punched the '*Start*' button more fiercely than was strictly necessary.

"No, this time it's different for Barry," insisted Lucy. "I know it and believe me, *she* knows it too. He's not weighing his chances like he does instinctively with any pretty woman. This time, Antonia decides where we go next. Not him and certainly not me."

"But she's a Tory!" exclaimed Anna, plaintively. "At least you've got Tom....."

* * *

Barry stood on the pavement in front of the house drawing deep breaths through a slim, dark cigar. Tom walked slowly towards him.

"Duty-frees from the States," said Barry. "I could give you a few packets if you'd like."

"No point, still don't smoke," came the reply, and they stood in silence for a few moments looking into the brightly-lit rooms. On the left, in the dining room, Anna and Lucy came and went clearing dishes, plates and glasses. To the right, Paul and Antonia sat facing each other in the living room, clearly in animated discussion.

"Got wonderful legs that girl," murmured Barry. "I can tell you they go on getting lovelier all the way to the top!"

"There was a letter for you today, from Penny," said Tom, quietly. "The first for some time."

"Ah, I was expecting there might be," replied Barry, still gazing appreciatively at Antonia.

"I've got it in the car if you want it."

"But do I? I'm sure I know what it'll say."

Tom turned towards him, looking faintly quizzical.

"I've only had to go up to Nottingham twice now since Christmas. Well it's hardly my fault if the needs of the business change...I have to go with the flow, you know. Anyway, poor old Penny-whistle has been getting a bit restless, starting making demands again – like they do!" sighed Barry. Tom stood next to him, watching Lucy re-enter the dining room and blow out the candles on the table.

"Make a wish, darling," thought Tom before turning to Barry and asking, "so where does that leave things, I mean with Penny?"

Barry dropped his cigar and crushed the butt, grinding it into the asphalt with his shoe.

"Up in the air, out on a limb; fucked if I know," he answered with a shrug. "You couldn't take her off my hands could you, old boy?" he asked, playfully.

"I don't think I'm..." began Tom.

"No, only joking," resumed Barry. "You're not in her league; but not to worry – I'll think of something..."

"So, do you want this letter or not?"

"Yeah, I'd better take it..."

Tom walked across to his car, unlocked the passenger door and reached into the glove-compartment. He handed the familiar, cream, envelope to Barry who had meanwhile flipped open the boot of a gleaming, new, BMW on the other side of the road. Barry tucked the letter under the carpet and slammed down the lid, waving cheerily back at Anna who was now summoning them from the front porch.

Chapter Eighteen

On the following Tuesday morning Lucy was surprised to receive a phone call at home from Penny. It was the first time they had spoken for many months.

"*Pen*! Darling!" shrieked Lucy when she realised who was at the other end of the phone-line. "Great to hear from you again, *Babes*! It's been simply ages. How're you doing? How's Crispin?"

"*Babes?* Wow, that takes me back a bit! I'm basically fine. Crispin should be away at school – he came home at the weekend and Gee's only just taken him back. Seems to think he's unhappy there, can't imagine why," answered Penny. "When you think what it costs...."

"Oh this is such an unexpected... you know I was thinking about you only yesterday, mmm yes, that's right, on the Bank Holiday. I was thinking how Barry doesn't get up to Nottingham so often these days, and regretting that I'd never managed to come up with him and spend a day with you..."

"Oh yes," said Penny, coldly. "Well, never mind, I'm coming south myself; later today in fact. I find I need some serious retail-therapy... How about we *do* lunch tomorrow?"

"I'd love to – hang on a mo – what's tomorrow? Wednesday! The Election's not 'til Thursday, of course. But I'm sure there's something else on...oh *knickers*, I'm supposed to be sorting-out stuff for the school jumble-sale...No fuck it! It's so long since we had a good old natter. Yeah, let's go for it!"

"Say, midday?"

"Yeah, kiddo; *High Noon* – somewhere in town? I'm sure I can park Alice with someone; call in a favour; you know how it is..."

"No, not really. We always had live-in help when Crispin was little, until he went away to school in fact."

"Oh, yes, well there you go! Anyway, where should I meet

you?"

"We always stay in that hotel next to Fitzroy Square, Do you know Fitzrovia?

"Fits what? Oh, the square! It's just along Warren Street isn't it? That'll be my nearest tube, and it's on the Victoria line..."

"I'm not sure, I always use cabs."

"Ha, yes, I remember. Is there anywhere we can go?"

"Yes, I'll book us a table at a little Italian I know around the corner in Cleveland Street. You can't miss it, aim for the Telecom Tower."

"Great. Look, give me your mobile number and I'll call you as soon as I pop up from the underground at Warren Street – or is Goodge Street nearer?"

"Lucy, darling, I've no idea..."

"Not to worry! Ooooh! I can't wait, it's been such ages!"

* * *

Penny recited her mobile phone number for Lucy to write down, ended with "Ciao!" then replaced the receiver and stared out of her bedroom window at the long sweep of manicured lawn leading down to the river bank.

'I'm going to miss this view,' she thought before turning away to complete packing her suitcase. She wished Lucy had not sounded so pleased to hear from her. She knew that what she planned would upset Lucy and end their friendship for a long time, if not forever.

'At least,' thought Penny, 'I've picked a restaurant I won't miss if Lucy makes a big scene and I find that I can't ever go there again.'

In the three, now nearly four, months since Christmas, Penny had grown increasingly irate with Barry's indecision and seeming neglect of their relationship. She blamed this largely on Lucy who, according to Barry, had produced some kind of hysterical breakdown at Christmas which she was now using as emotional blackmail to curtail the frequency of Barry's trips to Nottingham. According to Penny – and Cynthia strongly concurred with this assessment – Barry should by now have set her up properly, either locally or down in London, and divorces from their respective spouses should be well underway.

There had been nothing forthcoming from Graham to indicate that he would be putting significant properties in her name; so Barry had clearly got that all wrong. Meanwhile she had to endure Graham's constant questioning of where she was going, who she was meeting, when she would be back. She and Cynthia called this *'The Control Freak's Check-list'*.

"I'm sure he's ticking boxes on a clip-board when he phones me during the day," complained Penny to Cynthia, "and then I hear him creeping around on the landing outside my bedroom door every evening."

"Do you ever – you know - let him in?" Cynthia had enquired with a quiet, malicious, glee.

"Not since his birthday, last November – oh, and then again at New Year. Both times I was so completely pissed the old bloke who does the ruddy garden could have shagged me doggy-style and I'd have been none the wiser!" confessed Penny.

Cynthia, *bless her*, had found the perfect team of solicitors and a QC who could handle Graham's likely reaction once her affair with Barry was revealed. As for Lucy, well Penny thought that she herself could probably brow-beat Lucy into accepting a 'reasonable' settlement in about two hours, flat. After all, Lucy would be getting a nice little house in Clapham and some decent maintenance for the kids. Very little would change for Lucy, in fact, except that Barry wouldn't have to live with her any more...

Penny selected some more underwear for the trip and puzzled over two alternative dresses for evening wear. 'It's all for the best,' she re-assured herself, 'I just need to settle Lucy at a quiet table and explain to her gently how it's all over between her and Barry; *can't you see, he's with me now?* I mean she's got her kids – and she can't have any more – so that's OK....I know her instinct will be to hang-on to him...but she was always the one who claimed to be such a feminist at college – not me. Lucy, she recalled, had worn the T-shirt with *'This woman needs a man'* emblazoned across the front, and '...*like a fish needs a bicycle!*' across the back.

'Well, on your bike now dearie!' concluded Penny.

Outside she heard the tyres of a car crunching across the gravel driveway and she moved to the other window in time to see both Graham and Crispin emerge from the Lexus. Crispin wore his school uniform; his maroon blazer and cap contrasted vividly with the metallic blue of the car and the amber stones of the drive. Graham walked slowly to the back of the car and lifted Crispin's suitcase and brown leather satchel from the boot. The boy seemed upset and stood close to Graham who spoke a few words to him then lifted the boy's cap and ruffled his ginger hair. Crispin gripped his father around the waist and then jumped back when he glanced up and saw Penny at the window.

"I knew it!" she thought. "Poor little carrot-top. They probably got half-way to school before Crispin managed to sound sufficiently miserable and unhappy to persuade Gee to bring him back home. Well, I've done my best. If he wants to let Crispin become a day–boy that's their decision, not mine. I know I've said my piece. I'm not driving a thirty mile round-trip to his school twice a day. He'll just have to go somewhere more local. Anyway, he's Gee's problem now. "

* * *

The next day, on a cold grey London street, Lucy threw her arms around Penny when they met and Penny found herself reeling a couple of steps backwards.

"God, Penny you do look smashing!" gushed Lucy. "That's such a great jacket, bit revealing around the old cleavage 'tho, isn't it? And on a cold day too! Ever the fashion victim - I can see you haven't changed!"

"Less of the '*old* cleavage' if you don't mind," laughed Penny. "I think they're still holding up remarkably well – and not just because of the cold, thank you."

"They always did. And didn't you know it." Lucy threaded her arm through Penny's and then wondered in which direction they would need to start walking. "You really were the ultimate 'posh tart'," she bubbled, "and we *lesser mortals* always loved it when you vamped your way through the geeks at a party. I bet some of the sad little wankers have never recovered, even to this day..."

"The restaurant," announced Penny, guiding them across the street, "is just over there; with the hanging-baskets. Let's get out of this wind. Brrrr, you forget how it gusts and swirls around all these tall buildings."

Penny selected a table and they sat facing each other, the menus untouched in front of them, while she ordered their drinks. Penny sat back, trying to relax, expecting Lucy to launch into a long rigmarole of news about her children: how they were growing, what they were saying; all the usual kind of slightly self-deprecating parental reportage. Instead, Lucy offered Penny an American cigarette, leaned forward and with a huge smile across her face said;

"Well, darling, have I got news for you?"

Penny accepted the cigarette, smiled quizzically, and waited for her to continue. Lucy picked up Penny's lighter, frowning and rotating it in her fingers until she discovered how to spark the ignition. Penny stared back.

"I do hope you're not expecting me to feign interest in this boring bloody Election! You were always one of the *Reds under the Bed* Brigade, I seem to remember."

"I sometimes managed to be a Red *in the bed* too," replied Lucy, defensively.

"Oh yes, Bazza was a proper old Commie in those days, I seem to remember," said Penny. "My, how things change...you're still of the *bleeding heart* persuasion, I gather. Or is that your big news; you've seen the light?"

Lucy managed to light the cigarette and pout uncertainly before emitting a mouthful of smoke.

"No, nothing like that," she coughed. "Hold on to your hat, old girl, *I've* got a secret! Guess what?"

Penny blinked and frowned.

"Um, err, you're having a new kitchen?"

"No! God, am I normally so boring? No, think of something

much more exciting."

"Err, you've got a job?"

Lucy shook her head emphatically.

"Oh I don't know: you're planning to have a nose-job? You're having your tits done?"

Lucy frowned and shook her head again. Penny tried again;

"Err, you're on Crack Cocaine? No? You've rinsed all your credit-cards? You've been busted for shop-lifting? Give up, I don't know…"

"I knew you'd never guess," smiled Lucy, relaxing back in her chair and placing her hands on the table with the fingers interlaced. "This is it; I've got a secret lover! – There now; what do you think of that?"

Penny was so astonished she actually failed to light her cigarette and dropped her gold lighter onto the table. Her cigarette waggled up and down as her plush red lips puckered uncertainly.

"Don't look so shocked!" laughed Lucy. "Be happy for me!"

"But you're married!"

"Huh! Hark who's talking. So are you, but when did that stop you?"

"That's different; I mean we're different – horses for courses and all that."

"*Sisters under the skin,* we used to say."

"Did we? I thought that was something to do with wearing fur coats!"

"Penny!"

"Err, anyway; err tell me what he's like…"

"He's a really odd bloke…"

"No surprise there, then…"

"Definitely not your type at all, I'm relieved to say – and definitely not a bit like wicked old Brendan. But I think we're in love! It's all so exciting and utterly mad! It's all a horrible mess at home of course…but if I get to see Tom once a week or so it just about keeps me going."

"Wow!" breathed Penny. "Well done you! Is he good in bed?"

"Hey! Let's cut to the chase, why don't we?" shrieked Lucy. "Your priorities haven't changed have they? Actually, not bad I'd say – but of course I don't have your wealth of experience to draw upon... Oh, and this one can talk as well."

"No one I know, then," smiled Penny.

"Actually, I think you did meet Tom; when you and Graham stayed over with us the year before last, at Christmas. I'm sure he was there in the evening...I've been trying to remember..."

"Oh, good heavens! You weren't *at it* with him back then, were you?"

"No, no, I mean I probably always fancied him in that vague sort of way that you do, when you're married and stuff..."

"Not me; I'm never vague about it, dear," insisted Penny.

"But then one evening last autumn, when Barry was away in Nottingham – no doubt with *his* hands groping up some old slapper's skirt – we just sort of *came together* you might say!"

Penny coughed suddenly, cleared her throat and took a large gulp of gin and tonic. Clearly agitated, she stubbed out the cigarette she had only just lit.

"Does Barry know about this?" she enquired, sternly, long fingers crushing the white tube into a dainty ashtray.

"Jesus, no, don't be silly! It's not the kind of thing you tell the *old feller*, is it?"

"I guess not," whispered Penny, staring absently at the wall behind Lucy while trying to re-organise her own tumultuous thoughts.

"Penny?" asked Lucy, moving her head sideways, trying to meet Penny's eyes.

"Oh, sorry," she responded, "I was suddenly miles away... Let's order, shall we?"

The menu swam before Penny's gaze and she heard herself ordering something involving chicken.

"Oooh, That sounds nice," said Lucy. "I think I'll have the same, please."

The waiter departed and Penny tried to contribute once more to the conversation.

"I'm sorry, I can't picture this chap; *Tom* did you say his name was?"

"Err yes, Tom, Tom Cork. I can't tell you what a relief it is to tell someone at last. Just to speak his name; to be open at last."

"Tom Cork," mused Penny slowly.

"It's one of those names that sounds completely daft if you repeat it several times…"

"It does sound familiar. Maybe I did meet him that time. I'm usually terrible with names, but that one rings a distant bell, somehow…"

"I have to be careful not to mention him too often around the house. He's a mate of Barry's in an odd sort of way; they're not at all alike. But I sometimes catch myself about to say '*Oh Tom said so and so this afternoon….*' Mustn't give the game away. One careless slip could really let the cat out of the bag…."

"No one knows then?"

"I'm sure they don't. Except Anna – that's Paul's other half – she's twigged but she's had the good sense to maintain a diplomatic silence. She's never liked Brendan so I guess she'd probably say she couldn't blame me. She just gives me knowing looks sometimes. For all I know, she may even have the *hots* for Tom herself."

"Is he that attractive?"

"Well I think so; when you get to know him. Even Barry likes him – strange, that - but you know what men are like with each other; always having to be *one of the lads* , never being able to admit to having genuine feelings."

"Graham is never *one of the lads*, as you put it, but I know what you mean. For an otherwise articulate man, Graham has no ability at all to talk about his feelings. None whatsoever. So much so, in fact, I've begun to doubt whether he has any."

"Oh but he does, you can be sure of that," insisted Lucy. "Most men seem to have been rebuffed by their own fathers at some point in their childhood – I know Brendan was – and after that they daren't express their feelings because of the reception they fear they'll get…"

"Graham gets all intense and emotional; it's quite painful to watch, but then – nothing – *Pouf!* Gone – maybe he simply swallows it? There's none of what my friend Cynthia would call '*closure*'. Frankly, I'm not sure I want a man to talk too analytically about his feelings. It's all a bit wet isn't it, all that new-man, psycho-babble stuff? Now, Barry strikes me as having the balance about right. What you see is what you get with him, I imagine. I like that in a man. But Graham, well I don't know; talk about all lights blazing and no one home! He's amazingly articulate about money or with his pals at the golf club and all that; but alone with me he's just so feeble and awkward; I could scream... Actually, I do some times."

"I can imagine," chortled Lucy. "*A bugger when she's riled!*"

"What?"

"That's what Edward used to say about you."

"Oh, him! I'd forgotten about *him*; sorry you reminded me."

"Oh Pen; I'm so glad we can still talk so openly still. It's great; just like the old days!"

Penny stared at Lucy, who was again leaning back in her chair while the waiter silently offered her the wine list. Lucy looked totally baffled. Penny intervened, took the folder and scanned the names. Lucy watched with interest as she quickly selected an expensive Chablis. Penny met her eye.

"I don't know any of them," she shrugged, "but when in doubt I go for something a bit pricey." Lucy looked concerned, but commented brightly;

"That could almost be your philosophy for life."

"In a nutshell," agreed Penny. "But don't fret darling. This is my treat, or rather it's Graham's! We must drink a toast to the poor old sod when the bottle arrives. Anyway, now, do tell all. Like, how often do you manage to see this chap? It must be awkward with the kids in tow so much of the time."

"Oh, we have our ways; I sometimes wonder if the challenge and all the cloak and dagger stuff isn't part of the thrill. Of course, it can be nerve-wracking at times. Oh my God, Barry nearly caught us at it just before Christmas... I mean actually in bed, God! I can laugh about it now but it was really scary at the time. He's dead jealous; very possessive you know."

"Is he?" Penny observed dryly. "Is he really?"

"Oh but our best wheeze is our *driving lessons,*" Lucy held up two fingers from each hand and made the sign for quotation marks. "Brendan thinks they're a good idea and encourages them. Little does he know that all we do is nip round to Tom's house and ... and, well you know..."

"Shag?"

"Mmm, *make love* I'd prefer to say," giggled Lucy.

"No, dear, it's shagging; plain, old-fashioned *shagging*. We all do it – it's what makes the world go round."

"Penny, you are outrageous! This is all so new to me. Funny thing 'though, I met this woman the other night – a real ball-breaker I thought – and she said that I should try voting Conservative tomorrow; she said that I'd find it was nearly as much fun as committing adultery; *as if!*"

"Huh, I wouldn't go that far. The things they'll do to get people to vote...."

"No, I suppose the equivalent for you would be voting Labour."

"Ugh! I couldn't do that; I think I'd rather have another baby than vote for old slimy-chops Blair."

"Graham would probably divorce you on the spot if he thought you'd deserted the Tories."

"Hum, maybe worth a try then? Don't tempt me, darling... But seriously, when are you going to tell Barry?"

"Barry?" exclaimed Lucy.

"Yes, Barry – isn't that what you want to do?

"Err, no. Or rather yes; oh I don't know, I mean it's all so complicated. I mean I wouldn't trust Barry further than I could throw him. I did at first, you know, I wanted to believe he'd stay the course – but deep down inside I was never sure of him..."

"We're talking about you," insisted Penny. "What do *you* want?"

The waiter returned with a bottle and showed the label to Penny. She nodded and he poured a little into her glass and then stood back.

"Carry on," she snapped. "Just pour us two glasses, I'm sure it's fine." Then she eyed Lucy, expectantly.

"I don't know, I just don't know what to do for the best," sighed Lucy. "We are where we are. We muddle along; I see Tom when I can, he understands. He's very good with the kids; brilliant in fact. He knows the situation..."

"That's just it!" exclaimed Penny. "What is the situation?"

They both sat back in silence as another waiter brought their food. Plates were placed before them and dishes set upon the table. The waiter hovered nearby as if awaiting a further request; Penny waved him away.

"*Thank you,*" called Lucy to his departing back and then to Penny she added, "well, we just can't make plans...not at the moment."

"Why ever not? If you're happy with this Tom, why not just tell Barry and be done with it?"

"What? You are joking of course!" spluttered Lucy. "Tell Brendan? I should cocoa, mate!" Penny stared back, impassively and then skewered a small piece of chicken with her fork.

"Oh look Penny, you can't imagine what he's like," continued Lucy. "Barry's not all calm and collected like Graham, you know... There's no sweet reason with him. No shades of grey......"

Penny continued to stare at her, slowly and delicately moving her jaw as she chewed.

"Brendan would go ballistic!" stated Lucy. "He hates losing. He won't even let Emma win at draughts or Ludo... Christ alone knows how he'd react if he knew I was sleeping with Tom, but I predict *badly.*"

"You can't be sure," returned Penny. "I mean what if he's got someone else, got plans of his own?"

"Oh, I'm sure he has got someone, he may have several *other women* on the go, for all I know. With an ego like his to satisfy...I wouldn't be surprised. In fact, I did wonder if he wasn't shagging that Tory-bird Antonia who we met at Paul's the other night...I could just imagine him leering and saying to Paul, '*I'm only doing to her what Thatcher did to the country!'* Ugh! Men!"

Penny frowned and her mouth drew into a firm line;
"Tell him!" she demanded. "Or I bloody well will!"

"No, don't! I didn't tell you all this to get you involved," pleaded Lucy. Penny's expression softened and she smiled reassuringly.

"Don't worry darling," she cooed sweetly. "But I am *involved...* now."

"Oh, you're so kind," replied Lucy. "I should have known you'd take my side....but when it comes to Brendan, no one knows him like I do. He's such a creature of habit. Everyone imagines he's this great tearaway and adventurer. He encourages them to think that.

But really I know that he relies absolutely on having somewhere to come home to. A refuge - somewhere reliable; where he feels safe..."

"How can you be sure? What if he meets someone different, someone extra special?"

Lucy stopped eating and laid her cutlery together on the plate in a gesture of finality.

"To tell you the truth, Penny," she spoke quietly, "I can only see him leaving if he knew – I mean really knew – that he was going to have a son. He'd have to get some woman pregnant and he'd have to know it was a boy, and that it was his. He can be *very* focused you know. Can you imagine any fly-by-night dolly-bird or lap-dancer doing that for him? I can't.... Penny? Is there something wrong with your wine? You've gone very pale..."

Penny's mind raced; she imagined herself pregnant again and lying in some sterile clinic with her feet in stirrups and doctors prodding her vagina. She saw again that final, spinning, circle of blinding light and twitched involuntarily as she remembered the pain just before she passed out and Crispin was delivered by Caesarean Section. She stared bleakly at Lucy and looked increasingly pale as the colour drained from her cheeks. The wine glass trembled slightly in her right hand.

"No; why?" she answered suddenly.

"You've been holding your glass just under your nose for a while; you haven't taken a sip."

"Sorry, darling, I was listening to you; and thinking, but I really can't think what to say."

"You look so upset," said Lucy in her most soothing tone of voice. "I'm so sorry. I shouldn't have burdened you with all this."

"No, no, I'm glad you did. That's what friends are for, isn't it?"

"Promise you won't tell a living soul; not even Graham?"

"Oh darling," breathed Penny, starting to feel slightly better; a plan forming in her mind. "Who on earth would I tell? Certainly not Graham, I promise; he'd be the very last person...."

* * *

It was probably about one-thirty pm when Lucy apologised for having to leave and explained how she would have to be getting back to pick up the children. Penny sat drinking coffee until the waiter returned with her Amex card, then hurried the short distance back to her hotel. Within seconds of arriving in her room she was on the phone to Barry at his office.

"Now hear this!" chanted Penny in stentorian tones.

"*Penny-babes!*" burbled Barry, "hang on, I'm just going into the conference room.....That's better, we can talk freely now. You sound on good form."

"I am, oh I am," she trilled. "I'm just a simple lass from the provinces who suddenly finds herself foot-loose and fancy-free in the big city..."

"That's my girl; are you still up for it later this afternoon?"

"But, lover, don't you want to hear my news?"

"Let me guess; you snapped-up something reassuringly expensive in Harrods this morning?"

"Time to be serious, Brendan. I can call you Brendan, can't I? Like Lucy does."

There was a silence as she waited for him to reply. He made no answer.

"I had lunch just now with an old chum of mine from college; Miss Lucy Gardener, or should I say Mrs Brendan Sands...Correct; your wife no less."

"Oh, that Lucy," he said blankly, trying hard to anticipate what might be coming next.

"Don't you want to hear what we talked about, it was most interesting. We talked about men, of course, but surprisingly not just about you..."

"Go on. Naturally I assume you mentioned Brad Pitt and George Clooney in the same breath..."

"How about Tom Cork?"

"Corky? Why would you mention....."

"He and Lucy are lovers; have been since last year. You're not the only one playing away from home, darling!"

"Say that again!"

"Your wife, Lucy,"

"Yes, I know who my fucking wife is!"

"Well her; she has a lover. His name is Tom Cork. So if we're going to talk about your *fucking wife,* well that's who's *fucking* your fucking wife! And she thinks it's hilarious fun to hop into bed with him while you, poor sap, think they're out and about having driving lessons."

"The filthy, lying, two-faced little bitch! How could she? And with him! You wait 'till I get...You know who he is, don't you?"

"Well I must confess, the name did sound rather familiar, but I just couldn't place it: not for love nor money."

"Love nor money, *my arse!* It's his address we were using for your letters to me! I should think the name did sound familiar. He's known all about *us* since last summer!"

"Well he obviously hasn't spilled the beans to Lucy; that's a good sign, isn't it?"

"Good sign? You think that justifies him shagging her brains out? Why hasn't he told her? Or, if he has, what are they up to? I don't fucking believe this!"

"Now Barry, darling; please try not to be quite so unpleasant. Just calm down," soothed Penny, deliberately sounding as patronising as she possibly could. "Lucy did beg me not to tell anyone; but she was just so *bursting* to tell me her BIG secret! And I thought you'd want to be the last to know."

"Too fucking right. Wait 'till I catch that smarmy git Cork!"

"Barry, now listen to me, I only want to say this once," ordered Penny as firmly as she could. "I want you to take a deep breath and stop beating your chest like some alpha-male chimpanzee..."

"For Christ's sake, Pen!"

"Listen to me! I arranged to meet Lucy today because I've had it up to here with being *the other woman.* I had every intention of telling her about us and getting her to accept that it is all over between you two..."

"Now who's playing the alpha-male?"

"Listen. Here's what I want you to do; *do not* make a big song and dance about Lucy and her silly boyfriend. Just let it go; you've got me now; we were going to have to tell her sooner or later and now she's just made it so much easier for us. You can even tell the kids *'It's all Mummy's fault!'* if that makes you feel any better. It's what you would normally call a *'Result!'* If you'd only let yourself stop and think about it."

"Oh, yeah; be happy, why not? Some poncey bleedin' dipstick is poking my wife and you want me to say '*Well done, old boy. Jolly Good Show...no, don't mind me, you just carry on...* No fucking way!"

"Barry, you're not listening. Can't you see that this is exactly what we needed to happen? She can't make a scene if you leave her now..."

"I'll give her a fucking scene alright!"

"OK, that's it. You know where I am. It's about two o'clock now. If we have a future, lover-boy, you get yourself over here by three at the latest. Forget about Lucy and your pathetic macho posturing; *I'm* what matters now! I want you, here with me, within the hour; otherwise we're history! It's make your mind up time, darling. You've got to choose – me or her; now tell me, just how difficult is that?"

"Pen! Penny! Pen listen!" he called out, but she had gone and the line just fed him static.

"Fucking bitch! Fucking bastards, the fucking pair of them!" he yelled angrily and punched the wall so hard that blood sprang from beneath the broken skin on his knuckles.

"Ouch! Fucking bloody hell!" he swore again, bending almost double to nurse his wounded hand. "The poxy, cheating, two-timing, scheming little cow!"

Chapter Nineteen

Barry walked quickly across the office and fled into the washroom. Only Paul looked up as he passed; everyone else had heard him swearing and shouting but no one dared to enquire as to the nature of the problem. Barry ran the cold tap over his throbbing hand and stared at his reflection in the mirror. He pushed back the thick wave of dark hair which had fallen across his forehead. His face felt hot and the mirror showed him looking flushed. He splashed cold water onto his face and neck, then patted himself dry with a clean towel. He snatched a metal comb from his trouser pocket and swept it through his curls.

"I'm going out!" he called to Paul as he grabbed his jacket from the chair-back and then trotted down the echoing stone stairway and out to his car. He dialled his home number and listened to it ringing unanswered as he started the engine and pulled out into the traffic. The answering service cut in.

"Call me on the mobile as soon as you get in," he growled.

Halted in the traffic at the next red light, he scrolled down to Tom's home number and pressed the green button. The traffic moved off and his car lurched forward. Tom would, of course, be at work he realised. The answering machine began its recital and Barry left a message;

"Call me on my mobile as soon as you get back, you fucking slimy degenerate apology for a fucking slimy bleeding ponce! Oh, it's Barry, by the way – in case you hadn't guessed."

He felt a little better after that and concentrated once again on the traffic, flowing steadily towards Vauxhall. He noticed the signage for the Congestion Charge Zone and dialled the office with his left thumb.

"Madge? It's Barry. Do us a congestion charge for me BMW will you, I'm about to enter Ken's Magic Kingdom."

"Sure," replied the woman, "hang on a mo – Paul's got a message for you. Oh, OK. Barry are you still there? Paul says, '*Can you phone Antonia?*' "

"Ta," said Barry. "See you later."

At the next lights he scrolled down to Antonia's mobile number, it rang a few times and then she suddenly said,

"Hello my darling!"

"How're doing Babe? Hey, '*are you thinking what I'm thinking?*'"

Silence; Antonia did not reply. Barry waited a moment then resumed,

"I got your message, I was about to phone; are you alright kiddo? Sandra said you weren't in this morning."

"No, I had a doctor's appointment."

"You OK?"

"Oh yes, it's not like an illness...."

"What's not?"

"Pregnancy. Barry, I'm pregnant!"

"Christ!"

* * *

Smoke came off the tyres of Barry's car as he hit the brakes forcefully and skidded to a halt just a few millimetres from the rear of a stationary vehicle. The traffic was queuing for the lights at Vauxhall Cross. The driver behind blasted his horn and Barry dropped the handset of his phone.

"Barry, darling, are you there?" Antonia called, "Barry? Barry?"

He reached down into the foot-well in front of the passenger's seat and had to unclip his seat-belt before he could reach the phone.

"Bugger!" he groaned as his fingers skimmed the plastic casing.

"Barry, speak to me!" pleaded Antonia.

Barry managed to drag the phone across the carpet, his fingers curled around it just as a cacophony of car horns started behind him.

"Fuck off!" he yelled, snatched the phone and accidentally selected '*Loudspeaker*' by pressing the wrong button..

"Jesus fucking wept!" he blasphemed as a burly man in a paint-splashed T-shirt pounded on the roof of the car. Barry turned, snarling, in his seat and gave the man two fingers and a stream of abuse. The man punched the side window and the car rocked;

"You ain't s'posed to use a bleedin' phone in the car you stupid bleedin' twat!" yelled the van driver.

"Fuck you!" yelled Barry, slammed down the accelerator and executed a high-speed U-turn which forced the man to jump aside or have his feet run-over. Barry flung the phone down onto the passenger's seat and drove as fast as he could down the other side of the carriageway. The car lurched sideways as he suddenly turned left away from the traffic and zigzagged more slowly through the side streets before stopping and parking on a yellow line. The phone emitted a pathetic bleep and glowed briefly on the soft leather upholstery.

He realised that his heart was pounding, his breath came in savage spasms and he was sweating. He opened the glove compartment and reached inside, he pulled out a tissue and some chewing-gum. His eyes fell upon the keys to Tom's flat which lay gleaming on the dark grey leather. Barry held the phone with an unsteady hand and concentrated on re-dialling Antonia's number.

"Barry!" she cried. "What happened just now?"

"I was driving," he said quietly. "I nearly crashed!"

Antonia burst into tears;

"All I heard was you saying '*bugger*' and then '*fuck off*' and something else about Jesus. How do you imagine that felt?" she sobbed. "It's not how I expected the father of my child to respond to the news..."

Barry sighed and began a long heart-felt apology, trying to console her at every opportunity. The sound of her voice calmed him and he began to feel aroused, thinking of her sitting on her bed, beautiful, vulnerable and – above all – pregnant with his child. He explained that he had some complex negotiations to conclude that afternoon but promised that he would come to see her as soon as possible.

"I'll be there before dark," he whispered, "and we'll go out to celebrate, whatever you want to do, my darling!"

Barry rolled his wrist so that he could see the time on his watch. "Twenty past two," he noted. "And what did Penny say; '*Get here by three or we're history!*' Well OK, girlie, let's be history but let's make some history first; let's see if we can't cook-up a little confrontation they'll all remember!"

"Barry, are you still there, Barry?" sniffed Antonia.

"Always here for you darling, always," he replied. "But at this moment, I have to go. Looks like my meeting's about to kick off..."

"Love you!" she called.

"Love you too, angel-face," he whispered.

Barry called the office again.

"Madge – give me Paul, please.... Paul? Hi! What's the name of that school across the Common from you, the one where Corky teaches?"

"Why do you need to know that?"

"Never you mind; I just need to give him a message."

"Thrales something," replied Paul. "We went to an open day there with Jason. I think Anna called it Hester Thrale's High or The Hester Thrale Academy, something like that."

"Thanks," said Barry and ended the call.

He obtained the school's phone number from directory enquiries and politely asked the woman who answered if he could speak to Mr Cork, the History teacher.

"Connecting you to History..." she said, without a hint of irony.

"Err, hello?"

"I need to speak to Tom Cork, is he there?"

"No, he's teaching."

"It's very important....matter of life and death; can't you get him?"

"Hang-on, let me find his timetable; um, yes, he might be in here in about ten minutes – that's if he doesn't go straight to the Staffroom."

"Can't you find him for me?"

"Not really, hang on.....err I've just been told that he'll definitely be here at four for a meeting; then after that he's got the Year Nine parents' evening – he'll be in the Dining Hall for that, from five 'till seven-thirty."

"What's your name, *sunshine*? ...... Well OK, Trev, now you just listen to me," snapped Barry. "Take down this number, go find Corky and tell him he's got to phone Barry....yes that's right.... urgent! Have you got that? Good, then stop poncing about and just do it!"

Barry scrolled down the memory on his phone, found Graham's mobile number and pressed the green button.

"Graham? It's Barry, can you talk? Bit of a crisis I'm afraid."

"Yes," answered Graham, sounding concerned, "I'm at home with Crispin, as it happens – Penny's away in London..."

"Yes, I know. In fact that's why I'm calling..."

"Hang on old boy; I'm just going into the Study. Ah, that's better; the lad always has the TV on so loud. Go ahead."

"Look, there's no easy way to tell you this – and I may yet be proved wrong – but, well, they say there's no smoke without fire, don't they?"

"Barry? What's she done now?"

"Look, it may nothing, but – well I have had my suspicions again recently – but I didn't want to say anything, didn't want to alarm you..."

"There is a man, isn't there? I knew it!"

"All I can say is that she has checked out of the hotel..."

"But we're not expecting her back here until tomorrow night – so where will she be tonight?"

"Leave it with me," said Barry. "I'll track her down. The hotel porter called me when she said she was going. He knows all the cabbies; I'll bung him a few notes and find out where she went... I'll call you."

"I don't like the sound of this, not at all," grumbled Graham. "This can't go on. I want it settled; for the boy's sake as much as my own. It's beginning to affect his school-work. Barry, you do what you can, but we're coming to London. We'll be on the road in about twenty minutes. I'll call you from the car and you can update me... and Barry?"

"Yes, Graham,"

"Thank you, thank you so much. I know this is not easy for you, but you really are a good friend."

"Don't mention it old chap, wish I could say it's a pleasure...."

"Bye now, Barry. Catch you later."

"Hang on Graham, you still there? Good, see if you can find Penny's address book...."

"That should be easy enough, she keeps it in the kitchen – unless she's taken it with her. Are you on to something?"

"It's a long shot," said Barry clenching his teeth and trying to sound like a TV detective, "the initials *TC* might be important; see if you can find an address in London for anyone with those initials...It's worth a try...see you later."

* * *

Tom Cork, meanwhile, had finished his class and dawdled into the History Office with a large bundle of folders clutched in his arms. In fact he entered the room backwards, using his bottom to push down the lever-handle while finishing an exchange of words with a pupil outside in the corridor.

"I'm knackered!" exclaimed Tom, depositing the folders onto an already untidy desk, "I'm going to need Class 'A' drugs to get through this bloody Parents' Evening tonight."

Trevor looked up from his paperwork.

"There's been some 'geezer' – and I do mean *geezer* – on the phone for you. Someone called 'Barry'. He said it was very urgent and that he needed to speak to you; sounded quite rude in fact, and very aggressive."

Trevor waved the piece of paper bearing Barry's mobile number and Tom reached to take it from him.

"Not going to be bad news, I hope," muttered Trevor, inquisitively.

"Dunno; Barry does tend to exaggerate – probably just wants to borrow my car or something like that. Anyway, I'll call him;

then we'll all know!"

"Barry? Hello, it's Tom. You called?"

"Hello, you treacherous, two-faced, lying bastard scum-bag!"

"Barry?"

"It's about Lucy, you tosser! You've been shagging my wife behind my back."

"I wouldn't put it like that..."

"Fuck off! How would you describe it, you bleeding stuck-up git? You wait 'till I ...."

"Barry, calm down, you're upset."

"Upset? Upset? I'm bleeding livid! I trusted you, you cunt!"

"Where's Lucy?"

"I trusted you and this is how you repay me?"

"I haven't done anything to you, Barry. My feelings for Lucy have nothing to do with you, nothing at all."

"Don't talk to me about your *feelings;* gropings would be more like it. How d'you think I feel?"

"Calm down, Barry. Let me speak to Lucy..."

"Shut it! What about all the letters?"

"What about them?"

"Did you tell Lucy I was getting letters from Penny, and then use that as a trick to slime your way into her knickers?"

"I never mentioned the letters to Lucy. It was difficult, but I never told her anything about them. As far as I know, Lucy believes you're often unfaithful to her but I don't believe she either knows - or cares – who you sleep with."

"What do you mean, she doesn't care? It was the letters, wasn't it? They made you think it would be alright, didn't they? Come on, admit it! What's sauce for the goose is sauce for the gander. That's what you thought, didn't you?"

"OK Barry, now listen to me. I agree we need to talk, all three of us together; you and Lucy and me. I've got a Parent's Evening at school today so I won't be home until about eight at the earliest. Why don't you come round to my place then – or we could meet on neutral ground if you prefer..."

"Neutral ground? Fuck off! I'll see you when and where I want to see you – bastard!"

Trevor had been following Tom's end of the conversation with growing interest, especially when Barry had raised his voice and sworn at Tom.

"Anything wrong?" asked Trevor with pretend innocence.

"Fuck off!" exclaimed Tom and left the room, slamming the door behind him. The pile of folders on Tom's already chaotic desk moved geologically and then gradually, one by one, slid to the edge of the desk and dropped noisily onto the floor. Trevor watched with growing satisfaction.

Barry sat still for a moment, contemplating his own eyes reflected in the driving mirror. He checked the wing mirror and noticed a traffic warden appear around the corner of the street and start heading his way. He grimaced, started the engine, selected Penny's mobile number and pulled away from the kerb.

"Penny, darling! I'm trying to keep to your deadline," he assured her. "I had to drop everything at work…"

"Well, as you know, sweetie," giggled Penny, "I'm always ready to drop everything for you."

"Penny, this is serious," claimed Barry, trying to make his voice sound sombre. "I've just had a call from bloody Graham. What a bastard control-freak that man is."

"Tell me about it!" she scoffed.

"Look, he's having you watched at the hotel."

"What?"

"He's got some private detective following you. He knows you met Lucy earlier."

"So what?" challenged Penny.

"So I can't come and see you now, can I? Not without Graham knowing."

"Oh for fuck's sake!" exclaimed Penny. "I really have had it with him; this is just too bloody much!"

"It's OK, don't panic, dear," soothed Barry. "Good ole' Bazza's thought of everything, as per usual."

"What can we do? I *must* see you today, without fail."

"Here's what I want you to do. Put your hat and coat on – look as if you're going out shopping *again* – go down to Reception and ask the Porter to call you a cab; tell him that you're going to Tate

Modern for the afternoon. He'll remember that."

"OK," she repeated, "I get a cab to the Tate, then what?"

"No! Not the Tate. You must say *'Tate Modern'*, it's the new one; on the South Bank."

"I knew that," she lied. "Then what; are you expecting me to look at pictures?"

"No, 'course not, but I'll meet you there – you can't miss the main entrance, it's a sort of long, wide slope leading down into an enormous exhibition hall."

"What's on?"

"Fucked if I know... But I'll find you there and whisk you away. And I'll make damned sure we're not followed."

"OK, this had better work. I'm leaving now, see you there."

* * *

Tom walked into the staffroom and was relieved to find it looked empty. Tea and coffee cups had been left on every available surface but, unusually, there was no one loitering by the pigeon holes or slumped mournfully in any of the armchairs. He hurried across to the payphone on the wall in the far corner, pulling a phone-card from his wallet as he went. He dialled Lucy's home number and stood nervously, his back to the room, staring out of the window.

"Tom, hi! It's you," she began cheerily. "We don't normally get to hear from you at this time of day." He heard Emma whining *'Who is it?'* in the background and Lucy saying *'Only Tom'* in reply.

"Lucy...."

"Tom, what is it?"

"This is very difficult...you don't know yet, do you?"

"Know what?"

"Barry knows!"

"Knows what?"

"He knows..."

"About us? Gordon Bennett! Are you sure?"

"Yes!"

"Abso-blooming-lutely?"

"Yes, yes, yes!"

"Oh my good God! How?"

"Search me! He just rang me at school and started tearing lumps off me..."

"But how in hell....?"

"I do not know. I mean I haven't seen you since the driving lesson on Saturday – and if he'd figured anything out then he wouldn't have waited until now – would he?"

"No not Barry. He'd have confronted us as soon as...."

"Hasn't he called you?"

"There was a message to call him on the answering service – he just sounded grumpy – I played it back when I came in after seeing Pe....nny. Oh, no – she can't have; she wouldn't, would she?"

"Who? Wouldn't do what?"

"Penny, you know my old friend from Nottingham? She's in town – I had lunch with her and..."

"You did what?" screamed Tom; Lucy gulped with surprise at the volume of his voice.

"We just had lunch, and I told her about us.....OK?"

"No not OK; very much *not* OK!"

"Why - and anyway, how come you know so much about Penny all of a sudden?"

"Because, Lucy my darling, Penny is the *old tart* in Nottingham with whom your husband has been conducting an affair!"

"What? When did you find that out?"

Tom drew a deep breath, stared out of the window at the roof tops and the swaying trees, sighed and took in another breath.

"Tom? What is it? Who told you?"

"Lucy I'm terribly sorry, I've dreaded having to tell you this, but I've known since last summer."

Another pause; now it was Lucy's turn to draw a deep breath.

"I do *not* believe you! I just....I'm ....I'm completely lost for words. How the hell could you know that, and not tell me? After all that we've been through."

"I know because Barry told her to use my address for letters she wanted to write to him..."

"Love letters? From Penny? To Barry? That's downright unbelievable in itself. Good God above! Letters from someone who can barely write, sent to someone who can hardly read?"

"That's why he had a key to my…"

"So that he could pop round and pick up his little *billets doux* from his mistress? And you didn't bother to tell me? That hurts, Tom. That really hurts!"

"I couldn't!"

"Why ever not?"

"It would have been a betrayal; a betrayal of trust…"

"Hang on a minute, mate. What betrayal? Who the hell would you have been betraying?"

"Barry…"

"B'B'Barry? But you've been to bed with his wife! [*Emma, leave the room! No, right now! Go and see what Alice is doing. And close the door behind you!*]"

"Lucy, look we can't talk like this; I need to see you. You've got the kids there; I'm in the staffroom at school…"

"Just a minute, what makes you think I want to see you?"

"Lucy please don't; I can explain everything – you have to see…"

"All I can see is that you helped my husband have an affair, didn't see any need to tell me what was going on – *Betrayal Number One*. And then, you started having an affair with me – *Betrayal Number Two*."

"Who was I betraying then, in the second case?"

"Brendan, you idiot! You were sleeping with your best friend's wife! Do I have to sing you the fucking song?"

"God, Lucy, if only you knew the *angst* I've suffered over those fucking letters!"

"I don't want to know."

"But it was a question of principle…"

"Oh no; if you say *Moral High Ground* I promise you I will hang up, right now!"

"I could not tell you about the letters without first warning Barry I was going to tell you…."

"Why?"

"Because we are, *or were*, mates. I wasn't in love with you; I mean I didn't yet know I was in love with you, when the letters started…"

"But you were my friend – or did I get that wrong too?"

"Yes, I was your friend, always; and Barry will confirm I told him I was unhappy to be involved in..."

"Oh yes, I can just see Brendan stepping forward to give you a character reference on that!"

"Darling, when it started – I mean the letters – as far as I could judge, his adultery with Penny was an issue between him and you; it wasn't for me to tell you what your husband was up to with *your* erstwhile best friend."

"And later; after that, when it was *my* turn to commit adultery – with your *very* willing assistance - I seem to remember?"

"Well, then I still couldn't tell you without first telling Barry that that was what I was going to do."

"I'm not sure I follow your convoluted logic, but my question is still, *Why?* It's not as if you needed a second UN Resolution or to arrange anything involving the French!"

"What? No, I mean that if I warned Barry he would want to know why I had to tell you. If I hadn't told you in August, why did I suddenly have to tell you in October? He'd want to know what had changed..."

"And what had changed?"

"You; you had changed. I mean *we,* we had both changed. My feelings for you had changed, totally changed. I would have had to tell him that I was in love with you. But I couldn't could I? Going public on our affair had to be your decision – not mine. You had more at stake than I did..."

"Humph! God preserve us from men of principle! And now that silly old tart Penny has cut through your paralysing pseudo-moral dilemma at a stroke. I bet she wouldn't recognise a *Gordian Knot* if it bit her fat bum!"

"So when can I see you?"

"Don't know. I've got Brendan to face first. I'm certainly not going to phone him now! I won't let him dump me over the phone. Anyway, he'd better be ready to come clean about shagging Penny before he starts on accusing me."

"Be careful! Look, I've got one of these fucking awful Parents' Evenings tonight, I won't be home till eight. I must see you, I really must...."

"Don't know, I need to think – stay away from here; I will call you. Have you got that?"

"Yes, darling, I understand. I know how you must feel...."

"I doubt it. I doubt it very much."

"But Lucy...." Tom blinked and stared down at the handset he held clutched in his sweating palm. His lips moved but emitted no sound. He listened, shook the receiver vigorously and then listened again. Lucy had hung-up; all he could hear was the crisp, unwavering dialling tone.

"Fucking bloody bollocks!" exclaimed Tom to the seemingly empty room.

A newspaper rustled from behind a pillar over to his right and he heard the Headmaster's voice say;

"My word, Mr Cork, what a challenging social life you do lead!"

Chapter Twenty

Penny paid off her taxi and stood still, buffeted by the cold wind which pushed against the immense walls of the former power station. Feeling threatened by an imminent shower of rain and pursued by the chill, northern greyness of her life with Graham, she teetered on her high heels down the long concrete ramp towards the anonymity of the Turbine Hall. Above her, large black letters on an orange banner proclaimed '*COMING SOON : FRIDA KAHLO*'. Glass doors slid apart automatically and she was suddenly inside a huge, vibrant, industrial space. She heard a growling mechanical rumble as if some lingering echo of the departed turbines still reverberated from deep within the bricks and steel and concrete.

Bewildered, she walked past a chattering knot of school children and dodged wandering tourists who strolled along, gazing up into the great void above them. Instinctively she made for some stairs and quickly rose to the vantage point of a dark mezzanine platform. She spun round, expecting to see several pairs of eyes watching her. She wanted to know the face of whoever Graham had paid to follow her. The harsh sound of drilling and the high-pitched yelps of electric screw-drivers assailed her ears. On the vast floor below teams of workmen were hammering timbers and boards, preparing for some new exhibition. She turned again; a Japanese man raised his camera and blatantly photographed her before hurrying away, unsmiling. Powerless, she stuck out her tongue at his departing back; a saw-blade screeched and hammer blows echoed around the cavernous vault. Another group of school-kids babbled down the stairway; somewhere it seemed the ghostly turbine blades milled slowly on.

Penny looked to her left and spotted a gift shop through oblique glass walls. She hurried towards it, seeing ahead of her, in distant daylight, the grey sinews of the Millennium Bridge and a ferry-boat chugging along the river. She swept into the shop and rapidly selected a souvenir T-shirt and a box of colouring pencils for Crispin, ensuring first that the Tate logo appeared prominently on each pencil as well as on the box. From a rack next to the check-out she snatched six postcards:

"Four of these cards are of the same work; *'Whistler's Mother'*. You must really dig it!" said the neat boy at the pay-desk. Penny shrugged her shoulders and shook her head, puzzled why her choice could matter to him if it didn't to her.

"Err, fine, cheers," she mumbled and dashed out of the shop clutching her purchases in a bag which also proclaimed the gallery's identity. She hurried towards the daylight. In the dark under-croft a pigeon flew up, startling her. The wind was shaking a screen of silver birch trees; her high-heels tap-tapped urgently until she halted and glanced around. Out here by the Thames the wind felt even colder and Penny scowled at the milky-brown furrows scored across the seething river. Another pleasure-boat pounded past, a few determined tourists shivering on its wind-swept decks. No one lingered on the footbridge and, on the river-bank, passers-by all quickened their steps. It was a day for going places, not for pausing to spy, admire the ragged skyline or monitor the clanking heart of the huddled city.

Her phone rang and she snatched it from hand-bag;
"Barry! I've never felt so paranoid. I feel like everyone's watching me and reporting my every move to Graham. Get me away from here before I freeze to death." she pleaded.

"Some fucking springtime this is!" he exclaimed.

A black school girl yelled *'Hello!'* and waved down mightily to her from a balcony somewhere high on the towering brickwork; Penny hid her face and hurried away, keeping close to the wall.

"I'm waiting in the car, just by the entrance," added Barry, reassuringly.

"Can't see you; I'm walking past a restaurant," she called back. A diner looked up and stared at her, chewing a mouthful of food as he watched her pass. Barry's voice reached her again;

"That's right, keep going to the corner....There, I can see you now, look up....I'm here, over to your right....you're looking straight at me! The silver Beamer– behind the black cabs."

"Oh yes! Oh yes; I've got you!" she shouted.

Barry pushed open the passenger door and she fell into the car, her tight skirt riding high up her legs as she thrust her face towards him to be kissed.

"Drive away, drive away quickly!" she exhorted, "so they don't have time to get a cab!"

Barry was delighted that his own invention had worked so well. Penny was convinced that she was being followed. He could not resist asking her to look back to see if anyone ran to the cab rank.

"We'll be OK," she claimed, breathlessly. "They'll never get a cab to go south of the river."

"Darling, we already are *south of the river!*" he laughed.

"Are we? Well I wouldn't know; I get so confused."

Barry accelerated dramatically and turned sharply right into Southwark Street.

"A taxi! A taxi!" called Penny anxiously. "There's a black cab right behind us!"

Under the railway bridge the lights ahead went to amber and Barry accelerated again, the tyres squealing in protest as they lurched into a left turn and sped away down Blackfriars Road.

"We've lost them! They're stuck at the lights," chirped Penny. "Oh well done darling, well done!"

Barry smiled triumphantly and enjoyed the gentle pressure of Penny's hand in his lap as they drove along Lambeth Road towards the Albert Embankment.

"Where are we going?" asked Penny drowsily.

Barry tapped the side of his nose;

"Wait and see," he answered. "It's not the Ritz but a friend of mine is away this week and we can use his flat for the afternoon and then go out somewhere nice this evening."

"Oh goodie," smiled Penny, wriggling comfortably in her seat. "That's just what this girl needs – a nice warm bed then a rip-roaring night on the town. Put the pedal to the metal, Baz!"

"You're the boss!" he roared.

Penny's phone rang. She looked at Barry then reached into her handbag.

"Shit! What if it's bloody Gee?" she asked.

"You'd better look at the display; it should tell you who...."

"Oh!" she exclaimed, "it says, '*Barry home*'. That can only be Lucy."

"Corky must have phoned her," snapped Barry. "Don't answer it; let them stew."

"I'll press the button which signals '*I'm engaged*,'" quipped Penny and Barry scowled, accelerated fiercely and overtook two cars on the inside before having to brake sharply to avoid a bus. The phone emitted two beeps to indicate that a message had been left.

"Don't listen to it!" ordered Barry. "She'll only be bitching that you told me about her having it away with old bugger-lugs."

Penny giggled and her right hand moved to squeeze his crotch.

Lucy put down the phone and went upstairs to find the children. All three girls were in the bedroom which Alice shared with Cherie. The room was in even greater disorder than usual; drawers and cupboards hung open and clothes and toys were scattered everywhere. In the middle of the floor a large suitcase lay open and inside it was a growing pyramid of toys and clothes to which all three were busily contributing.

"Where did you get that case?" asked Lucy, quietly.

"Emma got it for us from the cupboard in Daddy's office," said Cherie, matter-of-factly. "It's our going away case."

"But why?" asked Lucy.

"Cos Emma says we're all going to live at Tom's house because you don't like Daddy anymore," said Cherie. Alice nodded and Emma stared impassively up at Lucy.

Lucy stood still for a moment that would later seem like an hour, then she slowly bent her knees and sank down onto the floor beside the three little girls. Her arms reached out to embrace Emma and Alice. Cherie clambered across the pyramid to fling her arms around Lucy's neck. Tears filled Lucy's eyes;

"No one is leaving. No one is leaving this house!" she sobbed.

"Then what about Daddy?" asked Emma flatly.

"I can't answer that," whispered Lucy. "We'll have to wait till he comes home, then we'll just have to see."

* * *

At the end of Wandsworth Road, they reached the lights where Barry turned left into Cedars Road. Ahead of them the green expanse of Clapham Common was intermittently brightened by flashes of sunlight. Penny glanced out of the side window as they swept onto the main road and noticed the distant outline of the bandstand, ornate and black against the bursting freshness of new leaves. A short distance further on, Barry swung the car into a side street on the right and cruised slowly until he found a parking space into which he could reverse.

"We're here?" said Penny, her intonation rising to make the words into a question.

"Yup," said Barry, "but just sit tight a mo, honey, while I call the office – we don't want them buzzing us for the next couple of hours do we?"

Penny smiled and flipped down the sun-visor so that she could check her make-up in the mirror. She fluffed her hair, lifting and tugging it with her fingers. Barry stared at his phone, switched on the car radio and opened his door.

"Stay in the warm, darling," he suggested, "I'm just going outside to get more bars on my phone."

"Be soon," muttered Penny, her lips stretched into an exaggerated oval as she applied fresh lipstick.

Barry buttoned the jacket of his dark suit as he strode a few paces across the road and dialled Graham's mobile; then he stood watching Penny through the back window of the car. Graham answered very quickly.

"South London," reported Barry, truthfully.

"I found an address; someone called *Tom Cork* in *London, SW11*, probably not far from where you live," claimed Graham.

"That fits," replied Barry, trying to sound clipped and gritty as he imagined he should. "What's your position?"

"I'm on the M1; I'd estimate an hour or more north of London..."

"Then it'll take you about another hour to get across the centre and down to Clapham – don't head for my place, 'though..."

"No, best not," agreed Graham.

"I know," suggested Barry, "can you get to Clapham High Street, it'll be signed as the A24?"

"No problem," answered Graham, "I know my way to the Oval, and then I'll keep on going south....."

"That's it. Well there's a McDonald's on the High Street – Crispin will spot it, I'm sure. Park up and call me when you're there; I'll come and find you. Oh, and Graham..."

"Yes?"

"Best not to call me 'till you're in Clapham. We don't want my phone going off at a delicate moment while I'm on, err... on *the case*, do we?"

Barry could barely stifle his laughter as he realised how close he had come to saying '*on the job!*'. He barely heard Graham say farewell and wish him luck, before the desire to roar out loud overwhelmed him and Barry snapped his phone shut, steadying himself against the rear of the car.

"You look mighty pleased with yourself, lover," said Penny as he ushered her through the gate and along the tiled path to Tom's front door.

"I'm so glad that old Colin is away up north; he's a journalist, covering the election you know. And *yours truly* has his keys...." grinned Barry, holding up the keys to Tom's flat.

"And are you?" enquired Penny as he opened the door.

"Am I what?"

"Mine, *truly*?"

Barry kissed her full on the mouth so that her newly applied lipstick transferred to his lips and he tasted its waxy perfume on his tongue.

Upstairs in Tom's flat Barry hurried Penny towards the bedroom hoping she would not hesitate at the sight of bachelor squalor. Penny removed her jacket and began to unbutton her blouse in one continuous movement.

"God! This place takes me back a bit; it's just like being at college all over again," she smiled, trying to flutter her eyelids and look wicked at the same time. "I love variety!" she squealed, kicking off her shoes and undoing a zip. She stepped out of her skirt with practised ease and put one stockinged foot up on the bed, inviting Barry to begin by unclipping her suspenders.

"Oh you little vixen!" he breathed and they fell to writhing pleasurably on the bed before Barry kicked Tom's duvet onto the floor and proceeded to make love to Penny in every position he could imagine. Penny was delighted by the vigour and inventiveness of his assault and she shouted her encouragement and whooped ecstatically half an hour later as the bed shook and the room resounded with his climactic grunts.

Barry let out one last roar of sexual release and slid heavily to the floor. Penny rolled over and smiled down on him as he lay sweating and panting on the carpet. She did not realise, of course, that Barry had just begun to take his revenge upon both Tom and Lucy by having raucous sex with her on Tom's bed.

"I think you broke Colin's bedside light when you kicked over the table, Bazza."

"Who gives a fuck?" murmured Barry, struggling to stay awake.

"Journalists drink, don't they?" suggested Penny.

"Course they do," confirmed Barry, his eyes still closed.

"Well, go see if there's anything drinkable in his 'fridge, will you darling? I need something cold and alcoholic."

"Huh; you've got me!" groaned Barry, rising reluctantly to his feet and shuffling, stark naked, into the kitchen. He swung open the 'fridge door and was surprised to find two bottles of sparkling white wine lying nicely chilled on the middle shelf.

"So sorry, Luce," he muttered as he lifted one bottle out, read the label and pressed its cold green glass against his forehead. He opened the freezer compartment and saw that its closely packed contents were heavily encrusted with ice.

"Dear me, Corky, your fridge needs to be defrosted....Here, let me help," and with that Barry pulled the electrical plug from its wall socket. The compressor gave a final shudder and Barry checked that the light stayed off when he opened the door.

He gave the bottle of *Cava* a vigorous shake and returned to the bedroom.

"No glasses I'm afraid," he announced, "But here's a little light refreshment!" He unwrapped the foil and twisted away the wire restraint. Seconds later the cork shot across the room with a satisfying 'pop' and a rush of bubbles splashed across Penny and the bed-sheet. He shook the bottle again and sprayed more of its contents across the wall and the carpet.

"Try that for size," he said, holding the now half empty bottle out for Penny to take. "Don't worry, darling. I'll go and fetch another from the fridge."

Barry returned with the second bottle, spraying more wine over Penny and the bed.

"I hope you're going to lick that up!" she squealed with delight as the cold wine coursed over her breasts and stomach. Barry grinned and took a refreshing swig from the bottle. Penny reached up to take it from him,

"Look," she smiled, "I've got just the lips for taking on big cocks and champagne bottles. Have you ever noticed the similarity in their shapes?"

Barry laughed and reached down to pick up Penny's handbag. She watched him quizzically, taking another sip from the bottle.

"Let's hear Lucy's message," said Barry, his thumb twitching as he accessed her message service.

"What's your PIN?" he enquired.

"6969!" she giggled.

"Fuck me! It is too!" laughed Barry as the recording of Lucy's voice began to play in his ear.

"Penny, you sad old tart!" she began quietly, *"I guess I always knew you were an alley cat and I just wanted you to know that really I don't mind – don't mind at all. In fact I'm surprised by how little I mind. I don't need to wish you happiness together; so I won't…..Just have to say that well, you probably really do deserve each other. I mean with your big bum and his big head your romance should last a lunchtime……you sad BITCH! Anyway, thank you and goodbye, you're welcome to each other*

– and I feel so much better now. Honesty is like that; you should try it sometime."

"The hypocritical little bitch," shouted Barry, handing the phone to Penny so that she could hear the message replay.

"You wouldn't think that she and her fancy man were banging away last weekend in this..." he stopped himself just in time from finishing with "...*very bed!*" Penny frowned, not hearing him as she concentrated on Lucy's message.

Barry emptied the second wine bottle and tossed it onto the crumpled duvet which lay between the bed and the window. Penny smiled, reached towards him and drew her red fingernails slowly down his back.

"Come here!" she said as he twisted around. Barry rolled on top of her then rose to his knees. He gathered her in his arms and lifted her bodily as he stood upright on the floor.

"Oh Bazza!" she gasped and flung her arms and legs around him, her ankles locking behind his back. Barry carried her through into the front room and planted her buttocks directly onto Tom's desk. Drawing breath, he noticed the cover of <u>The End of the Affair</u>, where it still lay on the floor. He stooped to pick it up and placed it on the desk before gripping Penny again and shifting her bodily onto the pages of the open book. He bent forward, kissing her deeply, letting her hands guide his re-awakened penis into the liquid bower between her legs. Barry grunted and thrust against her with his hips. Behind her his hands swept the desk clear of other books and papers, which all crashed noisily to the floor.

"Baz, oh Baz! Yes my Bazza!" moaned Penny, sinking her nails into his shoulders and squirming eagerly as he rocked against her and the whole desk vibrated against the wall. She shouted "Fuck me! Fuck me!" as loudly as she could and lifted her pelvis, twitching with pleasure in response to Barry's urgent pumping. The pages of the book creased and tore under their combined weight, absorbing bodily fluids in spreading stains. A large poster-print rattled on the wall and then fell forward, smashing to the floor with the sound of breaking glass. Penny closed her eyes and Barry sobbed, "My baby!" as he came.

Finished at last, Barry slid gently away from her and collapsed into the swivel chair. Languidly he raised one foot to the edge of the desk and pushed himself backwards. The casters skimmed briefly over the carpet, then snagged and stopped. Barry's weight and momentum toppled the chair over backwards, depositing him with his head and shoulders on the sofa and his legs knocking a bowl of flowers off the coffee-table.

Barry roared with pleasure to see the broken vase and the dark water dribbling onto the carpet. Penny stared at him with a guilty smile. Tom's phone rang.

"Christ! What time is it?" demanded Barry, clambering to his feet and returning to the bedroom for his watch. Moments later, Penny found him dressing hurriedly;

"I can't go out just yet," she began, "I need to bathe and tidy myself up."

"That's fine, take your time, darling," he answered reassuringly. "We've got all night. No, I just want to go and have it out with Lucy – I want to lay down some rules. She's not to let that wanker anywhere near my kids. So, look, have yourself a nice warm bath and then I'll be back and ready to party!"

"Hurry back; don't be too long!" she said, kissing him again and reaching to unhook Tom's dressing-gown from the back of the bedroom door.

"I'll start running the bath for you..." he called.

* * *

It was just before seven in the evening when Barry walked into McDonald's looking around for Graham. The brightly-lit interior was thronged with customers in shell-suits, hoodies or bulging Lycra, all guzzling burgers and fries or sucking drinks from huge wax-paper cartons. Graham and a small boy, who looked only about ten years old, sat at a table by themselves. They seemed isolated as if they had travelled through time and space to get there. The boy wore a startling maroon-coloured school blazer and sported a matching cap with a yellow band around its segmented crown. Graham wore a grey gabardine raincoat with epaulettes on the shoulders; the type that used to be called a 'trench' coat when anyone still remembered the trenches. There was an empty coffee cup on the table in front of Graham and a large, dark brown, trilby hat rested close to his fingers. The boy was painstakingly shredding a plastic box which had once held his hamburger. Barry approached, expecting to be repulsed by an invisible force-field which surely separated these two alien beings from the other denizens of the restaurant.

"Graham!" called Barry, "have you been waiting here long?"

"No, no; we've just had a little refreshment; but quite long enough, thank you. What news?"

"Well," began Barry, flicking his eyes from Graham to the boy and back again. "I think you could say we have located our quarry."

"It's OK," replied Graham, fingering the brow of his hat, "we can speak openly in front of Crispin. The lad knows his mother has been unwell and that bad people have taken advantage of her good-nature..."

Crispin tore the last recognisable portion of the box in half and then began to force all the fragments into Graham's coffee cup. Barry looked away.

"Well they're not far from here, within walking distance," he confirmed. "They were in the flat all afternoon. The man went out by himself not long ago, my guess is to get more booze or fags, and I expect him to return shortly..."

"Right!" announced Graham, rising to his feet and donning the ridiculous hat. "I think we'll watch and wait for a while and then, when I judge the moment is right, we'll knock on the door and introduce ourselves, formally, as it were."

The boy also stood and all three filed out into the street.

"This way," indicated Barry and led them along the busy street to the edge of the Common by Holy Trinity Church. The trio continued along North Side, past Graham Greene's old residence, taking the same route that Tom and Lucy had walked that evening last September when their own affair had begun.

Chapter Twenty One

In the Dining Hall of The Hester Thrale Academy, Tom stared coldly into the puffy face of Kelvin Spindle's mother. She looked like being the last of the Year Nine parents he would have to confront that evening. Behind her stretched the ranks of now empty chairs in considerable disarray where the hordes of parents had sat waiting their turn at the teacher's table. Tom glanced to his left and noticed that Trevor, like most of the other teachers, had now finished dealing with his queue and was smirking happily as he bundled-up his record-books and registers.

"......so you can see why he finds it all so bleedin' boring!" concluded Mother Spindle and folded her arms to await Tom's reply.

Tom frowned thoughtfully; he had not been listening to at least the last four minutes of her tirade and so had only the sketchiest notion of what had caused her to risk missing tonight's episode of *East Enders* .

"Well, that's very true," offered Tom. "I'll speak to Mr Hunter in the morning and see if we can't make Kevin an exception...."

"Kelvin," she corrected him. "His name's *Kelvin*!"

"Quite," groaned Tom, "Kelvin, as you say .... Do please remind him that my door is always open...any little problem..."

Mrs Spindle drew back and looked puzzled, she had been expecting Tom to offer some defence against her criticism of the National Curriculum in general and of his teaching style in particular.

"Well, then..." she said.

"Exactly," agreed Tom and pushed back his chair with a harsh scraping sound which he hoped would be sufficient to indicate that their interview was at an end. "Thank you so much for coming to see me."

"Humph!" replied Mrs Spindle and waddled away muttering venomously.

* * *

"That's the house," announced Barry as they stopped at the front gate, "She's in there...in the flat on the first floor."

"Right!" said Graham, grimly, "I think we'll cross over to the other side – pretend to be walking on the Common, that sort of thing – just until we've taken stock of the situation..."

"Good," said Barry, "well I'll let you take-over now. I've been here most of the afternoon and, frankly, I'm due a break."

"Of course! Of course!" agreed Graham. "I can handle it from here."

They shook hands and Barry walked quickly away, without a backward glance until, with a sigh of relief, he sank into the driver's seat of his car. Reaching into his jacket, Barry tugged out his phone and selected Antonia's home number.

* * *

Tom dodged between the tables and chairs, speeding up as he reached the corridor and breaking into a run when he emerged into the car-park and could see his car. He threw two plastic shopping bags containing folders and paperwork onto the backseat and drove towards Battersea as fast as he could. He was halted by a red traffic light outside Balham Underground Station and thought back to his researches last autumn into *The Blitz* and the flying bombs of the *'Doodlebug Summer'*. Passing Clapham South and turning left into The Avenue, he looked towards the Mount Pond and remembered telling Lucy how a V1 really had landed there, exactly as Graham Greene related in *The End of The Affair.* Tom thought of Lucy and saw again her dark curls trembling against the carpet that first time they had made love.

He knew that arriving back so late in the evening would present him with a parking problem and sure enough he was two streets from his flat before he found a space. Locking the car, he hurried along the street towards home, a carrier bag in each hand. Two figures stood at the edge of the Common, opposite his front gate. The man wore a hat and a long raincoat, giving him the appearance of a spy or a sleuth in some 1950's 'B' movie. The boy looked equally old-fashioned, wearing the nostalgic, cap-and-blazer ensemble favoured by pay-through-the-nose Preparatory Schools.

"Parkis? It can't be; Parkis and The Boy?" thought Tom, associating the strange looking man with the obsessively diligent private investigator whom Bendrix had engaged to follow Sarah. "Surely they should be down along Cedars Road, sprinkling traces of white powder on the doorbells of flats, trying to track down the ghost of Smythe."

Tom grimaced at the sight of the boy's pallor and the thinness of his white legs, visible between grey flannel shorts and crumpled woollen socks. The man noticed Tom and looked away, tugging the boy's hand as he did so.

"Poor little bugger," thought Tom as he reached the garden gate and kicked it open. He felt their eyes on his back as he strode down the path.

* * *

Feeling the need to pee, Tom hurried up the stairs, quickly unlocked the door to his flat and wandered first into the bathroom. He failed to notice that the light was already on and, without thinking, pulled the chord. The light went out and a woman screamed. Baffled, Tom stretched out his hand to pull the chord again, slipped on the wet floor and fell heavily against the toilet bowl. Before he could react, the light snapped back on again and he looked up to see a completely naked woman, dripping water and soap bubbles, standing directly over him, clutching the light chord. Their eyes met and Penny suddenly realised just how much of her he could see from down on the floor. She gasped, pulled the chord once more and splashed back into the bath yelling,

"Get out! Get out! Get out!"

Tom rubbed his head, then his eyes, and felt the dampness of the floor soaking through his trousers.

"You're still in here!" yelled Penny from behind him in the darkness.

"What?" asked Tom, struggling to rise to his feet.

"Go away!" she shrieked.

"I'm trying to," he growled, "but this *is* my bloody bathroom! You're in the wrong flat, lady."

As soon as he stepped into the hallway, Tom heard a swirl of water and a grunt as she threw her weight against the door and shot the bolt home.

"I don't know who you are," he called out, "but I live here and I need to use the bog, pretty pronto!"

"Barry said you're supposed to be away this week," she called back.

"Bugger Barry!" he retorted.

Tom looked into the bedroom and saw the dishevelled bedding and a woman's clothes scattered across the floor. Entering the living room he darted forward to rescue the fallen vase but realised it was broken and felt the remaining water spill through his fingers as he cradled the broken china. Then he took in the overturned chair and the chaos of books and papers on the floor below his desk.

"Christ all bleeding mighty!" he blasphemed and hurried back towards the bathroom. He hammered on the door.

"Give me a minute!" she yelled in response. Tom looked down at his trousers which were soaking wet all down one side. He quickly undid his belt and stepped out of the wet garment before striding across to the wardrobe.

* * *

Graham held the gate open for Crispin and they approached the house along the front path. They peered at the three alternative door bells which, confusingly, were numbered '1', '2' and 'A'. Graham pressed firmly on number one and a few moments later heard Jack Patterson grumbling his way towards the door.

"If you're canvassing for the bleedin' election, you can fuck right off!" exclaimed Jack even before the door was fully open. He reeled back at the sight of Graham and Crispin standing on the step.

"Oh my bleedin' good Gawd!" cried Jack, "It's the Law! What the 'ell do you two want?"

"Shennan's the name," announced Graham, "and I'm looking for my wife!"

"Well I haven't got her," snapped Jack.

"We know she's in there," insisted Graham.

"Fuckin.....Oh, hold on a minute, you'll be wanting upstairs. That's the local bleedin' knockin' shop! He's been at it all afternoon, you should 'ave 'eard the carry-on. Shoutin' and bangin' - my missus thought they'd have the bleedin' ceiling down on our 'eads at any minute! Fuckin' disgraceful I call it. If that's your wife mate, she needs taking in hand."

"Out of my way!" cried Graham, pushing past Mr Patterson and taking the stairs two at a time.

"She needs a right old slappin' – they both do!" called Jack. "Joanie, Joanie come out here, quick; Corky's having a *domestic*!"

Crispin moved to slip past and feared that Jack was about to stop him. The boy halted, looked around, then kicked Jack fiercely on the shin bone and scampered away up the stairs after his father. Jack bent low, rubbing his shin and yelling curses after the boy.

"Joanie," he cried, "the little bleeder's just kicked me...."

* * *

Penny emerged cautiously from the bathroom pointing Tom's nail scissors ahead of her as a defence. She wore Tom's blue towelling bathrobe and had Lucy's pink towel wrapped around her hair. Tom turned from the wardrobe, holding a pair of jeans in front of him,

"My name's Tom. I live here..."

Graham reached the first landing and pounded on the door with his fists.

"Police! Open up!" he shouted.

"What the hell?" began Tom, pulling open the door and jumping aside as Graham flew into the hallway. Penny screamed and dashed towards the front room. Tom saw a small, fast moving, red and white blur rush after her calling,

"Mummy! Mummy!"

Graham took off his hat and faced Tom squarely.

"I ought to have you horse-whipped," cried Graham.

"Parkis!" spluttered Tom. "What *the fuck* is going on?"

"You!" said Graham, poking him in the chest, "have had unlawful carnal knowledge of my wife!"

"I have never seen her before....I've just come home from work, you saw me! ....Oh, but hold up; her name isn't *Penny* is it by any chance?"

"You know damned well it is!" shouted Graham.

"Well she's been carrying on with Brendan Sands, that's Barry you idiot!" exclaimed Tom.

"Oh no you don't!" growled Graham. "It's entirely thanks to Barry that I've found your sordid little love nest."

"Oh, for fuck's sake," whined Tom. "Let's get her story shall we, before you go and murder the wrong bloke?"

They found Penny sitting on the sofa, shivering and sobbing and being comforted by Crispin who had also set upright the swivel chair. The pink towel had slipped down to her shoulders and Penny's wet hair clung limply to her forehead.

"Now then, young lady, I want the truth," began Graham, setting his hat down decisively on Tom's desk.

"Please stop yelling at everyone," cried Tom, dancing on one leg as he sought to remedy his trouserless state. "This will be a whole lot easier if you just calm down and listen as well as asking your questions."

Graham snarled but made no reply because Penny released an enormous sob which filled the room.

"Oh God, I'm so upset!" she wailed. "Barry brought me here to Colin's flat because he said you were having me watched at the hotel...."

"I'm not Colin, I'm Tom! This is my flat."

"I wasn't watching you, Barry was. And who is Colin?" demanded Graham. "Is he another of your paramours?"

"No. Colin is person who owns this flat; he's a journalist," sobbed Penny.

"It's my flat, I own it," insisted Tom. "Well, actually, my brother does…"

"No, Barry told me…."

"Bugger Barry!" snorted Tom, zipping his fly and remembering that he urgently needed to go to the toilet.

Graham pulled Penny's address book from the pocket of his coat and thumbed through it.

"This address appears in your book under the name of 'T. Cork'" he stated.

"Hurrah!" called Tom. "That's me T. Cork, Thomas Cork, aka Tom or sometimes even *Corky*."

"Aha!" lunged Graham, "so how come you are in my wife's address book, yet you claim that you don't even know her?"

"Because of Barry, don't you see – it all leads back to Barry! He gave her my address for the letters – to deceive Lucy, don't you see?"

"No I don't see! I don't see at all!" replied Graham angrily. "I'll tell you what I do see! I see you and my wife together in your flat, you with your trousers off, her in a state of complete *deshabille* at eight o'clock in the evening and evidence of,

of…."

"Of what?" insisted Tom.

"Of *goings on*! According to the brute downstairs you were *carrying on* all afternoon, and here she is; I mean, look at the state of her, and just look at your bedroom. It's disgraceful!"

Open-mouthed, Penny gazed pathetically around the room, her confused eyes moving from Graham to Tom and then back again. Her crying had spread her make-up and mascara into two black circles around her eyes. Her face was now as pale as Crispin's who still stood protectively at her side, gently stroking the top of her head. The robe had slipped open and both men could see her delicate pink nipples.

"Cover yourself up woman, for heaven's sake!" ordered Graham and she clasped the edges of the robe across her chest and held them tightly with one hand.

"I've been at work all day. At school; teaching. You and the boy were standing out there on the Common when I came home," protested Tom. "I had to change my trousers because the others got soaked when I went to use the bathroom; and I still do need to go pretty desperately, by the way."

Graham frowned,

"Penny? What do you have to say for yourself? Has this man only just come in?" Penny nodded, sniffled and sobbed.

"I'm sorry, I didn't catch that," insisted Graham.

"No, I mean *yes!*" she sobbed, "Colin – err I mean Tom – has only just come in. I was in the bath, that's why I'm undressed. He slipped on the floor. Go and look at the water if you don't believe me!"

"So, who was it? Who were you with?" rasped Graham.

They waited. Penny closed her eyes, bowed her head and sobbed quietly. Crispin stroked her head frantically until she reached up, clasped his hand, and murmured, "Gently, please darling."

"I'm waiting," said Graham, coldly.

"Isn't it obvious?" she whispered. "Even to you?"

"Say it! I want to hear you say it!" insisted Graham. Penny sniffed and snuffled. Crispin produced a large white handkerchief from his pocket and offered it to her. Penny blew her nose loudly and wiped black mascara onto the white linen.

"I confess," she began, "that I, Penelope Elizabeth Shennan, have reached the end of my tether....For God's sake Graham, I've had enough! You're suffocating me! Whatever I've done, you drove me to it! Look at the way we live! When Barry came along I thought he was my last chance! I had to take it! Can't you see that? He's so alive. He's fun to be with; I can't go on being one of your porcelain ornaments locked away in some display cabinet. It just isn't fair....So yes! Yes I did spend all afternoon in bed with Barry. He had me twice in the bedroom and then right there – on that desk. And I loved it! Do you hear me: I needed it and I *absolutely loved it!*"

Penny collapsed; bent double, wracked by sobbing. Crispin threw his arms across her back. Graham stood like a statue, staring over her head at the wind-rippled foliage of the trees stretching away across the Common. A tear sprang to his right eye and then another rolled from his left.

"I've been such a fool," he whispered hoarsely. "I don't know where or how...I'm going to need ..."

"You need me, don't you? You do still need me? Barry is just such a lying bastard..." choked Penny.

Tom felt embarrassed to be listening to this part of the conversation and silently withdrew, intending to relieve himself and get the kettle on ready to brew a therapeutic pot of tea. As soon as he reached the end of the hall his shoes splashed into the puddle of clear water which had spread from under the 'fridge and now reached across the kitchen floor.

"What the...?" he mouthed, opening first the 'fridge door then the freezer. A small waterfall cascaded down as soon as the door-seal was broken. He saw immediately the discarded plug, pushed it back into the wall socket, and jumped as the motor revived and began frantically pumping gas to return the system to its normal temperature.

"Barry, you spiteful fucking bastard," he growled, spreading newspapers and cloths across the flood. He grabbed the washing-up bowl and began dumping into it the sodden cardboard packaging which held the ruined contents of the freezer compartment.

Tom heard the rush of bathwater draining down into the gulley below the kitchen window and for a moment he feared another disaster. Dashing into the hallway he encountered Graham, standing very subdued outside the bathroom door.

"My wife's getting dressed, we'll be on our way soon..."

"I'm sorry about....well everything," said Tom. "Can I offer you a cup of tea?"

"No, but thanks all the same. We'll be heading back to the hotel; I'm a bit shaken actually...It's been a bit of a *to do*. Don't think I could drive all the way home tonight."

Tom nodded, wishing to appear sympathetic, and noticed that Graham had removed his overcoat and loosened his tie. Already he looked more normal. Crispin appeared. He too had changed; the cap and school blazer had gone and he now sported a T-shirt bearing an image of the Tate Modern drawn in yellow and red lines on a grey cloth.

"Can I have some paper, please sir?" asked the boy, clutching a box of coloured pencils also marked '*Tate*'.

"Of course," said Tom and led him through into the front room. On Tom's desk lay the remains of the postcards depicting *Whistler's Mother;* all four had been meticulously shredded. Feeling tired and numb, Tom stood at the window staring out across the Common waiting for Penny and Graham to leave. Crispin stood at the desk, drawing frantically on the paper Tom had given him.

After about ten minutes Graham at last called Crispin and then came into the room to ensure that the boy had picked-up his cap and blazer.

"Err, there's your overcoat, and the hat," mentioned Tom while behind him the boy slid all the blank paper and the coloured pencils into the 'Tate' bag. Graham frowned, stepped to where the coat lay on a chair and retrieved Penny's address book before turning again to Tom,

"Could you burn the coat and the hat?" he asked. "I never want to see them again; not ever."

Penny did not come to say goodbye. Tom heard them go downstairs and watched from the window as they crossed the road onto the Common and walked back towards Clapham Old Town. The two adults each held one of the boy's hands and he seemed happy to be walking between them at last.

"Goodbye Parkis," muttered Tom. "Goodbye Young Parkis! Goodbye Penny!"

* * *

The boy had left a single piece of paper on the desk next to the torn remains of the postcards. Tom turned it over and gazed at the child's drawing on the other side. Crispin had sketched the outline of a saloon car and had been busy colouring it blue when Graham had called him away. He had drawn the unhappy faces of a man and a woman in the front window of the car. The man wore a brown hat and the woman had ruffled red hair. Behind them, in a separate window was the face of a beaming child. Tom was about to feel glad that the child was smiling until he looked below the car and saw that Crispin had depicted the vehicle in mid-air, speeding over the edge of a cliff.

The phone rang.

"Lucy! Oh thank God it's you."

"Tom, have you seen Barry?" she asked.

"No, but I'd like to – I've had all-sorts going on here, I can tell you, and it's all because of *him*!"

"Well if he rings or turns up..."

"I doubt he will...But can I see you?"

"Not just yet. Simon's here with me. We're waiting for Brendan. Simon wants to speak to him, and so do I."

"And me? When might you want to speak to me?"

"Maybe not tonight. Don't press me, I need time. There's a lot to consider..."

"Where do you think he is?"

"Barry? No one knows. Simon thinks he'll be with Penny. Paul is sure he's with Antonia. Me? I don't know what to think – I don't even know if I care anymore."

"He's definitely not with Penny...."

"How do you know that?"

"Penny was here .....it's a long story, but basically she was here all afternoon with Barry; while I was at work..."

"Why?"

"Barry brought her here, made love to her in my bed and then again on my desk – you should see the mess!"

"I'd rather not..."

"Then he seems to have tried to set up a situation where I would come home, Penny would be flitting around in her undies and then Penny's old man would burst in through the front door...and shoot me, or something!"

"What? So that Graham would think you and Penny were lovers

and Barry would be in the clear....?"

"Exactly!"

"It didn't work did it?"

"Very nearly; I mean it was obviously never going to work in the long term...much too unlikely...Utterly *Bazza* 'though, when you think about it. Then it all became a bit of a bedroom farce, you know people coming and going through different doors, total confusion over identities – Barry had told Penny I was Colin..."

"Colin!" exclaimed Lucy. "Not Colin the old Trotskyite? Sorry, I shouldn't laugh..."

"No, go ahead, even I can laugh about it now; of course it wasn't quite so funny at the time. All it really needed was a vicar without any trousers to suddenly jump out of the wardrobe. It came close to that; those two nutters downstairs tried to put their oar in. It seems Penny and Barry made a lot of noise when they were humping...Upset our Mrs P. something dreadful!"

"Ugh! Too much detail," recoiled Lucy. "But that sort of behaviour is exactly what you'd expect from Barry; it's so animal. You know, like dogs marking their territory. He didn't piss on your bed did he?"

"Don't think so, but I've had to change all the bedding. It was all pretty grim. It was obviously important to him to fuck Penny in the same bed he knew you'd been in with me - and then to do it again on top of my books. One of them is completely ruined...all soggy and torn..."

"Which one?"

"Greene, *The End of The Affair*, strangely enough. For months it's been lying on the floor; Barry must have seen it, picked it up, and deliberately soiled it. Funny, I was thinking about it again on the way home too....."

"Must be a coincidence; Brendan doesn't do literary symbolism – does he?"

"Search me; he's your husband. This was certainly pretty literal..."

"*Was!* He *was* my husband. He's not after this, not after today."

"And Crispin; dear God, that poor little sod is going to need major therapy. It's unforgivable that Graham and Barry involved him in this."

"Oh it's unbearable....my three are all in pieces because they don't understand what's happening – and why the hell should they? So, I think we can safely assume that Barry's happily ensconced beneath Antonia's fragrant duvet and ..... "

"So, should I come round?"

"No you shouldn't. Don't keep asking that. It isn't just me that is involved with you... I come with a ready-made family."

"I know that; when did I ever make your children an issue or a problem between us?"

"No you didn't. You've been very considerate, but this situation is very disturbing for them. You can say that they are not a problem for you – but I have to decide if *you* are a problem for *them*. That's a tough one, and it can't be hurried. I'm not going to slip you in beside me as an instant replacement 'Daddy'. Real life doesn't go like that..."

Tom sighed loudly and could not think what to say. All he managed was,

"You're right of course."

"Mmm," breathed Lucy, "keep saying that and we'll get on fine..."

"I yearn for you," sighed Tom.

"Shouldn't it be '*I yearn for you, tragically*'?" she countered.

"Oh, yeah. Ex-PFC Wintergreen...."

"Oh Tom, is that all you ever do?" she mocked, "recognise quotations?"

"That-is-correct!" he answered, robotically. "*That's some catch, that Catch 22.*"

Chapter Twenty Two

The next day, 5th May 2005, was the date Tony Blair had chosen for Britain's General Election. Tom went off to work as usual, came home, picked up his polling card and went out to vote. By six in the evening he was back and standing in his front room, sipping tea and staring morosely out over the Common. His door bell rang.

"Oh what now?" he cursed, walking to the tall window situated directly above the front door. He raised the bottom sash and, assuming that the caller was a Labour Party worker reminding him to get out there and vote, he leaned over the sill and shouted,

"You're too late, I've already done it!"

Lucy's dark curls appeared as she stepped backwards from the front door, and her face smiled up at him.

"Me too; but do you think you should boast about it quite so loudly?"

"Lucy!" he mouthed. "Don't go away, I'll be right down."

Tom sat Lucy on the sofa and stood looking at her, one hand raised as if about to scratch his left ear.

"I can't believe you're really here, again – at last," he said.

"Well I am, so don't go on about it. You really have voted, haven't you?"

"Yes."

"Can I ask who for?"

"You can, but I'm afraid I can only reveal that if you agree to sleep with me."

"Mmm, that could explain why the opinion polls are never entirely accurate…"

"It could add a whole new meaning to *exit* polls!"

"Tom, be serious, please!"

"Sorry, ma'am. Oh, alright, you win, I held my nose and voted Labour, *again*. I voted for Martin Linton. He's probably a good bloke in private but I've never met him...."

"Did he canvass your vote?"

"No,"

"Will you see him between now and the next election?"

"Probably not,"

"What's his voting record like..."

"Absolutely appalling; on everything except hunting with dogs he's been pretty much a loyal Blairite..."

"Iraq?"

"Voted for the war!"

"University top-up fees?"

"Voted for them too!"

"Identity cards? Habeas Corpus?"

"Bit flaky, but at least he's not a lawyer...so you don't get quite the same in-your face hypocrisy..."

"And yet you voted for him – why?"

"I didn't vote for him."

"You just said you did!"

"I voted *against* the Tories."

"I suppose you think that makes it alright? *Well at least they're not the Tories* – bullshit! I mean; give me strength," fumed Lucy, genuinely angry. "And it appears my husband has legged it with the delectable Antonia – and she's a Tory isn't she?"

"But you can't blame our local man for Blairism and all the dodgy dossier stuff and the flaky cronies. Nor for Barry doing a runner, come to that."

Lucy frowned and scooped back her hair as if preparing for an argument,

"And talking of *flaky*," she began, "did you see Blair and Brown on telly last weekend? They were campaigning somewhere, together, and Tony walked up to an ice-cream van and bought two vanilla cones and gave one to Gordon...."

"So? I don't get it?"

"Gordon's had a flake in it."

"I think they both did."

"Well, what a photo-opportunity that turned out to be. I hope it comes back to haunt them," sneered Lucy.

"So," he enquired, "we still don't yet know about your vote...."

Lucy pouted thoughtfully, but made no comment.

"Well, come on," he encouraged, "who did you support?"

"I did not know what I was going to do, even when I had the ballot paper in my hand. That's a totally new experience for me. In every previous election I've known precisely who I supported. But not this time – and not just because of Blair – because of the whole 'New Labour' quagmire...the spin-doctors, the focus groups, all that manipulation they go in for."

"It would be ironical if I voted for New Labour and you didn't," said Tom.

"Well I didn't!"

"Oh, dear! Not Liberal Democrat I hope? You know that could let the Tories in here, don't you?"

"Of course I do, don't patronise me! I read down the whole list, going *Labour – No! Conservative – No! Liberal Democrat – No!* I admit I hovered over the Greens. I was tempted; their candidate was called Hugo Charlton – so on the paper it read *Hugo Charlton Green.* Did you know that Graham Greene had a brother – who was Director-General of the BBC in the 1960s – called *Hugh Carlton Greene?* Coincidence, or what?"

"Get away!" laughed Tom.

"It's true!" insisted Lucy. "At last I know something you don't...."

"So is that it? You voted Green? Even without the extra 'e'?"

"No, listen, I said I *hovered* over the Greens."

"Oh God, that only leaves the UK Independence Party. Please darling, no. Promise me, you didn't support UKIP." Tom threw himself down on his knees, pleading and begging in mock supplication.

"No! Don't be daft."

"So who then?"

Lucy breathed in and then out again, then leaned forward on the sofa, her hands clasped together and resting on her knees.

"I decided to send an important message..."

"Which was?"

"I wrote across the bottom of the ballot paper; *Come and visit your children, Brendan Sands, you selfish bastard.*"

"Ker-rist!" exclaimed Tom. "That was a bit sort of 'mad', wasn't it?"

"Well he won't answer his phone to me or to Simon. Paul says he came in to the office today and then disappeared saying he had to go shopping to buy clothes. And guess what, Antonia didn't go to work at all today."

"So he stayed with Antonia last night?"

"Damned sure he did! And not for the first time either, I bet. But I don't care. I don't care about him anymore. But the girls need to see him – they're very upset. They're not stupid. Kids always know when there's something wrong...And I've had all three at home today because the school is being used as a Polling Station...."

"But why write that on the voting paper? What was the point?"

"Because Barry will be at the count; he's been boasting for weeks that he's going to be one of Martin Linton's checkers or scrutinizers – you know the people who look out for spoiled ballot papers. It is electoral law that all the candidates have to see all the spoiled papers and agree that they really are spoiled. So, just when he's trying to impress Antonia with what a big cheese he is in the Labour Party, bingo! *Message for Brendan Sands! Message for Brendan Sands!*" she broadcast, cupping her hands around her mouth.

"My God, Lucy; that'll be quite a coup, if it works. I almost wish I'd thought of that myself: *Brendan Sands, please stop shagging your old tart on my bed! O*h, and PS, Can I have my keys back?"

"Change the locks, stupid. But I wonder how many other Battersea voters there are out there who might have wanted to get a message to Barry?"

"Err, well the fuck-wits downstairs were complaining about all the noise he made humping Penny...."

"So you keep saying," she snapped. "Hey, what ever happened to your Howard Hodgkin poster?" Lucy nodded to indicate the empty space on the wall next to his desk, marked by a rectangle of less-faded wallpaper.

"Barry," he answered. "Well Barry and Penny jointly, I mean as a couple...."

"As a copulating couple?" she giggled.

"'Fraid so," he confirmed. "But I think Barry was acting alone when he defrosted my freezer and broke my one nice vase...Why do you think he hasn't been back home?"

"Don't know, and now I'm tired of waiting in for him. It's certainly out of character for him not to have confronted either you or me yet, in person I mean. It'll be another one of his psychological games. Did he ever burble on to you about Sun Tzu?"

"Err, yeah, once, I think. I thought he made most of it up as he went along; it was all a bit like *'Confucius, He say...'* know what I mean? And, anyway, he has had a go at me – via Penny and Graham..."

"Maybe he really has found something with Antonia. Something he didn't get from me, and he knew he'd never get from the likes of Penny.....I'd love to tell Penny that *Bazza* was two-timing her with the *scrummydocious* Antonia!"

"No need," said Tom. "Poor old Penny was so humiliated by the state he left her in yesterday I don't imagine she needs any further...."

"Any further what? Don't expect me to feel sorry for her; her and her big fat bum!"

"I don't, but if you'd seen her kid, Crispin..."

"Anyway," said Lucy, brightly, "here I am! Here and now. Simon's gone home to get some rest and *good ole* Mary has stepped in to look after the girls for a while. You should be grateful to her you know; she thinks you're a good man. She told me you'd be much better for me than Barry. I had a long talk with her this afternoon – she's been through quite a lot in her life – and she persuaded me to come and see you."

"What a wonderful human *bean* she is, and so perceptive!" exclaimed Tom. "I'm just sorry you had to be persuaded."

"No, it's better. It means that I've thought it through. People don't always do that, do they?" she said, smiling again. "And also I'm here to ask if you are planning to stay up late this evening to watch the election results?"

"Err, what if I am," he answered, cautiously.

"Well, Paul and Anna are coming round to watch them with me – Simon has told them I mustn't be left alone in the house until we know for certain that Brendan has calmed down - and I, err, wondered if you'd, err, like to join us?"

"I'd love to. You could have phoned, you didn't have to come round..."

"Actually, yes I did," she smiled at him. "Paul and Anna won't be over until after half-ten and we've got at least an hour on our hands before Mary will be wanting to go home to her cocoa....."

"Oh Lucy, darling, this is an unexpected..."

"Pleasure?" she enquired.

* * *

Tom and Lucy walked through the evening light across the west side of the Common and down the quiet streets leading to her house.

"This town's not exactly been gripped by election fever, has it?" she commented. "I think I've seen one Tory poster, two Lib Dems and one Labour between your house and here."

"I know. I heard that the Apathy Party planned to put up posters, but I guess they just never got around to it," shrugged Tom.

"No, it's not apathy," insisted Lucy. "We've talked about this before, people really did feel *'None of the above'* when they look at the choice in this election."

"Wait 'til after the results are out," said Tom. "The spin doctors will get to work on what the figures mean. I bet we get lots of calls to change the electoral system away from 'first past-the-post' when they find out that it takes about four times as many votes to return a Liberal as it does to return a Labour MP."

"If the Tories lose for the third time running maybe even they'll want to change to some type of proportional system?" Lucy speculated.

"But if New Labour get back with a working majority, they're not going to change it are they? They'll say there's nothing wrong with a system that returns *us* three times on the trot."

* * *

Lucy let him hold her hand until they were nearly home. In the hall, Mary appeared and gripped Tom's arm before saying goodnight and kissing Lucy on the cheek.

"Goodnight, Mary," called Lucy, "and thanks for everything. I don't know what I'd do without all your help."

Lucy closed the front door and turned to climb the stairs,

"Go through and open some wine," she suggested, gesturing towards the kitchen. "Anna and Paul will be here any minute and I just want to check on the children...."

Tom carried the bottle and two glasses into the living room and sat down. The television was flickering with the sound off, familiar faces from journalism and politics mouthed silently, reminding Tom of tropical fish seen in close-up. A ticker-tape of news 'flashes' trundled continuously across the bottom of the screen. Tom imagined a comedy sketch in which one of the talking heads would peer over the apparent 'wall' and move his head in synch. with some headline tracking across the screen - then reach over with a duster and erase any information that did not suit his cause.

"They're predicting a Labour majority of 66, based on the exit polls," he informed Lucy as she came into the room.

"Oooh! Turn the sound up for this bit," she called out as the screen showed library footage from the moment back in '97 when Michael Portillo had been unseated from the Enfield Constituency. "I never tire of seeing that."

A hand tapped on the window and Paul pressed his face to the glass, looking immediately like some bank-robber wearing a stocking mask.

"God, you can always rely on Paul to frighten the horses!" said Lucy. "Be a darling and let them in, I've only just sat down. Ugh, look at that greasy print his nose has left on the glass. Oh really Paul, you are the limit!"

"I try," he called to her from out in the hallway.

Anna seemed particularly pleased to see Tom and kissed him firmly on both cheeks. Paul shook Tom's hand and patted his arm,

"Chin up, mate," he said encouragingly. Tom frowned and

shrugged, assuming that Paul was trying to encourage him to stay loyal to Lucy, whatever stunts Barry might attempt.

"I bet Barry's been wondering what happened," thought Tom. "He would have loved to have been a fly on the wall when Graham burst in on me and Penny last night. He must want to know how it went. Graham and Penny sure as hell aren't going to tell him."

Tom returned to the kitchen to fetch two more glasses and a can of lager for Paul. Lucy sent him straight back again with instructions to open the oven and bring in some sausage rolls and canapés which Mary had prepared.

"*Here's some I made earlier*," fibbed Tom as he minced across the room and laid the warm tray on the low table in the centre of the room.

"Tom, you're such a treasure!" shrilled Paul, responding to Tom's camp performance.

"Oooh, I shouldn't," sighed Anna, oblivious to what the men were doing.

"But you will," said Paul reaching forward to consume a couple of sausage rolls.

"Tom, be a darling and get some plates, will you?" smiled Lucy as Paul spilled a trail of crumbs around him.

Paul laughed and winked,

"Get used to it mate," he teased. "It doesn't take them long to get you doing all the fetching and carrying!"

"Well that's fine with me," proclaimed Tom and blew a kiss at Lucy.

"You'll learn, you'll learn," said Paul, shaking his head sadly from side to side. Lucy and Anna both made faces at him.

On the television, Jeremy Paxman was conducting a typically abrasive interview.

"Change channels, for fuck's sake," pleaded Lucy. "These two are just oozing too much testosterone...they're like rutting stags, only not as elegant!"

"Oh, God!" laughed Anna. "Look, there's a Dimbleby on each channel; shouldn't the Monopolies Commission look into that?"

Paul fetched another can of lager and slumped back heavily into his armchair, throwing his left leg over the arm-rest. Anna sat at one end of the sofa; Tom and Lucy were close together at the other. Tom's arm was around Lucy and from time to time she rested her head on his shoulder.

More talking heads populated the screen, this time speculating on which of the 'celebrity' politicians from Labour and the Conservatives might be vulnerable to losing their seats on even quite a small percentage swing. Someone mentioned that the Liberal Democrats had a tactic of 'decapitation' which meant that they were hoping to defeat 'top Tories' such as Oliver Letwin in West Dorset, Teresa May in Maidenhead and David Davis up in Haltemprice & Howden.

"Halt 'em at any price!" heckled Paul.

"They can't hear you, dear," called out Anna, adding as an aside to Tom and Lucy, "he sits at home sometimes chatting away to folk on the telly.....it's tragic, really."

"Emma asked me the other day if people on television could see her sitting at home..."

"I can remember asking that question when I was a child," admitted Tom.

"What did you tell her?" asked Paul.

"That Big Brother is watching you, of course," laughed Lucy.

"Mmm, many a true word," mused Anna, sipping more wine. "But the way this election has been covered, it's as if they really are trying to make it more like Big Brother – *let's vote on who gets evicted from the Big Brother House this week!* – it's kind of 'reality TV' for the chattering classes. It's what Portillo is famous for now, isn't it? Getting chucked out at Enfield."

"What's that one in the jungle," asked Lucy, "where people you've dimly heard of – like weather forecasters and people who do backing vocals – have to eat worms and spiders, wrestle in mud and do disgusting things with rats?"

Anna made a spluttering sound,

"It's called "I'm a celebrity, take me...something" she offered.

"Take me ...from behind, perhaps?" mooted Paul.

"Oh, do shut up!" snapped Anna.

"And then there's been Boris and his Dad; both trying to get elected as Tory MPs."

"What in the same constituency?" queried Paul.

"No you idiot. Miles apart – Boris is in Henley-on Thames and his father is contesting a seat held by the Liberals [*I think*] down in the West Country."

"Oh, not Liverpool then?" snorted Paul.

"I won't hear a word said against Boris!" insisted Anna. "We need people like him, he's good value!"

"Ah, but would you vote for him if you could?" asked Lucy.

"She bloody would, unless, of course, Andrew Motion was also running," sneered Paul.

Anna frowned at him and made exaggerated movements to fold her arms across her chest and adjust the angle of her head so that he was not even within her peripheral vision.

"God, the places they end-up in when they count the votes and announce election results," commented Tom, trying to keep the peace. "It used to be done on the steps of the Town Hall, but now! Ugh! Just look at that one: it looks for all the world like the corner of some warehouse in the arse-end of nowhere..."

"It's a *Leisure Centre*, stoopid," explained Lucy. "Look, look; there's some ropes, a climbing frame and some sort of trampoline behind that curtain on the left..."

"Huh! They should leave all the apparatus out – make the candidates bounce around or thwack each other with tennis racquets while they're waiting...." sang Tom.

"Hey, what about a display of beach volley ball..."suggested Paul.

"Shut up!" chorused Lucy and Anna simultaneously.

"Well exactly," continued Tom. "Using an odd corner of some gymnasium shows a lack of respect for the process – it lacks gravitas. The outcome is diminished when the result gets announced in such an amateurish way in such an unimposing context...see, the floor's marked out for badminton or basket ball."

"Yeah, like I said," interrupted Paul.

"....And the sound system is always crap, watch how they tap the microphones before they read the results..." continued Tom.

"No," insisted Lucy, "I think the opposite is true. I don't want it to be like *The Oscars*, you know all slick with lights and music; perfectly contrived for Prime Time TV on the West Coast or in

New York."

"That'd be different," puffed Paul, finishing his lager. "Instead of the boring old *Returning Officer* they could have some bimbo with enormous tits and a sequinned smile opening the envelopes: '*And the winner is....*' I'd watch that!"

"You're watching this!" snapped Anna.

"*Themediumisthemessage,*" decided Lucy. "The announcement at the end of the count must be seen to be made by '*The Voice of The People*'. It has to be impartial, and that comes over when it's delivered slightly nervously, preferably in a regional accent, by some local worthy who is getting his fifteen seconds of fame. We don't want jazz and razzle; we don't want slickness and PR. It must not seem impressive or professional. It's got to look like what it is – a bunch of ordinary, normal folk from the Library and the Council Offices sitting at long, wobbly tables counting the individual pieces of paper until they've got them right. It's all done in public – we don't want our politicians elected by acclaim - we want them to be made to line up on the stage – no matter how grand they imagine they are - and wait quietly behind the Returning Officer; along with Batman, a pantomime horse, a Dolly Parton look-alike, the guy from the Monster Raving Loonies and some weird little bloke with a moustache and a baggy tweed jacket.... That is all *so* important."

Lucy's vehement defence of contemporary electoral machinery stunned them all to silence. On the flickering screen, David Blunkett was being interviewed and had just begun laying into the Tories for using the immigration issue to attract the support of white, working class, voters. They heard the rattle of a key turning in the front door and someone entered the house.

Lucy went rigid and sat bolt upright. Tom rose slowly to his feet but, surprisingly, Paul was quicker and positioned himself between Tom and whoever might enter the room. A news flash blazed across the TV screen: '*Cons. Gain Putney – 6.5% swing Lab. to Con.*' it read. Anna gasped and pointed at the screen,

"Look, look at that!" she called.

Chapter Twenty Three

Barry strode into the room wearing a new cream-coloured suit with a blue shirt open at the neck and looking very suave and clean-cut.

"Hiya, folks," he called and smiled broadly.

"Brendan!" said Lucy and Paul in unison.

"It is I," he replied, bowing very slightly and opening the palms of his hands to the room.

"Have you heard the Putney result?" asked Anna, shrilly.

"Yup, know about that – and we're into a re-count here in Battersea. It looks a bit dicey; could go either way," he announced. "That's why....." Just at that moment, Barry's glance fell on Tom.

"What's he doing here?" he demanded, staring directly at Lucy.

"Now hold on, old chap," said Paul.

"Well if he's in here, why should Antonia be left sitting outside in the car? In the dark and cold? I'm going to bring her in too!" Barry spoke, and was gone.

Lucy looked from Paul to Anna and back to Paul. She seemed mesmerized and unable to speak. Tom put his hand on her shoulder and breathed with slow deliberation. On the television, the pundits had gone into overdrive analysing the Putney result; computer graphics flashed across the screen and lists of constituencies suddenly turned from *red background* to *blue background*. One of the '*anchormen*' danced like a Thunderbirds' puppet as he gesticulated to reveal the significance of coloured cubes, cylinders and ziggurats which were appearing to his left and right.

A draught of cold air played across the room and they heard the front door close once again. Barry came back into the room.

"You all know Antonia, don't you?"

There was a pause, and Antonia stepped into view looking very demure but still dazzlingly beautiful. Paul took the initiative,

"Great to see you, darling," he grinned. "Come and sit down, let Tom get you a glass of wine..."

"Just sparkling water, if I could please?" she asked quietly. Lucy studied her silently.

"Tom?" said Paul, "Oh, and bring lagers for Barry and me, as well, would you?"

Barry stood aside and Tom hurried to the kitchen. Barry guided Antonia gently with his hand and she settled hesitantly into an armchair, perching on the very edge of the seat.

"Hello, Brendan," said Lucy, looking into his face at last.

"Hi," said Barry and sat on the arm of Antonia's chair, his hand resting protectively on her shoulder.

"Bit grim at the count, is it?" enquired Anna after a silence. "Lots of long faces?"

"Not in Antonia's camp; they're all cock-a-hoop aren't they darling?" he answered. Antonia smiled but hesitated to speak. Barry pressed her shoulder encouragingly;

"Well it is up there with our target seats. I think our man Schofield is giving your guy a real run for his money..."

"And the Liberal Democrats," rasped Lucy from a dry throat. "How are they doing?"

"You didn't vote for them, did you?" sneered Barry.

"You know I didn't," she snapped. Barry looked puzzled. "Isn't that why you're here?" she asked, "You got the message I wrote on the ballot paper?"

"Not me!" proclaimed Barry, glancing at all their faces in turn, "What message? I actually popped in to say hello, make sure the kids are OK; that sort of thing..."

"They're in bed, fast asleep, you idiot – what did you expect? It's way after one in the morning for Pete's sake!" snapped Lucy. "Don't think you can...."

"Lucy, hold on..." said Anna firmly and Lucy stopped speaking, biting her lip in anguish. Tom offered Antonia a glass of water in which the bubbles continued to surge upwards. He held out a can of lager to Barry who took it and nodded without saying thank you. Lucy seemed to relax a little and consequently so did everyone else.

A voice from the television cut across the silence,
"We are watching an historic third victory, but it doesn't feel like a victory...."
"You can say that again!" shouted Paul.
"I'm sure he will," commented Anna. "Oh, look, look, there's Tony Blair arriving at his count in Sedgefield...God, cheer up Tony. Cherie looks well stressed too doesn't she? She must hate all this!"
"I think she's a lot brighter than he is, but she's so devoted to him she keeps quiet," suggested Paul.
"You don't know what you're talking about," cut in Anna. "Comparisons like that started back in 1992 with Glenys Kinnock – people used to say we'd have won that election if she'd been the leader rather than Neil."

"Anyway, as I was saying," Barry resumed, confidently. "There's loads of people milling around down at the Town Hall; they're counting Battersea, Tooting and Putney all at the same time. It turned out I wasn't needed at the Battersea count – Angus and Clive had got their wires crossed – and I didn't want to embarrass Antonia in front of her lot..."
"She's going to have to get used to that!" muttered Lucy.
"Lucy!" chided Anna,
"Sorry!"
"You said you'd sent me a message," said Barry forcefully. "What was that all about?"
"Nothing," replied Lucy, looking down. "I meant that I'd spoilt my ballot paper that's all."
"Why did you do that? It's going to be close, you know. Every vote counts!"
"Are there many spoilt papers, Barry?" asked Anna trying to sound bright and cheerful.
"No more than usual, as far as I'm aware," stated Barry, morosely.

"Oh yes there are," said Antonia. "I was told that there were lots more. They get shown to the candidates you know, in case of dispute or uncertainty as to the voter's intentions. You get people who carefully mark their cross exactly on the line between two names, that sort of thing...Or people who put numbers instead of a cross, as if we already have proportional representation.... Or else they write 'yes' and 'no', or something very rude, in the boxes..."

While they were talking, Tony Blair had made his brief acceptance speech at Sedgefield. When their attention returned to the screen his entourage were getting into cars for the drive to a nearby Labour Club where he was expected to address the faithful. The commentator remarked,
"If you'd watched his speech with the sound down, you'd think he had lost..."

"Brendan, I need to speak to you!" announced Lucy with sudden resolve which made everyone turn towards her. Anna started to rise but Lucy held out her arm to stop her,
"No," she said quietly, "just me and Barry, we'll go into the kitchen..."
Antonia twisted in her seat to see them leave the room; Tom sank back on the sofa and gazed forlornly at the ceiling. Paul, imagining himself as some sort of 'master of ceremonies' ushered them into the kitchen and shut the door behind them with a very positive click which seemed to echo through the whole house. Upstairs, a child coughed and snorted in her sleep. From the television a voice announced,
"We can go over now to Picketts Lock for the result in Enfield, Michael Portillo's old seat..."
Anna, Tom and Paul sat and watched as the candidates lined up behind the Returning Officer.
"God, I thought Twigg looked like a naughty schoolboy in '97 when he beat Portillo; but he's actually very tall isn't he..." commented Paul.
"He's lost it!" remarked Tom. "Look at his face and the smile on the Tory guy..."
"Oh yes!" exclaimed Antonia, her jewellery rattling as her right

hand flew to her lips.

In the kitchen, Lucy leaned against the sink unit while Barry walked to the far end of the room and sat down at the table facing her. Lucy's hands slid sideways along the edge of the work-top until her arms were spread wide. She was trying hard to look relaxed and casual, inside her stomach churned and her legs felt completely hollow.

"Well," she said, flatly, "that's us finished then, isn't it?"

Barry leaned back in his chair and looked at her. "Aren't you going to say anything?" she asked.

"What's to say?" he remarked casually.

"We are not discussing the quality of school dinners here, Brendan, we are discussing the end of our marriage..."

"It seems we are," he said coldly. "We've been living together since Blair became leader; maybe we've reached a natural conclusion..."

"Oh, time for a change is it?" sneered Lucy.

"Well we can't carry on like this......"

"Carry on? It's you who's been *carrying on*; all the time we've been together I've been expecting you to leave..."

"Glad I haven't disappointed you," said Barry, clasping his hands behind his head and tilting the chair so that the front legs lifted.

"I can't believe..." stuttered Lucy. "Do we or do we not have three daughters, all asleep upstairs in this house..."

"And your point is....?"

"Brendan! Those are our children; I gave birth to them, you fathered them!"

"Did I? Did I really? How can I be so sure?"

"Oh for God's sake!" exclaimed Lucy in a fierce whisper. "Of course they're yours! I was always faithful to you, just look at them. I see you whenever I look at any one of them."

"Well, that's nice for you. And I thought you'd been sleeping with sad old Corky; now whatever gave me that idea?"

"Only after," growled Lucy. "Only after you'd ....well you know what."

"So you admit your adultery?" asked Barry. "How could you even let him touch you? Touch you, you know, down there!"

"Don't!" she spat. "Don't you dare talk about..... talk about my womanhood! I know what you did with Penny in Tom's bed and all over Tom's books,"

"Oh, yeah! Oh, do tell me, how did that finish up by the way?"

"Remarkably well, according to Tom, and no thanks to you. He said things started to get better once they'd sorted out who everyone really was, and then they agreed that all the fingers of blame pointed at you. Now Simon's worried about the damage Graham could inflict on your reputation up in Nottingham...."

"He needn't be," smirked Barry. "Old Graham's hardly going to tell his chums in any detail what I did with his wife..."

"Oh, that makes me feel a whole lot better," groaned Lucy.

"OK, enough of this. Where do you think we go from here?" he asked, putting both hands on the table and letting the chair legs crash against the floor tiles.

"Down," she replied, "The only way out is down; someone has to tell the girls that you don't live here anymore..."

"What makes you so sure? Why do I have to leave? Why can't you ship out and stay with bugger-lugs?"

"I meant to say," growled Lucy, "that things can only get worse, but at least let's do our very best not to make them into a total disaster!"

"You think I can't look after the girls?"

"They need both of us. That's the whole stupid point. You'd know that if you understood the situation. At this age they need me living with them but they need to be able to rely on seeing you at regular intervals, even if you can't manage every day. It's not a question of what might best satisfy our egos; yours or mine. Above all else the children need consistency, or as much of it as we can give them in the circumstances. It's all a question of understanding, it always has been. That's why I'm here and, I think, that's why you and I need to keep talking...."

"When are we going to tell them? I mean, tell the girls?"

"Now that you've been back – which is good, by the way – I'm glad you did it and that we didn't just scream at each other down the phone or use Simon as an interlocutor..."

"What?"

"You know the sort of thing: I say: *Tell him blah blah!* And you reply, *Tell her blah de blah blah!* A dialogue of the deaf."

"I don't want to find bloody Corky is suddenly living here; that's not on..."

"You won't, he isn't. But they do know Tom and they do like him, I mean they're used to seeing him..."

"When I think how he's wormed his way...."

"Stop that! Stop now – you're not to do this. Tom won't be coming between you and the girls and you'd better not start poisoning them against him. They mustn't be made to take sides; in these situations kids always feel as if it's all somehow their fault..."

"You don't need to tell me that; you don't know the half of what I went through when my Mum and Dad .....no one does."

"Oh Brendan, that's why we've got to be so careful. Listen, they need to see you with Antonia; how and where is up to you - I'm not going to arrange it for you. But I will make a suggestion; make Emma feel special again first. The other two are following her lead. She can be off school tomorrow if you like; make a fuss of her, give her your time. She's desperate to see you..."

"I've been missing her too."

"She doesn't know that. She's more troubled by the thought that you've left her than that you've left me."

"Luce; hold on. I've got to sort out what to do for the best. I'm sorry it ended like this, you and me. I mean I don't know what I could have done different...maybe it's just me...Maybe I was always going to defeat the whole project?"

"Do you mean 'defeat', or do you really mean 'betray'?" she asked.

Barry frowned back at her, folded his arms defiantly but said nothing.

"Well look what's gone on," she continued, "you were unfaithful to me with Penny; and Penny betrayed me too – she'd been my best friend at college, remember? Then you made her betray Graham as well, and you made Tom betray me."

"Not so!" insisted Barry, "I didn't have to do anything to prise her away from Graham; she threw herself at me. And, the fact is, Tom betrayed me. He and you both betrayed me, together."

"No! Tom betrayed my friendship with him when he kept quiet about Penny's letters to you. And you knew it, but you didn't care."

"Well I paid him back; I had Graham thinking that Tom was having it away with Penny."

"Oh, right. So we can add Tom and Graham to the list of friends you've betrayed. Come to think of it, you even betrayed Penny at the end. A certain irony there, I feel."

"Only when the game was up. I only set her up when we were doomed anyway; I had to get her off me."

"You mean you ditched her when you'd fallen for Antonia's considerable charms," pronounced Lucy, coldly. "And you just did it in the cruellest possible way because you saw a chance to be spiteful to Tom. You knew if you took your revenge on him you'd also be getting back at me."

"We were pretty much defeated by then..."

"Who was?" she demanded.

"Penny and me, babe. You and me, babe. I think you and I were defeated a long time ago but we just didn't know it. You acted as if that was what you thought marriage was like.....you over-did the domestic drudgery."

"No," she said firmly, "we weren't always going to be defeated. Your raunchy little affair with Penny wasn't enough to defeat us.... My affair with Tom was; but then I wouldn't have turned to him – would I? - if I wasn't convinced you were ...well never mind what."

"I wanted us to last Luce, I promise you I really did. Look how hard I tried at Christmas. I made a huge effort and you chucked it back in my face...."

"Oh, that was your idea of trying, was it? Going somewhere far away, without the kids, and phoning for Room Service morning, noon and night?"

"I thought you looked tired. I wanted you to rest. I wanted us to be a couple again; like we were before...I wanted you to brighten up. I wanted to pamper you."

"Maybe you did. I don't doubt that you did. Even though you didn't behave as if I mattered to you as a person; maybe we could have lasted – sort of *weathered the storm*, as they say...."

"So why?"

"I could have got over you sleeping with Penny. In time maybe you would even have forgiven me for Tom..."

"Time? Some bloody long time…"

"But it's all an irrelevance now, it isn't going to happen is it?

"Why not?"

"I wasn't sure I'd lost you – and sure that you'd lost me – until…"

"Until what?"

"Until I saw you with Antonia. That's when I knew. At Paul's house last week. I've known since then....."

Barry stood up and gazed around, taking in the children's paintings on the wall and the clutch of bills wedged behind the radio. Lucy said nothing; she looked into his eyes and knew that he wasn't seeing her. He saw something far away and whatever it was, it made him look pleased with himself. His eyes came back to her and he gave her the very faintest of smiles.

"I don't know why I needed you to see that for me, Luce, but I did. It's almost as if, I didn't know….until you told me."

"Well just shut up, shut up right now!" she spat bitterly. "If I really did have to point that out to you I don't know how I've got this far without screaming…." She buried her face in her hands, squeezing her eyes tight shut to stop the tears and arching her fingers so that they pressed firmly against her forehead. Despite her concentrated effort, she felt the cold liquids of sorrow brim over inside her and begin to trickle slowly down her hot face.

A subdued cheer, the product of only three throats, went up in the other room. Barry raised his eyebrows and looked displaced, as if waking from sleep. Lucy made a guttural choking sound to expel the anger and frustration she felt. Her fingers swept through her hair and she shook a new energy into herself which enabled her to open the door and call out,

"What is it? What's happened?"

Paul shouted back,

"Battersea! We've held Battersea! It's Labour, but only after three recounts."

"Christ!" exclaimed Barry, moving past Lucy and walking back into the front room. "What was Linton's majority?"

"One hundred and sixty-ish," said Tom.

"That's all," confirmed Antonia. "Cut down to a piffling one six three! It would only have been one six four even if you *had* voted, darling."

"What? You didn't even vote?" asked Anna.

"Too much on, didn't get out in time..." muttered Barry, avoiding Paul's eyes and frowning at Antonia to be quiet.

Barry moved further into the room, resuming his place alongside Antonia who put her hand confidently on his knee. Lucy came back into the room just as Ian Hislop - staring into the room from the television screen and wearing his special *'I am baffled'* expression - was heard to enquire;

"Why are they all so depressed? What do they know that they haven't told us yet?"

"Now who says the people on TV can't see us?" demanded Lucy, giving a hollow laugh. "Come on, who knows anything else they haven't told us yet? No doubt Antonia slipped out to vote without waking you! "

Across the bottom of the screen the news flashes predicted a Labour majority of eighty two.

"We need to be going," said Antonia dryly, tapping Barry's knee and twisting around to see where Lucy was.

"Yes, OK," answered Barry, standing abruptly and offering his arm to Antonia as she rose from the chair. He stood still with Antonia at his side and drew back his shoulders. His eyes flickered nervously and he pushed his open fingers slowly through his hair as he sought to calm himself.

"I do have something else to say," he announced, "something important. I guess it affects all of you, one way or another..... And I want you to hear it from me..."

Antonia, Tom, Paul and Anna all focused their attention on Barry. Lucy stood by herself at the dark end of the room, looking down at her feet.

"It's Antonia," blurted Barry, "Antonia is pregnant; we are going to have a baby!"

No one spoke. One by one they remembered Lucy and looked towards her, even Antonia. Lucy looked up and smiled;

"It's alright," she said, as if acknowledging their concern, "I already knew."

"But how?" challenged Barry. "How could you know?"

"Oh, Barry darling," she sighed, "how could I not know? I was pregnant before we got married, remember? All you've done is modernize me; and so there I am – I'm Antonia....She's the new me. Look, I've been up-dated!"

"Oh, Lucy...." sobbed Anna.

"Don't start, Lucy. Just don't!" growled Barry.

"Don't worry, I'm not fighting; I don't want you anymore. I've had enough, more than enough. But remember, Brendan, I've lived with you through thick and thin for all these years – the Blair years, strangely enough – and now he's back for his *'historic third term'* – so they keep saying – and you've replaced me with, with..... her! And it doesn't even bother you that she's a Tory!" Lucy's lower jaw trembled as she sucked in a breath and continued, "As soon as I saw her I knew that Antonia was everything you'd always wanted; and everything I never was. I just couldn't.....It's not as if I didn't try.... And everything I'd once been counted for nothing; absolutely sod-all!" Lucy stood unnaturally still but vibrating with anger, her bony fists clenched tightly and drumming against her thighs.

Barry snorted,

"No, no, no; it's not like that! You've got that wrong!" he protested. "I moved on and you didn't; I mean you *wouldn't!* So you can leave her out of this, what went wrong was strictly between you and me..."

"Oh but she is involved...Very much involved. Think about it, think about what you've done. Her child will share its father with my children...They'll be step-sisters....Had you thought about that? What you do to me you also do to Emma, Cherie and even little Alice."

"They'll be fine," asserted Barry. "I'll make sure of that."

"And me," said Antonia. "I'm no threat to your children, Lucy. Please don't think that; I didn't intend..... here take my hand, please?"

Lucy glanced at Antonia's outstretched hand, the slender fingers and immaculate nails, the diamond bracelet around her wrist.

"Another time," said Lucy quietly. "Not now, just not right

now…I'm not like one of your hireling footballers, swapping shirts after losing a penalty shoot-out. The outcome of this affects my children, and that really matters to me."

"We're going," said Barry angrily and held the door open for Antonia to leave the room.

"I'll be keeping the girls off school tomorrow," said Lucy, hurriedly. "Make sure you come and see them. It's really important; especially for Emma!"

"He will," called Antonia. "I'll make sure he does."

"Yes," snapped Barry, "I will; I mean I was going to anyway!"

"Goodnight Lucy," said Paul, following the other two out into the hall.

"Lucy!" cried Anna, throwing her arms around Lucy and giving her a mighty hug. "We'll talk – tomorrow."

"Yes, OK," answered Lucy. "Bye for now…..I'll phone you, OK?"

The front door closed with a resounding thud. They heard Paul calling after Barry and Barry's cheerful *'See you later!'* before car doors slammed and engines revved. Lucy sighed and raised her hand to her forehead.

"Well, that's that, I suppose," she announced, crossing the room to turn off the television. "Didn't that go well? I mean, considering….." Her voice faltered and she fell silent, biting her lower lip. Tom sat slumped on the sofa, beginning to feel very tired but watching her with a questioning expression on his face.

"Should I go too?" he asked softly.

Lucy did not answer him, but gazed thoughtfully around the room.

"Do you remember this is where….where we first made love?" she asked, more calmly.

"I do; how could I forget?"

"Oh Tom," she sighed, "this was just so easy to get into, but now look at us. I've no idea what happens next, I really don't. The future has become all uncertain…."

Tom forced himself to smile;

"A bit like the past?" he asked.

"Yes, like the past," continued Lucy. "What was that all about? How could he and I have three children and then suddenly it's all gone....just vanished...beyond hope...nothing left?"

"But now at least *we* can decide things, you know," Tom whispered, "you and me! That's what's different; *we* now have a say! We don't just have to accept what others do to us anymore..."

Lucy frowned thoughtfully;

"Well, that's good. I mean I think it's good or it will be good – eventually." She stood above him, her hands on her hips. "Listen," she continued, "I'm going to bring down a blanket and a pillow. I think I want you to sleep on the sofa tonight. The girls can find you like *Sleeping Beauty* in the morning when they come streaming down to watch their cartoons on breakfast telly. If they find you here they'll be curious and excited..."

"I'm always glad to be a novelty..." laughed Tom, smiling up at her.

"When Alice finds you, she'll come all the way back up to tell me that you're here; then she'll trundle back down again and she'll probably sit on you..."

"You could do that too," suggested Tom, "or should I be bringing tea and toast up to you?"

"One step at a time please, *Mister* Cork, one step at a time, please," smiled Lucy. "The proper niceties have to be observed and anyway we're into '*An Historic Third Term*' now, don't forget. History is there to be made."

"Dear oh dear! Did you mean to sound like Yoda?" laughed Tom.

Lucy absent-mindedly picked up a wine glass and a plate from where Anna had been sitting. She took three or four small steps backward and perched uncertainly on the generous arm of a comfortable chair, facing Tom. She still held the empty glass and the plate.

"Those people on TV, and politicians, they treat us like children, don't they? They seem to think we can't cope with anything complicated. They're always reducing issues to simplistic slogans..."

"*Power to the People!*" chanted Tom. Lucy frowned.

"Actually I think a lot will happen in this third term that can't be made to seem simple – like ID cards you know - but we won't be expected to notice or even care about stuff like that. In fact they could use great big spectacles to distract attention from more serious things..." she suggested. "Just making us appear even more infantile..."

"That'll be the idea. Like a conjuror tries to make you look over here while the trick is going on over there," proclaimed Tom, losing his tiredness and suddenly becoming more animated.

Lucy held up her hand to quieten him, her eyes narrowed for a second and then she looked away, frowning down at a stain on the carpet.

"At the moment," she complained, "everything around me seems to involve deception. Deceit and deception!"

"I only meant sleight of hand, the sort of tricks that magicians do," said Tom, hesitantly.

"Oh! Magicians, eh?" sighed Lucy. "Like when some man with a top-hat, a cloak and a wicked grin entices a vulnerable woman to lie down in a long box and then begins sawing her in half? Everyone knows it's a trick – a deception – we just cannot believe our eyes.... "

"There's always a rational explanation," countered Tom, feeling compelled to sound reassuring but starting to worry where Lucy's speculation might be taking her.

"Not for the way I feel at the moment, there isn't," she replied. "My marriage was like being in that box. I had my head sticking out at one end and my feet at the other. Oh God, I bet Paul and Anna went away thinking *'Good old Lucy, she can cope. Breaking-up with Barry was what we've been expecting all along...She'll manage, there's Good Old Mary - and Simon - and now, of course, she's got Tom too...She'll bounce back in no time, you'll see!'*"

Tom sat upright but stared helplessly down at his hands. Before he could speak she continued - forming her words slowly and carefully as if extracting them from some distant, half-remembered treatise;

"That was it; everyone saw the box getting sawn in half. I was just the token woman lying inside it, permanently smiling. They thought I wasn't being hurt! Huh, I wish! And at the end of the trick the magician is supposed to help the woman climb out of the box to thunderous applause and cries of relief, to prove that she's unharmed. He's not meant to run-off with some other woman and start having babies!"

Lucy's shoulders drooped and her feet twisted in agitation.

"Well, take a look at me now, after all that's happened. I don't look sawn in half do I? I seem to be quite together." She paused, put down the glass, and ran her hand uncertainly down her chest and along her thighs. "But that's just another bloody deception. Now I know what the real trick was; I've been cut in half and no one saw a bloody thing!"

Lucy sobbed, letting the plate fall from her fingers, threw back her head and drew in a deep breath before addressing the ceiling directly above her;

"Where's *my* bastard magician?" she wailed then suddenly dropped her gaze and stared directly at Tom. "Was it you? Was it Brendan? Antonia? – or even poor 'tits-for-brains' Penny? There was no build-up; I heard no drum-roll, no crashing cymbals! But it happened, Tom, it was real, none the less. What if I now suddenly fall apart? Then everyone will see that the trick went horribly wrong....That the magician wasn't so clever after all. That the bastard's gone and left me sawn in two..."

Tom stood up, hesitated and then came over to her. She let him run his hands gently across her shoulders and then relaxed as they slipped under her arms and lifted her decisively. He held her close to him, using his body to support hers and saying nothing. His left hand cradled her head and pressed her face gently onto his shoulder.

"I'm here," he said at last. "For as long as you want me to be. Listen to me, Lucy, there was no magic and no magician. If your marriage to Brendan felt like being trapped inside a long box, then be glad it's broken open and you're out. You can live without Brendan, but you can't go through life without being deceived; deceptions are an essential part of finding out what's real. Without *deceptions* everything would be bland or else ridiculously simplified. Yes, you'd have The Garden of Eden but to make sense of the world – to have useful knowledge - we need the Serpent, Temptation and The Fall. Knowledge is dangerous, everyone knows that! Even in the Bible, it's what got us expelled from the Garden..."

"From earthly paradise?" she murmured into his woollen shoulder. "I don't know what's true anymore. You can fool some of the people part of the time....and part of the people some of the time....."

"I never set out to fool you, Lucy, but only you can judge whether I'm different from Brendan; or how alike we are." She uttered another muffled sigh; Tom paused and looked at her again before continuing, "Remember how you once said our relationship was *all pretend*? Well at least that's gone; there's no more make-believe.... I wish you could see yourself the way I do. I think all this has made you stronger too, but it may be a while before you realise by how much. Barry was good at undermining you, wasn't he? That was one of his tactics – that's got to stop..."

She lifted her face and her dark eyes searched his. She kissed his lips and felt comforted by his familiar warmth and the sound of his voice.

"Maybe you should try being the Magician for a change?" he suggested.

"What? With you as my *gorgeous* assistant? Welcome to *my* Magic Circle," she smiled enigmatically. Tom laughed and performed a clumsy curtsy. "Perhaps it's your turn to be lured into the box of tricks, Mister Silver-Tongued-Woolly-Jumper! No man escapes with either his trousers or his sanity from Lucy's mysterious 'cabinet of mirrors'!" she cackled, raising her arms and flexing her fingers as if casting a spell;

"*By the pricking of my thumbs*...oh God!" she cried, "why can't I become a Magician without turning myself into a witch? Did you see that? I slipped straight into being a witch casting an evil spell! Am I going to be *The Wicked Witch of Wandsworth* now? Antonia's the *Wicked Step-Mother,* surely? Oh, fuck it!"

Tom laughed and stooped to retrieve the fallen plate. Lucy spoke again;

"What does it tell you if a man who does magic tricks is called a magician, but a woman doing the same things would be a witch?" she demanded. Tom shrugged,

"I'm sure that the word 'magician' is rooted in wisdom, which is both male and female," he said. "Weren't the Three Wise Men in the Bible called 'Magi'? *Magi* comes from *Magus*, meaning a priest, a person whose knowledge of astronomy gave them power...enabled them to predict new moons and eclipses .....made them astrologers."

"But if they'd been female," she interrupted him, "unthinkable I know in those days; then they'd have been *witches*! How different would it make the story of the Nativity if three witches had turned up instead of three Wise Men? It would be *Son of* bloody *Macbeth,* wouldn't it?"

"Well, there it is," she said dryly. "Already I can see it's not going to be easy for me to return to functioning as a fully independent woman....and don't offer your help! That would only prove my point!" she snapped.

Tom looked crestfallen and felt a bit stupid, standing as he was in the middle of the room still holding the empty plate, which he now saw was decorated with the words of a nursery rhyme and a drawing of a cow jumping over the moon.

"Well for your next trick, my darling," he heard himself say, "you only need a blanket and a pillow."

Lucy softened, gave a little giggle and pulled him gently towards her.

"Hold me" she began.

"I am."

"No, hold me closer," she whispered and they stood holding each other in silence.

"Penny for them," said Tom.

"Don't mention that woman..."

"I mean your thoughts. Tell me what you're thinking, right now..."

"About Barry, actually."

"Why? What about Barry?"

"I was thinking you are holding me in Barry's house and I don't feel the least bit worried – no, not the least bit guilty."

"I've always thought of it as your house, not his."

"I'm amazed that he didn't even vote. After all his bombast about New Labour....it's truly amazing."

"Too busy, that's what he said he was..."

"Too busy seducing Antonia!"

"Wonder how long she's been pregnant."

"I'd say two months at least, for him to be so sure."

"Oh, not just since this afternoon then?"

Lucy scowled;

"Penny would never have done that for him," she said.

"Done what?"

"Got pregnant. Had his baby."

"She didn't stand a chance once he'd fallen for Antonia...."

"Neither did I sweetie, don't forget, neither did I."

"Speaking selfishly," said Tom, "I'm glad she's in the club. That explains why Barry didn't come round here yesterday beating his chest, or go over to my place, beating me up. Knowing she was *in the club* calmed him down. It made him stop and think."

"So, of the three of us; you, me and Barry..."

"Don't forget Antonia! We're a foursome now..."

"OK, four. Antonia will have voted Tory, let's assume."

"That's a safe bet."

"And you voted New Labour,"

"Which leaves?"

"Barry and I. But he either couldn't be arsed or *she* stopped him voting. I spoiled my ballot paper because I was so angry.... with *him!*"

"Oh no," laughed Tom, "not some fiendish Tory-plot to reduce the Labour turnout...?"

"No, but when every vote counted, Barry and I weren't any use, were we?"

"So I'm the only one who backed the winner! One of the slim majority! So it's thanks to me!"

"What is?"

"It's thanks to me we're *Holding Battersea!*"

Lucy pulled away from him.

"Does it matter?" she asked. "Does any of it matter? Who cares what we think? Who gives a toss what we say or do?"

"It would matter if Battersea had gone Tory!"

"Would it? Would it really? What would change? Name any three things that would be different for you if...."

"You can't look at it like that; it's important that we can vote out a government even if we don't..."

"Well now they can ignore us again until the next time."

"No they can't," insisted Tom. "They can't ignore me."

"Why not? Just watch them."

"No, 'cos I'm part of the slim majority. All parties will want my vote at the next election. They'll be out to seduce me, politically of course...."

"In your dreams, comrade!" she mocked.

"No, seriously. It's a key marginal now; that's how it is – I'm *holding* Battersea."

"They're not interested in you, your profile's all wrong."

Tom stepped away from her, frowning. The fingers of his right hand stroked down his nose.

"My profile?"

"No stupid, not that. Your demographic whatsit; you're too old, you're not a woman, you're not ethnic. You're just odd; *luverly*, but definitely *odd*!"

"Thanks very much."

"That's right, it is *thanks to me*."

"What is?"

"It's thanks to me you're holding me."

"Meaning?"

"I made the first move, remember? If I'd waited for you you'd still be home alone, drinking tea, shouting at the telly, with only your pillow to hold. And I'd be sitting up in bed, doing my knitting, cursing men..."

"Don't forget you've really put me through the wringer these last few months, you and Barry between you...."

"Have we, my darling?" she whispered. "This was never going to be easy for any of us; you, me, the children – even Brendan, damn him! – But I'm glad you're here now and I hope you'll stay, whatever happens. I know I'm sometimes difficult....Neurotic even, maybe a bit mad? Oh, you don't think I'm really mad do you? Barry did! He was always telling me..."

"Exactly. That's exactly what he would do. He undermined you for years, to control you. It suited him that way. He made you defer to him, made you think you needed him, when really he needed you far, far more."

She kissed him again; this time fiercely and passionately. She clasped her arms around him and rested her head on his shoulder so that her words went directly into his ear,

"Actually, I do sometimes have a struggle to control myself," she breathed, "but I'm glad at least tonight is over. Look at me; see? I'm happy now. How surprising is that? You've made me happy in your strange, elliptical way; suddenly I'm happy to be the woman, who's holding the man, who's holding Battersea."

"Tee tum, tee tum, tee tum, der dum!" recited Tom. "That sounds like the last line to some kind of demented, Blairite nursery rhyme. And don't let go. No, no! Without you...that man might be about to fall over..."

"What? Like this?"

END OF STORY

Lightning Source UK Ltd.
Milton Keynes UK
11 December 2009

147379UK00002B/7/P